Shake-Down: The Complete Cases
of MacBride & Kennedy, Volume 2

Frederick Nebel

Frederick Nebel

SHAKE-DOWN: THE COMPLETE CASES OF

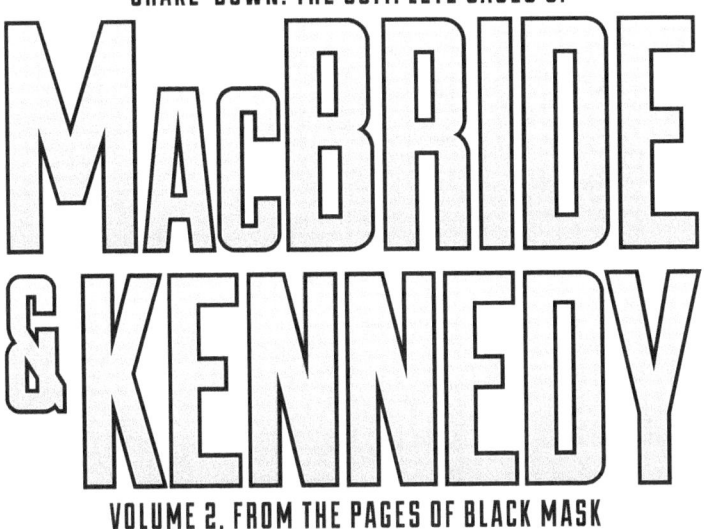

MacBRIDE & KENNEDY

VOLUME 2, FROM THE PAGES OF BLACK MASK

FREDERICK NEBEL

Illustrations by
ARTHUR RODMAN BOWKER

Introduction by
EVAN LEWIS

Series Editor
KEITH ALAN DEUTSCH

Another Volume in the BLACK MASK LIBRARY

Boston • Philadelphia • New York
2013

© 2013 Altus Press • First Edition—2013

DESIGNED AND PUBLISHED BY
Matthew Moring

BLACK MASK SERIES EDITOR
Keith Alan Deutsch

PUBLISHING HISTORY
"Introduction" appears here for the first time. Copyright © 2013 David Lewis. All Rights Reserved.
Owing to limitations of space, permissions to reprint previously published material appear on pages 364-365.

Published by arrangement with Black Mask Press/Keith Alan Deutsch (keithdeutsch@mac.com).

THANKS TO
Ed Hulse, Evan Lewis, Ken McDaniel, Rob Preston & Ray Riethmeier.

Visit altuspress.com for more books like this.
Printed in the United States of America.

Another volume in the BLACK MASK LIBRARY.

Table of
CONTENTS

Introduction

EVAN LEWIS

THIS has been a long time coming.
   Nebel fans like me have been waiting not just years—but *decades*—for this series to be reprinted.

   In the heyday of *Black Mask*, two series stood head and shoulders above the rest: Dashiell Hammett's adventures of the Continental Op, and Frederick Nebel's saga of Richmond City. Both authors excelled in their mastery of the hard-boiled style, the depth and humor of their characters, the richness of their settings and the varied scope of their stories. But while Hammett is now a household name, Nebel has been largely relegated to the shadows.

   The reason is simple. While Hammett and many of his contemporaries went on to write mystery novels, Nebel stuck to novelettes. As the pulps gave way to paperbacks in the 1950s, the novel became the dominant fictional form, rendering the novelette almost defunct. *Black Mask* writers like Erle Stanley Gardner, George Harmon Coxe, W.T. Ballard—and a guy named Raymond Chandler—remained in the public consciousness thanks to their books, while Nebel was remembered only by pulp collectors.

   Nebel was a skilled craftsman who put his own stamp on the hard-boiled school of writing. His prose, packed with crackling dialogue and keen characterization, is as fresh today as it was in the 1930s. Altus Press has brought the bulk of his detective writing back into print. Now, at long last, they introduce new legions of readers to his most important body of work—the adventures of Captain Steve MacBride and his pal, reporter Kennedy of the *Free Press*.

   When this series debuted in the September 1928 *Black Mask*, it was called "The Crimes of Richmond City." The title was appropriate because while this is the story of MacBride and Kennedy, it's also the story of a city. The series lasted nine years, and from first to last, Richmond City was portrayed as a living, breathing and growing metropolis—almost a character in itself.

Nebel's secret was simple. In writing about Richmond City, he was writing about his home town. The borough of Staten Island, New York, where he was born, was then known as Richmond. It comprised most of Richmond County, with Richmond Valley at one end, Richmond Terrace at the other, Richmond Creek in the middle, and joined by Richmond Avenue and Richmond Road. He took the harbor and residential areas of Staten Island and combined them with elements of the Bronx and Manhattan to create his own scaled-down version of New York. Richmond City seemed very real—because to Nebel, it was.

In the first volume of this series, comprised of stories published between September 1928 and February 1930, we saw Richmond City at its most violent. As the series began, crooked politicians and racketeers had such a stranglehold on the city that MacBride was powerless to act. It was only when his best detective quit the Force to fight fire with fire, that the grip is broken, and MacBride could start cleaning up. He did this with a vengeance. We saw pitched battles in the streets, usually with MacBride himself leading the charge, and the death toll was high on both sides of the law. While the worst offenders were weeded out, the corruption ran deep, keeping MacBride on the defensive. Things were so bad that the precinct house sometimes seemed the last bastion of law and order.

Now late in its second year, the Richmond City series is entering a new phase. In this second Altus Press volume, featuring stories published between April 1930 and February 1933, we see MacBride on the lookout for new rackets and new forms of corruption, hell-bent to nip them in the bud. Though he takes heat from other cops—and the commissioner himself—for overstepping his bounds, MacBride is on a crusade. And when his efforts finally earn him a spot at Headquarters, he must face the reality that some of his fellow officers are on the take.

The stories published between March 1933 and February 1935, to be collected in the third Altus Press volume, take on a more personal note. Rather than combating large scale corruption, MacBride and Kennedy often apply their talents to murder cases, and sometimes involving old friends. That group also includes "Bad News" (March 1934), in which MacBride is away on vacation and Kennedy takes the lead for the first time. This story, as you might expect, is the most comedic of the entire series.

With the series in its fifth year, MacBride beginning to feel his age. He gets more and more frustrated with the job, particularly when men he considers friends don't support his actions. "It just breaks my heart with gratitude," he says. "Some fine day I'm going to start out and systematically change the shapes of a lot of schnozzles in this man's town." In "Rough Reform" (March 1933), he remarks, "The longer I work at this job, the more I think I should have taken up farming." He's tired of the long, irregular hours, and sick of "the blood and intrigue" that goes with police work.

In the fourth and final volume, featuring stories published between May 1935 and August 1936, we'll see secondary characters assume larger roles, and the introduction of two new regulars. By this time Nebel had come to think of himself as a novelist and wanted to delve deeper into his characters. This results in longer scenes, and sometimes longer stories.

MacBride's two best detectives, Ike Cohen and "Mory" Moriarity, were introduced early in the series, but in the final years their personalities grew stronger, providing more comic relief. They're often found sneaking drinks in the station or matching quarters in the back of the police car, and both spend a lot of time in speakeasies. The medical examiner calls them MacBride's cowboys. Kennedy calls them his stooges. MacBride calls them apes or tramps, but trusts them implicitly. "I've got two palookas working for me," he sums them up, "who think of me first and then the department."

The new regulars also add to the comedy. One of these is Kennedy's wacky bartender pal, Paderooski. He's always ready to lend Kennedy an ear, and sometimes other essentials, like money or a gun. The other is MacBride's driver, Gahagan. He's an all-around dimwit and pays not the slightest notice to safety or traffic laws, but has an uncanny ability to get places in a hurry, and always delivers MacBride in one piece.

At this point in the series, the humor is welcome, because MacBride's moods have grown increasingly dark. He reaches the lowpoint of his career in "Fan Dance" (January 1936), when he finds himself suspended. "I ought to have been kicked in the head," he says, "the first day I ever put on a uniform." Kennedy's scenes are darker, too. Both the author and his characters seem to realize that Kennedy's drinking is out of control, posing a threat to his health and life.

Though Nebel had a long and varied career (a detailed biography appeared in Volume 1), his greatest legacy was the saga of Richmond City. To you who are about to enter the city limits and fight crime with MacBride and Kennedy, I offer a word of advice:

Hold onto your seat. It's going to be a wild ride.

Wise Guy

An alderman who does not want to play Gangland's racket calls for help of Capt. Steve MacBride.

Chapter I

ALDERMAN TONY MARATELLI walked up and down the living-room of his house in Riddle Street. Riddle was the name of a one-time tax commissioner. Maratelli was a fat man, with fat dark eyes and two generous chins. His fingers were fat, too, and the fingers of one hand were splayed around a glass of Chianti, from which at frequent intervals he took quick, sibilant draughts. Now an Italian does not drink Chianti that way. But Maratelli looked worried. He was.

The winter night wind keened in the street outside and shook the windows in a sort of brusque, sharp fury. Riddle Street is a dark street. Also a windy one. That is because one end of it disembogues into River Road, where the piers are. One upon a time Riddle Street was aristocratic. Then it became smugly middle-class and grudgingly democratic. Then proletariat. Other streets around it went in for stores and warehouses and shipping offices. But Riddle Street clung to its brownstone fronts and its three-step stoops. It was rated a decent street.

Maratelli stopped short as his five-year-old daughter bowled into the room wearing a variety of night attire known as teddy bears.

" 'Night, poppa."

Maratelli put down the glass of Chianti, picked up the baby and bounced her playfully up and down on the palms of his fat hands.

"Good-night, angel," he said.

His wife, who was taller than he, and heavier, came in and smiled and held out her arms.

"Give her to me, Tony," she said.

"Yes, mama," said Maratelli. "Put her to bed and then close that door. Captain MacBride will be here maybe any minute."

"You want to be alone, Tony, don't you?"

"Yes, mama."

She looked at him. "It's about...."

"Yes, mama. Please take angel to bed and then you, too, leave me alone."

"All right, Tony." She looked a little sad.

He laughed, and his ragtag mustache fanned over his mouth. He pinched the baby's cheeks, then his wife's, then marched with her to the inner door. They went out, and he closed the door and sighed.

He went over to the table, picked up the glass of Chianti and marched up and down the room. His broad, heavy shoes thumped on the carpet. He wore a henna-colored shirt, a green tie, red suspenders and tobacco-brown pants. His shoes creaked.

When the bell rang, he fairly leaped into the hallway. He snapped back the lock and opened the door.

"Ah, Cap! Good you come!"

MacBride strolled in. He wore a neat gray cheviot overcoat, a flap-brimmed hat of lighter gray. His hands were in his pockets and he smoked a cigar.

"Slow at Headquarters, so I thought I'd come down."

"Yes—yes—yes."

Maratelli closed the hall door. The lock snapped automatically. He bustled into the living-room, eyed a Morris chair, then took a couple of pillows from the lounge, placed them in the Morris chair and patted hollows into them. He spread his hands towards the chair.

"Have a nice seat, Cap."

"Thanks."

"Give me the overcoat and the hat."

"That's all right, Tony."

MacBride merely unbuttoned his coat; sat down and laid his hat on the table. He was freshly shaven, neatly combed, and his long, lean face had the hard, ruddy glint of a face that knows the weather. He leaned back comfortably, crossing one leg over the other. The pants had a fine crease, the shoes were well polished, and the laces neatly tied.

"Chianti, Cap?"

"A shot of Scotch 'd go better."

"Yes—yes—yes!"

Maratelli brought a bottle from the sideboard, along with a bottle of Canada Dry.

"Straight," said MacBride.

Maratelli took one with him, said, "Here's how," and they drank.

MacBride looked at the end of his cigar.

"Well, Tony, what's the trouble?"

The wind kept clutching at the windows. Maratelli went over and tightened a latch. Then he pulled up a rocker to face MacBride, sat down on the edge of it, lit a twisted cheroot and took a couple of quick, nervous puffs. He stared vacantly at MacBride's polished shoe.

Finally— "About my boy Dominick."

"H'm."

"You know?"

"Go on, Tony."

"Yes—yes. Look, Cap, I'm a good guy. I'm a good wop. I got a wife and kids and business and I been elected alderman and—well, I'm a pretty good guy. I don't want to be on no racket, and I don't want any kind of help from any rough guys in the neighborhood. I been pestered a lot, Cap, but I ain't gonna give in. I got a wife and kids and a good reputation and I want to keep the slate what you call pretty damn clean. Cap, I ask you to come along here tonight after I been thinking a lotta things over in my head. I need help, Cap. What's a wop gonna do when he needs help? I dunno. But I ask you, and maybe you be my friend."

"Sure," said MacBride. "Get it off your chest."

"This wop—uh—Chibbarro, you know him?"

"Sam Chibbarro?"

"Yes—yes—yes."

"Uhuh."

"Him."

"What about him?"

Maratelli took a long breath. It was coming hard, and he wiped his face with his fat hand. He cleared his throat, took a drink of Chianti and cleared his throat again.

"Him. It's about him. Him and my boy Dominick. You know my boy Dominick is only twenty-one. And—and—"

"Going around with Chibby?"

"Yes—yes. Look. This is it, and Holy Mother, if Chibby knows I talk to you—" He exhaled a vast breath and shook his head. "Look. I have lotsa trucks, Cap, being what I am a contractor. I have ten trucks, some big, some not that big. Chibby—uh—Chibby he wants my trucks for to run booze at night!"

MacBride uncrossed his legs and put both heels on the floor. He leaned forward and, putting the elbow of one arm on his knee, jack-knifed the other arm against his side. His eyes, which had a windy blue look, stared point-blank at Maratelli.

"And you?"

"Well—" Maratelli sat back and spread his hands palmwise and opened his eyes wide—"me, I say no!"

"How long has this been going on?"

"Maybe a month."

"And Dominick. Where does he come in?"

Maratelli fell back in his chair like a deflated balloon. "That is what you call it, Cap. He is very good friends. He thinks Chibby is a great guy. He says I am the old fool."

MacBride looked at the floor, and his eyelids came down thoughtfully; the ghost of a curl came to his wide mouth, slightly sardonic.

Maratelli was hurrying on— "Look, Cap. My Dominick is a good boy, but if he keeps friends with that dirty wop Chibbarro it is gonna be no good. I can't stand for it, Cap. And what can I do with Dominick? He laughs at me. Puts the grease on his hair and wears the tuxedo and goes around with Chibby like a millionaire. Dominick has done nothing bad yet, but if this Chibby— Look, Cap, whatcha think I'm gonna do?"

MacBride sat back. "Hell, Tony, I've had a lot of tough jobs in my day, but you hand me a lulu. It's too bad. You've got my sympathy, and that's no boloney. I'll think it over. I'll do the best I can."

"Please, Cap, please. Every night Dominick goes out with Chibby. Dominick ain't got the money, so Chibby he pays the bills. And where do they go? Ah—the *Club Naples,* and places like that, and women— Holy Mother, it ain't good, Cap! My wife and my baby—I ask you, Cap, for my sake."

"Sure, Tony."

MacBride stood up.

Maratelli stood up, his breath whistling in his throat. "But if Chibby knows I speak to you—"

"He won't," clipped MacBride.

He buttoned his coat, put on his hat and shoved his hands into his pockets. "I'll be going."

"Have another drink."

"Thanks—no."

Maratelli let him out into the street and hung in the doorway.

"Night, Cap."

"Night, Tony."

MacBride was already swinging away, his cigar a red eye in the wind.

Chapter II

JOCKEY STREET was never a good street. It was the wayward offspring of a wayward neighborhood. Six blocks of it made a bee-line from the white-lights district to the no-lights district, and then petered off into the river.

The way was dark after the third block, except for a solitary electric sign that winked seductively in the middle of the fourth. It projected over the sidewalk, and the winking, beckoning letters were painted green:

L U

C   B

N A P L E S

MacBride did not come down from the bright lights. He came up from River Road, up from the bleak, unlovely waterfront. He still walked with his hands in his pockets, and the wind blew from behind, flapping his coat around his knees.

A man in a faded red uniform with tarnished gold braid stood in front of the double doors. As MacBride drew near, the man reached back and laid his hand on the knob. He opened the door as MacBride came up, and MacBride went inside.

The ante-room was quite dim, and the sound of a jazz band was muffled. To the right was a cloak-room, and the girl came over to take MacBride's coat. But MacBride paid no attention to her. A man came forward out of the dim-lit gloom, peering hard. He wore a tux, and he had white, doughy jowls and thin hair plastered back, and he was not so young.

"Your eyesight bad, Al?" chuckled MacBride.

"Oh… that you, Cap?"

"Yeah."

"Cripes, I'm glad to see you, Cap!"

He grabbed MacBride's hand and wrung it. MacBride stood still, slightly smiling, his face in shadow, and Al laughed showing a lot of uncouth teeth.

This was Al Vassilakos, a Greek who went over big with the wops and who was on speaking terms with the police. Mike Dabraccio really started the joint, a couple of years ago, but Mike talked out of turn to the old Sciarvi gang, and Sciarvi told Mike to go places. Al was instated by Sciarvi himself, and when Sciarvi got himself balled up—and subsequently shot—in a city-wide gang feud, Al carried on with the club. He'd kept clean since then, but Sam Chibbarro, called Chibby, was back, and MacBride had his doubts.

It looked as if Al was a little put out at MacBride's imperturbable calm.

"You—you looking for some guy, Cap?"

"No. Just wandering around, Al. How's business?"

"Pretty good."

"Mind if I sit inside?"

"Glad to have you, Cap."

MacBride took off his overcoat and his hat and gave them to the girl. Al walked with him across the ante-room and opened a door. A flood of light and a thunder of jazz rushed out as MacBride and Al went in. Al closed the door and MacBride drifted over to a small table beside the wall and sat down. Al signaled to a waiter and motioned to MacBride.

"Snap on it, Joe. That's Captain MacBride from Headquarters. Don't give him none of that cheap alky."

"Okey, boss."

Al went over and put his hands palm-down on the table and asked, "How about a good cigar, Cap? And I've got some good Golden Wedding."

"All right, Al—on both."

"Hey, Joe! A box of Coronas and that bottle of Golden Wedding. Bring the bottle out, Joe."

"Okey, boss."

"Anything you want, Cap, ask me. I'll be outside. I gotta be outside, you know."

"Sure, Al."

Vassilakos went out to the ante-room, but he still looked a bit worried.

It didn't take long for MacBride to spot Sam Chibbarro. Chibby was at a big table near the dance-floor. Dominick was there, too. And MacBride picked out Kid Barjo, a big bruiser swelling all out of his tux. There were some women—three of them. One had red hair and looked rather tall. Another had hair black as jet pulled back over the ears. The third was a little doll-faced blonde and she was necking Dominick. MacBride recognized her. She was Bunny Dahl, who used to hoof with a cheap burlesque troupe and was for a while mama to Jazz Millio before Jazz died by the gun. The whole party looked tight. A lot of people were there, and many of them looked uptownish.

This Club Naples was no haven for a piker. A drink was two dollars a throw, and the *couvert* four. If a hostess sat down with you, your drink or hers was three dollars a throw, and her own drinks were doctored with nine parts Canada Dry. A sucker joint.

Joe brought the bottle of Golden Wedding and a fresh box of cigars. MacBride took one of the cigars, bit off the end, and Joe held a match. MacBride puffed up and Joe went away, leaving the Golden Wedding on the table. MacBride poured himself a drink and watched Chibby and his crowd making whoopee.

Presently Kid Barjo got up, wandered around the table and then flung his arms around Bunny Dahl. Dominick didn't like that, and he took a crack at Barjo, and Chibby stood up and jumped between them. Bunny thought it was a great joke, and laughed. Chibby dragged Barjo to the other side of the table and made him sit down. Barjo was cursing and looking daggers at Dominick.

The jazz band struck up, and Chibby took the red-haired girl and pulled her out to the dance-floor. Barjo sulked and Dominick seemed to be bawling out Bunny. Then Bunny got up in a huff and hurried through a door at the other end of the cabaret. Barjo jumped up and followed her. Dominick took a drink and lit a cigarette and turned his back on the door. But he kept throwing looks over his shoulder. Finally he got up and went through the door, too, not so steady on his feet.

MacBride took another drink and sat back. When the dance was over Chibby and the red-haired girl came back to the table, and Chibby looked around and asked some questions. He shot a look towards the door, cursed and went through it.

MacBride leaned forward on his elbows and watched the door. The jazz band cut loose, and the saxophone warbled. The two girls at Chibby's table were both talking at the same time, and both of them looked peeved. The small dance-floor was jammed.

Joe came over and said, "Everything okey, Cap?"

"Yeah," said MacBride, watching the door.

"Maybe you'd like a nice sandwich? Al told me to ask you."

"No, Joe."

"Okey, Cap."

"Okey."

Joe turned, swooped down on a table that had been temporarily abandoned by two couples. He swept up four glasses that were only half empty, swept out, and came back with four full ones. He marked it all down on his pad. A gyp-joint waiter has no conscience.

The drummer was singing out of the side of his mouth, *"Through the black o' night, I gotta go where you go...."*

Chibby came out of the door. He was frowning. He walked swiftly to his table, clipped a few words to the girls. They started to get up. He snapped them down. Then he turned and headed towards the ante-room.

"Hello, Chibby," said MacBride.

Chibbarro jerked his head around.

"Jeeze... well, hello, MacBride! Where'd you come from?"

"I've been here—for a while—Chibby."

"Yeah?"

"Yeah."

"Hell… ain't that funny!"

"Funny?"

"Yeah, I mean funny I didn't see you."

"That is funny, Chibby."

"Yeah, it sure is. See you in a minute, Cap."

Chibby hurried out to the ante-room. MacBride turned his head and looked after him. Chibby looked over his shoulder as he pushed open the door. MacBride squinted one eye. His lips flattened perceptibly against his teeth, and one corner of his mouth bent downward. A curse grunted in his throat, behind his tight mouth. He looked back towards the door at the other end of the dance-floor.

The two girls who had been sitting at Chibby's table were now walking towards the ante-room. MacBride watched them go out. A frown grew on his forehead, then died. Joe came in from the ante-room and stood with his back to the door. He was looking at MacBride. His face was a little pale. He backed out again.

MacBride turned in time to see the door swing shut, but he did not see Joe. He stood up and took a fresh grip on his cigar. He walked towards the door and shoved it open. He stood with the light streaming down over his shoulders.

"Goin', Cap?" asked Al Vassilakos.

MacBride let the door shut behind him. "Where's Chibby?"

Al was standing in the shadows, his face a pale blur. "I guess he went, Cap."

"Where're those two women were with him?"

"They… all went, Cap."

The red end of MacBride's cigar brightened and then dimmed.

"Al, what the hell's wrong?"

"Wrong? Well, hell, I don't know. They just went out."

MacBride turned and pushed open the door leading into the cabaret. He strode swiftly among the tables, crossed the dance-floor and went through the door at the farther end. This led him into a broad corridor. He stopped and looked around, one eye asquint. He pushed open a door at his left. It was dark beyond. He reached for and found a switch; snapped on the lights. The room was well-furnished—but empty.

When he backed into the corridor, Al was there.

"What the hell, Cap?"

"Don't be dumb!"

MacBride went to the next door on the right, opened it and switched on the lights. It, too, was empty. He came back into the corridor and bent a hard eye on Al. Then he pivoted and went on to the next door on the left. He opened it and turned on the lights. He looked around. It was empty. There was an adjoining room, with the door partly open.

"Jeeze, Cap, what's the matter?"

"Pipe down!"

MacBride crossed the room and pulled the door wide open. He felt a draught of cold night air. He reached around and switched on the lights in the next room.

A table was overturned.

Kid Barjo lay on the floor with a bloody throat.

"H'm," muttered MacBride, and turned to look at Al.

The Greek's jowls were shaking.

MacBride took a couple of steps and bent down over Kid Barjo. He stood up and turned and looked at the Greek.

"Dead, Al. Some baby carved his throat open."

"My God Almighty!" choked Al.

MacBride spun and dived across the room to the open window. He looked out. An alley ran behind. He jumped out and ran along, followed a sharp turn to the right. He saw that the alley led to the street. He ran down it and into Jockey Street. There was no one in sight.

He entered the Club Naples through the front door and returned to the room where the Greek was still standing. He looked at a telephone on the wall.

"Listen, Al. Did Chibby make a call in the lobby?"

"I—I—"

"Come on, Al, if you know what's good for you."

"I think he did."

"Okey. He called whoever was in here when he knew I was outside and they breezed through this window. And you've been stalling, you two-faced bum!"

"So help me, Cap—"

"Can it! There's one of three people killed this guy."

"Jeeze!"

The Greek fell into a chair, stunned.

MacBride called Headquarters. Outside in the cabaret the drummer was singing, *"That's what you get for making whoope-e-e-e!…"*

Out in the street the green sign blinked seductively:

L U

C   B

N A P L E S

Chapter III

SERGEANT OTTO BETTDECKEN was eating a frankfurter and roll when MacBride barged into Headquarters followed by Moriarity and Cohen, and Kennedy of the *Free Press.*

MacBride said, "Otto, that guy's full name was Salvatore Barjo; age, twenty-six; address, the Atlantic Hotel. Stabbed twice in the front of the neck." Bettdecken filled out a blue card and his moon face clouded. "Crime of passion, Cap?"

"Ha!" chirruped Kennedy.

"We don't know yet," said MacBride. "The morgue bus picked the stiff up and I closed the joint for the night."

"How about the Greek?"

MacBride shrugged. "He's free. I want to give him some rope first. He ain't tough enough to worry about. He came across with the names of the three broads. Mary Dahl—the one they call Bunny; there was a red-head named Flossy Roote, and the other broad, the one that was originally with Barjo—she's Freda Hoegh. Flossy's this guy Chibbarro's woman, and I understand Freda's a friend of Bunny's. Chibby lived with Flossy in a flat at number 40 Brick Street. We went down there, but of course they weren't there. I parked Corson on the job. Freda and Bunny have a flat at number 28 Turner Street, but they haven't shown up either. I put De Groot on that job. No doubt they're hiding out, along with Dominick Maratelli."

Bettdecken shook his head. "This'll drive Tony crazy."

"Yeah," said MacBride, and headed for his office.

Moriarity and Cohen and Kennedy trailed after him, and MacBride got out of his overcoat and hung it up. He started a fresh cigar and took a turn up and down the room.

Kennedy leaned against the wall and tongued a cigarette from one side of his mouth to the other.

"That guy Barjo always was a bum welter anyhow."

MacBride snapped, "Which is no reason why he should be knifed in the throat! And this young Dominick—"

"A wise guy," drawled Kennedy. "A young wop just out of his diapers and trying to be a man about town. I know his kind. In fact, I know Dom. Flash. Jazz. He's not the only slob this jazz racket has taken for a buggy ride. And take it from me, old tomato, he's not going to get out of this with a slap on the wrist."

Moriarity said, "The thing is, after all your gas, Kennedy, who—who did poke Barjo in the throat?"

"Well, first the broad—this Bunny Dahl—goes in," said Kennedy. "Then Barjo. Then Dominick. Well—I'd say Dominick."

"Nix," popped Ike Cohen, swinging around from the window.

"No?"

"The broad," said Cohen. "The other guys were just covering her. Cripes, from what Cap says, they were all pretty tight. And the broad, having not much brains, would be the first to pull a dumb stunt like that. What do you say, Cap?"

"Not a hell of a lot," growled MacBride. "I'll leave the theory to you bright boys. I'm just waiting till we nail one of those babies. But as for the broad rating no brains, I don't know. And I don't see where Dominick rates big in brains, either."

Moriarity sat on the desk, dangling his feet. He said, "Anyhow, I'm inclined kind of to think it was the broad. It looks like a dizzy blonde's work."

Kennedy laughed wearily. "Well, if it was, Mory, we'll have a nice time in Richmond City. All the sob-sisters will sharpen up their pencils. Bunny will put a crack in her voice and try to look like a virgin that this guy Barjo tried to ruin. 'I did it to save my honor!' Like that. As if she ever had any honor. Listen, I saw that little trollop in a burlesque show one night, down near the river and—"

"All right, all right," horned in MacBride. "We can imagine."

"Anyhow," said Kennedy, "I'll bet it wasn't the broad."

The papers had it next morning. Dominick Maratelli's name was prominent—"wayward son of Alderman Antonio Maratelli."

MacBride, who had gone home at two, was back on the job at noon. There were reports on his desk, but nothing of importance. Chibbarro and Dominick and the three girls were still missing, and none of them had been to their flats following the murder.

The city was being combed thoroughly by no less than a dozen detectives, and every cop was on the lookout too. The fade-away had probably been maneuvered by Chibby. MacBride thought so, anyway, and it struck him as a pretty dumb move on Chibbarro's part. For why should Chibby entangle himself in a murder with which, apparently, he was not vitally concerned?

Tony Maratelli blundered into Headquarters a little past noon. He was shaking all over. He was hard hit.

"Cap, for the love o' God, what am I gonna do?"

"You can't do a thing, Tony."

"Yes, yes. I mean—but I mean, can't I do something?"

"No. Calm yourself, that's all. Dominick's in Dutch, and that's that. I can't save him, Tony."

"But, Holy Mother, the disgrace, Cap! And my wife, you should see her!"

"I know, I know, Tony. I'm sorry as hell for you and the wife, but the kid pulled a bone, and what can we do?"

Tony walked around the office and then he sat down and put his head in his hands and groaned. MacBride creaked in his chair and looked at Tony and felt sorry for him. Here was a wop who had kept his hands clean and tried to attach some dignity to his minor office. His record was a good one. He was a good husband, a square shooter, and a conscientious alderman. But what mattered all that to the public when his son ran with a bum like Chibbarro and got mixed up in a drunken brawl that terminated in the killing of Kid Barjo, the popular welter?

"You go home, Tony," said MacBride. "There's nothing to do but hope for the best."

Tony went home. He dragged his feet out of Headquarters, and he looked dazed. This was tragedy, no less. It was the tragedy of a good man tainted by the blood of his kin. And it is the warp and woof of life; you can't choose your heritage, nor can you choose your offspring. A man in public office is a specimen eternally held beneath the magnifying glass of public opinion, and public opinion can metamorphose a saint into a devil.

The police net which MacBride had caused to be flung out, seemed not very effective. Three days and three nights passed. No one was apprehended. Kid Barjo was buried, and Moriarity and Cohen attended the funeral—not from any feeling of sorrow or respect for the newly dead. But—sometimes—killers turn up when the dead go down. That was one of the times they didn't.

At the end of a week the *News-Examiner* printed a neatly barbed editorial relative to the inability of certain police officials to cope with existing crime conditions. The innuendo was thrown obliquely at MacBride, who took it with a curse. The editorial made much of the fact that a representative of the law had been in the Club Naples at the time of the killing....

"Of course I was there," MacBride told Kennedy. "But I had no reason to suppose that a murder was in the wind. Drunks will be drunks, and I give any guy a decent break."

"Some folks think you're getting soft, Cap," smiled Kennedy.

"Yeah?"

"Yeah."

MacBride creaked in his chair and wagged a finger at Kennedy. "You tell those—folks, Kennedy, that I'm just as tough today as I was twenty years ago."

"Have you seen any more of Tony Maratelli?"

"No—not since the day after the killing. I told him to go home and calm down."

There was a knock on the door, but before MacBride could reply, it burst open and Sergeant Bettdecken stood there, a banana in one hand and his face all flushed.

"God, Cap, I just got a call from Scofield. There's hell in Riddle Street. Uh—the front of Tony Maratelli's house been blown off!"

"Ain't that funny?" said Kennedy. "We were just taking about him."

MacBride bounced out of his chair and reached for his hat and coat.

Chapter IV

THERE was a crowd in Riddle Street.

The night was dark, but the red glow of the burning house lit up part of the street. Fire engines were there, and hose lay like great black serpents in the lurid glow, and the black rubber coats and helmets of firemen gleamed as they shot water into the flames.

The water fell back into the street and froze and glazed the pavements. Behind the fire lines stood men pointing and talking; and there were women with shawls around their heads and with coats flung hastily over night-dresses. There were a few women with children in arms.

A sleek red touring car with a brass bell on the cowl drove up and the fire chief, white-haired beneath his gold-braided cap, got out and looked up at the flames and had a few words with a lieutenant.

Part of the house wall caved in with a muffled roar, and dust and smoke billowed, and some of the onlookers cried out. A couple of patrolmen kept walking up and down and pushing back those who tried to edge in beyond the lines.

MacBride arrived in a police flivver driven by Hogan. Kennedy was in the back seat with him. MacBride got out and shoved his hands into the pockets of his neat gray cheviot and looked around and then spotted Patrolman Scofield. Scofield came over and saluted and MacBride asked:

"Where's Tony?"

"In that house across the street—number 55."

"Anybody hurt?"

"Tony got a bash on the head, that's all. His wife wasn't hit, but she's pretty hysterical."

"Where were you when this place was blown?"

"Three blocks up River Road. I heard it and came on the run."

"I'll take a look at Tony."

He went into number 55. The hall door was open, and there were some people in the hall. The sitting-room was off to the right, and MacBride saw a white-coated ambulance doctor sitting on a chair and listlessly smoking a cigarette. Tony was sitting on another chair wrapped in a heavy bathrobe and staring into space. His wife was sitting on a cot, holding her baby in her arms and moaning and rocking from side to side. Several women were grouped around her, trying to comfort her, and one held a glass of water.

MacBride drifted into the room, looked everybody over with quick scrutiny, and then went over and stood before Tony. After a moment Tony became aware of his presence and looked up and tried to say something, but he could only shake his head in dumb horror. MacBride took one hand out of his pocket and laid it on Tony's shoulder and pressed the shoulder with brief but sincere reassurance.

"Snap out of it, Tony."

"Holy Mother.... Holy Mother...."

"I know, I know. But snap out of it. You're alive. Your wife and baby're alive."

"Like—like the end of the world...."

MacBride caught his toe in the rung of a chair and slewed it nearer. He sat down and took a puff on his cigar and then took the cigar from his mouth and braced the hand that held it on his knee.

"You've got to snap out of it, Tony...."

Tony winced. "Out of bed I was thrown... out of bed... like—" He groaned and put his hands to his head.

MacBride looked at the cigar in the hand on his knee and then looked up at Tony. "Were you asleep when it happened?"

"Yes... I was asleep. The wall fell in...."

"Did you get any warning beforehand? I mean, was there any threatening letter?"

"No—no."

"Well, try to snap out of it, Tony. I'll see you again."

MacBride got up and put the cigar back in his mouth and his hands back in his pockets. He looked around the room, his windy blue eyes thoughtful. Then he went out into the hallway and so on out into the street. He stood at the top of the three stone steps and watched the firemen pouring water into the demolished house. The flames had died, but the water was still hissing on hot beams.

Kennedy came out of the crowd, his face in shadow but the red end of a cigarette marking out his mouth. From the bottom of the steps he said:

"Now why do you suppose they chucked a bomb at Tony's house, Cap?"

"Who chucked a bomb?" said MacBride.

"Are we thinking about the same guys?"

MacBride went down the steps. "Yeah, I guess so. But I don't know why."

"Let's go back to Headquarters and get a drink."

"I'm hanging around a while," said MacBride.

Half an hour later water stopped pouring into the ruins. The firemen began to draw in the hose. The front of the building had disappeared. You could look into the lower and upper stories and see the debris.

MacBride went over and had a few words with the chief. He borrowed a flashlight from one of the firemen and went up the blackened stone steps. He climbed over the broken door and swung his flash around. He stepped from one broken beam to another and finally reached the living-room. The floor was slushy with black ashes that had been soaked by the water. The smell was acrid. He looked at the chair wherein he had sat one night and talked with Tony. It was burnt and broken.

He proceeded over fallen plaster that was gummy beneath his feet and reached a stairway. He climbed this and came to the floor above. The white beam of his flash probed the tattered darkness. Overturned chairs, beds soaked with water and blackened with soot. Tony's home in ruin…. He sighed.

There were three bedrooms, and he went from one to another, and looked around and meditated over several things, and then he went down by the cluttered stairway and worked his way back to the street.

He returned the flashlight to the fireman and said, "Thanks."

He stood on the curb, his chin on his chest and his hands in his pockets. Presently he was aware of Kennedy standing beside him.

"Where've you been, Cap?"

"Places," said MacBride.

"What did you see?"

"Things."

Chapter V

TONY MARATELLI stood by the window of number 55 Riddle Street and looked across at the epitaph of his home.

It was not a pleasant sight, in the sharp clear light of a winter morning. He could see the broad bed wherein he and his wife were used to sleeping; the smaller bed in another room wherein his daughter had narrowly escaped death; the other room and the other bed that were Dominick's….

Tony looked sad and haggard, and when a fat man looks haggard it is in a way pathetic. A couple of men were already at work removing the debris from the sidewalk, and a policeman walked back and forth, guarding what remained of Tony's possessions.

Of course, mused Tony, he would have a nice house again, somewhere. He had plenty of money. But—that house was an old one, and he had lived there for fifteen years—first as tenant, then as owner. It had been one of the milestones of his success as a building contractor. Wherefore its ruin made him feel sad. He pulled his heavy bathrobe tighter about his short, adipose body and sniffed.

He saw MacBride come down the opposite side of the street, pause to have a talk with the patrolman on duty, then run his eyes over the ruined house. Tony's eyes steadied. He licked his lips. MacBride was his friend, but....

The captain turned abruptly and crossed the street. Tony waited for the sound of the doorbell. It came. Mrs. Reckhow, who had been good enough to give him and his family shelter overnight, appeared from another room.

But Tony said, "It's for me, Mrs. Reckhow, thanks."

"All right, Mr. Maratelli," she said, and disappeared.

Tony went out into the hall and opened the door and MacBride said, "Morning, Tony," and walked in.

They came back into the living-room and MacBride took off his hat, looked at it, creased the crown and then laid the hat on a table.

"How you feeling, Tony?"

"Not so good. I feel rotten, Cap. Yeah, I feel rotten."

His black hair was tousled about the ears and he needed a shave and his jowls seemed to hang forlornly towards his shoulders.

MacBride, who had had only six hours sleep, looked fresh and vigorous. He went over by the window and looked at the men working on the sidewalk and then he turned around and looked at Tony.

"Tony," he said, and looked at the floor, pursing his lips.

"Uh?" came Tony's voice from somewhere in the roof of his mouth.

"Tony... about Dominick."

Tony wiped a hand in front of his face as though he were brushing away a spider-web. "Uh... you found him?"

"No."

"Oh... I thought you found him."

"No, I didn't find him."

"Oh." His voice was weary, coming out like weary footsteps.

MacBride brought his eyes up from the floor and fastened them on Tony's eyes and seemed to screw down the bolts of his gaze with slow but sure precision.

"We'd better talk plain, Tony."

Tony's eyes glazed and seemed to stare as though at something beyond MacBride's shoulder.

"Plain," said MacBride, his voice going down.

"Well...." Tony shrugged and looked around the room as if there was something there he wanted.

MacBride clipped, "How long was Dominick in your house before they blew the front off?"

Tony muttered, "Holy Mother!" and sat down heavily in a chair.

"How long, Tony?"

"Look, Cap! Could I go and give my boy up when he come to me for protection, crying like a baby? Could I? Didn't my wife she plead with me, too? But she did not have to plead, no. Dominick is my son, my flesh and blood, and if his father will not give him protection, who will? He is only the boy, Cap! He—"

"Now, wait a minute, Tony," broke in MacBride. "I can guess all that. What I want to know is, how long was he there?"

"Three days—just three days. But—I couldn't go tell you, Cap! The boy he ask me to protect him. He is sorry. He is sorry he got mixed up with that Chibby. He didn't do nothing, Cap. He didn't kill that box-fighter—"

"Who did?"

"I don't know."

"Tony...."

"Please to God, I don't know!"

A muscle jerked alongside MacBride's mouth. "Dominick knew! He told you!"

"No—no!"

"Tony"—MacBride's voice was like a keen wind far off—"Tony, I've given you every break I could. I know you're a good guy—the best wop I've ever known. But—you've got to come clean. Listen to me: I'm being razzed for that killing. You know why—because I happened to be in Al's joint when these bums got soused and Barjo got knifed. But aside from that—even if I wasn't razzed—I'd want the killer just the same—"

"But Dominick he didn't kill—"

"Don't go over that. He must have told something. What did he tell you?"

Tony spread his arms and looked as if he were going to cry. "Nothing, Cap." And he kept wagging his head from side to side. "Didn't I keep asking him? Sure. Didn't I beg him to tell me? But he don't tell. He just say he didn't kill Barjo—and he swear by the cross and kiss it. Cap, please to God, that is the truth!"

MacBride took one hand out of his pocket and rubbed his jaw and put the hand back into his pocket again. A flush of color was in his lean hard cheeks, and there was a cool subdued fury lurking in his wide direct eyes. His voice became almost laconic:

"All right, then. He was in your house. When did he get away?"

"It must have been when the fire started. I heard him yell from the other room, and then he was gone when I got there. He must have run right out. And now—now, where is he?"

"That's what I'm trying to find out. I knew he'd been there when I poked around after the fire. He must have left in a hurry. His dress shirt and his studs were on the dresser, and his tux was hanging on the wall. That's why I knew he'd been home."

"Yes, he didn't go out once. He was… afraid."

"Sure."

"And now—"

"His life," put in MacBride, "won't be worth two cents if Chibby and his crowd find him. That's why I want to know where he is. He must have run out on the crowd and come home. They're afraid he'll spring something. That's why they crashed your house."

Tony rocked back and forth. "And if I knowed where he is, Cap, sure I'd tell you. I don't want my boy murdered. God, if I only knowed where he is!"

"Listen," said MacBride, "where are you going from here?"

"I think we'll go to a hotel. The Maxim, yes."

"Okey. But remember—if Dominick gets in touch with you, tell me right away. The only safe place for him is in the jail."

"Jail!"

"Now calm yourself. Jail—yes. Let me know when you get in The Maxim."

"Yes." He got up, wobbling about. "Cap, you're my friend, ain't you?"

"Yeah, sure, Tony."

"Thanks, Cap—thanks!" His breath wheezed. "My poor wife, she is all bust up."

"Well, you're not helping her any by slopping all over the place. Buck up. Get a shave. Don't crack up like a damn' hop-head. For crying out loud!"

He laughed bluntly and slapped Tony on the back and went out.

Chapter VI

MORIARITY and Cohen were trying to get a kick out of playing two-handed Michigan when MacBride breezed into the office. They looked up once and then went on playing while MacBride got out of his overcoat. He came over and sat down and said:

"Deal me a hand."

Cohen said, "Well, how'd you make out?"

"Yes and no. Tony doesn't know a damned thing. But Dominick did come back to his house. He breezed when the place was blown."

"And didn't the kid tell his old man anything?" asked Cohen.

"No."

Moriarity said, "What makes you think Tony was playing ball?"

"I just know it."

Moriarity laughed. "Maybe you are getting soft, Cap."

"Lay off," said MacBride. "Tony's a square wop."

"Then why the cripes didn't he tell you his kid was home?"

MacBride looked at his cards. "You haven't got a kid, have you?"

"Not that I know of."

Cohen laughed. "There's a wisecrack for you, Cap!"

MacBride put four chips on the queen. "Then you wouldn't know, Mory, why the old wop didn't tell me. But he's square."

"Oh, yeah," sighed Moriarity.

"Go ahead," said MacBride, "razz me. I can stand it. If I took you guys and the newspapers seriously I'd jump in the river as a total loss. But you're all just a bad smell to me."

Moriarity laughed. "Poor old Cap!"

"Can that, too! And listen, you gumshoes. We want Dominick. He's lone-wolfing it somewhere. Even you, Mory, would realize that after he left Chibby's crowd and went back home, he wouldn't dare show his mug again with the crowd. You'd realize that, Mory—any dumb-bell would."

Cohen said, "Chew on that, Mory."

"And," said MacBride, "we want Dominick before Chibby or one of his guns nails him. They're after him; you can bet your shirt on that. He knows something, and they're after him."

"At least," said Moriarity, "it crimps Kennedy's idea that Dominick killed Barjo. I still say it was the broad."

Cohen snapped, "Hey, you, it was me first had the idea it was the broad."

"All right, grab the gold ring, guy—grab it."

"My idea may be crimped," said Kennedy, a new voice in the doorway. "But if it was the broad, why the hell should Chibbarro be going to such great pains to keep Dominick and the three girls and himself out of sight?"

"Now you've asked something, Kennedy!" chopped off MacBride.

Kennedy strolled in and said, "All right, Mory. I was wrong, let's say, on picking Dominick as the killer. I was wrong. Now, you bright young child, *why* is Chibbarro playing hide-and-seek?"

Mory put on a long face. "Well, if the broad was his friend—"

"Boloney!" chuckled Kennedy. "She was just a broad. Chibby wouldn't waste a sneeze on her if there wasn't a reason. If she killed Barjo, and there wasn't a good reason for his trying to hide her, that bum would have come right out and told Cap what she'd done. But he *had* to save her—*for a reason.* That's how much you know, Mory."

MacBride had to chuckle, and he looked at his right-hand men. "Boys, you're both good cops. In a fight, you're the berries. But take my advice and don't try to figure things out too closely. Not when this wiseacre Kennedy is roaming about."

"I'll put your name in the paper twice for that tomorrow," said Kennedy. "But get Dominick, and make him talk. I'm not saying the broad killed Barjo. I'm saying that *if* she killed him, then there's something bigger behind this job than just a ham welter getting a knife in his gizzard."

"Kennedy," said MacBride, "sometimes you're a pain in the neck, but today you're an inspiration."

"Three times in the paper tomorrow, Cap. Two more cracks like that and I'll see about getting you a headline."

"And another crack like that, Kennedy, and I'll plant my foot in your slats."

"Ah, well," grinned Kennedy, "boys will be boys. How about a drink?"

MacBride dragged out a bottle of Dewar's.

Chapter VII

IN a way of speaking, Dominick Maratelli was between the devil and the deep sea. That is reckoning, of course, on the conjecture of MacBride that Dominick had dropped the mob and that the mob was seeking him. The mob... and the law.

Moriarity and Cohen worked overtime on the hunt. Precinct plainclothes men worked too. And uniformed cops.

It was believed that when Dominick took hasty flight from the bombed house, he was broke. A man must eat. He must sleep somewhere. It was winter, and streets and alleys do not make comfortable lodgings.

Nor was MacBride idle. He too, roamed the streets and made inquiries at lunch-rooms, speakeasies; and most of his roaming was done during the dark hours. He went alone, looking into the twenty-five-cent-a-night flophouses, conning the bread-lines in North Street.

There was no clue yet as to the whereabouts of Chibby and the three girls. And MacBride was eternally aware of the fact that Dominick's life depended on who found him first. Tony kept calling constantly... but there was no news.

And in the middle of the next week there was an article in the papers relative to the fact that Antonio Maratelli had resigned as alderman. Of course, the political powers that be had asked him to resign—a request that was by way of being a threat. Tony made no kick. He was more interested in saving his son.

Kennedy said, "If you ask me, Cap, that young wise guy Dominick deserves to be bumped off. There his old man got a nice political job, and was kind of proud of it, and then this young pup pulls a song and dance that the old man has to pay for. The reward of virtue is most certainly a kick in the pants."

MacBride tightened his jaw a little harder and continued to roam the streets....

There was a black cold night when he wandered into a dark windy street and saw a familiar green sign blinking seductively:

L U

C   B

N A P L E S

As he drew nearer, he could hear the uniformed doorman beating cold feet on the cold pavement.

MacBride came up in the shadow of the houses and the doorman reached back for the doorknob. He did not recognize MacBride until the captain's foot was on the step, and then he seemed to hesitate in perplexed indecision.

MacBride looked at him and said, "Well?"

"Oh... hello, Cap. Didn't recognize you." He opened the door.

MacBride walked into the dim, stuffy ante-room and stood just inside the door and looked around. The coat-room girl came over but MacBride shook his head and she recognized him and bit her lip and retreated back into the gloom. A stiff white shirt-front came out of another corner of the gloom, and a voice said:

"Well, buddy?"

"I'm MacBride."

"Oh... yeah."

"Where's Al?"

"I'm Patsy. It's all right. What can I do for you?"

"Get me Al."

"Well, he ain't here right now."

"Where is he?"

"I dunno. He went out about an hour ago. If you want to wait for him—there's a little room off here."

"I don't want to wait for him."

"Well, I'm sorry, Cap."

Muffled was the racket of the jazz band.

MacBride turned and pulled open the door and stepped out and looked up and down the street.

The doorman was gone.

MacBride's hands were in his pocket, and the hand in his right pocket closed over the butt of his gun. He moved towards the narrow alley that flanked one side of the building and led to the courtyard in the rear. He looked down it and he flexed his lips and then he entered the alley and walked lightly but rapidly.

He reached the courtyard in the rear. He saw a door and a lighted window, but the shade was drawn down. He moved towards the door and grasped the knob and turned it and the door gave and opened on a crack. He pushed it wide and stepped into a corridor that was dimly lighted by shaded wall lights. He had been in this corridor once before. He closed the door behind him.

From the door farthest away on the right he saw Dominick step out, and behind him the doorman and Al Vassilakos. He started to rap out a command, but Dominick, who was on the point of making for the rear door, saw him and spun and ran in the opposite direction.

"Hey, you!" shouted MacBride.

He barged down the corridor past Al and the doorman. Through the door at the end he burst into the noisy cabaret. The jazz band was hooting and people were dancing. Dominick was running alongside the tables and making for the front. MacBride sailed after him, and the jazz band petered off and the dancers stopped and stared with amazement. MacBride bowled over a drunk that teetered into his path and reached the door to the ante-room six jumps behind Dominick. The door banged in his face, and as he flung it open he saw the front door slam shut.

He streaked through the ante-room and cannoned out in the cold dark street. He heard running footsteps and saw Dominick heading for River Road. MacBride took up the chase and pulled his gun out of his pocket.

"Hey, you, Dominick!" he shouted.

But Dominick kept running.

They were nearing River Road when MacBride raised his gun and fired a high warning shot. He saw Dominick duck and run closer to the shadows of the houses. He fired another shot, bringing it closer but still reluctant to kill.

Suddenly beneath the arc-light that stood on the corner of Jockey Street and River Road, he saw a uniformed policeman appear. At the same time Dominick cut across to the opposite side of the street. The policeman crossed too, to head him off, and then Dominick swerved back into the center of the street and turned around, ran this way and that, and finally stopped and crouched.

MacBride reached him first and clipped, "Now put your hands up, kid!"

"I—I'll—"

"You'll shut up! Is that you, Zeloff? Frisk him. I don't think he's got anything, but frisk him."

Patrolman Zeloff went through Dominick quickly and deftly. "Naw, not a thing, Cap."

MacBride took out manacles and locked Dominick's hands behind his back. Then he shoved his gun back into his pocket. Dominick was shivering with the cold. He wore no overcoat.

MacBride said, "Zeloff, go back to the Club Naples and pinch Al and bring him to Headquarters. I'll take this bird along in a cab."

"Okey, Cap."

"And close the joint."

"Sure."

MacBride grabbed Dominick's arm and walked with him towards River Road.

"For cripes sake, Cap, listen. Al hasn't done a thing—"

"Shut up. *Hey, taxi!*"

Chapter VIII

THE light with the green shade hung over the shiny flat-topped desk and the light umbrellaed outward over the desk and included in its radiance Dominick and MacBride, who sat and faced each other across the desk.

Dominick was thin and a black stubble was on his face and black circles were beneath his eyes, but there was also black mutiny in his eyes. He had on a shirt beneath his thin coat, but no collar, and his black hair was rumpled but still a bit shiny from the last application of hair oil.

"You," said MacBride, "you caused all this."

"Well, why the hell bring it up?"

"I intend bringing it up and up. You're just a wise guy who tried to run with big, bad boys. You worried hell out of your father and mother. Because of you your father's house was blown up. Because of you your father lost his aldermanic job. Now what the hell kind of a break do you suppose you deserve?"

"Did I ask for a break? Did I?"

"Of course not. But you're expecting one. What I want to know is, who killed Barjo?"

"I don't know."

"You mean you don't feel like telling me."

"About that."

MacBride leaned forward and put his elbows on the table and drew his brows close down until they almost met at the top of his nose. "Dom, my boy, you're going to spring what you know."

"Like hell I am."

"Like hell you are."

"Listen, you. I didn't kill Barjo. You've got nothing on me—not a thing! I didn't kill him."

"Why did you drop out of sight?"

"That's my business."

"Why did you sneak home and hide away?"

"That's my business too."

MacBride put his voice down low. "We know of course that Chibby is after you."

"You don't know anything."

MacBride snapped, "Listen to me, you little two-tongued dago! I'm giving your old man a break. I'm trying to give you a break—not because I like you—but because I like your old man! As for you, I think you're a lousy pup! But get this—get it!—I want Chibby or one of the broads was on that party the night Barjo got knifed. I don't care what the hell one I get, I want one of them! And you—you're going to play ball with me or, by cripes, I'll whale hell out of you!"

"I'm not playing ball!" rasped Dominick. "I was on that party, I know that. But I didn't do a thing to anybody. And I ain't going to squeal!"

"You poor dumb slob!" MacBride half rose out of his chair and planted his palms on the desk. "Don't you realize that Chibby wants to blow your head off? Don't you realize that we're the only guys can save you?"

Dominick was biting his lip and his black eyes were jerking back and forth across the desk. He shook his head. "I—I ain't going to say a thing."

The door opened and Patrolman Zeloff shoved in Al Vassilakos. "There he is, Cap."

"Okey, Zeloff. Hello, Al. What the hell are you looking all hot and bothered about?"

"This—this is a dirty trick, Cap!"

"Is it? Listen to me, Al. I've given you all the breaks you're going to get. You were harboring a fugitive from the law."

"I wasn't!" choked the Greek. "So help me, I wasn't. This guy came to me and asked me to give him some jack so he could blow the town. He didn't have no jack. I gave him hell for coming around."

Dominick cut in, "He didn't do anything, Cap. I went there and asked him for some jack, just like he said."

"Sure," said Al, waving his hand. "See?"

"All right, all right," said MacBride. "I see. But you've always tried to kid me, Al, and you'll warm your pants here a while. I don't like your joint. You're two-faced as hell. And I don't like you. Zeloff, put this guy in the cooler for a while."

"Okey, Cap."

"Aw, say, Cap," said Al, "give me a break."

"Break? I'm through giving guys breaks."

"Aw—"

"Come on, you!" snapped Zeloff, and pulled Al out into the hall.

MacBride swung around in his chair, sitting bolt upright, and threw his gaze across the desk like two penetrating beams of blue fire.

"You see the kind of a palooka you went to looking for help! The first yap out of him is to save his own face!"

"Well, d' you see me yapping?"

"Dominick..." MacBride said the word with deadly softness as he leaned back. "Dominick, I warn you, you're in for a beating if you don't come across. I don't care if you are Tony's son. I'm trying to give you a break, but maybe I'll have to break you first. You can be nice... or I can be—nasty. Do you get me?"

Dominick drew his face up tightly and pinched his brows down over his midnight eyes. "You can't lay a hand on me!"

"I don't—personally. I've got men who do it for me."

"Yah, you're just the bull-dozing cop I heard you were! Just a big flatfoot! Just a big, loud-mouthed tough guy!"

"Just," said MacBride, "that."

Dominick jumped up, a lean shaft of vibrating dark fire. "You won't beat me! You won't! By God Almighty... you *won't*."

"Unless you play ball."

The telephone bell rang. MacBride picked up the instrument.

"Captain MacBride talking," he said. "Yeah, Mory.... What?... No, no; go ahead...." He listened, his eyes narrowing "What's that address?... Yeah; 22 Rumford Street. Okey. I'll shoot right down."

He slammed the telephone back to the desk and went to the door and yelled down the corridor. A reserve came on the run.

"Shove this guy in a cell, Mike. I got a date with a good break."

He piled into his overcoat, grabbed his hat and went out into the central room. He called Hogan, and Hogan ran out to get the police flivver. MacBride was waiting for him on the sidewalk.

Chapter IX

RUMFORD STREET is on the northern frontier of the city. It is a hilly street, climbing up from Marble Road. A drab street, walled in by three- and four-story rooming-houses. Ordinarily a peaceful neighborhood.

The police flivver swung off Marble Road and labored up the grade. When it was halfway up MacBride saw an ambulance and a small group of people.

"That's it, Hogan."

"Yeah."

The flivver drove up behind the ambulance, and MacBride got out and saw a patrolman and the patrolman saw him and saluted.

"Second floor, Cap."

"Right."

MacBride entered the hall door and climbed the dusty narrow staircase. On the second landing he saw light streaming out through a door, and a policeman was standing in the door. He saw MacBride and stepped aside, and MacBride went into a small living-room.

Kennedy was sitting on a chair with his feet on a table and his hands clasped behind his back. Cohen was walking back and forth taking quick drags on a cigarette.

"Hello, Cap," he said, and jerked his head towards the next room.

But MacBride had caught sight of a doctor and a couple of uniformed patrolmen and Moriarity standing beside a bed, and there was a pulmotor working. He caught sight, too, of a girl's legs protruding from a nightgown, and then Moriarity turned around and saw him and shrugged and came out.

"It's Bunny Dahl," he said.

"What happened?"

"Gas."

"What—suicide?"

"Dunno. Ike and me stopped in a speakeasy just around on Marble Road. Kennedy was there, and we were just about to start a card game when Patrolman Cronkheiser came busting in looking for a telephone. It seems he was walking his beat down Rumford Street when a woman ran out hollering for help. She lives next door. She'd smelt gas and got up and went out in the hall, and then when she knocked on this door and got no answer she ran out and hollered and Cronkheiser came up and busted in. Bunny was laying on the floor, by one of them gas heaters—there it is."

"How is she?"

"Pretty rotten. They want to try the pulmotor because they think she may pass out before they reach the hospital."

MacBride went in and looked at her and then came back into the other room.

"Queer," he said.

"Yeah," said Kennedy. "Looks as if she got cold feet."

MacBride said nothing for a minute, and then he said, "I got Dominick."

Kennedy's feet fell down from the table. "Things come in bunches, like bananas, don't they? Where'd you get him?"

"Club Naples. He was feeling Al for some jack when I wandered in. I got Al, too. I don't like that two-faced Greek. I'm going to get something on him yet."

"Did he say anything?" asked Moriarity.

"No. The kid's got spirit. He won't squeal. But—he'll have to. Even if we have to beat him."

MacBride turned and looked into the other room and then he rubbed his hand slowly across his jaw. The doctor looked over his shoulder and beckoned, and MacBride came in and stood beside the bed.

"She's trying to say something, Captain."

"What's she trying to say?"

"About a chap named Chibby."

"Oh... Chibby."

MacBride sat down on the edge of the bed and took out a pencil and an old envelope. "Bunny," he said. "What's it all about, Bunny?"

"Chibby ... did it...."

"How?"

"He got me drunk... then he tied a rag around my mouth... so I couldn't yell... then he held my head down by the gas stove...."

"H'm." One side of MacBride's mouth drew down hard. He leaned closer. "Bunny, where is he?"

"I don't know.... Al knows."

"Why did he do this to you, Bunny?"

"Because I knew he...." Her voice trailed off.

The doctor said, "We'd better try getting her to the hospital. She hasn't got much of a chance."

"Okey." MacBride stood up. He went back into the other room and said, "Ike, I want you to go to the hospital with Bunny and hang around and see if she says anything more. Mory, you come with me to Headquarters. Al is in for hell."

He went out into the hall and down the narrow dusty stairs. Moriarity followed him, and Kennedy trailed along behind. They all climbed into the flivver, and Hogan started the motor and they drove off.

Chapter X

MacBRIDE had removed his hat, but his overcoat was still on and his hands were in his pockets. His face was gray and hard like granite, and his eyes were like blue cold ice, and he stood with his feet spread apart and his square jaw down close to his chest.

Kennedy sat on the desk with his feet on a chair and his elbows on his knees and his hands loosely clasped. Moriarity stood with his back to the radiator and a dead cigarette hanging from one side of his mouth.

Al Vassilakos sat in the swivel chair with the light streaming brightly into his white puffed face. It was a face that seemed to have been crudely molded out of dough. His knees were pressed together and his toes were turned in and pressed hard against the floor, and his pudgy hands gripped the arms of the swivel chair.

MacBride said, "You know where Chibby is, Al."

"So help me, Cap—"

"Shut up! You know where he is. I want to know where he is."

"Uh—honest, Cap—"

"Shut up! There's no time for stalling. You've been playing me for the fool and I'm sick of it. I want to know where Chibby is. I'll give you one minute to come across."

He took his left hand out of his pocket and crooked his arm and stared down at the watch on his wrist.

Al gripped the arms of the chair harder with his pudgy hands. His toes screwed against the floor. His white stiff shirt-front moved up and down jerkily. His lower lip, which had been caught under his teeth, flopped out and gleamed wet, and his nose wrinkled and his eyes bulged wildly. His breath was beginning to grate in his throat. His body was straining in the chair, and the chair creaked, and he was stretching his throat in his tight stiff collar, as if fighting for breath. Sweat burst out on his forehead and gleamed like globules of grease, and his whole face, that had been dead like dough, began to twitch and convulse as agitated nerve muscles raced around beneath his skin.

MacBride looked dispassionately at the watch on his wrist. Kennedy seemed interested in his hands. Moriarity's eyes were hidden behind shuttered lids, but he was staring at Al.

MacBride shoved his hand back into his pocket. "Minute's up, Al."

Kennedy looked up from his hands.

Al strained harder in his chair, his white face ghastly in the light that poured down upon it.

"Well, Al?…" MacBride drew his lips flat back against his teeth.

Al choked. "N-no!"

MacBride walked to the door and opened it and called, "Hey, Mike!"

He came back into the room and after a while a patrolman came in buttoning his coat.

"Mike," said MacBride, "take this guy upstairs and put him over the hurdles. You, too, Mory."

The policeman and Moriarity heaved Al out of the chair and

dragged him out of the room. Al was blubbering and breaking at the knees.

MacBride closed the door and sat down in the swivel chair. Kennedy lit a cigarette and shot smoke through his nostrils.

"Bunny sure got hell, didn't she, Cap?"

"Yeah. It's like that song about what you get for making whoopee."

"I wonder what's behind this. I wonder why Chibby tried to bump off the broad. Maybe *he* killed Barjo."

"Maybe."

They didn't talk much. MacBride started a cigar and sat back in his chair, and after a while Kennedy got down from the desk and wandered about the room.

Half an hour later the door opened and Moriarity stood there. He carried his coat under his arm.

"Okey, Cap."

"Yeah?"

"Yeah. Chibby's hiding out at 95 Hector Street with about six other guns."

"All right, Mory. Put your coat on."

Chapter XI

I T was a big, powerful touring car that left Headquarters and droned through the dark streets. Hogan was at the wheel. Beside him sat Moriarity and MacBride. In the rear were five policemen and Kennedy. It was half-past two in the morning. The dark streets were empty, and the big car plunged from one into another, and the men in the back swayed from side to side as the car bent sharply around corners.

"This is Hector," said Hogan.

"What's the number?" asked MacBride.

"The numbers begin here," said Kennedy. "That 95 should be about three blocks down."

MacBride said, "Pull up about a block this side, Hogan."

"Okey."

The car slowed down and rolled along leisurely, and presently Hogan swung into the curb and applied the brake.

MacBride got out first and looked up and down the street. The policemen got out and stood around him, and their badges, fastened to the breasts of their heavy blue overcoats, flashed intermittently.

"It must be on the other side of the street," said MacBride. "Come on."

They crossed the street and walked along close to the houses. The houses were set back from the sidewalk and fronted by iron fences, and just behind the fences were depressions and short flights of stone steps that led down to the basement floors. The street lights were few and far between, and the windows of the houses were darkened.

MacBride was saying, "We'll try to get in through the cellar."

They reached number 95 and went in through the gate and crowded noiselessly down the stone steps until their heads were level with the sidewalk. There were two windows, without shades, and the windows were dirty.

"They're supposed to be on the top story," whispered Moriarity.

"And it's four stories," muttered MacBride. "Let's try the windows."

They tried them, but the windows were locked. MacBride stood for a moment thinking. Then— "There's no fire-escapes in front. They must be in the rear. Let's find a way to the rear. The next block."

They came back to the sidewalk and walked on, took the next left turn and then turned left again into the street that paralleled Hector. MacBride counted the houses.

"You might have noticed," said Kennedy, "that 95 was the only four-storied house. The others were three."

"It should be about here," said MacBride.

He mounted the steps and rang the bell. After a few minutes the door opened and an old woman wearing a nightcap looked out.

"Madam," said MacBride, "we're from Police Headquarters. We'd like to pass through your house so that we can get to the one behind it in Hector Street."

"What's the trouble?"

"We're looking for someone."

"Well—well—all right. But waking an old woman up on these cold nights...."

"I'm very sorry, madam."

She led them through the hall and opened a door in the rear that led into a small yard. Beyond the yard was a low board fence. Beyond the fence was the back of the four-storied house.

"Thank you, madam," said MacBride.

"It's all right, but with my sciatica...."

MacBride and the cops and Kennedy passed out into the yard. MacBride scaled the fence and dropped down into the other yard, and the others were close behind.

"There's the fire-escape," he said, and walked towards it.

He was the first to go up. Whatever may be said of him, good or bad, he never hung back in the face of impending danger. If he planned a dangerous maneuver, he likewise led the way, remarking, with ironic humor, that he carried heavy insurance.

He climbed quite noiselessly, and the men were like an endless chain behind him, a dark chain of life moving up the metal ladders. The windows they moved past were black as black slabs of slate. The skirts of their long blue coats swung about their knees as the knees rose and fell with each upward step.

MacBride went slower as he neared the top landing. He stopped and looked back down over the line of men, and right behind him was Patrolman Haviland, and behind Haviland was Patrolman Kreischer, who was getting on in years. And looking at them, MacBride felt a little proud of them.

He looked upward and climbed slowly, and presently he reached the landing, and Haviland came up to crowd on one side of him and Kreischer came up to crowd on the other side. They all had their guns out. MacBride had his out, too, but he reached over and took Haviland's nightstick.

He looked at the window, and then he raised the heavy stick and smashed the glass. He struck four times, and then plunged in through the yawning aperture.

Somewhere in the darkness there was a shout. A split-second later a gun boomed and a flash of fire stabbed the darkness and a bullet slammed into the window frame. MacBride fired around the room and lunged across the floor. He heard a man scream. If he could find a door, then he could find a light switch, he reasoned.

Someone cannoned into him, and MacBride crashed against the wall. A gun exploded so close to his face that the smoke made him choke. He ducked and sprang away and banged into another twisting body, and ducked away again. He brought up suddenly against a door and then he groped around for the light switch. He could not find it. A body hurtled against him with such force that the captain went down.

Somebody pulled the door open, and the dim light from the hall filtered in. Two or three forms dived out through the door. MacBride leaped up and lunged towards the door and collided with another man who was trying to get out. Both went down under a rush of four policemen who had not time to recognize MacBride. MacBride disentangled himself in a hurry and heaved up as Haviland was on the point of swinging his nightstick.

"Hey!" shouted MacBride.

"Oh… you, Cap!"

Another man came barging out of the door behind a flaming gun, and one of the bullets put a hole through MacBride's new hat but did not budge it the fraction of an inch. Kreischer fired three times, and the man threw up his hands and screamed, and the momentum of his dive carried him over the banister and crashing down to the hall below.

And in the hall below the cops who had run down were fighting with the men who had opened the door and sought to escape. Somebody in the room had found the light switch—it turned out to be Kennedy—and the light revealed two gangsters lying dead on the floor and Kennedy mildly scratching his nose, as though he were trying to figure out why the men did not get up.

MacBride ran to the head of the stairs and saw the spurts of gunfire below. He forked the banister backward and slid down with lightning-like speed. He flew off the end and did a backward somersault, and as he was getting up Patrolman Mendelwitz toppled over him groaning and then slid to the floor like a bag of wet meal.

The fighting moved down the next stairway, and MacBride went after it, and Kreischer and Haviland came pounding down behind him. MacBride, going down the staircase, stumbled over a body, but caught hold of the banister and steadied himself. It was the body of a gangster.

MacBride looked over the banister and saw three gangsters backing towards the next landing below. He climbed over the banister, hung out a bit and then dropped. It was a fall of about fifteen feet, and MacBride landed on somebody's shoulders and created a new panic. He saw one of the other gangsters swing towards him, and he recognized Sam Chibbarro, and Chibbarro recognized him. The gunman swung his rod towards MacBride's head, but another body sailed down from above and crashed Chibbarro to the floor. It was Kennedy, unarmed, but effective, nevertheless. The third gangster turned and ran for the head of the next staircase, and Haviland fired along the banister and got him in the side and the gangster fell against the wall and then slid down to the floor.

Chibbarro flung off Kennedy and bolted, but MacBride, having knocked his own man out, dived for Chibbarro and caught him by the tail of the coat. Chibbarro cursed and tried to get out of his coat, and then he pivoted and his gun swung close. MacBride let go of the coat tail and caught Chibbarro's gun hand as the gun went off. The shot walloped the floor, and then MacBride swung Chibbarro's arm up and backward and clouted him over the head with the barrel of his own gun. Chibbarro went down like a felled tree.

Kreischer came up on the run, big-footed, and then stopped and watched Chibbarro fall. Then he looked at MacBride and grinned with his beet-red face.

"Himmel!" he said.

"I guess that's that, Fritz," said MacBride. "Hey, Haviland, how is Mandelwitz?"

"He's laying back here and cursing like hell."

"Okey. Then he's all right. Harrigan, find a telephone and call the hospital and then call the wagon. Hey, Sokalov, for God's sake, don't keep pointing that gun this way! It's all over. Put it away."

"All right.... I forgot, Cap."

MacBride looked around and saw Kennedy leaning against the wall and lighting a cigarette. Kennedy's hat was twisted sidewise on his head, and two buttons were gone from his coat, and his face was dirty. He looked comical. MacBride chuckled bluntly.

"How come you're alive, Kennedy?"

"There is a Providence," said Kennedy with mock gravity, "that watches over fools, drunks and bum reporters."

"I always said you were a bum reporter," put in Moriarity.

Kennedy spun away his match. "Imagine a guy like that!"

Chapter XII

DAWN was breaking, but the light in the office still streamed down over the flat, shiny desk.

Chibbarro sat in a chair within the radius of the light, his hair plastered down over his ears and forehead and a streak of dried blood on his cheek. His brows were bent, and he scowled at the top of the flat, shiny desk.

Moriarity stood with his back to the radiator, and Kennedy had reversed a chair and now straddled it with his arms crossed on the back and his chin on his crossed arms.

MacBride sat in the swivel chair and looked at Chibbarro.

"You did wrong, Chibby," he said, "to come to Richmond City. It's a tough town."

"Tough hell!"

"Tougher than you are, Chibby. I always wondered why you came here. I'm wondering now why you tried to kill Bunny Dahl."

"She was a chicken-hearted broad!"

"Bad… doing what you did, Chibby."

Chibbarro took out his handkerchief and blew his nose. "I been framed all around. That boy scout Dominick—"

"Didn't spring a thing."

"Bah!"

"It was Al."

"The lousy pup!"

MacBride leaned back and put his hands behind his head. "So you didn't kill Barjo."

"No, of course I didn't kill him! D' you think I'm a fool, to put a knife in a guy at a souse party?"

"I didn't think you were so much of a fool. But why did you try to put Bunny out of the way?"

Chibbarro turned his back on MacBride. "You can ask my lawyer all them things."

"That's all right by me, Chibby. But it won't help your case."

The door opened and Ike Cohen walked in. "Hello, Cap—Mory—Kennedy." He looked at Chibbarro. "Hello, Chibby, you small-time greaseball!"

"Go to hell!" said Chibbarro.

"Funny, you are!"

MacBride said, "What news, Ike?"

"The frail just died."

Chibbarro looked up with a start, and his dark eyes widened and horror bulged from the pupils. Then he pulled his face together and crouched sullenly in the chair.

Cohen drew a folded piece of paper from his pocket and handed it to MacBride.

"She regained consciousness long enough to spring this, Cap. It's signed by her and witnessed by the doctor and me."

MacBride unfolded the paper and spread it on the desk. He read it over carefully, then settled back in his chair holding it in one hand.

"Listen to this, gang," he said, and read aloud:

" 'I killed Salvatore Barjo. He was drunk. He followed me into a room in the Club Naples and tried to attack me. I picked up a paper cutter that was laying on the table and stabbed him. Then Dominick came in. Then Chibby came in. Chibby cursed hell out of me, and Dominick yelled at him and said I had to be got out of the jam. Chibby said like hell. Then I said he'd get me out of it or I'd tell what I knew about him. That's why he got me out of it. So we hid out. Then Dominick and Chibby got in a fight and Dominick skinned out. He was a good guy, Dominick. He didn't know what Chibby had up his sleeve. He thought Chibby was just a bootlegger.

" 'Then Chibby got his gang together and they hunted for Dominick to bump him off before the cops got him. Chibby thought Dominick knew more than he did. Chibby came here from Chicago. He was one of the Rizzio gang, and he came here to work up a white slave trade. He got me to work with him, and in the month here I helped him get twelve girls for houses in Dayton and Columbus. That was his real racket, but he wanted to try booze on the side, and he wanted to be friends with Dominick because his old man was alderman, and that might help.

" 'When we heard the cops had Dominick I wanted to go to Headquarters and get him out. I was sick of the whole rotten business. Chibby swore he'd kill me, and I dared him. I said I was going, and that I'd say nothing about him. But he didn't believe me. He got me tight and then he shoved my head down by the gas-heater. I guess he always was a bum.' "

"Hell's bells!" said Kennedy.

MacBride dropped the letter to the desk and got up and walked around the room.

"So that was it, Chibby," he said. "White slaving, eh?"

Chibbarro stared darkly at the shiny top of the desk.

MacBride said, "And you only protected the girl because you knew it was the only way of protecting yourself. God, but you're a louse!"

"Imagine this guy wanting a lawyer!" said Moriarity.

"Yeah," said Cohen. "Ain't he the optimistic slob?"

MacBride picked up the telephone and called a number. After a moment he said, "Hello, Tony. This is MacBride.... Now hold your horses. We've got the kid here.... Yeah, yeah, he's all right, and he'll get out after a while.... What's that?... No, I'm not going to comfort him. I'll leave that to you. If he was my kid I'd fan him.... All right, come around when you feel like it."

He put down the telephone and sighed and stared at it for a long moment.

Kennedy pulled a photograph out of his pocket and stared at it.

"She wasn't such a bad-looking frail."

MacBride looked at him. "Where'd you get that?"

"In her bedroom. We'll smear it on the front page of the noon editions."

MacBride went to the window and looked out and saw the red sun coming up over the rooftops. And it occurred to him, without any blur of sentimentality, that Chibby and Dominick and Al were small-timers, and that the girl—this Bunny Dahl—had been stronger than all of them put together.

Kennedy was saying, "It's tough the way sometimes a broad has to die to get her picture in the paper."

Shake-Down

Capt. MacBride follows a hunch and lands on a new racket—hard.

Chapter I

DURING the day life flowed through the street unhurriedly but with a certain quiet industry and purpose. Little Italy sold fruits and vegetables and spaghetti and groceries, and there were many small restaurants. After ten you saw only street lights and on rare occasions a pedestrian, footfalls echoing sharply on the sleeping pavement. Such a night was this one....

Spring had come in unobtrusively. It was still cool, but also mellow. No one was afield. It was shortly after midnight, and the store windows and the lit windows above them were black-laced and the stars shone.

Then the headlights of a car swung down the narrow street. The headlights stared straight ahead, as if uninterested in the old houses that walled in the street. The motor purred, the car rolled leisurely. It was a big car, a long one. In the middle of the block it seemed to move still slower, and swung in towards the right-hand curb, as though it were going to stop.

From the shadow of the tonneau spurts of flame suddenly leaped into the darkness with a rapid succession of brittle explosions. Glass snarled. Wood splintered. The motor of the car roared and the car picked up speed, thundered down the street, swung around the next corner and vanished.

Lights appeared in many windows like stars coming out after a storm. Windows grated open. One opened directly above the shattered store front. A bald head thrust out, a voice high-piped in Italian. Heads appeared in other windows. Shouted questions bounced back and forth, up and down the street.

At the corner around which the car had swung upon entering the street, was an arc light. Suddenly a figure appeared beneath it. Metal buttons shone on its coat, metal flashed on its uniform cap.

Patrolman Fogarty had his gun out, held away from his side, muzzle slanting upward, body half-twisted, legs arched. Dark eyes peered down the street, and a dark jaw jutted pugnaciously. After a moment he brought his legs together, let his arm drop to his side, the gun hanging motionless in his relaxed hand. He spat and began walking down the street, his eyes swinging up and down in short arcs as he looked from one side of the street to the other at the open, lighted windows.

"Where was it?" he kept yelling up at the windows, but nobody knew. Everybody was asking questions of everybody else.

Then Fogarty saw shattered glass glinting on the pavement near a street light. He quickened his steps, his tough police shoes smacking the cement loudly. He came to the demolished store front, stopped, put his hands on his hips and cursed shortly. Then he looked up at a bald head that was swaying from side to side and a mouth that was sputtering in Italian.

Fogarty waved his gun. "Aw, come down—come down."

The head popped from sight, Fogarty walked to the broken window, thrust in his head, saw only darkness. He stepped back, kicked at broken glass with his shoe, looked up and down the street, cursed petulantly.

A hall door beside the store opened, and a little fat man stood muffled in a large bathrobe.

Fogarty looked at him. "Well, pop, what happened?"

The man waddled out, looked at his broken window, held his head in his hands and groaned.

"I know—I know," said Fogarty, "but what the hell happened?"

"Look! Look!" cried the little fat man, thrusting his short arms towards the gaping window. "Look whata happened! I was sleepin' and it happened. Watcha t'ink o' dat, eh? Dey busta ma store all up. I heard-a da shots—bang-bang-bang—a watcha call mebbe da machine-gun—bang-bang-bang! Looka—ma store—all busta up!"

"Yeah.... Well, what's your name, pop?"

"Chieppa. Gabriele Chieppa. I runna da restaurant—gooda spaghet', gooda raviol'...."

Fogarty had his book out, but he turned at sound of a car rolling down close to the gutter. It was a small car, black and shiny. It drew in close to the curb and stopped. There were two men in front. The one at the wheel was uniformed. The other was not. The latter moved a red cigar end in the gloom and said:

"What's up?"

"Oh… that you, Cap?"

"Yeah. Heard the fireworks a couple of blocks away. Um. What's up?"

Fogarty said, "Far as I can make out some guys blew this front out with a machine-gun. This guy's name's Chieppa. He owns this joint."

"All busta up!…" Chieppa held his head again.

The door of the police car opened and MacBride stepped out. He put his cigar in the corner of his mouth, looked at the broken glass on the sidewalk, then looked at Chieppa. He went over and took Chieppa's arm.

"Let's go inside," he said.

"All busta up.…"

MacBride turned to Fogarty. "You hang around here. I'll report to your precinct." And to Chieppa, "Come on."

They went up a narrow staircase, reached a hallway, entered a living-room from which a scantily-clad woman retreated with two small children.

"Mr. Chieppa," said MacBride, "why do you suppose those guys blew out the front of your place?"

"I dunno!" Chieppa hunched his shoulders up beside his ears and spread his palms.

"Do you know who they were?"

"No—no."

"Has anybody threatened you?"

"No—no."

Chieppa suddenly began to wear a blank expression.

MacBride asked, "Who's your bootlegger?"

Chieppa started; shook his head. "I sell-a no booze."

"You don't have to kid me. This street is full of speaks."

Chieppa raised his palms. "I sell-a no booze. Ma wife no want-a me sell da booze. Spaghet', ravioli ... no booze."

MacBride sighed. "Got a phone?"

Chieppa led him to a phone. MacBride called the Second Police Precinct. "Hello, Sarge. This is MacBride. Just happened to be in this neighborhood when some eggs blew out the front of Chieppa's restaurant, 35 Boone Street.... Yeah. I'm reporting for Fogarty. He got here first. He's downstairs.... No, I don't know. Chieppa's dumb.... Yeah, looks like a bit of shake-down. ... Of course they got away."

He hung up and turned and looked at Chieppa. "You sure nobody threatened you?"

Chieppa shook his bald fat head so hard that his jowls wobbled.

MacBride shrugged and went downstairs. There was a small crowd there, and the lighted windows were still open.

MacBride said to Fogarty, "I reported for you. The wop's gone dumb. He's scared. Says nobody threatened him, but I'll look into that. I've got a hunch some guys haven't been getting the usual graft. Tried to scare him. Maybe they did. But if there's a gang muscling in around here, I'm going to nail 'em." He waved his hand at the broken window. "You better hang around, Fogarty, until morning."

"Okey, Cap."

MacBride climbed into the car and banged shut the door. "Shoot, Malone," he said.

Chapter II

HEADQUARTERS....

MacBride swung around in his swivel chair as Moriarity and Cohen came in. "Guys, Chieppa, a wop over at 35 Boone Street, got his joint slopped with machine-gun bullets last night. It's a break I've been waiting for. There's been rumor around for weeks that a gang is shaking down the spaghetti joints. I want to bust up the gang before it grows too big."

Cohen tipped his hat over his eyes, "Klausner won't like that. It's in his precinct."

"My old precinct," mused MacBride; then he snapped, "To hell with Klausner!"

"Yeah, to hell with him," said Moriarity. "I never liked that wet-blanket anyhow."

MacBride went on, "Chieppa seems like a nice wop. But he shut up like a clam. And he's not selling booze. He said so, and I'm inclined to believe him. It's come to a state, boys, where if a guy doesn't sell booze he's considered an outsider. And Boone Street stinks with speaks. Chieppa's scared. He knows damn well who slopped his joint, but he won't spring. Well... you can't blame him. You guys see what you can find out. I'll do the same."

They went out. After a while MacBride put on his conservative gray hat, lit a fresh cigar and left. It took him fifteen minutes to walk to the station-house in the Second Precinct. He went through the central room, nodded to the sergeant at the desk, and wound up in Captain Klausner's office.

Klausner looked up from a battered desk and said, "Hello, Mac-Bride."

MacBride sat down. "Morning, Klausner."

Klausner was big and red-faced. He had stiff sandy hair combed straight back from his forehead, and a clipped mustache stuck up under a big nose. His eyes were large, moist and unfriendly, and his voice was naturally hoarse. He hadn't much of a jaw, and his mouth was the weakest part of a face that at first glance looked strong.

MacBride said, "That shooting last night, Klausner...."

Klausner was reading a letter and he said, "I see you were on the job."

"Just cruising around in the flivver. Couldn't help hearing the shots."

"Yeah." Klausner waved a hand over the letter, but did not look up. "Nothing, though. Nobody hurt. What the hell!"

"That's the point, Klausner. It's where we disagree. That dago's been blown up as a warning. It means that a muscle gang is on the walkabout. Just dropped in to tell you that I'm looking into the matter."

Klausner sat back abruptly and made a face. "Why the hell can't you stop butting into other people's business?"

"Not butting. It's my job."

"I can handle my precinct!"

"We both can. Let's play ball together."

Klausner flung up a fat, freckled hand. "I can run it, MacBride. I can run it alone."

"Okey. What are you going to do about this shooting?"

"Do?" He smacked his palm down on the desk and tried to make his weak mouth look firm. "Nothing. It's small stuff. Nobody was hurt. Nothing."

MacBride took a drag at his cigar, then stood up. "Well, that's all I wanted to know. I'm working on it. So are Moriarity and Cohen."

Klausner glared. "You're a damn trouble-maker, Mac-Bride! You're not satisfied unless you're on the snoop! You stay to hell out of my precinct!"

MacBride went to the door but turned around before he opened it. "I'm Headquarters— at large, Klausner."

Klausner had risen, heels of hands jammed down on the desk, bulky arms rigid from shoulders to wrists, big head hunched between big shoulders.

"You're trying to ride me, MacBride!"

MacBride left the door and strode swiftly to the desk, took the cigar from his mouth and snapped off the ash with his little finger.

"Klausner, you can play with me, if you want. I'd like to have you. And the credit, it we break this trick, will go to your precinct. I don't need it."

"I'm running this layout, and I'm running it along my own ideas, and I'm not cluttering the blotter up with a lot of small-time tripe! And I'm just as tough as you are, MacBride."

"Okey," said MacBride.

He swung on his heel and strode out, went back to Headquarters.

Moriarity and Cohen came in about three hours later. Cohen shook his head.

"We been in twelve speaks in Boone Street, Cap, and not a glimmer. Everybody's got a tight lip. They get their booze out of the clear blue sky. Yeah, they just get it. And it's none of our business how they get it. Chieppa's joint is boarded up."

MacBride creaked in his chair, stared absently at the desk. "I had a chin with Klausner."

"What'd he say?" asked Moriarity.

"Says I'm butting in." He looked up, grinned with hard, strong, narrow teeth. "Says I shouldn't."

Cohen jingled change in his pocket. "Of course, that ends it then."

"Yeah," chuckled MacBride. "Sure." He went on, in a lower tone, "Klausner doesn't like me."

Cohen snapped. "And I know why—the big bum! The Second's too big for him. You made your rep there, Cap. They used to call it the Hell-howling Second. Now what? Well"—Cohen snapped his fingers—"he's trying to live up to the reputation you made. All he hears, I suppose, is, 'MacBride did it this way, MacBride did it that way.' Makes him sore. He's trying to be original. He hates the name of MacBride."

"Like a lot of other guys," nodded MacBride. "And he'll hate it more after I get through with this job. Keep fanning those speaks, boys. Something may break."

After lunch he hopped a taxi and rode for ten minutes. He got out in front of a restaurant in Jockey Street. It said *Roman Inn* in white letters on a black board above the door. He entered and went to a table in the rear. A waiter came out of the kitchen and MacBride said: "Hello, Tony."

"Hello, Cap."

When the waiter had delivered the dishes he returned to MacBride's table.

MacBride was poking with a knife at the glass sugar bowl.

"Tony, I'm looking for some dope."

Tony looked pained. He essayed a weak, "Yes?"

"Yeah. Who's running the booze in Boone Street?"

"Jeeze, Cap, I dunno."

MacBride kept poking abstractedly at the bowl. "Tony, a year ago I caught you frisking a drunk in the *Flower Pot*. I could have had you put on the blotter. I gave you a break because I knew that some time later you could give me some dope."

"Yeah, sure. I know that, Cap. I ain't backin' down. But I don't know."

"Find out."

Tony grimaced. "Aw, cripes, Cap—"

"Find out, Tony." He stood up and bit the man with an uncompromising eye. "I never let a crook go because I'm Santa Claus. I want an eye for an eye. Get me?"

"I—I'll try."

"You can find out. You know my telephone number." He jabbed the waiter in the ribs. "Give me a bum steer and I'll land on you."

MacBride did not stop there. He paid calls on two other men; one ran a fish market, the other worked in a warehouse. Both were men upon whom MacBride had something. They were catalogued in his mind among many others. The price of freedom was information. They were informers—stoolies, the underground grapevine of any police department, without which no cop can very well get along. MacBride did not look down upon them, did not hold them in contempt. Many he knew were going straight. It takes courage even to be a stoolie. These men were on his own private list. No one, not even his superior, knew who they were, just as he himself did not know the list maintained by either Moriarity or Cohen.

But it was Tony the waiter who telephoned on the following morning and made a rendezvous in a corner cigar store. MacBride went around and met him.

Tony said, "I got somethin', but maybe it's no good. I was sittin' with a broad in a speak, and we was talkin', and she says it's a rotten life. She says some girls gets all the breaks. She says her pal—the broad was her pal—was goin' with a swell guy. A new guy. Patsy Crane's the other girl's name. My broad says offhand that Patsy's crush was maybe gonna make it hot for some guys in Little Italy."

"Did you get the guy's name?"

Tony shook his head. "No. I asked offhand about it, but my broad didn't know. She just says that this guy was gonna rate big in Little Italy, and Patsy and him were puttin' up in class at the Willow Arms. That's all."

"You don't know under what name she's living there?"

"No. I just know she's living there. But my broad says she eats lunch a lot at the Ritz since she's been with this guy."

"Okey, Tony. I know her."

For the next two days running MacBride lunched at the Ritz, but did not see her. He tried a third time, and on that day he saw her. She was class—swank, but he used to know her when she hoofed in a cheap nightclub. She was alone.

When he finished eating he got up and went out into the lobby. He had to wait a long time—an hour. Then he saw her swaying out. He followed her and caught up with her as she was walking down the street.

"Hello, there, Patsy. Haven't seen you—"

She turned, stared, squinted, then stared again. "Why, if it isn't old Captain MacBride!"

"Old?" he grinned.

She laughed. "Well, you know what I mean."

"Sure.… I'm grabbing a cab. Take you anywhere?"

"Well, home."

A taxi sped off with them.

MacBride said, "You're looking swell, kid."

"You're looking swell yourself. How's the gumshoe trade?"

"Slow. Not a thing stirring, Patsy. We're having day-beds put in Headquarters."

She laughed, revealing fine white teeth. "Can you tie that!"

They kept kidding each other until the taxi drew up before the pretentious Willow Arms. MacBride handed Patsy out and elbowed her along into the lobby. He tipped his hat at the elevator. She got on and the elevator closed and went upward. MacBride walked towards the door, turned and came back and leaned near the elevator. When it came down he cornered the operator.

"That lady just went up"—he flashed his badge—"what's her name?"

The operator looked at him, then said. "Riggio."

"What apartment?"

"Thirty-one."

"Thanks," said MacBride.

He breezed out, whistling.

Chapter III

KENNEDY, newshound, came in and said, "Hey Cap, that guy Chieppa has gone places."

MacBride turned from the office window. "What?"

"Yeah." Kennedy took a butt from his mouth and spat at the ash. "Yeah. I ankled over there to get a human interest story or something, and the spaghetti-bender wasn't there. I got talking to his frau. She's not so happy you'd write home about it."

"What'd she say?"

"Not a damn thing." Kennedy looked as if he needed a shave, a clothes-pressing and a sleep. "Just said he wasn't there. Went to see his brother-in-law or somebody. Yeah, you know ... all these wops have brothers-in-law somewhere."

"What you think, Kennedy?"

"Me? I don't know, Cap. Just that the frau looked red-eyed and on the bum, and she was making a hell of a hard try to say as little as possible."

"She say how long he's been gone?"

"Nope." Kennedy sighed into a chair. "Don't tell *me* that everything's on the up and up. Something's cripes-all-crooked there, or I'm a slob. I went around to see Klausner, too."

"Tell him?"

"Nope. I sat around asking questions about this and that—you know"—he made a weary gesture—"about how things were after the shooting. What a guy! His tongue's all muscle-bound. So I blew—but I asked him on the way out if he'd ever heard of liver pills.... But, anyhow, old tomato, this Chieppa getting his joint banged in means something—and his being away means something else. Honest, the old woman ain't happy.... Any leads?"

MacBride said, "One, maybe. I'm working on it. But it's slow. No case. Look here, Kennedy. You're right, I think. There's a lot behind that shooting, and there'll be more, and I want to flop on the parade before it gets too big. There are some guys in this town think I'm a snoop. Maybe I am. To hell with them!" He doubled his fist, held it up, then snapped open his fingers. "Yes—to hell with them!"

He left Kennedy and went around to Number 35 Boone Street. The front was boarded up. There was a sign, *Closed For Business.* He opened the hall door and climbed the stairs, and after he had knocked above, Mrs. Chieppa let him in. There was a six-year-old girl hugging her skirts. MacBride patted the girl on the head and pinched her cheek. He smiled at Mrs. Chieppa.

"Your husband in, Mrs. Chieppa?"

She said, "No."

He had his gray hat in his hand and he looked at it, turning the brim up and down.

He asked. "Where is he?"

"He go his… brodder-in-law."

"Where's his brother-in-law?"

She was rubbing the head of the child that held her skirts. "I do' know. He just say he go there."

"When did he go?"

She looked down at the head of the child. Her bosom hung on a breath inhaled and held. Her voice almost squeaked. "Night before last he go."

MacBride took his eyes from his hat and laid them blankly on Mrs. Chieppa. "You know I want to be your friend, Mrs. Chieppa. What's wrong?"

She shook her head. There was a pallor creeping beneath her skin. The black pools of her eyes were not placid. In spite of which her left shoulder attempted a shrug of Italian unconcern.

"Gabriele will be back soon," she said.

"How soon?"

"Soon… I do' know… soon."

MacBride's eyes shed their blank look and became serious, friendly. "Mrs. Chieppa, you know there's something wrong. I know there's something wrong. What is it?"

She shook her head and said, in a muffled voice, that nothing was wrong.

MacBride sighed, patted the child's head, and left. He walked back to Headquarters and found Moriarity and Cohen.

"Now," he said, "I know there's something wrong. Chieppa went away night before last and hasn't turned up yet. His wife says everything's all right, but that's a lot of boloney. She looked scared stiff. It's hell, the way these wops keep a tight lip!" His voice toned down. "Listen. This one lead I have doesn't sound so hot, but I'm going to try it."

At about six that night he walked into the Willow Arms and took the elevator to the third floor. He got off and walked down thick, green carpets between tan, smooth walls. He stopped before a door marked 31 and pressed the button beside it.

It opened and he said, "Hello, Patsy."

She was surprised to see him. "Oh... hello!"

She had on a pale blue peignoir. Her hair was light brown, done in a permanent.

"Mind if I come in?"

She stepped back, looking a little troubled. As MacBride went in he saw a man appear in a doorway that led to a bedroom. The man had on a stiff shirt, a double-breasted black waistcoat and black broadcloth trousers. He looked at MacBride with bland dark eyes beneath heavy brows that met over a heavy nose. He was muscular, lean, and tall.

Patsy closed the door and said, "This is Joe Riggio. Joe, this is Steve MacBride—Captain."

"Hello, Cap," said Riggio, smiling.

"Hello," said MacBride, and went over to shake with him.

Then he turned to Patsy. "I was wondering if you could help me, Pat." He paused, picked a random name from his memory; said, "You remember Zoe Willy, of the old *Blues Club?*"

"Ye-es."

"Know where she is?"

Patsy seemed relieved. "No, I don't, Cap. I haven't seen Zoe in a year. Last time I saw her she said she was going to Dayton. I think she went. Anyhow, I never saw her after that."

"Some trouble?" threw in Riggio casually.

"Well, little bit. Not much. I just thought Patsy might know where Zoe is."

"Gosh, I'm sorry," said Patsy.

"That's all right, Pat." He turned to Riggio, smiled, and made a mental photograph of that dark, handsome face. Then he thrust out his hand. "Well, sorry to bother you." He shook and looked at Riggio's hand. He saw a white scar running from the junction of thumb and forefinger almost to the wrist. The hands dropped and MacBride walked towards the door. Patsy said good-bye, and he laughed and flicked her under the chin and went out.

Down in the lobby he made a telephone call. He got the *Roman Inn* and asked for Tony. When he heard Tony's voice, he said, "This is MacBride, Tony. Patsy's boy friend is a guy named Riggio.... Yeah, remember that name, and keep your ears open. I want to know if you hear anything about him."

He returned to Headquarters and went downstairs to the Bureau of Criminal Identification. He fooled around with the files. Riggio... Riggio.... He came to Rigolano, held the card up. It was dated four

years before. Stolen car. But somehow this guy Rigolano had pulled a suspended sentence. He'd been shot at by a cop... wound in the right hand. Out in the sticks. MacBride took the card and hunted through the picture files. He found a likeness of Rigolano. The likeness was also that of Riggio.

MacBride went back to his office, a little pleased, but not much. Finding that card did not make a case. It merely piqued his curiosity.

A little later the telephone bell rang. It was Moriarity.

"Cap, get this! I got a brainstorm before, I went over and hung around Chieppa's joint, and I was standing there about half an hour when Mrs. Chieppa came out. She was dressed up and she looked like she was going places. I tailed her. She got on a car and rode down Main. I got on the car, too. She got off at Jockey and I followed her down Jockey and into Waters. She went into a house at 48 Waters. I hung around across the street. After about five minutes I saw a window open on the second floor. A guy looked out, then closed the window. About ten minutes later Chieppa and his wife came out. I tailed them back to their place in Boone Street. What should I do, go up and see Chieppa?"

"No. Come over here."

MacBride hung up, rose and took a few swift turns up and down the room. An almost predatory light came into his eyes. Things were warming up.

When Moriarity came in, MacBride said, "How did Chieppa look?"

"Lousy. Needed a shave and I think he was bawling."

MacBride grinned a hard, tight grin. "What's it smell like, Mory?"

"Hell." Moriarity scaled his hat on the desk. "Smells like Chieppa's been detained at 48 Waters. Suppose we go down and talk to him."

MacBride shook his head. "No. You know damn well he wouldn't chirp. We'll not say a word to Chieppa. We're after this new gang, and Chieppa's probably too scared to help us. I'll find out something tomorrow."

He did. He found out that Mrs. Chieppa had drawn a thousand dollars from the bank on the day before.

Chapter IV

K LAUSNER looked up from his desk and saw MacBride coming through the doorway. He sat back and looked disgusted.

"Got a break," said MacBride, with a weird half-smile.

He sat on the edge of the desk, dangling a foot.

Klausner struck a match and held it to the stub of a cigar that drew down one corner of his mouth. He threw away the match and shot smoke through his nostrils.

"What am I supposed to say?"

MacBride planted a fist on the desk and leaned on the rigid arm. "Listen, Klausner, I've been working on this Chieppa case, and I've got a lead. Did you know Chieppa was away from home a couple of days?"

"I told you I wasn't bothering with that."

Three wavy wrinkles appeared on MacBride's forehead. "You've got to, Klausner!"

Klausner ripped his cigar from his mouth. "Damn it, haven't you anything else to do at Headquarters?"

"Sure."

"Then do it!" He pushed his palms towards MacBride. "Don't

bother me. Go 'way. I've got work to do."

"Your idea of work, Klausner, is holding down a chair! You get this! There's a gang growing in this precinct. I've warned you about it before. It's your business to look into it. Play ball with me, Klausner. We've stumbled on something hot. I want you to send some cops to an address in Waters Street. I'll go with them."

"I told you once, MacBride, that I can handle my precinct. I'm not going to waste my time on a wop that's only had his window shot out." He struck the desk. "Damn it, stay out of my precinct! Leave good enough alone!"

MacBride stood up. "I've tried to get you to play with me, Klausner. But you're thick. You won't do it. You hate me like a louse. You're sore. One of the mistakes of the Department was when they made you captain, and a bigger one was when they put you in this precinct. All right, big boy. Play alone. But I'm going to bust this precinct wide open. I'm being paid to prevent crime, and there's a gang shaking down in little Italy, and it can't go on.

"Not that I give a damn about the jack involved, but you know as well as I do that when that racket starts it usually winds up in trouble and a lot of guys get hurt. All right. To hell with you. Stick right here if you want, but don't yap if I make a jackass out of you. And that's what I'll do!"

Klausner rumbled, "Watch your step, hard guy—watch it!"

"Yeah, and I wouldn't be a bit surprised if *you* knew a lot about this racket!"

Klausner heaved up and stuck out as much of a jaw as he had. "You watch that tongue of yours, too!"

"Yeah? And what the hell do you think you could do about it?"

"I'll—"

"*You'll!* Pipe down! Tie a rock to that tripe and chuck it overboard. You're not fazing me."

Klausner's lips got wet and little white semi-circles appeared on either side of his nostrils. His freckled fists looked like lumps of spotted pale meat. His big red face trembled.

MacBride sliced him up and down with a look of contempt, pivoted, and left him shaking with rage.

MacBride stopped in the doorway, leveled an arm at Klausner. "And you try cramping my style, Klausner! Try it… and I'll put you in the hospital!"

He sailed out of the station-house like a mean wind.

He walked five blocks in the throes of burning anger. When that wore off, he stopped in a cigar store, loaded his pockets with cigars, lit one, and felt a little better. He stood for a couple of minutes on a corner, deliberating. Then he yelled for a taxi.

"Jockey and Waters," he said.

He sat back and filled the car with smoke. He rolled down a window to let the smoke out. He had wanted Klausner to come in with him, because then it would have looked better for the precinct. But Klausner was sore. Insisted on playing lonesome. Well, to hell with Klausner!

MacBride got off at Jockey and Waters, paid the driver, and watched the taxi spin off. Then he looked down Waters Street. It was not a pretty street. It was cobbled. It was narrow. No house had more than three stories, and all the houses were old. A lot of the stores were empty, the windows dirty. There was a pool-parlor. A garage. There was a store that sold paper and twine. There was a barbershop—a lunch-room next to it.

Number 48 was a dirty red brick house, with one stone step and then a vestibule. MacBride looked up. There were only two windows on the second floor. The vestibule door was open. So was the hall door. In the hall was an old baby carriage. MacBride smelled garlic and heard a baby cry—on the main floor.

He climbed the stairway. There was a brown carpet on it, but in places that carpet had been worn through to the wooden steps. He reached the corridor above and stopped to get his bearings. He moved down the corridor towards the front. There were doors on the right only. On the left, the stairway that went up to the top floor. He figured that the door nearest the front led to a room whose two windows looked out upon the street.

He went right up to that door and knocked. His coat was open. He felt the gun in the holster on his hip but left it there. He heard somebody moving inside. He heard the lock click. Then the door opened.

An old woman stood there, smoking a cigarette. Ragged gray hair smeared her head. A brown face, wrinkled and cavernous, beak-nosed, loose-mouthed. She had no teeth. She was humpbacked. She looked like a sack of meal tied in the middle.

MacBride said, "Well, well, Sister Annie!"

The loose lips undulated and the cigarette bobbed. "Cripes, where'd you come from, Cap?"

He shoved in and slapped the door shut with his heel. He rolled his cigar from one corner of his mouth to the other and looked down humorously at the misshapen old woman. He chuckled.

She peered up at him with pale, washed-out eyes that were near-sighted. She thrust her bony leather-colored hands into the pockets of a soiled tan sweater. She cackled, and the cigarette bobbed again, and her face became tied up in a lot of wrinkles.

"You're sure a sight for sore eyes, Cap!"

He grinned "Am I? Hell, Annie, I thought you were dead long ago. Let's see… I haven't seen you in—what is it?—five years."

She took the cigarette from her mouth and waved a charred clinker of a hand upon which glittered, oddly enough, a couple of old diamond rings.

"Yeah," she hacked, "there's only a few of us left."

He chuckled abstractedly and looked around the room. Everything in the room was like the woman—slipshod, decrepit, unclean. There were a kitchen and a bedroom beyond.

She was eyeing him covertly with her pale, squinty eyes, one side of her nose wrinkled, one side of her mouth pulled up, the cigarette drooping from the other side.

"What's the racket now, Annie?"

She snorted raucously. "Racket? Cripes!"

He faced her suddenly. "Why the hell do you suppose I looked you up?"

Her eyes blinked. She shook her head. "How the hell do I know?"

He made a blind stab. "Some girl told me you were living here."

The loose mouth twitched "Yeah?"

"Yeah… sure."

"Well, I'm living here, ain't I?"

"Sure. What else are you doing?"

She rasped, "If you know, what the hell are you asking for?"

That stumped him. But he played along, saying, "This girl seemed to know what she was talking about."

Sister Annie threw her butt to the floor and stamped on it. "Ah, go to hell!"

"We've got a lot of pictures of you at Headquarters, Annie, and your name's no stranger to the blotter. Suppose I take you to Head-quarters—for old time's sake?"

"Ain't you the wisecracking—?"

"Your tongue's as sloppy as it always was," he grinned. It was a fixed grin that did not include his eyes.

Sister Annie spat on the floor. Then she blew her nose. Her pale eyes squinted hate at him as she slopped across the floor and took a drink of gin straight. She smacked her loose lips after the drink and eyed him coldly, craftily.

"Too —— bad you can't let an old woman alone!"

The fixed grin stayed, and still stayed out of the eyes. But he said nothing. This seemed to make her madder. She shook bony fingers at him.

"Well, what are you gonna do—what are you gonna do?" she yammered.

He said, "You're pretty old to pine away in jail, Annie. Want to tell me things?"

"I got nothing to tell you!"

"Oh, no?"

"You heard me!" She came towards him belligerently. "You want to take me to Headquarters? You want to?... Go ahead, take me. See if I care. See what you'll find out. See what the hell you'll find out." She struck her chest. "I'm no greenhorn, MacBride!"

He looked at her for a moment. Then he turned and crossed to a telephone. He picked it up and caught her pale burning eyes again—held them. He said into the mouthpiece:

"Information."

Her eyes lost their anger and became wary.

"Information?" said MacBride. "Give me the number of the Willow Arms, 272 Willow Avenue."

But he did not take his eyes off Annie's eyes.

"What's that?... Western 0440. Thanks." And to the operator, "Western 0440."

Annie tongued her lips and then made them tight, and new fire burned in her eyes.

MacBride said, "Hello, Willow Arms. Connect me with Mrs. Riggio's apartment."

Annie scowled. There was malevolence in that scowl. Her breath whistled through her nostrils.

"Hello, Patsy. This is MacBride.... Listen, are you dead sure about what I asked you last night?... I mean, you're not kidding me, Patsy.... Well, that's what I wanted to know. Honest to God, eh?... Okey, Pat."

As he hung up, he kept his eyes riveted on Annie. Baffled rage was in her eyes now.

MacBride smiled thinly. "I've been checking up, Annie. Suppose you and I go around to Headquarters and talk it over."

Sister Annie snarled, "That—!"

"Who?"

Veins stood out on her forehead. Her eyes narrowed. "You still can't make me talk, MacBride!"

He jerked his head. "Put your rags on, Annie."

"I got 'em on!"

"Then let's go."

He drifted to the door and opened it, bowed with mock courtesy. "Before me, Annie."

She slapped her loose shoes towards him, stuck out her tongue, spat at his feet, called him a dirty name, and went out into the dark hall. He closed the door. She was shuffling towards the staircase. MacBride started after her.

Something hit him on the head and the world seemed to explode in his eyes.

WHEN he came to he lay for a few minutes staring up into the gloom. Then he sat up. Then he touched his head. He said, "Ouch—hell!" and closed his eyes hard. Then he opened them and got up.

He pushed open the door, left it open. He looked around the room. Some articles had been cleaned off the table. He went into the bedroom and saw a lot of bureau drawers open. There was nothing in them. He wanted to touch his head again but didn't. It stung. He went into the kitchen and put it under the cold water faucet. That felt good. There was a clean towel left and he dried his head, careful of the bump.

Then he looked at his watch and figured that he'd been out for almost an hour. He went back into the hall, found his hat, brought it back into the room, dusted it off, recreased it and put it gently on his head.

He returned to Headquarters and found Moriarity and Cohen playing penny ante.

"I just got socked," he said, banging the door behind him.

Cohen said, "Who—Klausner?" and to Moriarty, "Up two."

"Bump you two more, Ike."

MacBride took off his hat and bent down over the desk. "Look."

Cohen looked. "What'd he do—paste you with a spittoon?"

MacBride walked around the desk and hung his hat on a clothes-tree. He turned and rubbed his hands together. "We got a break, boys—we got a break!"

Cohen snickered. "Hell, you always get that way after a crack on the dome?"

"You're all wrong," said MacBride. "Listen. You remember Sister Annie?"

"Sure," said Cohen.

"Listen. She's in town. At that place in Waters Street, Mory?"

Moriarty showed interest. "Oh, yeah?"

MacBride leaned on the desk between them. "Yeah. I got her all hot and bothered. I didn't know what the hell I was talking about, and out of a clear sky I said a girl had tipped me off she was there. That worried her, but she's just as tough as she always was. I was feeling my way. I took a Brody and called up Patsy Crane and made a trick speech. Annie fell for it, and called Patsy a dirty name. Then she shut up."

"What about Patsy?" asked Cohen.

"She's living with a guy named Riggio. I got some information about Riggio that he was rating some tomatoes in Little Italy. I've been stumbling in the dark, but I think something's going to happen. I've got a good hunch that Sister Annie is somehow hooked up with Riggio and a racket we don't know about. Riggio is on the blotter for a stolen car job about five years ago... he was Rigolano then. But he's clean now, so far as a case is concerned.

"Well, I was going to bring Annie over, to see what would happen. I was going out in the hall with her when some guy socked me and I went out like a light. He must have trailed me there, or come up and heard me talking to Annie. Anyhow, I got mine, and they breezed."

Cohen said, "Chance for Klausner to razz you."

"I've been razzed before.... But there you are. Sister Annie thinks, the way I figure, that Patsy sprung something, and she'll look for blood. But that'll blow up when she finds out that I wasn't talking to

Patsy about what she thought I was. Riggio can back Patsy up, because he was in the apartment when I went there with a goofy fable about a broad I used to know named Zoe Willy. When that blows up, they'll try to figure out how ever the hell I found Annie's hideout. And what'll they do? Hell. Suspect Chieppa."

"The poor wop," said Cohen.

MacBride said, "So I want to plant one of you guys around there. We've got to protect the wop, even though he won't open his trap. They've probably threatened him and his family and you couldn't jimmie his jaw."

There was a knock and a policeman put his head in and said, "Sergeant says some guy called you on the phone about an hour ago. Says call the *Roman Inn.*"

"Okey," said MacBride; then to Moriarity and Cohen, "There's no telling what those guys might do, so we'll have to take care of Chieppa."

The phone rang, and MacBride answered it; hung up and said, "Be back... Commissioner," and went to his office.

The Commissioner said, "What the hell are you picking on Klausner for, MacBride?"

"Am I picking on Klausner?"

The Commissioner scraped a thumbnail with a knife. "He's put in a complaint that you're barging all over his precinct looking for trouble; that you've been very insulting to him; that you're gumshoeing around looking for something that doesn't exist; that, generally speaking, you're creating a nuisance because some inconspicuous Italian got his store-window in the way of a few shots."

"Did he put all that in writing?"

"No. He paid me a personal call.... Lay off him, MacBride. Don't worry him that way."

MacBride chuckled. "Sometimes I don't know whether to laugh at Klausner or push him in the nose. Listen, Mr. Commissioner. I'm on the snoop. I don't deny that. But I'm after something. It began with a hunch, and I always tail my hunches. I'm going to turn something very soon—so help me."

"Turn it quick, then. I don't want to be annoyed by complaints from the precincts. I like you, MacBride. I know you're valuable. Only don't go riding rough-shod. As much as I like you, I'll land on you if you create a disturbance without showing some result. I mean it." He waved a hand. "That's all."

MacBride went out and got all steamed up on the way to his office.

"Imagine," he shouted at Moriarity and Cohen, "that guy going to the boss! I'm a general nuisance, guys! Me! Okey, I am, then. I feel like being a boil—I feel like being a boil all over Klausner's dirty neck!"

He slammed into his swivel chair, grabbed the phone and called a number. "Hello, Tony. You called me up. What's up?... I see. Yeah.... Okey. I'll remember that. S' long."

He sat back. "This Riggio is hanging out a lot in the *Garden Club*.... Ike, you'd better keep an eye on Chieppa's place tonight. Meantime I'll see about getting a couple of cops to work shifts on watching it. The Commissioner's a little sore. If we flop down on this I'll get hell and maybe leave-without-pay into the bargain. Mory, you keep cruising Little Italy."

MacBride ran his hand through his hair and half-rose with a grunt when his hand touched the sore spot. He flopped back and cursed. He was not in a rosy frame of mind.

Moriarity and Cohen went out and MacBride sat and gnawed meanly on his cigar. He might have felt better with his fist in close and not harmonious proximity to Klausner's jaw. There is a lot of psychology in a crack on the jaw.

He went out to eat at six in a restaurant around the corner. His appetite was not good. The Commissioner landing on him had a bad effect. He felt like going over and pinching Patsy Crane and Riggio, but he knew he had nothing on Riggio. A pinch was no good unless you were sure of a case. He suspected Riggio, but that was not enough. At any rate, he felt like doing something. Even his sense of humor was low. If only he could pick a fight with Klausner.... He cursed. That was senseless.

In the end, he went for a walk. A walk always soothed a man; pounding the dark streets was by way of being a tonic. It was cool tonight, and misty. Damp winds rolled through the streets, and the street lights were swollen globes of wet nebulous radiance. This was a beat he used to pound in the old harness days.

He turned a corner and saw the words *Garden Club* picked out in blue electric globes. He strode passed it, paused, deliberated, then turned and retraced his steps and walked in. There was a lot of lattice work in the lobby decorated with imitation vines.

Pete Lachetto was a small wop in a lot of white shirt front.

"Hello, Pete," said MacBride.

"You're a stranger, Cap!"

"Just poking around."

"How about a drink?"

"Thanks, Pete—no."

He peered through the lattice work and ran his eyes up and down the tables. He saw no one he knew. He grouched out, leaving Lachetto perplexed.

A taxi had drawn up to the curb. A man was paying the driver. MacBride saw his back. It was the back of Klausner, in plain clothes, off duty. MacBride strode swiftly off into the mist, but looked over his shoulder and saw Klausner enter the *Garden*. MacBride stopped and leaned against a pole. From where he stood the lighted sign was only a smear of radiance in the dark mist.

He crossed the street and leaned against another pole. The taxi drove off.

Five minutes later Klausner came out of the *Garden* and walked swiftly down the street. MacBride moved after him. Klausner came to a main artery where automobiles were streaming past. MacBride saw him get into a taxi. MacBride got into another and told the driver to tail the first. It wasn't easy because of the traffic. But the driver followed it across town and into upper Willow Avenue. MacBride began to get a hunch.

It wasn't wrong. He saw Klausner's taxi swing in towards the Willow Arms. He told his own driver to keep going and pass the other car. As they drove past he saw Klausner entering the Willow Arms. He told the driver to stop at the next block. He got out and paid his fare and walked back towards the Willow Arms.

He entered the lobby and went around to the elevator. It lifted him smoothly to the third floor. He got out and walked down the corridor, looked at the door marked 31 but did not stop. He continued down to the other end of the corridor until it made a right turn. He stopped there, hid around the turn, and watched.

After about ten minutes he saw Patsy appear in the corridor. Klausner appeared with her and they walked towards the elevator. When they had got in, MacBride bolted down the stairs, reached the lobby, looked about and then headed for the door. He saw Klausner and Patsy walking up the street. He followed. They turned many corners.

Presently they were in Grove Street, which is a quiet residential street. Cars were parked here and there, lights faint in the mist. MacBride could barely see Klausner and Patsy, half a short block away.

Suddenly two bursts of flame stabbed the mist near a parked car, and at the same time the car lurched away from the curb, motor roaring.

Chapter V

MacBRIDE thought he saw Patsy fall. He saw Klausner jump back.

But the big car gathered speed.

MacBride tugged out his gun and stepped behind a tree. He raised the gun and aimed it at the right side of the windshield. He pulled the trigger and the gun convulsed in his hand. The car roared by, and a scream rose with the roar.

MacBride hugged the tree and saw dimly one figure writhing behind the wheel and another figure reaching over to get control of the reeling car. As he saw this he also saw two tongues of flame snap from the rear of the car and heard the slap of lead against the tree. He fired at the flashes. The car was swaying but it kept going.

MacBride flung a look in the other direction. Klausner seemed to be bending over Patsy. MacBride looked after the touring car. It was halfway across the sidewalk, stopped. He gripped his gun and started after it. But it started again, swinging around a pole and back on to the street.

MacBride stopped beside a small black flivver coupé. He jumped in and found the key in the switch. He turned it and started the motor, threw into gear and tooled the car away from the curb. He saw the tail-light of the touring car go around to the right. He reached that corner and went around to the right also. The red tail-light was ahead, getting smaller rapidly. MacBride slammed the accelerator down to the floor and let the engine have its head.

He put his gun on the seat beside him because it took two hands to manage the wheel. Even then it was rough going. He kept sounding the horn. The cross streets were frequent and bad, and he trusted to luck. Brakes of other cars screeched to avoid a collision.

Automatic traffic signals began to appear. The touring car paid no attention to them. Neither did MacBride. A traffic cop yelled and cursed. The touring car swung into a boulevard. MacBride followed it and picked up speed again. The boulevard was wide and there were many cars afield. The touring car thundered past them and MacBride and his flivver howled after the touring car.

At an important intersection the touring car swerved to avoid a smash, climbed the curb, left it again and continued on the boulevard. MacBride snaked his flivver around the back of the car that had almost been hit, heard a flung oath, but kept his eyes on the touring car's tail-light.

Then the big black car swung left, had the traffic light with it, and continued down a slight grade. MacBride reached the corner just as the lights changed, but he bullied a car out of the way and tailed the touring car down the street. There were no traffic lights here, and the street was narrow. He knew this street led to the freight yards near the river. The touring car could not lose him, and yet he could not overtake it. But he hung on grimly.

He saw two red lights blinking alternately beyond the touring car and knew that those lights marked a railroad crossing. But the car ahead did not slacken speed—nor did MacBride. He saw the touring car crash through lowered gates and heard the snarl of splintered wood. He had the accelerator jammed down and he was hunched over the wheel.

He bounced over the crossing in the glare of a locomotive's head-light and heard it roar by a foot behind him. His heart jumped into his throat and hot sweat burst from his pores. He gritted his teeth and thought about his wife and daughter.

There was the red tail-light ahead, and MacBride felt cobbles beneath the flivver's wheels. Warehouses walled in the narrow road. There were parked trucks and moving trucks and the sound of horses' hoofs striking the cobbles. The narrow street emptied into a much wider one that met it at right angles, and on one side of this street were piers and sheds and the river, and more trucks rumbling through the mist.

Then he saw the touring car careen to one side to avoid a turning auto truck. In missing the truck, the touring car sideswiped a horse-drawn wagon moving in the opposite direction, skidded sidewise, slammed its rear end against an iron light-pole and turned over.

MacBride spun his wheel to avoid the panic stricken horses, felt the flivver skid beneath him, and hung on while it turned round and round and jolted to a stop with its rear end against the curb. He shut off the ignition and jumped out with his gun.

The overturned touring car was fifty feet away, and he ran towards it. He saw men running away from it—counted three of them. He shouted, and one of them turned and fired. The bullet clipped the cobbles beneath his feet and he swung up his own gun and cut loose. The man who had fired took a header and his gun bounced away over the cobbles. He was screaming as MacBride lunged by in pursuit of the other two.

The two were fast. They dived into a dark street that led away from the river, and MacBride galloped after them, keeping close to the buildings. He blew his whistle as he ran. A gun flamed and a bullet whined past his ear and shattered a dark store window. He dropped behind a garbage can and fired over it. It was difficult to see.

Then he heard one of the men shout, and saw beyond them, in the glow of a corner light, the figure of a cop. The cop ducked behind the pole and a split-second later one of the gunmen fired in that direction. The cop returned the fire almost instantaneously, and one of the gunmen yelled and fell down. The other ran towards a door and tried to open it. It was locked. He pounded on it.

MacBride crept up along the buildings. He was close when the last gunman darted from the door and sped across the street, zigzagging. MacBride aimed low, pulled his trigger and got the man in the legs. The man buckled, fell against a fire-hydrant, shouted, "Don't, for God's sake!" and dropping his gun, hugged the hydrant with both arms.

MacBride yelled up the street, "Hey, it's all right! I'm MacBride! We got these guys!"

The cop stepped away from the pole, keened his eyes, started down the street gingerly, his gun still raised. MacBride lit a match and cupped it before his face. The cop drew closer, recognized him and relaxed.

"Okey, Cap. I got one, I think."

"Yeah." MacBride waved towards the hydrant. "There's the other necking a hydrant. Let's look. Got a flashlight?"

"Yup."

They crossed the street and the cop put his flash on the wounded gunman.

MacBride knelt down. "Well, you bum, how do you like this?"

"I'm wounded. Jeeze, I'm wounded!"

"Sure. If you wasn't, you'd be putting lead in my belly."

"God… it hurts!"

"What the hell do I care!"

It was a young face, pale, thin, shiny-eyed beneath a rakish cap. The right leg was bleeding at the calf.

"You're damned lucky I didn't plug you in the guts," said MacBride; then added, "Or maybe you aren't." He stood up, said to the cop, "Lend me your light till I look at the other bum."

He took the flash, threw the beam ahead of him and walked across the street. He swung the beam down on a motionless form that lay in the gutter. Glassy eyes stared into the white eye of the flash. Lips hung loose. There was blood all over the neck.

MacBride walked back to the hydrant. "You got him in the throat."

"Dead?"

"Hell, yes. Here." He handed the cop the light. "Stay here with this guy. I'll go back to the river. I knocked over another guy and there's a car there. I'll phone an ambulance. And the morgue bus."

He walked away down the street and reached the wide road that paralleled the river. He turned left and kept walking and soon he saw a small group of men in the middle of the street. He reached the group and found a cop asking questions.

"Oh, hello, Steinfelt," he said.

The cop looked up. "Oh, you, Cap! What the hell happened?"

"Plenty. Anybody in that overturned car?"

"One guy, but he's dead. There's a flivver, too—"

"I came in that. I tailed these birds from Grove Street, and, boy, what a ride they took me for…. Let's see. This guy cold?"

"Stony."

MacBride looked at the dead face, shook his head. "So far, I don't know any of these birds. Wait'll I look in the car."

He strode away over the mist-wet cobbles and found another group around the car. He lit a match and looked in through the broken windshield. The face he saw there was also strange. He stepped back and told the crowd to clear out. Crowd-like, it only moved away, and not far.

He went over to one of the piers where there was a light shining in a watchman's window. The watchman was standing outside. Mac-Bride asked about a phone, and the watchman took him into the office. He called a hospital, called the morgue, and then called Headquarters. Bettdecken was at the desk.

"I'm down on River Road, Otto. There was a shooting in Grove Street… some guys in a car. Patsy Crane fell down, I think. Klausner was with her. Maybe it was a pinch. I followed the car down here and it got wrecked and I shot it out with three guys. I killed one, Kerney killed another, and the third is wounded. I don't know the bums…. Klausner report anything?"

"Not yet," said Bettdecken.

"Okey."

He hung up and went back to the wrecked car. He lit a fresh cigar and told the crowd to clear out. The crowd merely backed up a few feet. In five minutes an ambulance arrived, and MacBride hopped in and rode with it to where Kerney was standing beside the wounded gunman. They put him in the ambulance. They put in the dead gunman also but took him only as far as the overturned touring car, where MacBride and Kerney hauled him out. The ambulance went off—Kerney with it.

When the morgue bus came, it picked up the two dead men by the car, rolled on to pick up the third, and sped away.

MacBride drove the flivver back to Grove Street, found the owner, apologized, and went to Headquarters.

Chapter VI

HEADQUARTERS was lively.

Sergeant Otto Bettdecken, rated the fattest man on the Force, heaved around on his chair behind the desk. A couple of cops were arguing furiously. Kennedy, at sight of MacBride, did a brief clog, then grabbed MacBride and kept turning him around and feeling his body.

"Where are the bullet holes, old tomato?"

"Ah-r-r, Kennedy, you jack, lay off!" chortled MacBride, and with bear-like playfulness shoved him away.

Moriarity popped out of a corridor, spotted MacBride, stopped short, and exhaled, "Cripes! And he walked in by himself!"

Some more cops appeared from the reserve room, and everybody hemmed in MacBride. Bettdecken erupted behind the desk to say, "Hey, Cap Klausner called up. That broad is in a horsepital with two slugs in her."

"Where's Klausner, Otto?"

"He called from the horsepital just after you called. I guess he'll be over."

MacBride barged through the crowd and headed for his office. Moriarity and Kennedy followed him, and MacBride paced up and down, trailing clouds of cigar smoke. Kennedy fell in step on one side and Moriarity on the other. All three went up and down the room as though they were going somewhere.

"Who were they?" asked Kennedy.

"I wish I knew," said MacBride.

"How'd it start?"

"By me tailing Klausner from the *Garden Club*. Looks as if Klausner was working on his own. Looks as if he pinched Patsy. Anyhow, he took her out of her apartment."

Moriarity said, "Maybe the Commissioner landed on him and he had to get somebody."

MacBride clipped, "I knew Patsy was mixed up in it."

"Yeah," said Moriarity. "Maybe this'll give Klausner a rep."

"But you got one guy alive?" asked Kennedy.

"Yeah. As soon as I see Klausner I'm going over to the hospital and have a chat with this guy. Never saw any of the guys before. They're imported, it you ask me. I'd like to lay my paws on Riggio—and Sister Annie."

"What's all this about?" asked Kennedy.

"You'll see when I get 'em." MacBride suddenly stopped. "Who the hell started this cross-country walk?" He dropped into his swivel chair.

Kennedy blew out his cheeks, "I'm glad that's over."

Five minutes later the door banged open and Klausner stood there.

"Ah, there you are!" said MacBride. And then to Moriarity and Kennedy, "Outside, boys."

They went out, not overjoyed.

Klausner walked heavily around the room and then stopped and looked at MacBride.

"Well," he said, "I hear you were on target practice."

"Yeah. Didn't you see me?"

"No. I didn't know what was happening. I was too busy with the broad."

MacBride grinned, not pleasantly. "Was your gun locked up?"

Klausner scowled and flexed his lips. His hands closed and opened. "I'm no fool. What the hell would have been the good of me trying to fan a gun?"

"It still surprises me that only the broad got hit. What did you want her for?"

"That's my business. D'you think you're the only guy can gumshoe around and make a pinch? I told you I was working on my own. I am."

"You sure are. Is the broad sick?"

"Kind of. But she'll come around, they said. I dragged her into a house after the shooting and telephoned an ambulance."

MacBride put his elbows on the desk. "Look here, Klausner. We'll have to work this case together. It's as much mine as it is yours."

"What I want to know is," rumbled Klausner, "how the hell did *you* happen to be in Grove Street when the party started?"

"I'll tell you. I tailed you from the *Garden Club*. I saw you come out of the Willow Arms with Patsy. I kept on tailing the two of you."

Klausner's red face became redder. "Why?"

"Force of habit. Why did you pinch her, Klausner?"

"On a tip that she had something to do with the Chieppa job."

MacBride smiled crookedly. "I thought you'd forgotten about that."

Klausner snarled, "I had to do something after you kept showing your mug in my precinct and raising hell."

"Who tipped you?"

"A tip is a cop's private business."

"That's right—yeah, that's right." MacBride leaned back. "I got one guy in the hospital. You've got Patsy. Between us we ought to be able to spring something big."

"Between us—hell! I'm still working alone!"

MacBride stood up, grinned his hard tight grin. "I think I'll have a talk with Patsy."

"You stay out of my yard, MacBride!" roared Klausner. "If you don't, I'll see the Commissioner in the morning."

"This," said MacBride, tapping the desk, "is tonight. I'm not going to sleep all night. There are a lot of things look funny as hell to me, Klausner. They're so funny I can't explain them. This case is mine as much as yours. I tailed that car and cleaned up that mob, and I'm going to get the big shot of that mob—"

"You're riding me, MacBride—you're riding me!"

"Yeah? Maybe I am. I like it. I'm getting so I like riding a big bum like you. You're yellow, Klausner. If you wasn't, you would have yanked your gun and put some bullets in the back of that car. You—in the Second Precinct! Holy cripes, what a joke!"

Klausner's eyes bulged with rage. He took a swing at MacBride. Without moving his feet MacBride ducked and laughed shortly, then put the palm of his hand against Klausner's jaw and shoved him over a chair. He opened the door.

"Get out, Klausner—go on, get out."

Klausner stumbled to his feet, his lips wet, his fat nostrils shaking.

"Out, bad smell," said MacBride, jerking his head towards the door.

Klausner lunged out, saying, "You'll see—you'll see!"

MacBride took a casual kick at Klausner. "I'll see, all right. And so will you."

Klausner lugged his heavy feet down the corridor.

Chapter VII

AT two in the morning Patsy lay in bed complaining because they wouldn't give her any cigarettes. She complained too because she had to lie on one side. A nurse tried to talk reason with her, and she told the nurse to go a lot of places—particularly, hell. She looked a bit yellow and washed out, but for a girl who had got tangled up with hot lead she was exceptionally vociferous, and in no uncertain terms.

When the door opened and MacBride came in, she closed her mouth and looked at him with fever-bright eyes. He closed the door and looked at her with mouth smiling and his blue eyes quizzical.

He said, "I've been trying to see you for three hours, kid."

"Why didn't you send up flowers?"

"The stores were closed."

He picked up a chair and carried it over to the side of the bed. He sat down on it, and then looked up at the nurse.

"Mind going out a few minutes?"

The nurse said, "She's feverish, Captain. Don't disturb her too much."

"Okey."

The nurse went out.

Patsy said, "For God's sake, give me a butt."

He held up a dead cigar. "Only smoke these."

"Hell!... Well, give me a drag on that."

He lit it and handed it to her. She took one puff and almost choked. "God!" She threw it on the floor.

MacBride put his heel on it, and waited till the spasm was over. "Now... Patsy...."

She looked at him. "Yeah... now. Now what?"

"What did Klausner want you for?"

"Listen." Her lips curled. "Are you trying to double-cross Klausner?"

"I'll double-cross anybody who deserves being double-crossed. I've got no conscience, kid. Why did Klausner want you?"

"He said it was a pinch."

"Why a pinch?"

She showed her upper teeth unpleasantly. "I don't know. He said we'd talk it over at the precinct. I argued, but—well, it was a pinch."

MacBride appeared to think that over, but he was really formulating a big lie. "Look here, Patsy. You got in wrong with the mob. I had a long talk with Sister Annie. I happen to know that Sister Annie and your friend Riggio are in cahoots. Why wasn't he in the apartment when Klausner turned up?"

"He was out. He went somewhere. I haven't heard of him since."

MacBride put his palms on his knees and leaned forward. "He left you flat, Patsy."

"I figured that out long ago."

"All right. You're done with the mob, kid. Riggio dropped you because Sister Annie told him you'd spilled something to me. When I telephoned you I was in Annie's place. I *didn't* tell her you'd spilled anything. But she took that for granted when she heard me talking to you on the phone."

"That was a hell of a trick!"

"I'll admit that. But I'm a cop and I was out after information. That line about Zoe Willy was a trick too. I wanted to see the guy you were living with. Now—you're in hot water. I can make it easy for you. That's a promise. I'll see you don't even go up for questioning. If you're broke, I'll stake you and give you a ticket to anyplace you want to go."

"That's another line."

"My eye! Listen, kid. The mob tried to get you once. They'll try again—when you get out. You've got only one friend." He tapped his chest.

"Friend—hell!"

"All right. Let's say you've got only one guy who can come between you and another bullet. That's more like it. Riggio can't do it. If he could, those guys would never have nailed you. And maybe—maybe, kid, he wasn't against their nailing you."

Her eyes darkened. "I'll take you up, MacBride. Not because I like you, but because you can do for me what you can do. Those bums were after me. Riggio called me up about six and told me to meet him for dinner at the *Garden Club*. But his voice was funny—all choked up. I told him to go to hell and I told him that if he came around the apartment I'd bounce something off his head. I was scared. I figured they were after me. I wasn't going to move out of the apartment.

"Then Klausner came for the pinch. I had to go. He was nervous all the way. I crabbed about why didn't he get a cab. And as we came up to that touring car, I remember Klausner stopped to look at his watch. Then hell broke loose, and I remember that as I went down, I saw Klausner still staring at his watch, though how the hell could he see it in the dark?"

A thin smile was on MacBride's face. His blue eyes were narrowed keenly.

"What do you think. Patsy?"

"Damn it, I think Klausner put me on the spot!"

MacBride said quietly, "Go on, kid."

"Riggio used to say that they were smearing some guy on the Force, and that's why the racket was easy. He never said the guy's name, though. They were muscling in all over town, but they couldn't muscle in on Chieppa. His wife didn't want him to handle booze or women. The main thing was women. Sister Annie handled that. She placed the women in the wop restaurants and got a rake-off on what they got from the suckers. The hostess racket. There's sixty broads spread around in fifteen restaurants, but the racket's young, and they hope to get more.

"Riggio and his guys gave strong arm protection and handled the booze. They told Chieppa that if he didn't come across they'd chase him out of town, and that if he said anything to the cops they'd get him. They blew out his place, and then they picked up Chieppa and made his wife come across with a thousand dollars. They had him scared stiff."

MacBride sat back and blew out a breath. "Well, I'll be damned!" Then he said. "Where do you suppose I can find Riggio and Sister Annie?"

"The mob had some rooms over the *Garden Club*. But for God's sake, don't get killed! Not that I give a damn, except that it's up to you to give me a clean bill."

MacBride got up and said, "Okey, Kid. I'll be back to get the addresses where these hostesses hang out."

"And bring some butts."

"Sure."

Chapter VIII

BETTDECKEN was asleep at the desk when MacBride sailed into Headquarters. MacBride slapped him on the head.

"Come on, Otto, snap out of it. I want six cops.... Where's Moriarity?

"Uh—in your office, I guess. You want—"

"Six cops," said MacBride.

He strode down the corridor and found Moriarity sleeping on the desk in his office.

"Hey, Mory!"

"Ya-ah?"

"Up, guy."

"Huh?"

MacBride dragged him off the desk. "Mory, we're going out for a bit of hell. The *Garden Club*. I got a tip that Riggio and Sister Annie are there—and maybe some more."

Moriarity had a hard time waking up. MacBride slapped Moriarity's hat on his head, dragged him to the door and dragged him on down to the central room. Cops were coming out of the reserve room, buttoning their coats and trying to look wide awake.

"Malone," MacBride said, "get the squad car."

"What's it all about, Cap?" asked Bettdecken.

"A raid. Say, this is hot. Riggio and Sister Annie in on a new racket in town—the hostess racket. They're handling broads for the restaurants.... Come on, boys, get dressed. Snap on it. More later, Otto."

He led the way out of Headquarters and his men stood around him at the curb, waiting for the squad car. It shot out of the driveway and they piled in, MacBride and Moriarity squeezing in beside Malone.

"All right, Malone. The *Garden Club*. Park a block this side of it."

The squad car tried out its lungs in first, jumped to second and slipped contentedly into high. Malone bent it around the second left turn and Moriarity lit a cigarette, yawned out smoke, shook his head and said:

"Cripes, I'm sleepy!" He added, "Let's stop for a drink somewhere."

"Forget it, Mory," said MacBride.

"There's a speak right down the street here—"

"Lay off. You'll wake up."

"Ah, hell."

The squad car lunged through quiet streets. They passed a taxi beside which stood a group of men singing *Sweet Adeline*. Behind the group of men was a single yellow light upon a house wall that marked a speakeasy.

"I wish I felt that way," said Moriarity.

"Right next," said MacBride, "and over to Kendall, then down Kendall and park where it crosses Chester."

"Okey," said Malone.

The car swung into Kendall, purred along and stopped just before it came to Chester. The *Garden Club* was on Chester.

MacBride got out first and took a look up Chester to see it dark and gloomy except for the infrequent street lights. The cops moved around him.

"You guys stay here a minute," said MacBride. He walked up Chester on the side of the street opposite the *Garden Club*.

There was one floor above the restaurant that had three windows. The shutters of the three windows were closed, but slivers of light could be seen on two of them. Beside the restaurant was a hall door that was part of the same house. MacBride crossed the street and tried that door. It was locked.

He walked back close to the buildings and stopped and looked at a half dozen high boards that shut off an alley between two houses. Then he continued until he reached the corner where his men waited.

"Door's locked but there are lights upstairs," he said. "I'll ring the bell and get Pete Lachetto to come down. Three of you guys climb a board fence down here and hurry around to the rear of the *Garden*. Rest of you hide in an open vestibule across the street. Come on. You, Mory—you stay with me."

They moved along Chester Street. When they came to the board fence three cops scaled it. The other three cops crossed the street and disappeared in an open vestibule. MacBride and Moriarty walked the rest of the way to the *Garden* and MacBride pressed the bell-button.

He and Moriarty stepped back to the middle of the sidewalk and looked up at the shuttered windows. They saw even the slivers of light go out. A couple of minutes passed. MacBride pressed the bell again and again stepped back to the center of the sidewalk. Presently a voice came down from one of the shutters.

"What you want?"

"Hey, Pete, this is MacBride. Come down a minute, will you?"

"You, Cap?"

"Yeah, Pete. Make it snappy. I can't stay long."

A pause; then, "All right."

Two minutes later the door opened and Pete Lachetto, muffled in a bathrobe, collarless, but with his stiff shirt front showing, looked out and said:

"Jeeze, I was sleeping a drunk off, Cap. What you want?"

"Let's talk upstairs, Pete."

"Ah, listen. I got a friend up there. Mightn't like it."

MacBride rubbed his jaw with his hand and then suddenly the hand shot down to grab Pete's wrist. At the same time Moriarty lifted a gun from his pocket and poked it against Pete's stomach.

Pete tried to laugh it off with, "Hell, Cap, this ain't right, hell."

"Quiet, Pete. Inside."

There was a light in the hallway. Stairs and a banister climbed to the next floor. But MacBride took out his manacles, clipped one bracelet on Pete's wrist and the other to a rung of the banister on the lower hall side.

Then he looked at Moriarity and nodded and they went up the stairs, MacBride first with his gun before him.

Suddenly the lights in the hall went out.

MacBride and Moriarity were at the head of the stairs. They dropped to the stairs and remained motionless, so close they could hear each other's breathing. Nothing happened. They heard footsteps somewhere beyond the walls. Two—three—five minutes passed.

Then there was a shot, muffled. Someone cursed out loud and feet pounded.

MacBride whispered, "They tried to get out the rear."

"Yeah," whispered Moriarity.

They heard a window bang open.

"That's in front," said MacBride.

"They can jump to the pavement."

"Boys across the street'll get 'em."

From the street they heard somebody shout, "Hey, you!"

Bang went a gun.

MacBride leaped up and stood in the upper hall. He felt Moriarity brush against him. Inside a voice cursed. A door flung open and feet rushed into the hall. MacBride got in the way of a running body and fell with it against the banister. Arms wrapped around him. He and the body went over the banister and hit the stairs, legs and arms tangled up.

In the upper hall a gun exploded.

MacBride and the man locked with him went tumbling down the staircase and landed in the lower hall. MacBride felt strength against him, and he had a stout right wrist gripped in his left hand while a stout left hand gripped his own right wrist. Hot breath smoked against his face in the darkness. Both were on their knees, toiling mightily, and when MacBride rose, straining, the other rose with him and they heaved against the wall. MacBride got a kick in the shins and then a knee in the stomach.

"Tough belly," he muttered, and kicked back at the man's shins.

A lot of feet came down the stairs and hurried past for the hall door. Out of the tail of his eye MacBride saw two shapes framed against the lighter darkness of the street; and then those two shapes were in brief silhouette against two gun flashes. These flashes were followed by two shots a little more distant, and one of the figures fell down. The other turned and ran back into the hall, back to the rear, and then a door banged.

MacBride and his man fell down again, rolled over and over.

A shot banged in the rear.

There were two voices coming down the stairs—a man's and a woman's.

MacBride got his knee on the forearm of the hand that held his right wrist and pinned it to the floor. He twisted his hand and then wrenched it free. He raised his gun and banged the barrel down against a jerking head, and the head thudded against the floor. He struck it again, and then felt the body relax beneath him. He had no trouble removing the man's gun.

As he was rising two cops came in the front door. There were feet pounding up from the rear. There were feet coming down the stairs.

"Now listen, Annie, cut out fighting me or I'll have to bust you!" That was Moriarity on the stairs.

"Hey, Cap," a voice shouted in the darkness.

"I'm here," said MacBride. "I'm all right. How about some light on the subject?"

One of the cops who had come in the front door snapped on a flashlight and the first one the beam landed on was MacBride, hatless, with his hair plastered over his forehead and a smear of blood on his cheek.

The footsteps coming from the rear developed into a cop who said, "We got two guys out back. One dropped from a window before and the other just busted out the back door. Hummel and Gary've got 'em."

The beam of light jumped up the stairs. Moriarity was almost at the bottom, with Sister Annie.

He said, "I found her trying to hide under a bed."

She told him what she thought his mother was.

The beam of light left them, swept around, paused on the huddled figure of Pete Lachetto, still manacled to a banister post. It lowered and crossed the floor and stopped on the bloody face of the man whom MacBride had knocked cold.

"Hell!" said one of the cops.

MacBride chuckled without humor. "The funny part about it is that I'm not so surprised."

That bloody face on the floor was Captain Klausner's.

The beam leaped up and stabbed the farther darkness of the corridor as some shapes came through a door. A cop was dragging a man. Another cop was shoving a man before him. This man blinked at the light.

MacBride said, "Hello, Riggio."

Chapter IX

"**A**T about three o'clock this morning a gunfight between policemen and gangsters broke out in the *Garden Club,* a restaurant in Chester Street owned and operated by Peter Lachetto. This was the culmination of long days of sleuthing conducted by Captain Stephen J. MacBride, of Police Headquarters, which began when Gabriele Chieppa's restaurant, in Boone Street, was riddled with bullets on the night of April twenty-sixth.

"At about nine last night Captain MacBride happened to be in Grove Street when four gangsters in a touring car shot at and wounded Miss Patricia Crane, of the Willow Arms, who was at that time in the custody of Captain George Klausner, of the Second Police Precinct.

"MacBride fired at the touring car as it started off and wounded the driver, who died a few minutes later, but another gangster got control of the wheel. MacBride followed in a machine which he found unattended at the curb. The gangster's car was wrecked on River Road, but three of the gangsters succeeded in getting out. A running battle followed, in which MacBride killed one on River Road and wounded another in Harker Street. The third was killed by Patrolman Kerney, who came at the sound of MacBride's whistle.

"Following clues, MacBride broke into the *Garden Club* this morning and with the assistance of six policemen and Detective Michael Moriarity, shot it out with gangsters headed by Joseph Riggio, alias Rigolano. Apprehended with them was Sister Annie Ross, an old character known for her connection with houses of ill fame five years ago.

"The most astounding result of this battle and the incidents leading up to it, is the fact that Captain Klausner is in jail accused of accepting graft from Riggio and Sister Annie. It is alleged that he received weekly payments from Riggio for allowing Riggio and Sister Annie to circulate 'hostesses' throughout the restaurants in his precinct. These girls were imported from various cities and shifted frequently from one restaurant to another. Twelve of them have been apprehended by detectives and two of them have admitted that they were hired to sell their charms in the various restaurants, under the inducement that they would receive police protection.

"This is not a new racket, but it is the first time it has been known to occur in Richmond City, and from all accounts it is believed to have been in operation for no more than a month. Credit for nipping it in the bud goes to Captain MacBride, who through diligence and perseverance revealed its sordid existence and at the same time revealed the complicity of Captain Klausner."

That was Kennedy writing in the evening edition of the *Free Press*.

Klausner got fifteen years.

Patsy got a stake and a ticket to Hollywood.

MacBride got a month's leave—with pay.

Ten Men from Chicago

Captain MacBride meets a gang from the Pineapple City.

Chapter I

THE Police Commissioner took his cigar from his mouth and waved it in front of his chest. "This... this Quagliari, now. You know him, MacBride?"

MacBride said. "I've run across him now and then. Not much. Seems he's been keeping his hands clean."

"Reformed crook, though, eh?"

"Yes, he did a stretch. About being reformed.... Well, yes, I guess you might say that—to date. A guy never knows, though. He's been president of the Neighborhood Club for the past year. Last Christmas he got up a lot of baskets of food for the poor and he had a bread-line for a week in Race Street. And for a living"—MacBride shrugged and linked his hard strong fingers on his hard flat stomach—"well, he runs an employment agency for guys who have been up against it.... What's the matter? Quaggy been getting out of step?"

The Commissioner put his elbows on the arms of his chair and his fingertips together just below his chin. "No, not exactly. It is about Quagliari, though and 'Boss' Dillon, the political chief—mainly about Dillon."

The ghost of a sneer appeared on MacBride's face.

The Commissioner saw it and smiled with his tongue in his cheek.

He said, nodding, "I know how you feel about Boss Dillon, Mac-Bride. Well, listen to this. There's to be a private banquet at the Neighborhood Club tonight. A testimonial to Boss Dillon, the man with the big heart, the man who put many another man in office. Quagliari's throwing it, apparently. Dillon gave Quagliari many a break. And maybe the dinner would seem all right if it were not for the fact that among those slated to be present is a former Assistant State's Attorney. You know him... Pohly."

MacBride blinked. "Why, Pohly and Dillon had a falling out six months ago."

"That's just it," said the Commissioner. "This has all the earmarks of reconciliation. You remember that bit of scandal when Nick Piciulo was up for grand larceny. Pohly tried the case for the State. He was rated a damn good trial lawyer. There was a lot of rumor around that Boss Dillon was behind Pohly and that he had his hooks in Judge Marsden, too. Pohly made a fool out of himself in that case, and a lot of us thought he did it deliberately. Something went wrong somewhere.

"It looked to me as if Pohly tried to get the case thrown out of court by his own deliberate bungling, and then Judge Marsden dropped a bomb-shell by demanding a new trial and another lawyer for the State. Pohly got kicked out of his job. Then a month or so later Marsden resigned, and some believed that it was under pressure from Boss Dillon. And of course Pohly blamed Dillon for the loss of his job, because we are to suppose that he had relied on Dillon to fix Judge Marsden before the trial. Now Pohly's a criminal lawyer."

"And a sly one," said MacBride.

"Yes. Another thing puzzles me is why none of us have been invited. I have an idea that many celebrities of the underworld will be there. And I'm wondering whether this party is being really staged for Boss Dillon or for the fact that Dillon and Pohly have become—or are to become—reconciled. Now I want you to sort of drift in there. You won't have to give any reason. Well, you were just walking around the neighborhood, heard that a party was being thrown, and you just dropped in to say hello."

"And what am I to do there?"

"See who's present. I want to get a line on this Quagliari and also on Boss Dillon. We can rest assured that anybody there will be a friend of Quagliari. This party is being kept quiet The papers will not get it. I got wind of it through one of my under-cover men. A reconciliation between Boss Dillon and Pohly means something. It may be the prelude to graft, since Pohly will doubtless meet racketeers there and perhaps get their future cases. I don't want you to make any trouble. Just drop in, look around, have a drink, and try to get the lowdown on the whole affair."

"Okey," said MacBride.

"That's all."

MacBride stood up, took his hat, said, "I'll report to you in the morning," and started towards the door.

The Commissioner called out, "Remember, MacBride, don't pull any rough stuff."

MacBride turned on the threshold, grinned. "I'll be a lamb among wolves, Mr. Commissioner."

THE Neighborhood Club had its rooms in Jockey Street. The ground floor used to be a store at one time, but now the plate-glass windows were painted, and behind them were card rooms and a billiard room. The banquet rooms were upstairs, and could be reached either through a hall door directly from the street or from the rooms below.

It had many honorary members among the political crowd, and as a matter of fact it was first organized, back in 1919, for the express purpose of rounding up votes for the notorious Billy Penrose, who became mayor in that year and first put Richmond City on the map as a hot-bed for grafters. Penrose was shot to death a year later in the bedroom of a River Street call-woman, and a day later a son was born to his wife. The shock killed the wife.

Since that time quite a few of the club's members died in the chair. Others became ward-heelers, and there were some who went into business and moved out of the neighborhood, and two became first-rate prizefighters, one rose to Municipal Comptroller and was in office only fifteen months when he became embroiled in a gigantic payroll padding scandal and got kicked out on his neck.

MacBride came down Jockey Street at about ten-thirty. He came

on foot, having dropped off a trolley on Main Avenue, four blocks away. He was smoking a cigar. He wore a dark gray spring topcoat and had his hands in his pockets.

As he approached the Neighborhood Club, he could see a lot of cars drawn up alongside the curb. He could see four lighted windows on the second floor, but the shades were drawn. There were some chauffeurs hanging around the cars at the curb.

The hall door was partly open, and the hall itself was brightly lighted. It ran back to a door on the ground level, and halfway back was a staircase that hugged the right wall and led upstairs. As he entered the hall door, MacBride heard the muffled drone of voices and convivial merriment, and he stood still for a moment, appearing to meditate.

Then he started up the stairs, and as he neared the top he could see a few men hanging around in the upper hall, leaning on the banister and smoking. They were rough-looking customers and they glanced down at him and then looked hastily at one another. MacBride nodded genially enough as he reached the top, and looking past them, he saw a door open and one end of a banquet table and about six men, all talking and gesticulating and drinking what appeared to be red wine.

"You got a pass, bud?" said one of the three men in the hall.

"No," said MacBride. "I just dropped in for a drink."

"You gotta have a pass."

MacBride opened his coat and showed his shield. "How's this?"

The man looked at it, then looked up at MacBride's face. " 'Fraid it ain't enough, Cap."

"Go in and tell them MacBride would like a drink."

The man snapped over his shoulder, "Ed, go in and say Captain MacBride wants a drink."

Ed went inside and came out a minute later with Quagliari.

"Hello, Cap," said Quagliari.

"Hello, Quaggy."

Quagliari was a gaunt, hollow-cheeked wop, with steady black eyes and a mouth that slashed tightly across a cleft chin. He had black hair that was naturally wavy and a forehead that looked as if it had some brains behind it.

"What you want, Cap?"

MacBride shrugged. "Just dropped in."

Quagliari bent his brows and then unbent them and sucked in his left cheek with a droll smile. "You want a bottle?"

"Hell, no. I don't have to grub bottles. I just dropped in for a drink and a hello. Heard you were staging a blow-out. Happened to be in the neighborhood."

Quagliari raised his hand and put it behind his head and rubbed the back of his neck, while his chin went down against his chest, hiding his bow tie.

"Jeeze, it's kinda private party, Cap."

"I'm sorry, Quaggy."

"Have a bottle, won't you?"

"No." MacBride took his cigar from his mouth, regarded it, then raised it and blew off the ash and put the cigar back in one corner of his mouth. "Give Boss Dillon my regards."

Quagliari raised his eyes and his head, and he looked awkward with his arm crooked up behind him. His expression made it patent that he was surprised to know that MacBride was aware of Dillon's presence. He got tired of holding his arm up and let it fall back to his side. Then he shook his shoulder.

"Well, maybe it ain't so private. Come on."

MacBride followed him into a large room. There was a long table in the middle of the room and around the table sat about twenty men. The dishes had been cleared away, and now there were plenty of bottles—wine, whiskey and cordials—and a few boxes of cigars. The talk was noisy, and only a few looked up when MacBride and Quagliari entered.

Boss Dillon looked up and his eyes opened wide and his jaw fell, but only for the briefest of moments. Then he raised his hand and grinned and MacBride took it and shook briefly.

"Well, well, MacBride, this is a surprise! How are you?"

"Fine. How are you?"

"Very well, thank you. We're having a little party here. Will you have a drink?"

"Sure."

A waiter brought a chair and wedged it in beside Dillon, and MacBride sat down. He noticed Pohly sitting directly opposite him. Pohly nodded and smiled with restraint. He was a thin man, with sleek brown hair, and sallow skin drawn tightly over pointed cheek-bones. He had small eyes that flanked a knifelike nose, and large ears that stuck out from his head. He was a homely man, and a shrewd one.

MacBride took Scotch with a shot of seltzer, and ran his eyes up and down the table. Hymie Goldman was there—Hymie had long been suspected of being a fence. Alderman Tony Pisanti, sticking to dago red and looking happy. District Leader Skoog, nursing a bottle of Cointreau and trying to give the impression that he had a refined taste. County Clerk Marcus, Dillon's shadow and yes-man. A couple of blue-jawed guys with close haircuts whom MacBride had never seen; they drank Scotch straight out of water glasses. Henry Kofchur, owner of the Metro Paper Bag Company. Nat Levine, the big-shot gambler. Bud Glazer and Sam Hannaman, beer and alky barons with plants in Pennsylvania. A tight-faced, slit-eyed man on either side of them. Half a dozen neighborhood merchants... and others whom MacBride didn't know.

"Just a sociable little party," Boss Dillon was saying at MacBride's shoulder. "It hasn't been spread around, you know. I'm a plain man, MacBride. There's nothing high-hat about me. I'll eat, drink and be merry with anybody. But—of course—it wouldn't be politic for news of this party to be around at loose ends in the town."

"Of course," nodded MacBride. "Sure, I understand."

"I was surprised to see you come walking in."

"I was surprised myself. I saw a lot of cars outside and I felt like being chummy."

"You don't always feel that way, Cap."

MacBride grinned. "That's right. I don't."

Dillon laughed good-humoredly and clapped MacBride on the back. MacBride laughed with him. Dillon poured out another drink for MacBride.

"How are you, Pohly?" MacBride called across the table.

"First rate, Cap. How are you?"

"Jake."

Dillon jerked a thumb towards Pohly and said, "He's a good sport, Cap. Too bad we had an argument once. I like Pohly. We're friends now."

Quagliari had resumed his seat at the other end of the table. Men on either side of him were talking, but he seemed not to hear them.

He seemed to have drawn within himself, and from time to time he flicked MacBride with his dark large eyes. Alderman Tony Pisanti started to sing a song about Napoli, but Quagliari told him to shut up.

Boss Dillon was getting drunker and merrier and he shouted, "This is a fine party, Quaggy! You're a splendid host!"

"Thanks, Boss," said Quagliari. "I'm kinda proud to have you here."

Sam Hannaman told an off-color story and the room shook with bawdy laughter. After that Boss Dillon suggested a toast to Hannaman, and everybody stood up with their drinks. They were all drinking—MacBride among them—when two men jumped into the room.

"Keep standing, you guys, and lift your mitts!"

Chapter II

SILENCE struck the room like a sudden, swift and paralyzing plague. Every man stood with his drink still, near his lips.

The two men, both masked, fanned the crowd with their guns while six more likewise masked, filed in and surrounded the table.

The man who had first spoken, spoke again, "Just drop them glasses. Hey, you—I didn't say put it on the table—I said *drop it!*"

Glasses crashed to the floor.

"Get those mitts up, and snap on it!"

All hands went up. MacBride's went up, because there was a gun pressed against his back.

The leader snapped, "There's two guys taking care o' those babies in the hall. We'll take care o' you. There ain't nobody going to get hurt unless they crack wise." His voice dropped. "All right, buddies. Frisk these guys."

"My God!" breathed Boss Dillon.

MacBride said nothing. His lips were flattened against his teeth. He felt his gun being taken from its holster. He did not move—did not utter a word. To make a false move would be to start the hold-up guns popping, and a lot of people would be hurt.

He saw Boss Dillon frisked of his rings and watch and of the money in his wallet. He saw Quagliari frisked. And he saw Pohly, stiff and tense, while a gunman went over him. He saw Pohly try to argue.

"Quit it, you!" clipped the gunman.

Pohly's lips were hueless, his face a frozen mask. Alderman Pisanti bewailed the loss of his wedding ring. The two hard-faced men with the short haircuts were chewing their lips. Nat Levine, the big-shot gambler, sneered as one of the gunmen took a solitaire off his finger and a diamond cluster stick-pin from his tie. District Leader Skoog said, "Aw, say, that watch is a present from my sister." And the gunman said, "Listen, wisenheimer, if you don't shut up I'll take out your gold teeth."

The leader stood at the foot of the table, motionless, his gun pressed against his hip. From time to time he snapped out brisk orders to his men. His eyes missed nothing. His men took everything—money, jewelry, guns, and two knives. They worked swiftly, deftly, and for the most, silently. They worked after the manner of men who knew their trade.

Nat Levine said, "Hell, this reminds me of Chicago!"

"You ain't wrong there, brother," said the leader. "That's where we come from."

One of the gunmen said, "There's a dick in this mob, boss."

"Yeah?"

"Yeah. This guy. A captain."

"Don't that give me a jolt!" chuckled the leader. "Hey, gumshoe, how the hell do you like this?"

"Pretty neat," said MacBride.

"Ain't it!"

"Hang around town a while and you'll learn something."

The leader laughed. "Brother, I been brought up in Chicago!"

"Yeah, and this is just the burg to come to if you want to be brought down."

"I ain't got time to talk." He turned to his men. "All right, buddies, if you got everything we'll breeze. And listen, you guys," he said to the others, "don't make a chirp for five minutes. Back up there, all of you—and stay there."

Quagliari's guests bunched in the back of the room, and the leader stepped beside the door. He clipped to his men:

"Out, buddies."

They filed out. The leader waited until the last had gone. Then he sneered.

"So long, angels!"

He stepped out and closed the door after him.

Those inside the room remained motionless. Every man was disarmed and therefore helpless. Some were still pale with fright. Only now did some realize it was safe to lower their hands.

MacBride walked out to the center of the floor. Then he jumped to one of the windows, drawing the shade aside.

"They must have come in and gone out the back way. Is there a back way, Quaggy?"

"Yeah. There's a yard behind, and then a wire fence, and on the other side of that is an alley that goes to the next street over."

MacBride turned and looked at the men. He did not say anything. His eyes kept moving back and forth.

"My God!" breathed Boss Dillon.

MacBride asked, "Where's a telephone?"

"Downstairs," said Quagliari.

"Wait!" yelled Boss Dillon.

"Huh?" said MacBride.

Dillon was mopping his face. "We've got to think up something."

"I've got to report to Headquarters."

"Wait," persisted Boss Dillon, shaking his head. "Not yet. Listen, for God's sake, I can't afford the publicity! Nobody knew I was here. If the papers get hold of it, they'll ride holy hell out of me!"

"Me too," said Alderman Pisanti.

"Oh, you're not that big," scoffed Dillon.

"And how about me?" asked District Leader Skoog.

Dillon held his head and walked up and down. "My God! My God!" He stopped short and took a drink. Then he pivoted and stared at MacBride. "Cap, come into another room a minute."

"Listen," said MacBride, "if I don't report this right away, I'll get hell."

"Just a minute, MacBride."

The three men who had been in the hall burst into the room but nobody paid any attention to them. Dillon led MacBride into another room and closed the door. He was still mopping his face.

"Listen, MacBride, can't we hush this up?"

"Why the hell should we hush it up?"

"Why? Think of my position! The papers are aching to smear me. My God, you saw a lot of the men in there! It's all right for me to know them, but I can't be seen mixing socially with them. Levine, Hannaman—those others. Can't you see?"

"How can we hush it up? We can't."

"We've got to. Those bums came in the back way and went out the back way. Not even the chauffeurs downstairs know what's happened. The only ones who know are those of us who've been robbed. My position is precarious, MacBride. I'll go to any length to keep this quiet."

"How about the birds in the other room?"

"What do you mean?"

"Well, a lot of them have no positions to worry about."

"I'll fix them, MacBride—I'll fix them."

"How do you know they'll be fixed?"

Dillon waved his hands. "Don't you worry about that. I'll attend to that."

"Listen, Dillon, I wouldn't trust most of them no farther than I could see them. And what the hell would happen to me if I didn't report this and it leaked out later that there'd been a stick-up here? I've got a position, too—not as big as yours in a way, but just as important to me personally."

Dillon held his head between his hands again and rocked it from side to side. "What a mess—what a mess!"

"What strikes me is that you're an awful jackass to come to a joint like this."

"But it's happened, MacBride—it's happened. For God's sake, don't report it. Leave those other men to me. I'll talk to them. There were only a few heavy losers, and they're good sports."

"I'm not worrying about the heavy losers," said MacBride warmly. "I'm worrying about the small fry—the mutts out there. I won't take a chance on them. There's no telling when they'll come up against me, and they'd spring this as sure as hell. My job means a lot to me."

"I'll see you through, Cap, so help me!"

"You can't see me through, Dillon."

"What do you mean?"

"You know damned well you'd have all you could do to see yourself through. You're in this and you've got to weather it. It won't kill you. You didn't commit a crime. All the papers can do is razz you for a while, and if you lose your job, you've got lots of money and you can go ahead and retire. If I lose my job, I've got nothing."

He turned swiftly and went out into the main banquet room. The men were drinking and talking volubly, all at once. Dillon came plowing in behind him, red-faced, sweaty, agitated.

Pohly sneered. "What the hell have you guys been cooking up in there?"

MacBride put a withering eye on Pohly. "What the hell do you think we've been cooking up?"

Quagliari came over with a glass in his hand. "Jeeze, Cap, what do you think of it—what do you think of it?"

"I think it was a pretty slick job."

Pohly said, "It was so damned slick that it looks phony to me." And he stared at Dillon as he said it.

"What do you mean by that, Pohly?" snapped Dillon, his fists clenching.

"Not a damned thing!"

Quagliari was scowling at Pohly. "That sounds like a crack outta turn, Pohly."

Pohly drawled, "Was I talking to you, Wop?"

"You were talking to my friend," said Quagliari.

"Well, when I talk to you, open your trap!"

Quagliari colored. "I gotta mind to—"

"You pipe down, Quaggy," broke in MacBride. "And now show me that telephone."

Dillon reached out a hand and caught his breath. MacBride walked past him. Pohly was staring at Dillon with hard, narrowed eyes.

He muttered, "If I thought you were two-timing, Dillon—"

"Don't be a fool!" snapped Dillon.

MacBride went downstairs and called up Headquarters. When he returned to the banquet room he had a pad and pencil in his hand. He looked around at the men scattered about and said:

"Names, now—and everything that was stolen."

Dillon dropped to a chair, exhausted, wet with perspiration. Pohly leaned against the wall smoking a cigarette, his small, beady eyes never straying for long from the Boss.

"My… God!" murmured Dillon in a broken whisper.

Pohly chuckled. It was a dry, brittle chuckle, seeming to linger just back of his thin, tight lips. Smoke drifted out of his nose, hung around his face, and through it he appeared strangely satanic.

OF COURSE the papers got it and howled to high heaven. They hadn't had much news in a week, and most of them gave it black headlines and the right-hand column. But only the principals at the banquet were named: Boss Dillon, District Leader Skoog, Alderman Tony Pisanti, Nat Levine (famous sportsman), County Clerk Marcus, Frank Quagliari (reformed gangster making it his life's work to urge other unfortunate stragglers to go straight).

"Well," said Kennedy, "it was a polished job." Kennedy was a news-hound with a scent for under-cover facts that couldn't be beat. He was also a staunch admirer of MacBride.

"Like clockwork."

"Ten men from Chicago, eh?"

"Seems so."

"I wonder, Cap—now I wonder if by any stretch of the imagination that trick could have been framed. From all accounts, those guys made quite a haul. I can't get over the fact that Pohly and Dillon were there. You know I always had an idea that when Pohly was Assistant State's he was working in cahoots with Dillon. I had an idea—but I may be wrong—I always had an idea that Dillon was subsidized by certain racketeers and that Pohly came in for a nice slice of graft too. That's all theory, but I don't think it's so wrong."

"I don't think it is, Kennedy—to be frank. This job was smooth—and the fact that there were ten men puzzles me. You know dam' well that gunmen rarely travel in a gang that big. But, I ask you, if there was a frame-up somewhere, who the hell was framed—and why?"

"How about Quagliari?" asked Kennedy.

"What do you mean?"

"Well, he invited, say, Dillon and Pohly. He knew that they would bring along some big shots—Nat Levine is Pohly's friend—and Hannaman had two thousand bucks taken from him. Levine said that ring and stick-pin of his are worth twelve thousand, and he lost eleven hundred in cash besides. This employment agency of Quagliari's looks to me like a blind. Of course, he gets some guys jobs, and he plays Santa Claus to the down-and-outers on occasion. He cuts a nice sob-figure for the tabloids. A great-hearted guy who knew the dregs of life and is now living clean and making a name for himself in the neighborhood. The kids think he's some tomatoes. The women rave about him. He's pretty clever—and if he is straight, then I'm wrong."

"Kennedy," said MacBride, "you have a knack of putting into words a lot of convictions that I have planted in the back of my head. But if Quagliari was behind that job, he certainly used his head. And we can't touch him—not yet. I've got my men fanning the city, but my hopes aren't high. Those ten guys were strangers so far as I'm concerned."

For the time being Boss Dillon went into retirement, refusing to see reporters, claiming that he was ill. MacBride's men scoured the city, picked up all suspicious-looking characters, dragged them to Headquarters and quizzed them. A day passed, and then another, with no results, not even the slightest of clues.

On the third day MacBride walked into his office bright and early and found a package on his desk. He took off the brown wrapping paper, upon which the name and address had been printed in pencil, and found an oblong cardboard box of the type in which shoes are packed. This was tied with a piece of twine. He snapped the twine. He opened the box and found a lot of tissue paper. He pulled it and it came out bodily, wrapped around something weighty. He tore the tissue paper apart and found a gun. He looked at the base of the butt. It was his own gun, with the police marking.

He sat down before his desk and put the gun on the desk and stared at it, his fingers tapping. The police marking of course could not be removed, therefore the gun was of no use to anyone except MacBride, who had reported its loss. After a short minute he picked up the box in which the gun had come and turned it over and over in his hands. One end of the box showed certain signs of having been scraped; the paper sticker which one usually finds on shoe-boxes had been removed. He picked up the cover. There was nothing on it except a blue triangle.

He put the box in one of the desk drawers beside a bottle of Bacardi and went around to see the Commissioner. He showed the Commissioner the gun and said:

"Well, I got it back."

The Commissioner sat back and looked at the gun in MacBride's hand and said, "Who gave it to you?"

MacBride grinned. "I wish I knew. It came through the mail."

"How about the address?"

"Printed—in pencil. No good. Came in a shoe-box, but the name of the brand of the shoe was torn off."

"If you could only trace the box...."

"Yes. I'll see what I can do about it."

The Commissioner took a drag on a cigar and streamed the smoke through his nostrils. "I'm glad I sent you to the club, MacBride, and yet I'm sorry if some of the criticism hits you. The *Morning Express* waxed kind of sarcastic. Have you read it?"

"No. Just the *Free Press.*"

"They were sensible. But the Express... well, read it."

He shoved a newspaper across the desk, and MacBride saw an editorial penciled off. There was a left-handed jab at himself.

> ... *and it certainly doesn't please us to find that Captain MacBride, touted as a staunch opponent of crime, corruption and graft, was among those present in the Club. According to testimony, it appears that he did not report the hold-up to Headquarters until almost half-an-hour after it had been committed....*

Dull red crept into MacBride's lean cheeks. He laid the paper down. He laughed shortly, crisply.

"Kind of a kick in the pants, isn't it?" he said.

"Yes," said the Commissioner vaguely. Then he added, "It was kind of long, Captain... half an hour."

"There were a lot of things to talk about."

"Yes, I suppose so." The Commissioner picked up a sheaf of letters. "I suppose some of the boys there tried to bribe you to keep the thing quiet."

"I didn't say so."

The Commissioner chuckled. "It's all right, MacBride. I believe in you. I sent you there. Only it's too bad this sheet took you under the hammer."

"That sheet can go to hell."

"Sure. Well, I'm busy, Captain. If you'll pardon me...."

MacBride went back to his office, a little hot under the collar. He sat down and pulled open the drawer and took out the shoe-box. He placed it on the desk and stared at it. He stuffed his pipe and lit up and continued to stare at the cardboard box. Presently he put it back in the drawer, rose and got into his dark gray topcoat and took his conservative gray fedora from the clothes tree and sailed out of the office.

Chapter III

TEN minutes later he walked into a huge department store, accosted a floor-walker and asked for the shoe department. It was pointed out to him, and he went over and met one of the clerks, a small, old man, who asked him to take a seat.

"No, thanks. I'm Captain MacBride, from Police Headquarters. I wonder if you could tell me what make of shoe comes in a box that has on the cover a simple blue triangle."

"A simple blue triangle.... Let me think." He appeared to think, having quite a time of it. He mumbled to himself and wandered over to the files of shoe-boxes and ran near-sighted eyes up and down and across. He came back, his forehead wrinkled. "I don't think I know. Wait—there's a trade journal in town called the *Shoe Merchant.* Maybe they'd know."

MacBride got the address and went out.

The offices of the *Shoe Merchant* were in Commerce Street, and

MacBride was received by the advertising director, to whom he told the object of his visit.

"A blue triangle? Why, yes, it's a rather dear shoe—sells for fifteen dollars for men and considerably more for women. The reason is because they are made to order—for people with fallen arches, exceptionally high insteps, or foot deformations. General department stores and shoe dealers don't handle them, as a rule. I believe there are a few in this city."

"Could you tell me who are the distributors?"

"I think so. Just a moment."

When MacBride left he carried the addresses of the only three stores in the city that handled the Blue Triangle Shoes. He went back to Headquarters and found his right-hand men, Moriarity and Cohen, sneaking drinks out of his bottle of Bacardi.

"See where I'll have to lock this office up," he clipped.

"Now, now, Cap," chided Cohen.

"We only had a drink apiece," said Moriarity.

"Well, now you'll do some running around," said MacBride, pulling out the shoe-box. "See this? Well, my gun came back in it this morning."

"How thoughtful of the mutt who took it," grinned Cohen.

MacBride went on. "I've been trying to check up, and maybe we'll get a break. Made-to-order shoes come in a box like this, and I've found out that there are only three stores in the city that take orders for them. I've got the addresses here. You guys take 'em. You go to these stores and check up on the people who have ordered shoes and got them delivered in the past month. Bring back all the names and let me look them over. Ten to one nothing will turn up, but we can take a chance, and it's about time you guys did some work anyhow.

"Now get out of here. There's the addresses, and see if you can do this job without stopping in any speakeasies on the way."

They laughed and went out. There were a lot of letters in the basket on the desk, and MacBride got down to business. About half an hour later Sergeant Bettdecken, outside at the desk, called up and said that Nat Levine had dropped around. MacBride said it was okey for Levine to come in.

The gambler drifted in genially. "Hello, Captain. Popped in for no reason really—or maybe a bit of a reason. Any news?"

"Not a bit."

Levine breathed money. He sat down lazily. "I see some of the papers razzed you too."

"All in the game."

"Yeah, I guess so. I was a heavy loser, you know. I'd like at least to get that ring back. She was a neat piece of ice. Funny—that stick-up."

"What do you mean?"

Levine smiled, shrugged. "Maybe nothing. But when a job is pulled off as neat as that, a guy gets to thinking somebody was inside on it."

"How'd you come to go there!"

"Pohly."

"Good friend of his?"

"Kinda."

"Pohly looked sore as hell—and he said he lost only two hundred. I didn't think he was such a bad loser."

"I guess two hundred was a lot to him. He ain't had such good breaks lately. He lost heavily in the market crash too. Stick to cards, say I. Well…." He stood up, re-creasing his tan snap-brim hat and then putting it on carefully, with a swanky tilt over the left eyebrow. "Well, if you recover some of my ice, Cap, I'll slip you a present."

"Forget the present, Levine. I get along on my salary."

Levine laughed. "Still a die-hard, eh?"

"Still got old-fashioned ideas… only a few of us left."

"Yeah, yeah, that's right."

Levine drifted out and MacBride went back to work.

At two o'clock Moriarity and Cohen returned with a long list of names and addresses which they placed before MacBride. He squared off before the list. He studied each carefully, turning each name over in his head. He waded through the list slowly. Suddenly he sat back with a rigid forefinger jabbed alongside one of the names.

"Look at this, boys," he said.

Moriarity and Cohen looked over his shoulder.

"That one?" asked Cohen, pointing.

"Yes, this one," said MacBride.

"Oh, that one," said Moriarity.

"Yes," nodded MacBride. "That one. H.I. Goldman. Hymie Goldman."

"The fence?" asked Cohen.

"The fence," said MacBride. "And Hymie was at the party."

Chapter IV

HYMIE GOLDMAN'S store was in Brock Street. The window was filled with a lot of cheap novelty jewelry and curios of soapstone and imitation jade and ivory. The interior was gloomy and small, with a showcase flanking one wall.

When MacBride entered Hymie was sitting on a high stool at the rear of the counter, looking at the insides of a watch beneath a bright white light whose radius did not extend four feet beyond him in any direction. He was a small, thin Jew with brown dry skin and greased black hair pulled back tightly from his forehead. The hair was thin on top and you could see his scalp through it. He was about forty.

"Hello, Hymie."

"Hello, Cap," Goldman said offhand, and went on looking at the insides of the watch.

MacBride leaned on the counter. "Having a hard job?"

"No. Except some guys expect a ten dollar watch to run for years."

"Is that a ten dollar watch?"

"I sell 'em for nine-fifty."

"Can't expect to get a good watch for nine-fifty these days."

"Tell the world. How you been?" he asked, squinting at the watch.

"Okey. You?"

"So-so."

"Guess that stick-up the other night gave you quite a jolt."

Goldman listened to the watch, stared into space abstractedly. "Me? Kinda. Not much. I didn't lose much. Fifty bucks. Hell, look at some of the guys."

"Yeah."

"Any leads?"

MacBride shrugged. "One—maybe."

" 'At so?"

"Yeah."

Goldman looked at the watch again through a glass screwed into one eye. "Glad to hear that, Cap."

"I didn't think you would be."

"Hell, why not?"

"You're the lead."

Goldman, still peering through the glass, probed the watch with a needle and said, "That's funny."

"I thought it was too."

Goldman took the glass from his eye, laid it on the counter, snapped the back on to the watch, set the watch, listened to it, then rubbed it off with a strip of chamois, attached a tag to it and reaching back, placed it in a pigeon hole. When he turned to face MacBride again he lit a cigarette and a droll smile crept across his lips, making the cigarette wobble. "What's the dope, Cap?"

"I may be all wrong, but I'd like to look through your safe."

"Safe? Why?"

"Do you mind if I look through it?"

"Of course not. But, why?"

"Well, I want to look through it."

"A safe's supposed to be a man's private property, Cap."

"Sure. I know all that."

Goldman took a puff on his cigarette and then looked at it vacantly. "What did I ever do to you?"

"Not a thing."

"Then what's the idea?"

MacBride's voice quickened. "Listen here, Hymie, you're in a hole and there's no dam' use in your stalling. You can play ball with me nice, or you can play nasty, but no matter how you play you've got to come across."

Goldman was still unimpressed. "I'm in the dark."

"How about the gun you sent me?"

"What gun?"

"My gun."

"Where the hell would I get your gun?"

"That," said MacBride, "is what I want to know."

Goldman laughed. "Jeeze, this gives me a kick!"

"Listen, Hymie. I've got an idea some of you guys know about that stick-up. You sent me my gun, you dumb animal-cracker! You sent it in a shoe-box and you were wise enough to tear off the labels. But I happened to get a brainstorm and traced down the make of the shoe-box right to the store that two weeks ago sent you a pair of specially made shoes. You should have scraped off the blue triangle on the cover. Hell, cops are noted to be dumb, but sometimes we get a break, and I got one, and you're going to come across."

"I think you're all wrong, Cap, and I think you're trying to dish me up a lot of tripe."

"We can settle that by looking in your safe."

Goldman's face did not change, but his voice got raspy. "Well, dammit, if you want to play rough with me, I'll play rough with you! My safe's my private property, and you'll have to show me a search warrant."

MacBride smiled a bleak, cold smile. "So that's it. Well, we'll see about that too. I'll tell you what I have got, Hymie. I've got a blanket warrant, and I'm going to use it on you."

"What do you mean—a pinch?"

"Sure. And it won't take me long to get the search warrant. Put on your hat and coat." He added, "First, shove that telephone over here."

He called up Headquarters and got Sergeant Bettdecken on the wire. He said, "Otto, send a cop down to 54 Brock Street.... No, there's no trouble. I just want him to hang around here."

He hung up. Goldman was putting on his coat.

"Thanks for the break, Cap."

"Don't mention it."

Chapter V

GOLDMAN was locked up at Police Headquarters. MacBride did a lot of running around and secured a search warrant a couple of hours later. He returned to his office and made a number of telephone calls. Inside of half an hour there arrived Nat Levine, District Leader Skoog, Alderman Tony Pisanti and Sam Hannaman, the beer baron.

"Just wait here a minute," said MacBride.

He got Goldman out of the cell, showed him the warrant, and said, "Now you'll go along with me and we'll open that safe."

He stopped in his office to get his hat and coat and told the men waiting there to come along. They all went out, accompanied by two policemen, and drove around to 54 Brock Street. Patrolman Grotsky was leaning outside the door.

At a word from MacBride Goldman unlocked the door and everybody filed in.

Levine was smiling. "What, do I get my ice back, Cap?"

"I don't know."

Goldman had tightened his face and drawn into himself. He went into the back room, knelt down before the safe, spun the knob a few times, and then pulled open the heavy door. He got up and stepped back.

MacBride bent down, pulled out all the drawers he could find and placed them on the floor. The collection of stones here had nothing in common with the junk in the window. MacBride drew his notebook from his pocket.

"Here," he said, "I have a list of names and also a list of the articles stolen the other night. I wish you men'd get down here and see if you recognize any of your stuff."

"I can see my solitaire without getting down," said Nat Levine. "In that third box from the end, Cap. See it? Hell, you can't miss it!"

"This?" MacBride held up a diamond ring.

"No other." Levine looked at Goldman. "Well, you louse-faced—!"

"Ah!" cried out Tony Pisanti. "My wedding ring!"

"Now, hold on," said MacBride. "You can't take that stuff yet. Hey, you, Hymie, come over and pick out all the stuff that was stolen and I'll check it off on my list. This stuff will have to go through Headquarters first as a matter of course."

MacBride and the two policemen took Goldman to Headquarters, and MacBride took him on into his own office. Moriarity and Cohen were there.

MacBride said, "Sit down, Hymie."

Hymie sat down.

MacBride sat down. "Well, Hymie?…"

A crooked smile drew across Goldman's lips. "You know damned well, MacBride, that I'm not talking."

"You know the penalty for receiving stolen goods?"

"Sure. Am I crabbing?"

MacBride put his elbow on the desk, closed his fist at the end of his upright forearm, and planted his chin on his fist.

"Hymie, somebody is in for a lot of hell. There were ten guys in that stick-up job, and we're to suppose they came from Chicago. It was one of the best-oiled jobs I've ever seen. I want one of those eggs, Hymie. I want a conviction. We've got to get a conviction on this job.

The public and the press are howling for a conviction. We found all the stolen jewelry in your safe. You know who pulled that job, and you're going to spring what you know. We've got you cold, so you might just as well give yourself a break."

Goldman's smile became almost derisive: "Do I look dumb? Do you think I'm going to spring what I know and get taken for a ride when I get out?"

MacBride stared at him for a long moment. "Hymie, my boy, have you ever heard of a rubber hose?"

"Yes."

"It's a great old little toy. Moriarity over there has a special talent for using it."

"Yeah?" smiled Goldman.

"Yeah."

Goldman reached into an inside pocket and drew out a long white envelope. From the envelope he drew a folded sheet of paper and tapped the desk with it.

"This, MacBride, is signed by a doctor. It says that I have a bad case of heart trouble, that I'm kinda ill—very ill—and that any violent physical action might kill me. Read it."

MacBride read it. He folded it slowly, thoughtfully, and pushed it back across the desk. He did not say a word. He did not look at Goldman. He squinted at the flat shiny surface of the desk. Then he reached for the telephone, called a number.

"Hello, Doc. You busy?… Good. Listen, will you do me a favor?… Uhuh. Yeah, I wish you'd come over to Headquarters.… Will you?… Thanks."

He hung up; said, "Mory, take Hymie downstairs. Dr. Ames is coming over."

An hour later Dr. Ames walked into MacBride's office. They shook hands.

"I just examined that man, Cap."

"How is he?"

"Sound as you."

"Honest?"

"Sure. You worried about that letter? Nonsense. Goldman bought it. That doctors' graft, Cap."

"Thanks, Doc."

The police doctor went out. Cohen moved away from the wall.

"What should I tell Mory?"

"Tell him to play kick-the-wicket with Hymie." He stood up, tight-jawed. "I'll be down in a minute."

Chapter VI

SERGEANT OTTO BETTDECKEN sat at the desk in the central room eating a frankfurter-on-roll. A clock ticked on the wall behind him. Bettdecken was a large man, with fat rosy cheeks and heavy jowls that overlapped his tight standing uniform collar. From time to time he raised a bottle of home-brew from behind the desk, cast searching eyes around the large room, and took a generous swallow. After each swallow he sighed with that profound air of a man serenely at peace with the world and thankful for the small creature comforts which it bestows upon mankind—and especially police sergeants.

There was the sound of hurrying footsteps. A door banged. Bettdecken hastily put the bottle of home-brew out of sight, dragged his fat hand across his mouth and bent serious eyes on a report sheet before him.

MacBride came into view muscling into his overcoat. Behind him were Moriarity and Cohen. Moriarity was buttoning his vest. Cohen carried Moriarity's jacket and topcoat.

MacBride clipped, "Hymie's back in the cell, Otto. He sprung. We're going out for Quagliari."

"Quag—"

"Yeah. If we need the wagon, I'll ring you."

He passed out of the central room. Cohen was at his heels. Moriarity was behind Cohen, getting into his topcoat. In the street, MacBride looked up and down.

"We'll walk down to Townsend and flag a cab."

They walked briskly. It was early spring, and the night was cool, damp with mist that came in from the not distant river. The stars were small and far away. There was a bit of moonlight, but the moon itself was hidden somewhere beyond the houses. They reached Townsend; walked another block before they got a taxi. MacBride gave the address to the driver, then climbed in and pulled down one of the spare seats, facing Moriarity and Cohen in the darkness.

Moriarity lit a cigarette, bending his head and cupping his hands over the match against the damp wind that blew in through the open cab window. The taxi bounced and swayed and all three men rocked from side to side in unison.

"Quagliari," said Cohen with a hard little laugh in the darkness.

"Yeah," said Moriarity.

"It's like Kennedy said," put in MacBride. "Once a bum, always a bum."

"Sure," said Cohen.

"He threw the party," went on MacBride, "and got a nice crowd there, and all the time he's arranged with these imported Chicago guttersnipes to pull the stick-up. What a double-timing dago pup he turned out to be!"

"Something tells me he'll put up a fight," said Cohen.

"We won't waste words," MacBride told him.

After a few minutes Moriarity said, "Well, anyhow, Cap, the papers can't crab so much now that all the jewelry is got back."

"That's not enough. We want a conviction."

The taxi was slowing down. The driver was leaning out trying to see the house-numbers.

"What number was that?" asked MacBride.

"Twenty-two."

"We'll get off here."

"Okey."

The taxi stopped and they got out and MacBride gave the driver fifty cents. They were at a corner and the taxi started off and swung around to the left. MacBride and his two men crossed the intersection and kept on straight ahead.

"What was it—thirty-eight?" asked Cohen.

"Yeah," said MacBride. "There it is."

It had three stone steps, a red brick front, three stories. They climbed the three stone steps and pushed into the vestibule. MacBride tried the inner door, but it was locked. Beside the door was a white button with the word Janitor beneath it. MacBride pressed that and then leaned against the wall. Moriarity looked at his cigarette, took a puff, looked at it again, then dropped it and ground it under his heel.

Cohen said, "It ain't"—he yawned—"it ain't a bad neighborhood, though."

"It ain't so bad," said Moriarity.

"No, it ain't so bad," added MacBride.

The latch began clicking. The door opened. A short old fat man, with thin tousled white hair and a corn-cob in his mouth, looked at them with sleepy eyes and huddled in a voluminous bathrobe.

MacBride said, "We'd like to see Mr. Quagliari."

"Upstairs... second floor... the door at the back of the hall."

They went in and the janitor closed the door and padded off down to the basement door as MacBride and his two men climbed the staircase to regions above. There was a red carpet on the stairs, fastened down with brass strips that clicked loosely beneath the men's feet. The place had a warm, old, intimate smell.

They reached the hall above and looked around and then MacBride pointed to a door at the rear and they went back and MacBride knocked. The three men looked at one another, and Cohen grinned and Moriarity put a thumb beside his nose and rubbed it reflectively. MacBride looked around at the walls and the ceiling, and then looked at the door again, and again knocked.

Moriarity looked gloomy. "Ain't in, guess."

"Yeah," murmured Cohen.

MacBride said, "Well..." in a vacant voice, and turned away. But he turned back again and half-heartedly tried the knob.

The door gave.

"Well!" breathed Cohen.

MacBride pushed the door open, and looked into darkness. The meager light from the hall went over his shoulder and lay dimly on the floor. He reached around on the wall inside the door but found no light switch. Cohen took a cigarette-lighter from his pocket, snapped it on, and walked in with the flame held above his head. They saw a chandelier, and MacBride found the cord and pulled it, and the lights came on.

"Jeeze!" clipped Cohen.

MacBride pivoted.

There was a man lying on the floor. Cohen bent down and looked at him more closely.

"Dead," he said.

He opened the man's vest. The shirt beneath was blood-soaked around the stomach. Cohen tore open the shirt. The man had been shot in the stomach.

"Never seen him before," said Cohen.

Moriarity bent down and picked up a bunch of keys. He jangled them in the palm of his hand. "He probably had a key to this joint."

Cohen looked up. "He's all dressed. D' you think he was shot in here?"

MacBride shook his head. "No. Not logical. If Quagliari'd shot him here he would have taken him out and dumped him somewhere. Wonder who he is. Look in his pockets, Ike."

Cohen went through the dead man's pockets. He found a worn pin-seal wallet and dumped out the contents on the table. They found a lot of thumb-marked cards.

"Mostly Chicago addresses," said MacBride. "This guy came from Chicago. A hundred-odd bucks. A Pullman stub."

Cohen clipped, "Somebody coming!"

Moriarity jumped over and closed the door.

They could hear the click of shoes on the brass strips that held down the stairway carpets. They faced the door. MacBride pulled out his gun. So did Moriarity and Cohen. The clicking stopped and they heard footsteps in the hall outside. Then a key grated in the lock, the door shook—opened.

"We've been looking for you, Quaggy," said MacBride.

Quagliari hung in the doorway, his mouth dropping open. His dark eyes shot from one to another of the men and then dropped to the body on the floor. The muscles on his face twitched.

"Come in and close the door, Quaggy," said MacBride.

Quagliari came in, nodded towards the body. "What the hell is this?"

MacBride grinned. "That's what we want to know."

"What happened?"

"That's what we want to know."

Quagliari stared at the body, bending his brows down over his nose.

MacBride said, "We came here to pinch you, Quaggy. We found this."

"Pinch me?"

"Sure."

"For cripes' sake, I didn't kill this bird!"

MacBride shook his head. "Not for this job, Quaggy. For the Neighborhood Club stick-up."

"What!"

"Hymie sprung."

"Hymie?"

"Yeah. We pinched him and he sprung. We found the jewelry in his shop. He said you gave it to him."

"The lousy kike!"

"Ain't he, though? Ike, clamp on the bracelets."

Cohen put one of the bracelets on his own wrist and the other on Quagliari's. Quagliari looked at the bracelets.

"What a break!" he chuckled.

MacBride said, "Who's the stiff?"

"Damned if I know."

"Don't be funny. He had a key to the door. He was dead when we got in. He's from Chicago. Who is he?"

"Well… Dink Buffo."

"Was he in on the stick-up?"

"Sure."

MacBride squinted. "You're coming across pretty nice, aren't you?"

Quagliari grinned. "Sure. And I'm in a position to give you a good break, if you'll give me one."

"What are you talking about?"

"There's nine guys downstairs who may come up any minute. I said I'd be right down. If you don't want to get slaughtered, use your head."

MacBride batted not an eye. "The other nine guys from Chicago, eh?"

"I don't like these bracelets," said Quagliari.

MacBride turned to Moriarity. "Mory, walk along the hall to the front window and look down."

Moriarity went out, and MacBride could see him walk to the window at the front of the corridor. Moriarity came back in.

"There's a big touring car down there. Some guys are standing around."

Quagliari didn't look worried. "No sense getting yourselves killed, guys. Those lads are waiting for me."

"Suppose," said MacBride, "you go to the front window and yell down that they should came back later."

"No." Quagliari shook his head. "You see, I came up here to get fifteen thousand dollars, part of what we got from Goldman for the jewelry. Then I'm to go down to these guys and split it. They want it in a hurry. They're leaving town. If I tell 'em to go away, that'll just make them come up."

"Where's the money?"

"Behind that picture on the wall."

MacBride went over and moved the picture and a wad of bills fell to the floor.

"You simply got to come to reason," said Quagliari, "or you're done. Let me go and I'll blow the town too."

"Let you go down," said MacBride, "and tell those guys that we're up here and then have them come after us? Ain't you bright?"

"You guys go down first. If you just walk out and mind your own business, nothing 'll happen."

MacBride shrugged. "Yeah, and while we're walking down you can yell out of the window what's up."

"Why should I?"

"Because we'd be taking fifteen thousand bucks with us. Because you know damned well that if you told them you'd let us walk out with it they'd very likely give you the works."

Quagliari looked at MacBride for a long minute. He chewed his lip and seemed vexed. "Say, if I told you I thought I knew who killed this guy on the floor, would it give me a break?"

"You could lie about that, too," said MacBride.

"Jeeze, you're a suspicious guy!"

"I sure am," laughed MacBride, humorlessly. "You know damned well, Quaggy, that I've got an idea that you know something about this killing, and that I'll get it out of you eventually. I don't have to buy you off. How do I know that you didn't kill him and then go out and come back again? We can plant the job on you in order to make you come clean. Where's your telephone?"

"I got none."

MacBride took a turn up and down the room—cracked fist into palm. He was in a hole. Nine gunmen were downstairs, and to try to take Quagliari out would be suicide plain and simple. And at any moment those guns might come up. He and his men were trapped just as much as Quagliari was trapped. There was a street lamp in front of the house, and if he walked out without Quagliari to get some aid, some of those birds would surely recognize him. There was one chance, long and dangerous for himself.

"Mory," he said, "you and Ike will have to go out. They won't know you. Go out and get to a telephone and tell Headquarters to shoot around a squad car. I'll stay here with Quaggy and lock the door."

Cohen said, "But suppose they come up?"

"I may be able to hold 'em long enough. Unlock the bracelet from your wrist and put it on mine."

Cohen grumbled as he did it. The bracelet clicked on MacBride's wrist.

"You're a dumb cop, MacBride!" snapped Quagliari.

"Yeah," muttered MacBride.

Moriarity and Cohen were lingering.

"Get out," clipped MacBride. "Snap on it!"

They went out.

MacBride locked the door and turned and looked at Quagliari.

"I think I'll fix you to the bed instead," he said. "I may have a fight on my hands."

He took the bracelet from his own wrist, made Quagliari lie on the bed, and fastened the bracelet to one of the metal posts.

Then he sat down on a chair and lit a cigar and laid his gun on the table. He laid his hand on the gun and puffed and waited, watching the door.

Chapter VII

TEN minutes passed.

Then there were sounds on the stairway.

MacBride did not budge. His hand closed around the butt of the gun, but he did not move it from the table. The cigar stuck out straight from the left corner of his mouth, and a thin, blue-gray column of smoke rose perpendicularly and mushroomed above, writhing sinuously among the three lights of the chandelier.

Footsteps came up to the door, and then someone knocked. Mac-Bride looked towards the bed and shot Quagliari a glance that recommended silence. Quagliari lay motionless, looking sidewise at the door.

"Hey, Quaggy," someone called.

Quagliari swallowed but said nothing. MacBride was looking at him.

The doorknob rattled.

"Hey, Quaggy."

MacBride looked at the door with steady blue eyes.

"Hey, Quaggy. This is Joe and Dave. You in there?"

Quagliari took a long breath while his tongue came out and moved across his lower lip.

The voice was lower. "Dave, go down and get that janitor."

The metal strips on the stairway clicked again.

MacBride stood up silently. He reached up his left hand, caught hold of the light cord, looked at Quagliari, and snapped out the lights. He moved cautiously over behind the bed, putting it and Quagliari between himself and the door. He leaned down and whispered:

"If you're wise, Quaggy, you'll stay quiet."

He could hear Quagliari's breath coming out. The bed-spring creaked.

A couple of minutes later there were footsteps again. MacBride heard the voice that had done the talking before:

"Looks like something's wrong. You better open it."

A key grated in the lock.

The door opened. MacBride saw the janitor and behind him two other men. The janitor came right in. He knew where the light cord was and he pulled it.

"Stick up your hands," said MacBride.

He stood behind the bed, his gun leveled across Quagliari's prostrated body.

The janitor was so frightened that he reeled sidewise, hit a chair and fell violently to the floor. One of the other men, who had started to come in, flung back into the hall and started to run.

"Hey, you!" yelled MacBride.

The other man had his hand in his pocket and the pocket jerked and flame and lead tore through the cloth. The shot hit a metal post of the bed and rang sharply after the explosion. MacBride made a brief, quick movement, pulled his trigger and sent a shot slamming into the man's chest. The man jerked backward, twisted his mouth, shook his head, opened his mouth wide, as if to yell.

MacBride cannoned past him into the hall, jumped to the head of the stairway, saw the other man near the bottom. The man was half-twisted around. He fired up. MacBride blinked as the shot gouged out the plaster on the wall an inch from his head. He held his gun low and fired with a businesslike snap. He saw the man fall down the remaining steps. He ran down after him.

The man was threshing about on the floor. He got up, staggered along the lower hall.

"Hey!" yelled MacBride.

The man looked back, saw MacBride at the foot of the staircase, stumbled backwards, bringing up his gun.

MacBride shook his head, but there seemed no use, so he fired again and his bullet got the man right below the chin. He stood, squinting, while the man swayed on his feet. The man had a look on his face that was half-surprise, half-terror. He stuck out his tongue in a manner that would have been ludicrous if it were not tragic. Then he suddenly collapsed like a deflated balloon.

A split-second later there was a clatter of shots out in the street. One of them smashed the window in the front door. MacBride looked back up the stairs, started to go up, then changed his mind and ran towards the street door. He reached it hugging the wall and looked out. There were two cops at the base of the stoop. There were two others crouched by the touring car and firing down the street.

MacBride opened the door and stepped out. The two cops at the base of the stoop started.

"Me," said MacBride.

There was a cop across the street, hunched behind a telephone pole. MacBride saw the muzzle of his gun spit flame into the night. There were two forms lying in the middle of the street. There was another lying in front of the touring car.

One of the policemen near MacBride said, "There's four more behind that stoop three doors down."

"Where's Moriarity and Cohen?"

"In an areaway across the street— There goes one o' their guns now!"

Red death burning in the darkness....

MacBride looked up and down. "Listen," he said. "I'm going to get those babies. I'm going to jump out and get on the other side of that car. When I say the word start firing at that stoop till I clear the sidewalk. All right. *Now!*"

The guns barked as MacBride leaped across the sidewalk, reached the back of the car, then worked around to the off side. For a moment he crouched there. Then he crept forward, opened the front door and released the emergency. He closed the door again, bent down and began pushing the car. It rolled slowly. One of the cops on the other side of the street must have divined his plan, for he started across on the run. A shot got him and he crashed down on his face.

The car was moving slowly towards the stoop behind which the four gunmen were hiding. Presently it was abreast of it. A fusillade of shots crashed into it, but MacBride remained crouched as he moved along with the car. Then he reached in and yanked the emergency. The car stopped.

He fired around the back of it. Three jets of smoking flame leaped from his gun. He heard a scream. He ducked back as lead hammered into the car. One of the rear tires blew. He reloaded his gun. He moved this time to the front of the car, got down on hands and knees, crawled around the fender, peered through the spokes of the wheel that was flush with the curb, and cut loose. He emptied his gun.

He saw two men reel out of the shadow of the stoop and fall across the sidewalk. He saw another crawl out and then collapse. The fourth, still in the shadows, was yelling for mercy....

Chapter VIII

QUAGLIARI sat in the office in Headquarters, his manacled hands lying on the shiny, flat-topped desk. Moriarity leaned against the radiator. Cohen sat in a chair with the back tipped against the wall. MacBride sat facing Quagliari.

"So those guys were from Chicago, eh?"

Quagliari shrugged. He looked disgusted.

"So tough," went on MacBride, "that we had only one cop wounded, and he'll get over it. Now what about Buffo, the guy I found killed in your flat?"

"What about him?"

"You said you had an idea who killed him."

"I have."

"Well?"

"Pohly."

Cohen brought his chair down on all fours with a bang. Moriarity walked away from the radiator to get a better look at Quagliari.

"Pohly!" repeated MacBride.

"Yeah. Buffo had a letter to sell Pohly for five thousand berries."

"What about it?"

"It was a letter taken from Pohly the night of the stick-up. It was a letter written to Pohly by Boss Dillon. Pohly was in Columbus at the time, and Dillon wrote him to hurry back. It was when they were in cahoots. Dillon wrote him that Nick Piciulo had to go free, and there was three thousand in it for him to bawl the case up so it would get thrown outta court."

"I thought you were Dillon's friend?"

"I was as long as I could use him. But he was getting scared lately and told me I'd have to shift somewheres else. I got sore at first. Then I got an idea. I threw that party for him to show there was no hard feelings."

"And framed it with Buffo and his pals to stick it up."

"Sure," nodded Quagliari.

"But about Pohly and Buffo now?"

Quagliari shrugged. "Well, we picked Buffo to call him up and tell him he had the letter to sell. Buffo wasn't known here, and we figured that Pohly would play ball nice. They met last night and Pohly gave Buffo five thousand berries. It took us about an hour to find out the jack was counterfeit. Buffo got sore and went after Pohly today. The only way I can figure it is that Pohly got him."

MacBride stood up. "Recess," he said, "while I look up Pohly."

He put Quagliari in a cell, took Moriarity and Cohen and went out and caught a taxi on Townsend Street. Fifteen minutes later they got out in front of an apartment house, went in and were whisked up in an elevator to the tenth floor. MacBride rang the bell six times, then went downstairs, got out the manager, flashed his shield, and said he wanted to look in apartment 1006.

They found Pohly in bed, very pale.

"Hello, Pohly," said MacBride.

"Hello, MacBride."

"I think we want you for the killing of a wop named Dink Buffo.
"Is that right?"

"It sure is," said MacBride. "Quagliari's locked up, and he told me
a long story about a certain letter and about your giving Buffo five
thousand for it. What's the matter, you sick?"

Pohly snapped, "For God's sake, if you had a bullet in the side you'd
be sick too!"

"You shot?"

"Yes." Pohly licked his lips. "Buffo shot me. I walked out of the
lobby this afternoon and he came up to me with his hand in his pocket.
I knew what that meant. He had a coupé parked up the street and he
made me get in it. We drove out to the country, and he said I'd have
to come across with five thousand in *real* money. He stopped the car
in a lane in the woods. I said I didn't have five thousand. I'd managed
to uncatch the door, and I took a long chance by jumping out and
hopping into the woods. He fired and I fell down, and then I drew
my own gun and fired up at him as he came running towards me. He
fell down and I got up and beat it through the woods. Hell, I'm not
going to live long now, either, if you ask me."

"How about a doctor?"

"I had one—a friend of mine. He went about half an hour ago. I'm
not giving his name. I told him to keep his mouth shut about this."

"Where's that letter?"

Pohly shook his head. "I'm not giving that up."

MacBride said over his shoulder, "Look around, boys."

They went to it. They searched Pohly's clothes, pulled out the bureau
drawers, then found some keys and went into the living-room and
opened the drawer of the desk there. Moriarity came into the bedroom.

"Maybe this is it."

Pohly groaned and then cursed.

MacBride asked, "Well, why the hell did you want the letter,
anyhow?"

"Why? Dammit, I was going to sell it to Dillon after that party
for ten thousand dollars! I could still have sold it to him. I need the
money. And Dillon always was a big bum! He turned yellow as hell
at that Piciulo trial, and I got the dirty end! He swore that Judge
Marsden would play ball—and the Judge didn't."

MacBride sighed and shook his head. "It always gives me a pain, the way grown men like you, who are supposed to have more brains than us ordinary guys, always get yourselves into such a hell of a tangle. Money. Graft. You'd sell your very souls for money. Common honesty means nothing to you—"

"Oh, hell," cut in Pohly peevishly, "are you going to sit there and preach?"

MacBride's jaw tightened. "No." He stood up. "Mory, call the hospital, so we can send this guy there."

"GOOD morning, MacBride," said the Commissioner.

"Good morning, Mr. Commissioner," said MacBride.

The Commissioner leaned back from his desk. "I've just been reading your report. It's a long one."

"There was a lot to tell."

"Yes. I want to congratulate you. We've been trying to pin something on Boss Dillon for a long time, but we never hoped to be so fortunate. This letter of his is damnable evidence. His future is ruined. A man of his years cannot start over again. And Pohly— who once was hand in glove with him—it's ironic to think that Pohly's testimony will help ruin the Boss forever. And I'll wager that Pohly himself will get twenty years."

"And Quagliari."

"Yes—and Quagliari. And Hymie Goldman." The Commissioner laughed. "By George, MacBride, it was a priceless haul!"

When MacBride breezed back into his own office, he found Kennedy of the *Free Press* slouched in a chair.

"Old tomato!" grinned Kennedy.

"Thanks for the write-up, Kennedy."

"You notice I mentioned your name eight times."

"Was it eight?"

"Yeah," drawled Kennedy. "Ain't that worth eight drinks."

With a low, good-natured growl MacBride dragged out the bottle. "Another form of graft," he rumbled. "I often wonder, Kennedy, with all the drinking you do, when you ever work."

"Work," said Kennedy, moving lazily towards the bottle, "is the curse of the drinking classes."

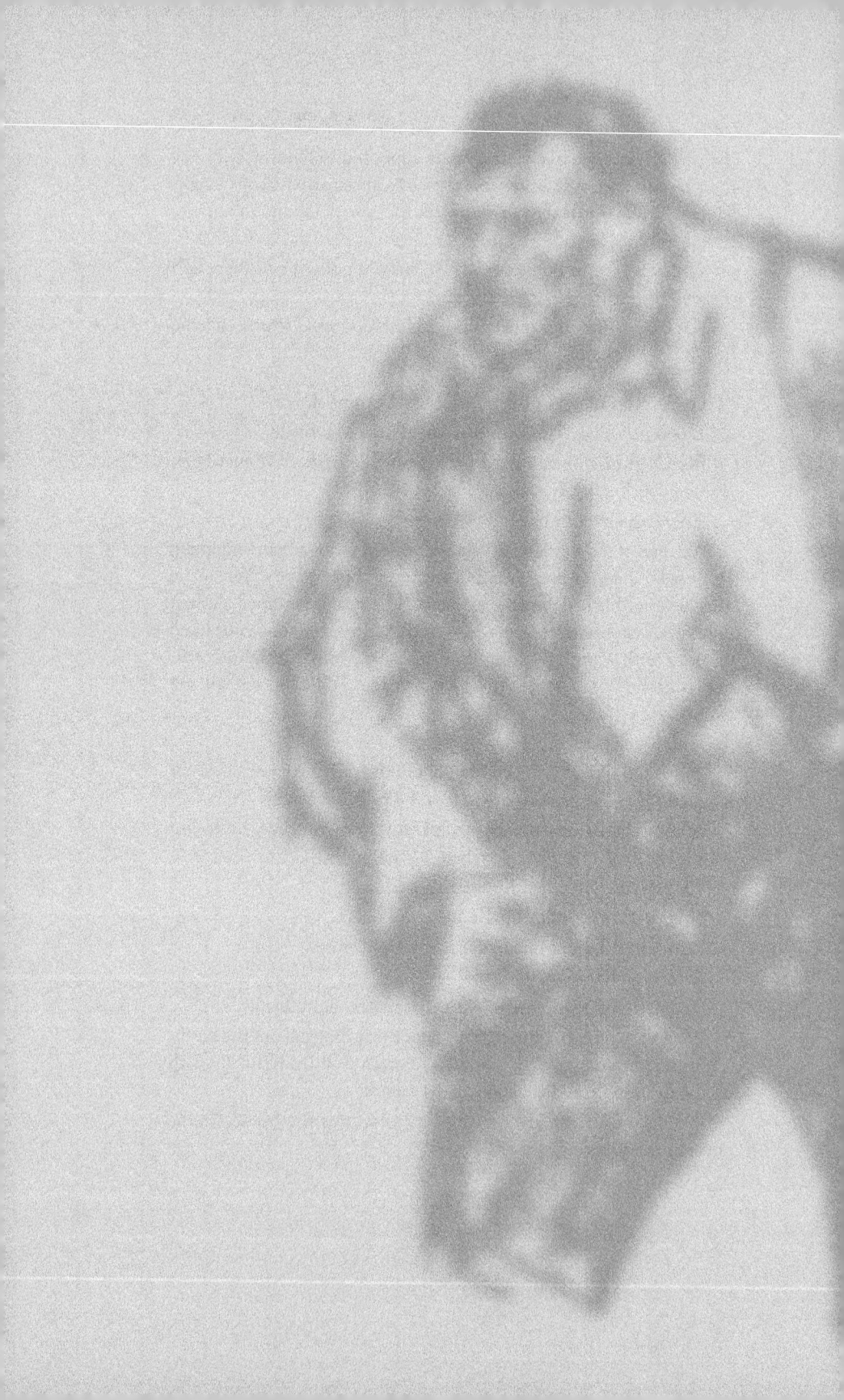

Junk

Capt. MacBride tackles Richmond City's turbulent waterfront.

Chapter I

CAPTAIN STEPHEN MacBRIDE sat in his office at Head-quarters, although it was getting on towards midnight. Idly, but at the same time gently, he cleaned and polished his .38 service revolver. A row of new cartridges lay on the desk before him.

Ice and snow incrusted the window panes. The river was not far distant, and up across the ragged network of tenement and warehouse roofs a rowdy wind hooted and shrilled.

The latch clicked and the door opened on well-oiled hinges. A man of medium height and slight build drifted in—a young man with a young-old face, lazy eyes. His hands were thrust into his overcoat pockets. He shut the door with a kick of his heel, ran his tired eyes over the room.

"Not a bad dump, Cap," he droned, "on a night like this."

MacBride did not look up. He squinted down along the barrel of his revolver—asked, laconically, "Who let you in, Kennedy?"

"Nobody. Let myself in." Kennedy got his overcoat off gradually and hung it up. He added, "The guy at the desk downstairs was making a date over the wire and I didn't want to bother him. How's tricks?"

"So-so."

Kennedy stopped by the desk, helped himself to a cigar from a humidor and slouched down in a chair facing MacBride. "Find time heavy on your hands, eh, Cap?"

MacBride loaded his gun, held it in the palm of his hand, stared at it meditatively. "I'm ready, Kennedy—ready when things break."

"The *Free Press* is hard up for news."

MacBride pulled back his coat and sheathed his gun. "They'll get news, Kennedy. The river's been quiet for years, but somewhere, somehow, something's started."

"How," ventured Kennedy, "do you suppose it started?"

"How the hell do I know?" MacBride chuckled. "But a junk war is brewing. And the junk business, hiding a multitude of evils, is one of the biggest rackets in the city."

"Don't I know!" agreed Kennedy. "Cripes, you see a dirty bumboat plowing up the river. There's a dago in it, collecting junk." He laughed, and repeated, ironically, "Junk! Junk, in their lingo, means anything from the rear left wheel of a baby carriage to a dock-load of copper ingots or a car-load of virgin telegraph wires. And there's a broken-down horse hauling a wagon with a couple of bells on it. Old paper, bottles, tin-ware. What they collect in the daytime has nothing to do with what they collect at night.

"It seems small, a piker's business, but on a large scale there's millions in it and they're organized to scoop it up. And every now and then there's plunder that's worth something.

"And now there's been a break in the junk gang business of Richmond City. Some guy has got sore at somebody else and is starting in to say it out loud.

"That fight last week proves it. Two gangs meet on Pier Four at midnight and hell busts loose. It's over in no time. The cop on the beat, being no dumb-bell, stands in a pier-shed down the way and waits till it's over. The gangs split and take their wounded and dead—if any—with them. Now who were the guys in those gangs?"

"That," said MacBride, "is why I am on this special little job."

"Blood was spilled," went on Kennedy. "The dock was smeared to hell with it."

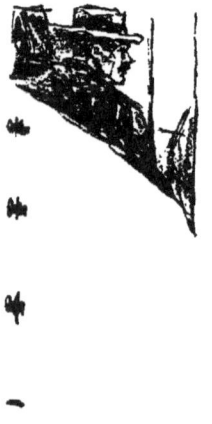

"We combed the hospitals and all the doctors within a mile. Not a clue. I've got men all over the river, watching."

Kennedy scoffed at the last. "A lot they'll do. Your first clue, if you get any at all, will be through more blood. They don't want the law to butt in—neither side wants that."

The telephone bell jangled. MacBride picked up the receiver, said, "MacBride talking," and then listened. Then he said, "H'm. I'll look into it," and hung up.

Kennedy's eyes had steadied.

MacBride stood up. "You'll have to blow, Kennedy."

"What's up?"

"I don't know. Toddle along. Go out and grab a sandwich and a mug of coffee."

"Look here, Cap—"

"Now, Kennedy." MacBride raised his hand, then jerked his thumb towards the door. "Breeze."

Chapter II

THE door opened.

A gruff voice said: "In, mister." MacBride had made a half-turn on his swivel chair.

A young man, well dressed and carrying a tweed cap in his hand, entered. He looked nervous, and his eyes darted about the room. Two men came in behind him—Detectives Cohen and Moriarity—and a uniformed patrolman followed.

Cohen said, "This is the guy, Cap."

MacBride nodded. "Take a seat," he said to the stranger, and motioned to the empty chair beside his desk.

The man sat down.

"Your name?" MacBride asked.

"Felton."

"Now tell me about it."

Felton moistened his lips, glanced at the patrolman and the two detectives. The bright desk-light showed every line on his young face—no expression, no matter how slight, went by unnoticed. He turned to face MacBride.

"Well, it's like I told these men, Captain," he said. "I was driving home along the waterfront. There's no crosstown traffic there and I did it to avoid traffic. At Railroad Street, where the tracks are, I was held up by a freight train. It was cold, and there was a lunch-wagon nearby, so I pulled up on the side to get a cup of coffee.

"I sat at the counter next to this man. His plate was empty and he kept looking out the door. Then he said something about he guessed the buses had stopped running. The counter-man laughed at this, and so did I.

"Finally the man buttoned up his coat and said, 'Maybe I can bum a ride down,' and I said I would take him. I had some packages in the front seat beside me, and I was going to throw them in the rear, but he said that was all right, he'd pile in the back.

"So he got in the back and we drove off. We talked back and forth, but not much. Then he didn't talk at all, and I figured he was asleep. About twenty minutes later I heard a whistle blow and pulled up. I saw a cop coming over.

"He said, 'Hey, Buddy, if you don't look out that souse you got with you'll fall out.' It was this officer here," he nodded to the patrolman. "So I looked around and saw this man hanging over the side of the car. I said, 'He ain't drunk. He's tired.' So the officer, here, shook him and then cursed. 'Tired!' he said. 'Hell, he ain't tired. He's dead!'"

MacBride nodded.

"I see," he said, and turned to the patrolman. "That right, Epstein?"

"That's how it was, Cap. The feller had been shot through the heart from the left side."

MacBride returned to Felton. "Never saw the man before?"

"No, sir."

"Any cars pass you on the road—I mean, come up behind you and go by?"

"Yes—several. I've only got an old flivver touring, and it makes a lot of noise. He didn't yell or anything. I didn't hear him, or anything like a shot."

MacBride studied Felton for a long moment in silence. Then he got his address, where he worked, and where he had come from when he stopped at the lunch-wagon. He lived out in Hillside with his mother and father, and held a minor position in the Hillside Savings Bank. He'd been up to see a girl that night and had left her at her home at ten-thirty.

"It must have been almost eleven," he said, "when I stopped at the lunch-wagon."

MacBride turned to the others. "And none of you know the dead man."

Three heads shook negatively.

MacBride sighed, bit his lip, then said, "All right, Felton, as soon as they check up on you downstairs, you can go. We may have to get in touch with you again. Go with him, Epstein. Give the names to the desk and have 'em phone to his house and one of the officers of the bank."

Felton and the patrolman left. The two detectives sprawled in chairs.

MacBride said, "I think the kid's right. Somebody plugged that guy with a silenced rod from another car. The bums must have spotted him at the lunch-wagon and tailed him down Railroad Street. What did you find on him?"

"A rod—a .32, loaded full," said Moriarity. "Forty bucks—no identification—and these." He passed over two theatre ticket stubs. "Found 'em in his vest pocket. The New Empire."

"Burlesque," said MacBride. "The odds say he was with a man." MacBride stood up. "I'll take a look at him."

He found the man downstairs, covered with a blanket. He placed his age at between thirty and forty. Clean-shaven, lean but rugged. Not an indoor face.

"Better get him to the morgue," MacBride said. "Let's see. The New Empire is about four blocks east of Railroad Street. The first show is out at ten. He must have been to that one, then walked over to put on the feed-bag.

"Mory," he turned to one of the detectives, "you take these stubs and chase over to this dump. Find the seats and look around. It won't hurt to look around. Cohen, you and I'll run up to this lunch-wagon. Step on it, Mory!"

Fifteen minutes later MacBride entered the lunch-wagon with Cohen at his heels. The place was empty but for the counter-man, who sat on a stool drinking coffee and reading a paper.

"Yes, sir!" he chirped. "What'll it be, gents?"

"No eats," came back MacBride. "We're from Headquarters."

"Oh-o!" The counter-man perked up.

"You remember a fellow in here about eleven tonight waiting for a bus?"

"About eleven—why, yes, sure, guess I do. He got a lift, though—"

"Exactly. And he was plugged fifteen minutes later."

"Gawd!"

"Yeh. A young fellow gave him a lift. Remember that?"

"Yup—yes, sir, I do."

"Jake on that. Now listen. When did this fellow come in—I mean the one who got the works?"

"Gee, I don't know exact. Well, anyways, it wasn't later than ten-thirty— might ha' been five or ten minutes before that."

"Come in alone?"

"Yup—yes, sir, he did— But hold on." He rubbed his hands together and wrinkled his forehead. "Look. He opened the door, see? But before he closed it, he leaned out and waved to somebody, and he yelled, 'You leave that to me,' and then sat down smilin' to himself like he was pleased."

"Didn't call a name out?"

"Nope—no, sir, he didn't."

"All right. That's that. Well, so long. Come on, Cohen."

They went out, got into the flivver, and Harrigan headed for the New Empire. Only a single light was burning in the lobby when they arrived, and MacBride saw Moriarity speaking with a couple of men.

Moriarity came out to them. "The seats weren't used for the second show, Cap," he said. "I didn't find much. Only an empty box of cigarettes."

He handed over the empty box. MacBride took it carefully, opened it.

"Good!" he muttered.

"What?"

"The tin-foil's still inside, Mory! Fingerprints. Hop in!"

Sleary, the fingerprint expert at Headquarters, was rudely awakened from a deep, contented sleep.

"Wait till morning, Cap," he protested.

"Do it now," clipped MacBride. "It's either the marks of the man at the morgue or the bird he was with."

Sleary went to work. MacBride and the two detectives went upstairs and sat down to wait.

Time dragged by.

The telephone rang. Moriarity reached for it, but MacBride said,

"I'll take it."

He took it, muttered his name, listened. His jaw hardened, his eyes narrowed.

"O.K. Doc," he said, and hung up.

Moriarity and Cohen wore expectant looks.

MacBride faced them. "That guy at the morgue certainly must have been somebody when he was alive. He was carrying a gun wound not more than a week old in the right side—bandaged up." He cracked fist into palm. "Tried once and missed. Tried again—and got him."

"That scrap on Pier Four last week—"

"Right, Cohen!" bit in MacBride. "I'll bet this bird was in on it."

The door opened and Sleary scuffled in, yawning. "Guess you get a good break, Cap."

He placed a series of photographs accompanied by fingerprint records, upon the desk. The three men leaned close.

"This," he drawled, shifting his chew and pointing to the photographs, "is a series of likenesses of the bozo that opened the pack of butts you gave me. I believe him and you have met before."

MacBride took one look and then struck the desk with a doubled fist. "Boys, we certainly have got a decent break. The fellow who was bumped off went to the New Empire with Little Abie Moskovitz!"

"Abie's no killer," said Cohen.

"Of course not," agreed MacBride. "I've a hunch this thing is linked up with the row that's brewing on the river. Little Abie's been out of trouble for over two years. But he's a fence. He's running a second-hand clothing store on Water Street, and his brother, Big Abie, runs that eating joint a block away. They're known the length and breadth of the waterfront, and what they don't know about the river isn't worth knowing. I'm calling on Little Abie right now."

"Let's go," chimed in Moriarity.

"Sit tight—both of you," came back MacBride. "This is no big parade. Grab a bite to eat, take a nap. You've both been up overtime. I'll work this job alone tonight. If I need help I'll draft the cop on beat or send in an S.O.S."

"Well heeled, Cap?" asked Mory.

MacBride tapped his coat. "Plenty. If my wife calls up, tell her I'll be home some time before noon. Ask her if I should bring anything from the city."

"Jake, Cap."

"Jake."

Chapter III

OUT in the street, MacBride drew up the collar of his overcoat against the sharp bite of the wind. He jammed his hands into his pockets and strode briskly towards the arc light on the next corner.

At the intersection he hailed a nighthawk taxi, settled down and started a fresh cigar. When the taxi swung into lower Water Street, which paralleled the river, MacBride got out, paid his fare and started walking.

Street lights were not numerous. He passed blank-faced stores and nondescript rooming-houses. Across the wide cobbled street were the piers. Sheds loomed darkly, and beyond them the river rolled to the sea, murmuring and mysterious.

MacBride slowed down presently, looked around.

There was Little Abie's shop; second-hand overcoats, seamen's supplies, shoes, pocket-knives, playing cards—and behind all that, what? A narrow doorway and one narrow show-window crammed with odds and ends piled one on top of another. And Abie was rated around five hundred thousand in cash and air-tight bonds.

Abie's rooms were upstairs—cramped, narrow quarters. Abie had crossed the police once, but had wriggled off with a suspended sentence. After that he had sold out, remained apparently idle for a year, and then started anew.

MacBride rapped at the door. The sound re-echoed sharply in the dark, silent street. Minutes passed. MacBride rapped again, loudly, insistently.

An upper window creaked open.

"Who is it?" croaked a sleepy voice.

"Open up, Abie," called MacBride. "Want to have a chat with you. MacBride—Headquarters."

"Now I should open up?"

"Right now, Abie."

MacBride waited, and soon the lock on the door clicked and MacBride entered.

"Light up," he clipped.

Little Abie found the switch and turned on a dull light.

"Now we'll go upstairs," said MacBride.

They went up, and MacBride found himself in a small, cheaply furnished living-room, the walls of which were decorated with rotogravure prints of famous Follies beauties. There was only the one door by which they entered.

Little Abie drew his bathrobe closer about his scrawny body and stood in the middle of the floor, rubbing his hands slowly together. He was a little bent at the shoulders. His hair was a dusty gray, so thin that it revealed his scalp. His lips were thin and well-nigh colorless. He had skin like dried parchment, and small, shrewd eyes flanked a beak of a nose.

"Vell…?"

"Well, I'll tell you, Abie," clipped MacBride. "The guy you went to the New Empire with was bumped off."

"Vhat guy who vent to the Empire mit?"

"Act your age, Abie. You know me. If I didn't know what I was talking about, I wouldn't be down here. Now don't try to pull anything like that. Who was this bird?"

Abie's shoulders went up to his ears and he spread his bony hands palmwise. "It's a fact, Cap, I don't know vhat you're talking about."

"Boloney! I've got you cold. We found the ticket stubs in the fellow's pocket. We found an empty cigarette box under one of the seats and your fingerprints are on the tin-foil that was inside. I'm not saying you did the man in—not yet. This guy was shot once in that scrap on Pier Four, and I want to know who he is, what's going on along the river, and where you figure in it. You're in a hot spot and you better come clean."

If Little Abie was cornered, he didn't show it. He drew a cigarette from his bathrobe, lighted up and took a long drag. His beady eyes jerked up and met MacBride's steadily. There was something malignant and dangerous in that pinched face—even in repose. The thin lips curled ever so slightly.

"Cap, better you take a tip from me," he croaked. "Dere iss somet'ings in life vich a cop like you vould be better should he steer clear off. You have a body, so—unidentified at the morgue. Vell, vhat t' hell. Dot's enough, no? Leave it like it is, Cap. It vould be much better for all dose vhat is concerned."

"What do you mean, Abie?"

Little Abie's stare grew more concentrated, two pin-points of strange fire that bored into MacBride's. Suddenly he spat, almost vindictively: "Hands off!" His thin body quivered.

MacBride measured him. One eye squinted. "Hands off, hell!" he growled. "You can't bluff me, Abie."

A ghost of a smile, satanic and fleeting, crossed Little Abie's face. "No?" There was mockery in that. "No? Vell, maybe I can't bluff you, Cap. But, on de odder hand, you can't bluff me."

MacBride's jaw hardened and he rocked on his feet. "Listen to me, you wise little kike. You're talking big, aren't you?" MacBride glowered at him.

"Well—got an iron-bound alibi as to where you were between eleven and eleven-thirty?"

"I vas on de trolley car—den here—"

"Can you prove it?"

Little Abie backed up, his mouth working, his frown darker than ever.

"My lawyers is Finklebaum and O'Shay—"

"Try 'em. But just now, get your pants on, boy, and come for a buggy ride."

The interval that followed was hollow with silence.

Then a light blinked overhead. MacBride looked up. Four globes were on the chandelier. One had been lighted when MacBride entered. It was another of the four that had blinked.

MacBride snapped his gaze down to Abie. Abie had backed up. His hands were clasped together against his stomach. His face was immobile, the eyes shining like two shoe-buttons.

The light, blinking again, drew MacBride's attention. He listened, flung searching glances about the room. There must, he reasoned, be some way of answering that signal. He espied a switch on the wall—two buttons just inside the door. He tried one and the light in the room went off. Hastily he pressed the other button and relighted it.

The signal switch must be elsewhere. In the corner was a roll-top desk, with the top closed. He crossed over, pushed back the top. There he found another switch—two pearl buttons beside each other.

He was about to press one when he heard a light thud, like a door closing, but the sound did not come from the direction of the single door. He swung about, his gun drawn.

Little Abie was gone!

Chapter IV

SNAP-JUDGMENT, a trained mind at work in a pinch, caused MacBride to swing back towards the desk and jab his finger against one of the two pearl buttons. Something would happen, he judged, if the signal reached the other end before Abie.

His eyes, more alert now than ever, swept the room and clamped on the spot where Abie had stood. There MacBride saw a small, cheap rug, rumpled, and a closed trapdoor.

MacBride yanked open the trap. At first, pitch darkness yawned below, but by concentrating his gaze, he could make out vaguely the counter and the skeleton work of the grilled cage in which Abie spent most of his daylight hours.

Glass crashed somewhere below. Like a cat, MacBride dropped down to the counter in the store, and then to the floor. Above him the trap swung shut of its own accord. He found the light switch and turned on the lights.

The sound had come from the rear. He ran in that direction. In the back was a small storeroom, and as he burst into it a gust of cold night air struck him, and he saw a figure, too tall to be Abie, dart to one side.

MacBride ducked, too, and barked, "As you are, buddy, or I'll bust you wide open!"

"That you, cap?"

MacBride snorted, "Cripes, Kennedy, what you doing here?"

"Just poking around. I tailed you from Headquarters, cap. What's up?"

"I don't know. Did you see Little Abie?"

"No. I saw you go in and waited so long I thought you were in Dutch."

"You better clear out, Kennedy. There's something damned queer going on here, and you might get lead in your pants."

"I'm in, cap, and I'm going to see it through. I crashed the joint."

"All right, if you must, Kennedy. Little Abie handed me a fade-away, but there's somebody else around here doing some signaling. Follow me."

MacBride led the way upstairs and into Little Abie's living-room. He stopped short as he crossed the threshold.

A woman, dressed in an expensive mink coat, sat in an easy chair smoking a cigarette. Diamonds glittered on her hands. She was good-looking and chic, but in a brassy, hard-boiled way. She did not appear in the least perturbed. She eyed MacBride coolly for a moment and then cracked a smile.

"Well, big boy, you're new to me. Where's Little Abie?"

"Where'd you come from?" snapped MacBride.

"Gawd, but you're tough!" She blew smoke through her nostrils. "Not so fast, big boy. It ain't going to get you anywhere."

MacBride came in with Kennedy and closed the door. Then Mac-Bride said, "You're new to me, girlie, too."

"Well," she chuckled, "sit down and take the load off your feet. Who's your boy friend?"

"That's him," replied MacBride.

"Well, well!" she said. "You know, mister, I've a hunch you're the big king pin in the bowling alley."

MacBride grinned, and he had a grin that women usually liked. "That so?"

"Sure thing. This is a surprise, if I'm right. I've been trying hard to meet the big cheese. I've been after Little Abie to fix up an introduction, but he always sidestepped. Where is he, anyhow?"

"Downstairs, hunting up a drink," MacBride ventured.

"I thought he'd never answer my signal. Well, I've got the lowdown, anyhow."

"I guess—" began MacBride, but at that moment the signal light blinked again.

"H'm," murmured the woman.

"I guess it's all right," said MacBride, moving towards the desk.

"Sure. Give him the O.K. button," nodded the woman.

MacBride pressed one of the buttons, Kennedy was eyeing him quizzically, and the brief look that MacBride shot him was one of warning. Kennedy dropped his right hand casually into his coat pocket.

Suddenly the light went out, and the room was plunged into Stygian darkness.

"What the hell is going on here?" the woman wanted to know.

"Maybe a short circuit," essayed MacBride.

"I don't like this," the woman complained. "There's something funny about it."

Her skirts rustled and the end of her cigarette glowed red in the gloom.

Silence followed.

Then, it seemed out of nowhere, a low voice said. "Snap out of it, sister! These guys are bulls!"

"Gawd!"

A chair scraped.

MacBride dived for the woman, but she must have known the place better than he, for she eluded him. He tumbled over a chair and Kennedy knocked over the table.

MacBride tore out his lighter and thumbed it. The dim light revealed the disorder of the room, but no woman.

"She didn't go out through the door, or down that trap," MacBride said. "And where was the guy that wised her?"

"Search me," said Kennedy.

He lighted matches and they moved about, tapping the walls.

MacBride muttered, "Here it is."

Kennedy came over.

"Listen," said MacBride, tapping the wall under the mantel. "Eh?"

"Guess so, Cap."

MacBride pressed. A small door swung open silently on a pivot.

"Cripes!" exclaimed Kennedy.

"Goes somewhere," said MacBride. "Little Abie got out and warned the guy at the other end of this. Wish we had a flashlight. Look around for a candle, Kennedy."

Kennedy searched. In one of the desk drawers he found one, and lighted it.

"I'll carry it, Cap."

"Kennedy, you'd better go home to bed. You don't know what's at the end of this."

"Neither do you, Cap. Go ahead. I'll carry it."

MacBride stepped out on to the rung of a ladder. Kennedy followed. They descended about thirty feet, where the ladder ended, and stood upon damp ground. Kennedy cupped a hand back of the candle.

MacBride led the way down a tunnel. He had to bend over a little. A cold, damp draft blew in his face, and caused the candle to sputter. There were not many turns, but the passageway took a gradual decline.

MacBride's hand was clamped hard on his gun, and the light from the candle danced weirdly on the dark walls of the tunnel. Beads of moisture stood out on the walls.

"I hear water," muttered Kennedy.

"The river," said MacBride.

The air, if it grew colder, also became clearer. They came to a ragged opening, and heard clearly the river lapping against the rocks. Then they saw a fretwork of piles. They were under a pier.

"Look!" whispered Kennedy, pointing.

MacBride looked. Dimly he saw a dark shape moving out across the water, and heard the muffled chugging of a gasoline engine.

"For the time being," gritted MacBride, "they win all the marbles. But Little Abie's one guy we want."

Chapter V

BEFORE returning to Headquarters MacBride called up and had a policeman sent over to stand watch at Little Abie's shop. The swinging door that led to the passageway was nailed up, and the shop and all it contained was in the hands of the law.

A quiet search was started for Little Abie, and a net spread where he might show up. MacBride did not call on Little Abie, but he arranged to have his lunch-room watched night and day. He also gave orders to have his men at vital points along the river, and every patrolman on the waterfront received special instructions. They were told to report immediately any suspicious occurrence, no matter how slight.

MacBride went home for a bite to eat and a brief sleep, and was back at three in the afternoon. Not a murmur had been heard from the river during his absence. Nor had the man, who had been killed in the machine, been identified.

Kennedy dropped in.

MacBride said, "I've hunted through the gallery, high and low, but I didn't see any picture that looks like the woman. Still, I've an idea I've seen her somewhere, I don't know where or when."

"I was thinking the same, Cap. Suppose we run over to the newspaper and scout the 'morgue.'"

"Good idea."

It proved no easy task. What they were looking for was a photograph, and they left nothing unturned, working from the current date backwards. They covered a year and started on the second year, and it was well after dark when MacBride grunted and sat back and spread a paper before him.

"Look at this, Kennedy."

Kennedy yawned and came over. "It's her," he said.

"Grace Devore."

"Yup."

"Listen. In April, last year, according to your paper, she got in a jam at the Twinkle-Toe Roadhouse. It was some party. She was escorted by a bird named Klinsic—you know him, Kennedy—and in the party were the Misses Glovack, Halsey and Dennison, and the Messrs. Brant, Avel, and Huber—three enterprising young bootleggers.

"Klinsic, if you remember, ran a big feed store on River Alley, and he was worth a lot of jack. Well, the party was getting gay, when this guy Gilano crashes in half-cocked and wants to know what Klinsic is doing with his girlfriend.

"The fight starts, and Gilano gets beaned with a bottle. He died two days later. Klinsic had a good case, and the roadhouse manager backed him up. But something we never found out caused Klinsic to sell his feed business and drop out of sight, and the gal faded with him.

"I didn't know he was back in town. I'm saying I think he is, because the woman is. Well, we've got her placed, Kennedy, and it now remains to locate her. So we've got two leads—Little Abie and Grace Devore."

"Yeah," nodded Kennedy. "And then there's that big cheese of the racket she took you for."

"That's so, and it can't be Klinsic or she should have known it. Well, I've got the river blocked, and I'll bet every bum on both sides is cursing hell out of me. I'll make this thing so air-tight that it will blow up from inside."

Back in Headquarters, he called Moriarity and Cohen, his aides.

"You boys start out and comb every hotel in town," he said. "I'm looking for Peter B. Klinsic—it may be, 'and wife.' He's never used a fictitious name, and he has no record. He got out of that scrape at the Twinkle-Toe Inn clean. Snap on it, boys."

When they had gone, MacBride settled down and re-read the old newspaper account of the fight at the Twinkle-Toe.

The clatter of the telephone bell interrupted him and he picked up the receiver and muttered his name.

"Yes, MacBride," drifted in a quiet voice. "I'm calling from a midtown booth. I notice you've put the clamps on the river. Now be reasonable. Let up—ease away, friend. You'll have to loosen right away or you'll regret it. I mean what I'm saying."

"I don't know who you are," came back MacBride. "But you can go plumb to hell!"

And on that he hung up and went back to reading the newspaper.

Moriarity and Cohen reported well past midnight, and the report was—failure. Klinsic was not staying at any of the hotels.

"Tomorrow," said MacBride, "comb all the agencies that handle the renting of apartments, and if you fail there try the furniture stores. This guy is in town somewhere!"

He picked up the telephone and called the sergeant downstairs. He said, "You've got the river all patrolled, Dave?... Good. Keep everything tight, and if there are any reserves cluttering up the place spot 'em on the waterfront.... Yes, some wiseacre called up before and tried to buffalo me.... You said it, what a chance!"

HE was back on the job at four the next afternoon, and he was not seated ten minutes when Moriarity and Cohen blew in full of news.

"We get a break, Cap," grinned Mory. "A guy by the name of Peter Klinsic has rented a three-room furnished apartment in Wellington Court. He rented it a month ago."

"Great work!" beamed MacBride, and reached for his hat and overcoat. "Mory, you come with me. Ike, you stay on tap in case anything happens on the river or if they see anything queer at Big Abie's place."

Winter dusk was settling, and a light snowfall twisted white banners through the street. The wind had an edge, and a man's breath spumed out in silver clouds. The fallen snow was soft and dry, and footfalls crunched on it.

MacBride's special flivver drew up and the captain and Moriarity climbed into the rear. Harrigan, the driver, roared his motor and whisked off.

Wellington Court is a notch shy of being exclusive, as things go in Richmond City. A three-room apartment runs to about three hundred a month. It has the advantage of being quietly, and at the same time centrally, located. All apartments are outside affairs, and in the center of the octagon-shaped building is a garden of spruces, and there is some statuary, and a fountain.

MacBride and Moriarity strode through the gardens and up the wide staircase that led to the foyer entrance. Here a six-foot dignitary in blue and gold trappings refused to notice them. MacBride and his aide breezed into the foyer, and headed for a mahogany desk behind which sat a telephone operator.

"Is Mr. Klinsic in?" asked MacBride.

"I'll see," she said, reaching for a plug.

"Hold on!" MacBride clipped. "We're from Police Headquarters." He flashed his badge. "Now do you know if Mr. Klinsic is in?"

"I believe he is," she replied.

"All right. Don't bother plugging in. What's his apartment?"

"Forty-two."

"Thanks. Come on, Mory."

They entered the elevator and were whisked up to the fourth floor. They got out, walked down the corridor and stopped before apartment forty-two. MacBride rapped.

A minute passed. Then the latch clicked and the door opened. A man looked out. He wore a dressing gown.

"We'll come in," said MacBride.

"I beg pardon but—"

"That's all right," went on MacBride and pushed in, showing his badge. "Don't get excited, Klinsic. You don't remember me, but my name's MacBride, and this playmate of mine is called Moriarity."

Klinsic was a well-set man of forty-odd, dark-skinned, black-haired, jet-eyed, capable-looking. The jet eyes flashed.

"What does this mean?" he snapped.

"It means—well, just a little talk. I want to see you and your friend Grace."

Klinsic frowned. "What are you talking about? She doesn't live here."

MacBride turned to Moriarity. "Scout around for a woman's trappings," he said.

Klinsic was assuming a nonchalant air that fitted him well. He put a cigarette between his lips and snapped on a patent lighter.

"I remember you now, MacBride," he said. "You handled that mess at the Twinkle-Toe."

"Right. And I'm afraid I'm out to handle another mess in which you're going to figure prominently."

"I don't see the point."

"That's a lot of tripe. Don't pull it on me, Klinsic. This girl friend of yours is in it too."

Klinsic gushed smoke through his nostrils and smiled, highly amused. "Hell, MacBride, but you're on a cold trail."

"I'm on the trail of you and Grace Devore and Little Abie Moskovitz. It's cool now, but it will get hot."

Klinsic's eyes narrowed and he regarded MacBride speculatively.

Moriarity drawled: "No woman's duds here, Cap."

MacBride swallowed his disappointment. "All right, Mory." He stood up. "My error, Klinsic. Come on, Mory."

As they went out of the foyer, MacBride said: "Mory, you hang around and keep tabs on him. If he comes out, tail him. He's a hard guy to handle. He knows a lot."

"Jake, Cap."

They walked to the end of the block before separating. MacBride turned the corner and kept walking. Soon Harrigan drifted along in the police flivver. MacBride climbed in and they headed back for Headquarters.

Sergeant Shane met MacBride as the latter crossed the central room on the way to his office. Shane looked grave, and there was a tenseness evident in his whole body.

MacBride slowed down and frowned quizzically. Shane was opening and closing his hands.

"Well, Dave?"

"Cap—" Shane moistened his lips. "Cap, some pups heaved a bomb at your bungalow—"

"My God!"

MacBride sucked in a harsh breath and his eyes widened, the color fled from his face.

"Dave—" He jerked forward, one hand outstretched.

"It's all right, Cap. Your wife's in the hospital, cut up by flying splinters—but no need to worry. Your daughter wasn't home."

"What hospital, Dave?"

"Grove Manor Memorial."

MacBride spun around, plunged out through the door and into the snow-carpeted street. He ran down the block, caught a taxi, and shouted the address.

He rushed headlong into the hospital. He found his wife in a room beneath white sheets, bandaged but conscious. His daughter was beside the bed. He clasped her in one arm and with the other gripped his wife's hand. His wife smiled up at him wanly.

"Any pain, darling?"

"Not much—the doctors helped me."

A doctor came in. "Not as bad as it looks, captain," he said. "Your wife was stunned. Most of the cuts are superficial."

"Thank God!" murmured MacBride.

He stayed there for two hours, and then the nurse recommended that he should go. He took his daughter with him and they rode back to the bungalow.

The little vine-clad veranda was only a memory. It had been blown away, and a ragged hole was in the front of the house.

MacBride's daughter cried where she leaned in the crook of his arm. He patted her head.

"There, baby. We'll rebuild it. You stay over at Mrs. Conway's tonight and then spend most of your time with mother."

"Dad, you will be careful!" she cried.

"Yes… I'll be careful."

She did not see the interplay of lights that shone in his keen, narrowed eyes, a lump of muscle quivering at either side of his wide, grim mouth.

"You'd better stay at Mrs. Conway's too, dad."

"No, baby," he replied. "I'll take you over there. There are a few little things I have to attend to at Headquarters."

Fifteen minutes later MacBride was bound for Headquarters. The cigar in his mouth was dead—it had been dead for the past hour. MacBride stared straight ahead, silent, motionless; and his face was granite hard.

Chapter VI

A RIVER is a thing of mystery—dark, inscrutable, restless as the souls of the men who ply it after sundown.

MacBride, standing on a pierhead at midnight, regarded it as something inimical. His overcoat was bundled closely about him. Cohen stood near him, tapping his feet to stimulate circulation. MacBride was touring the waterfront personally, checking up on the watchers, too keen to be in the midst of things to stay in his office.

After a time he turned and headed inshore, stopped at a telephone booth and called Headquarters.

"Moriarity's reported by phone," said Shane. "He told me to tell you he's tailing that guy. Guess you know who."

"Yes, Dave," replied MacBride.

"He said he's tailed him to Big Abie's," went on Shane. "He's watching the joint from an alley across the way."

MacBride said: "Thanks, Dave," and hung up. And to Cohen, "It's getting warmer. Come on. Mory's tailed Klinsic to Big Abie's."

He strode out into the street, hailed a taxi, and Cohen hopped in after him. They went booming up the waterfront street until MacBride yelled, "Pull up!"

The two men alighted and proceeded briskly on foot. A block farther on they turned into a side street. A few doors away, on the opposite side of the narrow street, was Big Abie's place. MacBride slowed down and presently espied an alley running between two ancient brick buildings and obliquely across the way from the lunch-room.

He stopped at the entrance of the alley and muttered, "Mory?"

"Here, Cap," came a low reply.

MacBride and Cohen eased into the dark alley and were alongside Mory. The patrolman on watch was with him.

"He's been in there about twenty minutes," explained Moriarity. "I saw them go in a back room."

MacBride said, "I'm going over and walk in, boys. I think it's about time. Come on." To the patrolman, "No, you stay on watch."

He led the way across the street; banged open the door and barked at the counter-man, "You stay where you are."

He did not stop but went right on towards a door in the rear, pushed it open and looked in.

Big Abie, a huge mountain of flesh, was poking at a small cylindrical stove with one hand and shoving in fresh kindling with the other. He was considerably younger than his brother, and native born. He swung around, a heavy nether lip drooping.

"Huh?" he grunted.

"Ten to one, Big Abie," said MacBride, "you've been expecting a visit from me for a long time. I've got a bad habit of picking out late hours."

Big Abie rubbed his nose and put down the poker. He looked slow and dull, phlegmatic. "What you want, Cap?"

"Want to see the guy came in here about half as hour ago."

"Guy?" Abie seemed not to understand.

"Guy named Klinsic," nodded MacBride, and then snapped forward and yanked open the stove door.

Smoke billowed out. MacBride grabbed the poker, stuck it into the stove and hooked furiously at something. Out that something came, and MacBride stamped out the flames with his feet. Then he picked it up. It was what remained of a gray sweater.

"Yours, Big Abie?" he snapped.

"Well...."

MacBride turned on Moriarity, "Collar this bird!"

Moriarity drew his gun and stood beside Big Abie.

MacBride swept the room with quick glances. Cohen joined him. They ransacked the place.

Then MacBride clipped, "The back door, Ike." And both dived for the door and swung it open.

The chill of the night struck them. The door looked out into a littered yard covered with snow. MacBride had a flashlight this time. He snapped it on, sprayed the beam out into the dark.

"Footprints," he muttered. "Two pair." He turned and yelled, "Keep him collared, Mory!"

"He's salted, Cap."

"Come on, Ike," MacBride bit off and started out into the yard, bent low over the footprints. Then he knelt down. Cohen knelt beside him. Then both looked at each other.

"You say the same, Ike?"

"Blood—yup."

Both jumped up and went off at a run. The tracks led to a hole in the fence, and into another yard. They followed them into an alley that came out upon a dark, dismal street. Down at the end of the street the tail-light of an automobile was just disappearing around the corner.

"On the jump, Ike!" muttered MacBride, and both galloped down the street and out on to River Road.

Up ahead they could still see the solitary red light receding. Down the road the headlights of a car were approaching. Both men waited until it drew nearer and then leaped out. It proved to be a roving taxi and they jumped in.

"Follow that tail-light," said MacBride, "but not too close."

The taxi started and maintained an even speed of thirty miles an hour. After about ten minutes the tail-light ahead swung to the left and drove along closer to the long line of pier-sheds. The taxi kept to the right. Finally the tail-light disappeared.

MacBride said to the driver, "Don't stop. Here's four bits. Slow down and we'll hop off. You keep going. Good-night."

MacBride leaped and Cohen followed. The taxi kept rolling on, and the two men ran across the street into the shadows of the pier-sheds. Both drew their guns.

They walked rapidly yet warily, their hands tense on their drawn guns. Soon they slowed down and proceeded more cautiously. They crept past a huge pier-shed where the shadows were black as pitch.

MacBride peered around the corner. The car stood there, all lights doused. A little farther away, at the brink of the bulkhead, two dim figures were moving about. MacBride touched Cohen's arm, jerked his head.

They started out, guns leveled.

"Up, you birds!" barked MacBride.

The two figures dodged. A dagger of flame split the gloom and snow spurted alongside Cohen's right foot. MacBride fired and one of the figures reeled sidewise and hit the ground with a thud.

The other darted and fired at the same time and MacBride's hat was knocked on one ear but not off his head. Cohen's gun boomed twice. The dark figure staggered and started to run. He turned as he ran and fired wildly. Cohen fired again and the figure fell, rolled over and lay motionless.

"That's that," said MacBride under his breath.

They walked over. Both men were dead. "Faces I've seen before," observed MacBride. "Bud Goss and Joie Griffin—tough nuts."

"What's this?" asked Cohen.

Another form lay on the ground. It was partly wrapped in a blanket. Attached to it was a length of rope, and at the other end of the rope was a huge stone. MacBride snapped on his flashlight and leaned down.

"H'm," he muttered. "Klinsic."

"They must have got him," observed Cohen.

"Knifed him," said MacBride, "in Big Abie's. Then lugged him down here and tied a stone around his neck, to pitch him in the river. Now—"

He paused to listen. A moment later two uniformed policemen appeared on the run with drawn guns.

"Easy, boys," called MacBride.

"We heard shots," said one.

"You did," came back MacBride. "The trail gets hotter. Bud Goss and Joie Griffin. We got them. This other stiff—Klinsic—was knifed in Big Abie's. I caught Big Abie burning a sweater. Must have been blood on it. All right. You boys stick to your post. Help us load these birds in the car."

The three dead men were piled into the car.

"Hop in, Cohen, and drive," said MacBride. "We'll go back to Big Abie's. There's one guy in for no birthday party!"

Chapter VII

BIG ABIE'S place was locked up and Moriarity left inside to watch.

Big Abie himself was taken to MacBride's office, at Headquarters, where Kennedy was taking a nap. When they tramped in, Kennedy sat up, lit a cigar, and looked interested but said nothing.

MacBride flung the partly burnt sweater on the desk. Big Abie was slammed into a chair by Cohen.

"Now, big boy," said MacBride dangerously, "you're in for it. Klinsic was knifed in your back room. We got your friends and we finished them. This thing has come to a head. We want to know where Little Abie is, and where the woman Grace is. We want to know what's going on along the river and who is swinging the big racket. There's blood on that sweater, and the sweater's yours. Now start broadcasting."

Big Abie's face was heavy. His jowls hung limply. He shook his head. "Can't talk till I see my lawyer."

"Who was Klinsic—I mean, where did he fit in?"

Big Abie shook his head. "Can't talk."

"You realize, don't you, that you're in a fine position to get the chair?"

"I'll take them chances. But I ain't talking now."

"Was Klinsic the big gun behind the game?"

"Ain't talking."

MacBride's hands worked slowly. It was always the way. A crook or a gunman could hire brains and more often than not those brains beat the law. He looked at Cohen. Cohen lifted an eyebrow. MacBride nodded, then turned to Kennedy.

"Kennedy, go downstairs a while."

Kennedy grinned. "Sure, Cap."

Half an hour later, when Kennedy returned to the office, Big Abie was gone and MacBride and Cohen were wiping perspiration from their faces.

"Well," drawled Kennedy, leaning back indolently against the door he had closed, "did he come across?"

"Not all the way," replied MacBride. "He's holding back, and he went only so far. He's pretty hard. Klinsic was not his boss—nor Little Abie's. Klinsic was the big gun behind the other side. He came to Big Abie's looking for trouble—so Abie said.

"He was looking for the woman Grace. He went to Little Abie's, and when he found the place boarded up, he went to Big Abie's. Big Abie told Klinsic he didn't know anything. Klinsic pulled a gat, and just as he did Joie Griffin and Bud Goss came in the back door. Klinsic's automatic jammed as Goss knifed him. That's Big Abie's story.

"But as to what big game is going on along the river"—MacBride shrugged—"he refused to come across. It's something big, so big that Big Abie will take his chances on a beating or anything else. We'll indict him, and the State's Attorney will try to hang first degree on him or I'm all wrong."

The telephone rang. MacBride picked it up, listened, crouched over it. When he slammed back the receiver he leaped to his feet at the same time and dived for his overcoat and hat.

"That," he called over his shoulder, "was Shafer, the cop on watch at Pier Ten. He's been using a pair of night-glasses. Says three small boats are hanging around a schooner out in the river. He thinks they're junkies. Come on, Cohen."

He was already on his way out the door. Cohen was at his heels and Kennedy followed. Harrigan was roused from a deep sleep and he started off to get out the police flivver. They all crowded in and Harrigan raced the car down the street, skidded around the first corner and went howling up River Road.

"If we get at the root of this," said MacBride, "ten to one we'll find a store of stolen rubber, tin and wire, and God knows what else. The telegraph company's been complaining all along. Bales of rubber mysteriously fall overboard and junkies are on the job like flies around a dead horse."

"But," put in Kennedy, "there's something bigger than just lost rubber or telegraph wires."

"No doubt," agreed MacBride. "But whatever it is, it will lead to the rest—the petty jobs that grow and amount to something in a year's time—the loot that's hidden away or being changed into something else. Easy on the curves, Harrigan!"

The car almost turned over, and Harrigan gritted his teeth and straightened out. The motor rattled wildly, and the wind clapped and whistled. Harrigan slid to a stop in front of Pier Ten and MacBride was the first to leap out.

He ran through the huge, partly open door, nodded to the watchman and went on down the vast interior, where barrels and cases were stacked in solid rows. Cohen and Kennedy were behind him, and in short time they came out on the end of the pier, where Patrolman Shafer was industriously using his binoculars.

"They're still out there, Cap," he said. "You can't see 'em with the naked eye and you can just about see 'em with the glasses. Three motor boats, I figure, and they were running without lights. See them up there alongside the schooner?"

MacBride took the glasses and looked. Then he lowered them, and said: "Ike, go out to the telephone in the watchman's booth and relay the word up and down the river that some junkies may try to land. Collar anybody—I don't care who—that tries to land, and I don't care how innocent he may look. Get me some reserves from Headquarters. Tell them to board the police boat that's at Pier One and have the boat head up this way. Fast, Ike."

MacBride swung his glasses towards the schooner. It was dark out there—no moon, no stars. The water was black as ink. The three small boats still clung to the schooner's side. Presently MacBride saw another dim shape moving across the water. A second followed this, and then both slowed down and lay at some distance from the schooner. The customary lights were absent.

But suddenly MacBride saw a quick flash from one of the newcomers. It looked as if it might have come from a flashlight, and complete darkness followed it.

Then MacBride said, "One of them's moving away from the schooner." And after a moment—"Now another's starting. The whole three are going and so are the two that came last. Taking off a cargo this time of night, in boats without lights, means something we might be interested in. Then the way those other boats are lining up with the three, looks like they were meant for a guard, and if they need a guard, they're expecting trouble."

He lowered the glasses and looked around.

"We ought to get in on this. Let's see—"

Then suddenly streaks of gun flame ripped through the darkness; and a volley of sharp reports came to them, across the water.

MacBride raised his glasses again. "See those other boats? That's another going out to hi-jack—we got to get out there. Shafer, beat it to the phone and see if that police boat has started."

The whole river re-echoed with gunshots. Burst after burst went up as the new group of boats came out of the darkness to head off the flotilla that had left the schooner.

As they waited impatiently the waterfront was a madhouse. A riot call had been sent in by a patrolman and every available man from Headquarters and the nearby precincts came tearing to the scene. Horns tooted and police whistles blew, and intermingled with these and the many sounds of a milling mob, came the sharp reports of guns on the river.

"The three boats, Ike," yelled MacBride. "They are almost out of sight. They're the boats I want. They are aiming to slip out of the fight and hide away somewhere. I'm going to take a machine and then get a boat and meet them upriver. Come on, Ike. We can't wait for the police boat."

"I'm with you, Cap," said Kennedy.

MacBride started to protest, but changed his mind, shrugged and started off.

A half mile up the river, he commandeered a big motor launch. It was lying at a pier and was the property of a steamship company. With him were six policemen gathered on the way up, and one of them said he could run the boat.

The little company representing the law slipped out into the shadows of the river. The motor purred beautifully. Sometimes it stopped while the men listened for sounds in the darkness. Downriver the guns were still working.

"See anything, Ike?"

"Not yet, Cap."

The motor purred again. The craft moved. All eyes searched the gloom, and all ears listened.

"Over there," muttered a policeman, and pointed.

MacBride squinted. "Looks like 'em." He turned to the man at the wheel, and the latter nodded. "Get to 'em with all you're got. Boys, keep low!"

The motor roared and the craft plowed ahead. Spray flew, and a frothy wake boiled astern.

MacBride crouched in the bow. The three shadows loomed nearer, and gradually these shadows materialized into three small boats. The first one was towing the other two, and towards this one the launch steered.

The leader of the three boats made a sharp turn, but the launch followed the turn and MacBride snapped on a big spotlight. Four figures in the leading boats shrank back. MacBride fired a shot over their heads. No men were in the other two boats.

"Stop your boat!" yelled MacBride, and fired another warning shot.

The leader's clutch was thrown out, and the launch eased alongside. The policemen crowded the rail, and MacBride and two others swung into the junkie. Handcuffs clicked.

"Now," said MacBride, "we'll take your junk ashore."

The four men carried junkie licenses. They put up no argument, and the boats were towed in by the launch.

In the two small boats MacBride found a cargo of twisted iron and lead.

"Junk," he mused. "I wonder if I've been kidded."

"Any rags, any bones, any bottles today," sang Kennedy.

Chapter VIII

THE gang war was over. Riddled boats sank and the men swam for the shore, and there were policemen waiting to help them out of the water and into patrol wagons. Some did not reach the shore, and many had met violent deaths during the hot exchange of pistol and machine-gun fire.

MacBride, having left a guard of six men over the three boats he had captured, returned to Police Headquarters, a somewhat weary and disappointed-looking man. Kennedy was with him. They walked into the central room and Sergeant Shane looked up.

"If they keep bringing any more prisoners in," he said, "we ain't going to have room." He jerked his thumb towards the ceiling. "Friends of yours upstairs, Cap."

MacBride climbed the stairs, pushed open the door of his office and sagged in. He dragged to a stop and stared with eyes that were heavy with fatigue.

Moriarity was parked in the swivel chair, and facing him were Little Abie and Grace Devore.

"Greetings, Cap," nodded Moriarity. "Good you left me at Big Abie's place. These two pulled up in a car. They didn't know Big Abie was collared. They knocked at the back door. And here we are."

"Good," muttered MacBride, and bit the end off a cigar as he dropped into a chair. He eyed first one and then the other of the prisoners, and then lighted his cigar and inhaled deeply. "So," he said, "we got you."

"Yes, you got us," snapped the woman. "Just by a good break."

"Suits me," agreed MacBride; then added, "Now until you're spoken to again, keen your trap shut."

"I'll say what I feel—"

"Shut up!" barked MacBride. After a long, hard stare, he shifted to Little Abie. "Well, the racket's up, Abie. We've got the junk that was taken off the schooner and about twenty prisoners—yours and the other gang's. We've got your brother, and if you don't come across it will go hard with him. He's slated for the chair, but we may let him off with life if you come across."

Little Abie was nervous—and cornered. He looked at the woman. She cut him with a bitter stare. He shifted uneasily.

"You better not," said the woman.

He turned to her, hands spread. "Gracie, I got to. Big Abie is in bad, and vhat can ve do?"

"You keep quiet," she said.

MacBride broke in with, "Mory, take her outside."

"Listen, you guys," she cried. "You're all a lot of big bums! I want to stay here and listen to what's going on."

"Take her out," reiterated MacBride wearily.

Moriarity urged her towards the door.

"Little Abie," she cried, "if you—"

"Out," said Moriarity, and pushed her through the doorway.

MacBride regarded Little Abie. "Now, spring it."

Little Abie writhed and squirmed. He was in a corner, and none knew it better than he. Keep quiet and his brother would burn. If he opened up, he had MacBride's word that what leniency could be extended would be shown Big Abie, but he would have to come through all the way. He knew MacBride.

MacBride sat, smoking steadily, and let him work it out. In a very few minutes, Little Abie wilted. Discounting Little Abie's endeavors to exonerate himself for the greater crimes, his story stacked up like this:

Among the horde of lesser scavengers, two rival gangs of junkies had been organized to pick up the choicer morsels and to prey upon the individuals. Klinsic was the head of one; no other than Little Abie headed the other.

They agreed to a division of waterfront territory and in the main kept to the agreement. Until recently there had been no warfare between them.

Then Klinsic, with the Devore woman, took a trip to South America. In Rio, a man fell hard for her and disclosed to her a wealth of gold he had accumulated in the mountains. He wanted to marry her.

Klinsic appeared, murdered the man and stole his cache of gold. To get it out of the country, he melted scrap iron and lead around it and shipped it as junk by schooner to one of his men in New York.

Klinsic and the Devore woman fell out. He thought she was left stranded in Rio when, as a matter of fact, she sold some jewelry and took a steamer north ahead of him.

She sought out Little Abie; and two gangs waited for the schooner's arrival—one to receive the fortune in junk; the other to hi-jack it.

Their first clash came when Klinsic tried to land the junk at Pier Four. Then, both gangs lay back, fearful of the police and waiting for things to quiet. The man, given a ride from the lunch-wagon, was the mate of the schooner and was shot by Klinsic's men when they found him going around with Little Abie.

When MacBride tightened up on the waterfront, Klinsic decided to run his cargo in at any cost. He gave orders to his men and started out, himself, to get the Devore woman, who had given the plant away.

"Well," growled MacBride, when Little Abie paused, licking his dry lips, "that's that for the State. Now, who were the rats that bombed my place in Grove Manor? Come across with that!"

"It must been Klinsic's men," whined Little Abie, "you see, I don't know noddings about that. And you know *I* vouldn't do such things to you, Cap."

MacBride growled something unintelligible.

There was a commotion outside the door. It whipped open and Grace Devore burst in, her face contorted with rage, her hair disheveled. Moriarity lunged in after her, grabbed her.

"She gave me the slip, Cap," he panted.

Little Abie hid his face in his hands.

Grace shook a fist at him. "You told—you told, you damned little kike. You dirty—"

Moriarity clapped a hand over her mouth. She struggled fiercely.

Little Abie cried, "Gracie, don't you should be so hard. It vas for Big Abie's sake. I have money, Gracie. I vill give you lots—"

"You're a piker," she screamed through Moriarity's fingers, "compared to what *they* were worth. Ha, you little fool. D'you think I ever fell for you?"

"Take her out, Mory," snapped MacBride, "and keep her out. She's slated for a vacation as the guest of the State."

Little Abie was almost in tears, "I worshiped her—"

MacBride clapped him on the back. "That's the least of your troubles, Abie."

Little Abie never looked more bent as he was taken out of the room and down to a cell below.

MacBride slumped into a chair, relaxed.

Kennedy opened a drawer in the desk and pulled out a bottle. He poured two drinks and then sat on the edge of the desk.

"Put that under your belt, Cap," he drawled. "The big racket's over. You're top-dog now. You'd better go some place and sleep. You need it."

MacBride studied the glass of liquor, then downed the contents at a gulp. He stood up, flexing cramped limbs. Dawn was breaking over the ragged sky-line of tenement roofs.

He went to a closet and hauled out an old overcoat. He muscled into it slowly, then drew on a cap.

"See you tomorrow, Kennedy."

"Get a good sleep, Cap."

"Can't sleep, Kennedy. Got to go out and see the wife."

The door clicked softly behind him.

Beat the Rap

Capt. MacBride hangs a rap on some under-cover killers and defies them to beat it.

Chapter I

CRAIG SQUARE is on the hoodlum North Side of Richmond
City, where the old brownstones have gone to rooming-houses
or areaway speaks, and you can buy alcohol in any drug-store. The
back of any barber shop is liable to be an alky-cooking joint, and the
dagos no spikka English if you're not in the know.

The municipal stretch of a state highway crosses Craig Square east
and west. North and south runs Hummel Street, named after a Semetic
alderman who tried to step into big-time and got his diaphragm
blown out in the process. On the Square are automatic traffic lights
that alternate every thirty seconds.

Half a block south on Hummel stands the Old Town Hotel, popular
in certain circles because of a broad-minded desk-clerk. Its red brick
is dirty, but the huge plate glass window always shines darkly. The
doorway is narrow, with a brass name plate on either side.

At exactly three on that blustering March day the north and south
traffic lights turned red. At precisely the same time three black touring
cars rolled north on Hummel and slowed down as they came abreast
of the Old Town Hotel. A man had come out of the door and taken
two steps down the stone stairway. He wore a blue overcoat, snug-
fitting, and a derby. He paused. His lips tightened and horror welled
suddenly in his eyes. He spun and dived back towards the doorway.

From each of the three touring cars a Thompson sub-machine
hurled streams of lead across the front of the hotel. The plate glass
window collapsed violently in a snarling shower of glass. The man
was caught in the doorway and died with thirty bullets up and down
his back. A woman, with a little child, stood petrified ten yards from
the doorway, while the child clung screaming to her skirts.

The motors of the touring cars roared, and as they neared the broad
intersection the red lights became green and the cars crossed the

Square at fifty miles an hour.

A man huddled against a stoop on the opposite side of the street repeated the license number of the last car with palsied lips.

A cop came pounding up the sidewalk from the south, his overcoat flapping about his legs. Some windows grated open and faces appeared timorously. The man in a huddle kept repeating the license number. The door in the hotel could not swing shut because the man in the derby was caught there.

The cop's shoes crackled on shattered glass and he stopped short and looked at the woman who was kneeling on the sidewalk hugging the child.

"You hurt?" the cop asked.

The woman's lips blubbered.

The cop stamped towards her and seemed angry when he bent down and repeated the question. Then the woman shook her head. "N-no."

"Oke," said the cop, and swung to look at the doorway.

A police flivver hurtled up to the curb and stopped so short that its rear end yawed around. MacBride sat next to the chauffeur drawing on a pipe and running his eyes across the hotel front.

"Were you here, Swartzman?" he asked.

Startled, the cop pivoted halfway up the stone steps. He shook his head. "No. I was down at Hummel and Waterford."

"Seems to me," said MacBride, "that some of you guys could spend a little time out of a speakeasy."

"I wasn't—"

"Says you!" MacBride stepped from the flivver, shifted his pipe across his month and eyed the woman still on her knees. He went towards her, his hard features relaxing. "You hurt, missus?"

"N-no. I—I'm just—scared."

He reached down a strong arm and helped her to her feet. He picked up the little child and held her against his chest "You can rest up inside," he said. He carried the child in one arm, used his left hand to guide the woman into the hotel, saying, "Just step over that guy. Hey, Swartzman, get this stiff from blocking traffic."

"Yes, sir."

MacBride eyed him wearily. "And I thought you were on peg post, Louie—at Hummel and the State road."

"Jeeze, I was, Cap—but I just—"

"Okey, Swartzman—okey. Song and dance some other time."

His long-chiseled face was heavy when he entered the lobby of the hotel. Three men were just getting up from behind chairs. One lay sprawled on the floor, his face a bloody welter. A clerk stood shaking behind the desk. MacBride led the woman to a chair and placed the child in her lap.

Then he tilted his gray fedora, shoved his hands into the pockets of his neat gray topcoat, and moved his polished black shoes across the floor. He stopped and looked down at the man lying on the floor. He turned and looked at the man Swartzman had dragged in from the doorway.

"Who is it?" he asked.

"Rocco."

"Oh," said MacBride. "So it's Rocco."

"He ain't got no spine left, Cap."

"He never had a hell of a lot anyhow, but—" He turned and eyed the desk-clerk. "Any idea who was behind the heavy artillery?"

"No, sir."

MacBride turned to the three men who had risen from behind as many chairs. "You guys?"

They shook their heads. He peered keenly at them. "Hello, Butcher."

"Hello, Cap," growled a short, thickset man.

"You might have an idea, Butcher."

"I ain't."

"The old theme song, eh?"

"Hell! I was just sittin' there—"

"You'll bury your dead, Butcher, but I'll bury the guys did it. Get that."

He went back to the woman and said: "Missus, did you by any chance get the license number?"

"There was three cars. I didn't—"

"See any of the men?"

"I—I saw one behind—a big gun. I'd know him again if I ever seen him."

MacBride took down her name and address, then said to the cop: "Swartzman, help this lady down to 324 Hummel and come right back. Come right back, Swartzman—which don't mean a bracer in Donkey Joe's."

"Yes, sir," the cop gulped.

A man appeared in the doorway and MacBride sized him up. "What d' you want?"

"Are you—a detective?"

"Yeah, kind of."

"I saw the shooting. I was walking down the other side of the street. I saw the shooting. I got the number of the last car. It was A-41141."

MacBride wrote it down. "That's an easy number to ball up."

"It's right, though. I kept repeating it. And the car was black with a tan top and there was a rent on the back of the top and the left rear mudguard had a dent in it—a big one."

"You've got eyes, mister. Name?"

"George Plannet, 93 Housman. I work with the Meteor Radio Company—repair man."

"Okey, Mr. Plannet."

He put his book back in his pocket and surveyed the death and debris with tired, bitter eyes. He looked up at the desk-clerk.

"Get Headquarters. Ask for Inspector Starin." He shifted his eyes to Rocco. "So they got your boss, eh, Butcher?"

"Yeah," came Butcher's thick voice.

MacBride went to the telephone. "Hello, Inspector. MacBride.... Rocco got rubbed out at his hotel about ten minutes ago.... Nope, not a thing—except the license number.... I'll be seeing you.... Well, there was another guy got his face blown out. I'll take 'em both to the morgue.... G'-bye."

Butcher was saying: "Jeeze, he was a great guy, Rocco was."

"Swell," MacBride said. "I'll send flowers."

Chapter II

POLICE Headquarters....

MacBride looked up from his neat flat desk when Moriarity came in wearing a disgusted look.

"What I told you," Moriarity growled. "The plates were swiped from a Buick in a Jockey Street garage three nights ago. I got in touch with the guy owned them. He'd reported the lift the same night."

"Okey," MacBride nodded. "I figured they were phony plates. But look here, Mory: I got in touch again with this guy Plannet. He says the car was a Packard, with a sort of V-shaped dent in the rear left mudguard. Cruise around the garages that specialize in rolling out dents, and cruise the auto-top repair places. The Packard had a rip in the top. Those places roll out dents, too."

"You figure it was a bent car, Cap?"

"No, I don't think it was stolen. If it was, we'd have a report on a car found abandoned. On the jump, Mory. Cohen go after that woman?"

"Yeah. Well, be seeing you."

Moriarity turned and pulled open the door. Kennedy of the *Free Press* stood there, smoke from a limp cigarette mushrooming against the brim of a faded, misshapen fedora.

"Thanks," Kennedy said wearily, and strolled in. "Hello, Cap. They do tell me Rocco will have a big funeral, attended by one state senator, two magistrates, a Special Sessions judge, three aldermen, and the mayor disguised as four Hawaiians. Who said the meek shall inherit the earth?"

"Are you drunk, Kennedy?"

"No, but that gives me an idea. How about a drink?"

MacBride hauled out a bottle of Dewar's and Kennedy took half a water glass full. "To your health, Cap. And to the damnation of your enemies, so long as you serve Scotch like this. Who killed Rocco?"

"He was accidentally killed by some small boys playing cowboys and Indians with bows and arrows."

"That's funny. I didn't know Dazzy Nagle was up on archery. Or his little boys."

MacBride's eyes steadied. "What are you talking about, you drunk?"

"Me drunk?" He placed his fingers affectionately around the neck of the bottle as he eased himself on the edge of the desk. "Well, then I was just fooling, Stephen, old sock. It's a fairy story. Listen, but don't believe a word of it. Rocco owns—did own, pardon me—Rocco owned the Old Town Hotel. He had the beer and alky trade sewed up on the North and West Sides. He really owned the Stonemasons and Plasterers Union, and every pushcart merchant in Little Italy and Kike Town paid him tribute. He had his hand in the cheese business.

"He was a great friend of Magistrate Selianos and Alderman Angelan. Who runs the South Side? Dazzy Nagle. The East Side? Lug Neri. Well, last month there was a big meeting at the Congress Place Hotel. The lords and underlords of gangdom gathered. A truce was declared for the occasion. Nagle was there. Neri was there. And of course Rocco. They agreed on certain territories after Rocco had tried to make a combine of three with himself as commander-in-chief. Neri was half-willing. He's not so big anyhow. But Nagle rates, and Nagle said no. So they compromised, had a banquet, and left.

"Last week somebody crossed the railroad tracks and shunted off two boxcars loaded with Canadian rye. They were Nagle's. Some guys had beaned the crew of a switching engine at three in the morning and taken the two cars for a three mile ride and unloaded them on the main line. It damn' near caused a wreck. Who did it? It was on the border between Neri's and Nagle's territory. Let's say that Nagle figured Neri would never have done it on his own. Neri always kept to the hunkies. Let's say that after the truce meeting, Rocco, seeing that Neri would have joined him if Nagle had, went to Neri and quietly took Neri under his wing. If Nagle figured that way, who, then, played cowboys and Indians in Hummel Street this afternoon?"

Kennedy raised the bottle. "Do you mind?"

"Why don't you run that fairy story in the paper?"

"Because some of these punks would think it was true and my boss has got sick and tired of having his place shot up. My imagination does run away with me at times."

"Yeah," said MacBride. "I'd advise you, Kennedy, that if you must get drunk, do it here, or lock yourself in your room and throw the key away. If you get plastered in a speakeasy, your imagination might run away with you again and I'll have to send flowers."

Kennedy smiled with his young-old face and his dreamy, insinuating eyes.

"I can see, Cap," he drawled without moving his lips, "that you don't believe in fairy tales."

The door opened and Cohen said, "I got this Mrs. Schlemmer, Cap. 'S okey to bring her in?"

MacBride stood up, saying, "No. I'll go out." He looked down at Kennedy. "You stay here. Or go home."

"I'll stay, old sock."

MacBride went out and Cohen showed him Mrs. Schlemmer, who had witnessed the shooting. MacBride took her arm and they went upstairs to the Bureau of Criminal Identification. The woman was nervous in these great echoing halls. MacBride spoke kindly to her, in an offhand tone, asked about her child and her husband and finally led her through the large room where the files were kept.

"I want you to take your time," he said. "Look at the faces carefully."

He began turning the big metal pages that hung bookwise from the walls. He had a vague idea of what section to choose first. Before Mrs. Schlemmer's searching eyes passed a parade of faces the like of which she had never witnessed even in the most lurid movie.

Finally she gulped. "There—there!" Her finger pointed.

"You're sure?"

"Yes—yes. I would never forget that face." She shuddered.

It was a broad face with a plowshare jaw, a wide, thick-lipped mouth and pale button eyes. In profile, the lower jaw was projected forward.

"Thanks, Mrs. Schlemmer," MacBride said. "You can go home. We may call you again to identify the man when we get him."

Cohen mused: "Bat Jukes, eh?"

"Don't tell Kennedy."

"I thought Bat went out to Kansas City to run the machine-gun squad for Big Time Herman Goss."

"Yeah. And the Kansas City police think he's still there. He was with Rocco for two years. He came back to pay Rocco for an old deal."

"Is he on his own or is he Dazzy Nagle's new typewriter man?"

MacBride stared keenly into space. "I don't think, Ike, that Bat would come all the way from Kansas City just to blow out the front of Rocco's hotel. Let's go downstairs."

When they returned to MacBride's office Kennedy had gone. MacBride picked up the bottle. It was empty.

"The tank!" he growled with rough good humor.

Cohen was lighting a butt at the window. "Pipe this," he said.

MacBride went over, looked down and saw Kennedy assisting Mrs. Schlemmer across the street.

"Anyhow," MacBride said, "she doesn't know the name of the guy she identified."

The telephone rang. MacBride answered it. "Yeah, Mory.... Uhuh.... Yeah, he would say that.... Okey. Well, come on back."

He hung up. "The Packard had the dent rolled out in a place at 46 Terrence, and the tear fixed. At four o'clock this afternoon. One guy brought the car there. He wore colored goggles and a chauffeur's uniform. That's all the guy knows." MacBride rapped his knuckles on the desk impatiently. "Okey, then, Ike. See if you can root out Bat. Get your stoolies working. I'll get mine and I'll have Mory get his."

"What are we going to pick him up on?"

"Anything. I've got it. That grocery store stick-up three days ago out in Ellenville. Be nice with him, Ike, if you get him. We can get rough later. But if we accuse him right off of this kill he's liable to go nutty and fight. Besides, the woman may be wrong. Breeze, Ike."

For two days MacBride and MacBride's men—and their stoolies—hunted for Bat Jukes. You will know about Bat Jukes if you've followed the reign of crime in Richmond City. He began his career as a strike-breaker, becoming illustrious—in certain strata—through his use of a baseball bat as a means of coercion. Later he got fancy and dipped his bullets in garlic.

But Bat didn't show up. Either the stoolies were stalling or Mrs. Schlemmer had fumbled her identification.

On the third day, towards dusk, MacBride sat behind his desk and creaked in his swivel chair. Moriarity faced him.

"Seems," MacBride said, "that I ought to pay a call on Dazzy Nagle. He might know."

The door opened and Sergeant Bettdecken said: "There's a guy to see you, Cap."

"Who?"

"Bat Jukes."

Chapter III

I HEAR you been lookin' for me, MacBride," Jukes said.

He was a whale of a man dressed in loud clothes. His pale eyes were both quizzical and hostile beneath his craggy brows.

"Sit down, Bat," MacBride said.

"Sure." He sat down expansively, planting his pigskin gloved hands on heavy knees. "If you guys want to talk to me, why the hell don't you ask me 'stead of sendin' your stoolies?"

MacBride smiled. "We weren't sure you were in town, Bat. Kansas City give you the air?"

"Hell. She's a tank town. Well, what's on your mind?"

"A little job out in the West End. Ellenville. Grocery store stick-up. Guy got away with two hundred and socked the grocer in the kisser just for fun. Another guy gave us a pretty good description. It sounds like you."

"Oh, yeah? When'd it happen?"

"Five days ago."

Jukes leaned back and laughed throatily. "Guess again, Cap. And since when have I gone around stickin' up small fry? That's a pansy's job."

"Anyhow, Bat, suppose we let the guy take a look at you?"

"Nix. Nah. Where do you rate that crap? Me stickin' up a grocery? Jeeze, that's rich!"

MacBride stood up, "You think you're a wise guy coming in here, Bat. Okey. But you're going to let this guy take a look at your pan. Mory, go out and get him."

Jukes heaved out of the chair, bending his craggy brows. "Who the hell do you cops think you are?"

"Shut up, you punk," MacBride bit off. "Don't try to get snotty around here. Go ahead, Mory. When you get back take the guy down to the shadow box. Then call me."

Mory went out leering at Jukes.

"Now sit down, Bat," MacBride said. "Time enough to blow off if the guy identifies you."

"Okey, Cap—okey. But you bums can't hang nothin' on me."

"I'd like," said MacBride, "to hang a shiner under your eyebrow."

THE shadow box was down in the basement. There were rows of seats in a darkened room. At one side of the room was a small narrow stage with a white mesh in front of it. The stage was lighted. Anyone on that stage could be seen from the seats but could not see anyone in the seats.

MacBride sat in the room off the stage waiting for Moriarity and Mrs. Schlemmer.

"Listen," Jukes complained, spreading his pigskin-gloved hands. "I gotta date. I can't be wastin' time on a lotta cheap cops that's got a lousy idea."

"Horsefeathers, Bat."

The door swung open and a cop looked in. "Cap. Moriarity." He jerked a look over his shoulder.

MacBride got up, sensing trouble. "Stay with this gorilla, Henny."

MacBride went out and found Moriarity standing with his hands in his pockets and wearing a sullen look.

"Nothing doing, Cap," he growled.

"What do you mean?"

"She ain't there."

"Well, where is she?"

"The whole family moved two days ago. I was speaking with the people on the second floor and they said the Schlemmers were dispossessed for not paying the rent."

"Well, hell, didn't they leave a forwarding address?"

"Nope."

MacBride let an exasperated breath whistle through his nostrils and slammed a knotted fist into an open palm. "Some guy pulled a fast one! Okey!" His blue eyes keened. "I'm going to look into this. And I'm going to hold Bat."

"Jeeze, what can you book him on?"

"I'm not going to book him! I'm going to hold him on suspicion! For twenty-four hours."

Bat Jukes took the news and went into a towering rage. "You guys can't do that!" he reared. "I got my rights! Damn you, MacBride, let me get aholt of my lawyer!"

"Like hell, Bat. You'll cool your pants till I find the guy can identify you."

"That's a lot of hooey! You know damn' well you ain't got no guy can do it! And I ain't gonna stand for it, you lousy flatfoot!"

MacBride took one quick step and grabbed Jukes by the collar with his left hand. His right fist loomed in front of Jukes' face. MacBride's wide lips were curled against his teeth, his brows were bent.

"Another word out of you, you dirty punk, and I'll shellac you!" He hurled Jukes halfway across the room.

Two cops slammed Jukes into a cell.

GRIM purpose was in the set of MacBride's jaw when he left Headquarters on his own. His stride was purposeful, his heavy-soled shoes striking the pavement with sharp echoing rhythm. His teeth bit hard into the stem of his old briar.

At 324 Hummel Street he made inquiries. The renting agent of the four-story house had his offices at 485 Waterford Avenue. To that address went MacBride.

Mr. Bergman rose from behind a roll-top desk and looked over small spectacles. He had a gray, dry face, thin, hueless lips, and thin mouse-colored hair.

"You want to see me?"

"Yes. I'm Captain MacBride, Police Headquarters. Two days ago you dispossessed a family named Schlemmer from a flat at 324 Hummel Street."

"Yes, we did."

"Where did they go?"

Mr. Bergman shrugged. "I don't know. We don't keep that kind of records. Their rent was two months overdue."

"In hard times like this," went on MacBride, "when flats are hard to rent, do you ordinarily dispossess a person who's two months behind?"

"We saw no prospect of getting the money, since the head of the family was out of work."

"How long did they live there?"

"Three years."

"And this was the first time they fell down on payment?"

Bergman looked around. "I believe it was."

"Then do you think it was humane, or on good sense, that you acted as you did?"

Bergman tightened his lips. "Just what are you getting at, Captain? By law we have a perfect right to dispossess any family that defaults on payment of rent. Our personal reasons have nothing to do with the matter. It was a matter of form, of business."

MacBride's cold blue eyes were fastened rigidly on Bergman. "Have you any other families overdue that way?"

"Why—yes, I believe we have?"

"Two or more months in arrears?"

Bergman took a breath. "Approaching two months."

"Mr. Bergman," MacBride said, raising a forefinger. "I'm going to get a writ permitting me to look over your books—unless you're willing to have me look at them now."

"I don't see any reason for permitting you—"

"All right. I'll be back with the writ in half an hour."

He swivelled decisively on his heel and started for the door.

Bergman was saying stridently: "There's no need for a writ. We dispossessed them because, besides being overdue in their rent, the man Schlemmer got drunk on several occasions and annoyed other tenants. We dispossessed them because—"

"Wait!" MacBride came towards Bergman with a heavy tread and a lowering look. "Have you or have you not any rentals that are two months or more in arrears?"

"Why—yes, we have, but on the other hand—"

"Never mind the other hand!" snarled MacBride. "I think, Mr. Bergman, you're a liar!"

"Why?" cried Bergman.

"You dispossessed those people for other reasons than you stated. Get this, mister. I am very much interested in the Schlemmers. I want to know where they are. What is your salary here?"

"Two hundred a month?"

"Have you any stocks or bonds?"

"I—why, no. I—"

"Have you any other source of income but your salary?"

"N-no. I still don't see—"

"Where do you bank?"

"The Water— Damn it, you have no right to—"

"All right. The Waterford State Bank. I'll use your telephone, please."

MacBride called Headquarters. "Hello, Mory. MacBride.... Listen, I want you to go down to the Waterford State Bank and find out if Mr. Marcus Bergman has made any deposits in the last week.... Yeah, that's the name. And call me right away, Mory. I'm at—" and he added the phone number.

He banged the receiver back onto the hook and glared at Bergman. Bergman's face looked drier. MacBride sat down, knocked out his pipe, restuffed it and lit up. He snatched up a newspaper and assumed a passing interest in the front page.

When Moriarity called, MacBride listened, nodded, said: "Thanks, Mory," and hung up. He hung up slowly and looked across the instrument at Bergman.

"Mr. Bergman," he said incisively, "how come you deposited five hundred in your bank the day before the Schlemmers were chucked out?"

Bergman's nostrils quivered. "I don't see that it's any concern of yours."

"Mr. Bergman, have you ever seen the inside of Police Headquarters?"

"No."

"It's kind of worth seeing. Put your hat on."

Chapter IV

THE afternoon sun streamed in through the window and across the mouse-colored head of Bergman, who sat in MacBride's office, his collar half-open, his tie out of place, sweat on his face. His thin shoulders were hunched up alongside his ears, and he licked at his hueless lips.

Cohen leaned against the radiator. Moriarity leaned against the wall, using a jack-knife to scrape his fingernails. MacBride faced Bergman across the neat flat-topped desk. His fingers were loosely interlocked, his head thrust forward, his keen eyes clamped on Bergman's.

"Then you accepted five hundred dollars to dispossess the Schlemmer family?"

"Y-yes."

"Who gave you the five hundred?"

"I don't know. Two men came to my office. They didn't give any names. Both were young—not over twenty-five. They were well dressed and talked pretty well."

"What did they say?"

"Well they asked me if I was the renting agent for the house at 324 Hummel. I said yes. They asked me if I knew a party there by the name of Schlemmer. I said yes. They asked me if they were good tenants, if they paid their rent. I said they were overdue. Then one of the men drew out a roll of bills and said he wanted them dispossessed immediately. He counted out five hundred dollars and laid it on the desk. 'That's for your trouble,' he said. I hesitated and told them that I couldn't do it. They smiled and one of them said, 'Yes, you can. And do it now. Or else—' They smiled again, in a kind of hard way. Then they went out, leaving the money. So I did it."

"And you've no idea where the Schlemmers went?"

"No."

MacBride flexed his lips. "Didn't it occur to you that these men were kind of queer to make a demand like that?"

"Ye-es, it did."

"In other words, you accepted a bribe to chuck out a family that were in a bad way financially."

"I—I—yes, I suppose—"

"Of course you did. Mr. Bergman, I can make you lose your job and have you thrown in jail in the bargain. I'll do both if you don't help me." He stood up. "Come along."

They went up to the Bureau of Criminal Identification and began going through the gallery of portraits.

"If you see a picture of either of the men," MacBride said, "point him out."

Ten minutes later Bergman pointed to a picture of a youth. "That looks like the one who offered me the money."

MacBride noted the file number and went to the array of card indexes. When he returned he said:

"All right, Mr. Bergman, you can go. Don't mention to anybody what happened. Don't say I brought you here. Keep it under your hat."

Bergman was shivering. "Thanks, Captain. I'm sorry I did that, but—"

"Get along. I may have to call you again."

Back in his office. MacBride looked at Moriarity and Cohen. "It was Dancer Frank."

"Hell," Cohen said, "he's Nagle's right-hand man."

"Sure," MacBride smiled. "But we haven't got Dancer. We have got Bat. And we've got to get the woman to identify him."

"What I can't see," Moriarity said, "is how the hell they ever found out the woman told you in the first place."

MacBride lowered his voice. "That's something I've been laying awake about since it happened, Mory. But"—his voice quickened—"we've got to find the woman. Get the telephone book, Ike. Make a list of all the storage houses in the city. Then call 'em up."

Moriarity and Cohen got together. For a solid hour they made telephone calls, and finally gave it up.

Cohen said, "Try advertising, Cap."

"No good." MacBride paced the floor with his hands clasped behind his back. He stopped short, leveled his arm. "Try this. Get a list of second-hand furniture dealers. See if one of them bought some furniture since the Schlemmers were dispossessed."

They went to work on the telephone books again, got a long list and began calling. At the end of half an hour Cohen took an interest in the conversation he was holding. He made notes. He hung up and smiled, leaned back importantly.

"The old Yiddish luck," he said. "One Israel Rosenbloom, of 46 Market, got wind of the dispossess and sent a man around while the furniture was on the sidewalk. To buy at cut-rates, of course. Well, the Schlemmers decided to sell some of it. They sold twenty dollars' worth, with the promise the dealer would send a truck. They paid back a dollar and a half to have the rest taken to a two-room flat in number 606 Billings Street."

MacBride lunged across the room for his hat and coat. "Great work, Ike! Hang around, both you guys."

BILLINGS STREET is tatterdemalion. The pushcart vendors are eternally at war with the ragtag shop owners, and once in a while the city street cleaning department finds its way into the frowsy neighborhood.

In all the hodgepodge of pushcarts, ashcans, scrawny children and half-dressed riffraff, MacBride was a clean-cut figure striding along with his pipe belching smoke. A fight was going on between two youngsters, fists were flying. MacBride slowed down, squinted, but did not stop. He was not a man to bother with petty things. His feet picked up speed and he was back at his old formidable gait.

There was a stone stoop generously draped with dirty-faced kids, a slatternly woman with a baby in arms, and an unshorn man smoking a pipe.

"Does Mrs. Schlemmer live here?" MacBride asked.

"Search me," said the man.

The slatternly woman said: "Ah, I guess they're the new ones on the fourth floor—in the back." On general principles she scowled at MacBride. It was a neighborhood that was clannish for no good reason. It resented outsiders.

MacBride went up the creaking stairway, the smell of damp rot strong in his nostrils. What a miserable hole! He attained the second landing and tramped towards the rear. He knocked at a door and Mrs. Schlemmer opened it. The odor of boiling cabbage assailed his nostrils.

"Hello, Mrs. Schlemmer," he said.

The woman squinted. "Oh... hello."

"I didn't know where you'd moved to. You should have got in touch with me."

"Well, you see, sir, we were dispossessed—right sudden, and I was so mixed up, I didn't know—I forgot—"

"I see. Well, that's all right. What's the matter with your little girl?"

He nodded to the child, who had a flannel bandage around her throat.

"Sore throat. This place is damp, but we had to move somewhere, and—"

"That's too bad." Entering, he saw beads of dampness on the scarred and stained walls. His eyes lingered on the chid. Oddly enough, his eyes became dreamy—a rare thing with the hard-bitten skipper. It brought him back, long ago and far away, when he was a rookie on small pay and his wife and daughter lived on starvation funds in a run-down flat. Sickness, and doctor's bills, and his daughter down with the grippe....

"She can't talk, sir," Mrs. Schlemmer was saying.

"H'm. Too bad, too bad. So you were dispossessed?" His eyes, usually keen as a shaft of cold blue flame, softened on the haggard woman. "By the way, has anyone—annoyed you?"

"No. Except we were dispossessed so sudden. Jake—Jake's my husband—Jake wanted to go down and fight the agent, but—well—that wouldn't done no good. Jake's out looking for work now. It's hard. He can't lift heavy things like he used to. Six months ago he fell from a lumber stack."

"Gosh. Well, I was going to say, Mrs. Schlemmer, I wonder if you could come over to Headquarters and identify the man you saw fire the big gun?"

"Well, I got no one to leave Nancy with. I don't know none o' the neighbors yet. If Jake was here—" She shrugged. "I can't leave Nancy."

"No, of course not. Well—"

There were heavy footsteps in the hall. A big man, broad-shouldered, came in and stopped short. He wore a threadbare coat and there was brown stubble on his face.

"This is Captain MacBride." Mrs. Schlemmer said; and to MacBride, "This is my husband."

"Hello, Cap," Schlemmer said. A glimmer came into his eyes.

His wife said: "Captain MacBride wants me to go to Police Headquarters to identity—"

"Nothin' doin'," her husband cut in. "Look here, Captain. You got to keep my wife out o' this. It's dangerous. I know about that murder, but damn it, you ain't goin' to drag her in it."

"She'll just—"

"I know what she'll do. She'll identify a guy and then before he comes to trial she'll be bumped off—or my kid will. I know these gangsters."

MacBride said: "I know how you feel, Mr. Schlemmer, but this is necessary. A murder has been committed. It's up to the State to get and convict those responsible. And it's up to any good citizen to assist the State."

"She ain't goin'," persisted Schlemmer. "She's had enough trouble with me out o' work and the kid sick. And listen, mister. I ain't dumb. We were dispossessed too sudden for it to be on the up an' up. Somebody paid somebody else to do it. And we're not goin' to be put on the spot because that dago Rocco got bumped off."

"I promise police protection," MacBride said. "If your wife identifies this man, from that moment on I'll have you protected night and day by a plainclothes man. You'll come to no harm—none of you. But your wife will have to come to Police Headquarters."

"She won't, I tell you!"

"Mr. Schlemmer, she will!" His words were blunt, but in his heart he sympathized with the man.

THE stage was set. The seats in the shadow box were plunged in darkness. Mrs. Schlemmer stood in the center of the room, her hand resting on the back of a seat. MacBride stood beside her, supporting her by the arm.

The door at the side of the stage opened and Moriarity led Bat Jukes out into the brilliance behind the white mesh.

"Toe that line, Bat," he said. "Look straight ahead."

"This is a frame—"

"Shut up. Button your overcoat. Put your hat on."

"Ah, you guys—"

"Pipe down." MacBride said from the darkness. "Raise your head. All right. Now face right…. Right again. Now left, you dumb-ox! Right, with your back to me!… Okey. Now right again…. Now front. Keep your head up! Take your hat off."

Skeins of shining sweat on Bat's face gleamed in the brilliant light.

MacBride leaned close to Mrs. Schlemmer. He put his ear near her whispering lips. Then he stood erect.

"Okey, Mory," he said. "Take him to the desk for booking."

Bat Jukes roared, "What are you guys doin'? Where's the guy says I stuck up that store? Where's he? Gimme a look at him and I'll—"

Moriarity planted a hard knee where it was most effective. Bat Jukes went stumbling from the stage into the arms of a waiting policeman.

Bat Jukes, denying all charges, coming through six hours of shellacking battered and still maintaining his innocence, was turned over to the office of the State's Attorney.

Chapter V

MacBRIDE held a match to Kennedy's cigar and looked the reporter in the eye.

"You know, Kennedy," he said, "I always figured you for a drunk, a wiseguy, a bit of a grafter in a nice way—and a white guy. A white guy, Kennedy."

"Well," Kennedy said, inhaling languidly, "my old man was Irish and my mother was a McNulty. There's no trace of the dinge, the quadroon or the octoroon in my blood. Not a bad cigar." His lazy eyes held a provocative twinkle.

"By white, Kennedy, I mean on the up and up—with me."

"Dear father, dear father, what have I done?"

"Cut out the burlesque wit. Somebody wised up somebody else that Mrs. Schlemmer came down here just after the shooting and picked out a picture in the gallery. When she left, I saw you walking across the street with her."

"I make it a point to help children, ladies and dogs across streets."

"Have you come to the point where you make it a point to two-time on a cop that was always willing to give you the shirt off his back?"

Kennedy leaned back on his heels. His eyelids drooped till he seemed about to go to sleep on his feet. A slow smile crept across his lips.

"Excuse me, Stephen. The astral body of my city editor just appeared. I must be going."

"You listen to me, Kennedy!" MacBride gripped his arm and shook him violently.

Kennedy's slow satiric smile lingered on his lips. His lazy eyes almost closed.

He drawled, "Stephen, no rough stuff. I'm under the doctor's care."

"You answer me, Kennedy."

Idly Kennedy reached up and adjusted MacBride's tie. "Cap, old tomato, you're a believing soul. Your cops are good hard-working guys, all of them. Once in a while they drop in a speak for a snifter. But by and large, they're all honest and upstanding. You look in a mirror and say, 'I am Steve MacBride. I've never accepted a bribe. I've been true to my job.' And looking at yourself, you say, 'I am the prototype of all policemen.' That makes you feel upsydaisy."

A low liquid laugh started way down in Kennedy's throat, chortled through his smiling lips.

MacBride dropped his hand from Kennedy's arm.

"What do you know, Kennedy?" he muttered.

Kennedy drifted to the door, opened it and stood there in his wrinkled topcoat, his battered fedora.

"Nothing," he said; and as he backed out, drawing the door shut, he said. "Ask Louie Swartzman how he liked the two hundred dollar party he threw at Pomano's the other night." The door closed on Kennedy's quiet chuckle.

MacBride stood staring at the closed door, his lips pressed so tightly together that a mound of muscle bulged at either corner. His strong, square-tipped fingers flexed themselves against his palms. Tiny points of fire seemed to flash phosphorescently across his eyes, and the crow's-feet at the corners rippled.

A breath exploded, bursting his lips apart.

"By God!"

His eyes lashed themselves to blue-blazing fury.

BAT JUKES' lawyer, the notorious Archie Kline, famed throughout the country for his brilliance and his scathing tongue, filed a plea of not guilty in his client's behalf. Assistant State's Attorney Bellows, a die-hard, roared his murder-in-the-first-degree. It promised to be one of the quickest trials on record. Bellows raked up Jukes' past, leaving no stone unturned. And he was to bank everything on the testimony of Mrs. Schlemmer, the State's star witness.

"She must be guarded," he said, "as if she were a queen in danger of assassination. It must be seen to that no one approaches either her or her husband in an effort to buy them off."

Behind the ample bosom of Mrs. Schlemmer there must have beaten the heart of an amazon. With a quiet stoicism she promised to stand by the State. Life had knocked her from pillar to post, ground her on its ragged edges. Yet in this time of imminent danger she became cool and collected and quietly grim in her purpose.

"She will hang Bat Jukes," said the Assistant State's Attorney.

WITH MacBride, something more personal had entered into the case than murder on a large scale. A growing suspicion gnawed its way into his heart and remained there, burning slowly. It kept him awake, marched tirelessly with him by day. It became an obsession, until finally what at first had been a stinging suspicion became in his mind almost a palpable truth.

One night he took a street car and rode out to the edge of town. Alighting, he walked down an elm-lined street. He climbed the porch of a modest little house and pressed the bell-button. A white-haired woman, neat and smiling, opened the door.

MacBride touched his hat. "How do you do, Mrs. Swartzman. I'm Captain MacBride. Is Louie in?"

"No, he's not, Captain."

"You expect him in?"

"Well, not till late, I guess. He dressed up and went out—put his tuxedo on."

"Thank you. I just wanted to see him. Good-night, Mrs. Swartzman."

He retraced his steps to the street car line. Tuxedo! Humph! Cops going out in tuxedoes these days. Pretty fancy. He returned to Headquarters and sat around brooding. Sergeant Otto Bettdecken came in and said he and some boys were sending out for hot dogs and they had a new batch of beer. Would the skipper like to join the party?

"No," growled MacBride.

And when Bettdecken had gone MacBride poured himself a stiff jolt of Golden Wedding and downed it neat.

At half-past ten he put on his conservative gray topcoat and went out. He walked swiftly through the dark streets. His pipe bowl was a red smoking eye in the darkness. He drew savagely at the stem till the hot smoke burned his tongue.

It took him twenty minutes to reach a street in which a sign scrawled in neon lights said:

POMANO'S

He rolled past the liveried doorman and barged into an anteroom hung in seductive red drapes. A couple of sleek men in evening dress drifted towards him.

"Table for one, sir?"

"No. I just want to look the place over."

He rolled past them and stood in the arched entrance to the night-club proper. There was a gang. There was blatant jazz hurled out by a negro orchestra. There were dazzling lights, and gay paper streamers, and men and women wore funny paper hats, and there were bottles on tables and drunken laughter and drunken dancing and feverish hilarity.

At a big table halfway down the room MacBride saw Swartzman. The cop looked clean-cut in his tux. A paper Napoleonic hat was cocked over one eye, and a girl lay in his arms. There were half a dozen others at the table, chairs for three or four more. It looked like a wild party.

MacBride signaled the headwaiter. "Tell Louie Swartzman somebody wants to see him."

"You?"

"Yeah."

Swartzman came down the floor unsteadily, waving to other tables, laughing. He almost walked into MacBride. He chuckled and slapped MacBride on the shoulder.

"Come join party, Skipper."

"I want to talk to you, Louie."

"Hell, why talk when can drink? C'mon, be sport, got nice-sh dame f'r you 'n' everything—"

A man tapped MacBride's arm. "What's the idea, stranger?"

"'S all right," Swartzman said. "He-sh friend mine. Cap'n Steve MacBride, good guy, gonna have drink, make whoopee."

"Get your hat and coat, Louie," droned MacBride.

"Huh? Ain't goin' no place. Why get coat 'n' hat?"

The headwaiter said: "Listen, Cap. It's Louie's party—"

"He'll pay up to now. Pay your bill, Louie."

"Ain't goin' no place. Why pay bill?"

"Listen," the headwaiter said, "why bust up the party?"

"You keep your oar out of this!" MacBride barked.

They got Louie's bill while MacBride forced him into his overcoat. The bill was two hundred and twenty dollars. MacBride saw Louie give the headwaiter a roll from which the latter peeled off the amount. Then Louie gave a fifty dollar tip.

MacBride dragged him outside and heaved him into a taxi-cab. He sneaked him through a rear entrance in Headquarters and unseen got him into a room on the second floor. The room was soundproof. MacBride locked the door.

Louie fell into a chair and started to go to sleep. MacBride punched him awake. Louie stared at him with bleary eyes.

"Hic—hello, Skipper."

MacBride's voice was low and hard: "Hello, Louie. Who paid you to sneak off your beat the day Rocco was rubbed out and the Old Town Hotel drilled?"

"Huh?"

"You heard me, Louie. They couldn't have made a clean getaway if you'd been on beat where you should have been. How much were you paid and who paid it?"

Louie's eyes widened. "I don't know what you're talkin' about— Me—paid?"

"You can't throw parties at Pomano's on a cop's salary, Louie. You're going to come clean before you leave this room."

Louie frowned. "Ah, don't know what you're talkin' about. You're crazy, Skipper."

"Says you." His voice was still low, deadly. "You're going to come clean, Louie. You always were a hard guy. You got a great kick out of shellacking a guy. I mind the time you picked up a drunken bum and walloped his ears with your stick till they were rags. The guy's in the insane asylum as a result. You hear me, Louie? You're going to talk!" He raised his fists. "Or I'll use these on you."

Louie started. Out of his sodden stupor he gathered some inkling of MacBride's cold determination.

MacBride was saying: "Somebody wised up the gang that Mrs. Schlemmer saw Bat Jukes in one of the cars. Nobody knew that but you. You were on the scene. I had you take the woman home. You might have got away with it, Louie—but the money went to your nut. And you're going to spring, kid—you're going to spring!"

"Me? Ah, you're crazy, Skipper!"

"Get up, Louie."

"Listen, you can't try any rough stuff on me—"

"Get up. You two-timed on us, Louie."

Louie got to his feet, his mouth agape, his eyes bulging. MacBride caught him by the throat.

"Who paid you, Louie?"

"Nobody paid me. I tell you—"

MacBride hurled him across the room. Louie crashed against a chair and went down with it. He leaped up, terror in his eyes.

"Damn it, you can't do this! I'm a cop—"

"You won't be after tonight."

MacBride crossed the room slowly, his jaw set. He lifted Louie off the floor with a terrific blow to the jaw. While Louie was toppling MacBride hit him again. The cop lay panting on the floor. MacBride hauled him to his feet.

"So help me, Louie, I'll put you in the hospital!"

"Leggo. I don't know a thing—"

MacBride's fist crashed between his eyes and Louie went hurtling backwards, covering his face with his hands. The wall stopped him abruptly and he buckled to the floor. He started to crawl. MacBride put him on his feet again. He clipped Louie on the jaw. He battered him around the room, tore off his coat, his collar, his shirt. He did it coolly, grimly, but his heart was thumping and the hot blood of rage stormed through his veins. This was a traitor, a man who had two-timed on the shield.

Louie began screaming. MacBride had seen him dress a suspect down on more occasions than one. Louie had delighted in it. Louie had invented new ways of making a suspect talk. MacBride saw him now as a groveling, blubbering wreck.

"My God!" Louie cried. "Cut it out! You're killing me!"

"I'll just about, Louie. Who paid you?"

The question was accompanied by a blow to the jaw that sent Louie clear across the desk and on to the floor beyond. MacBride stalked him and started to haul him up again.

"Don't—don't!" Louie screamed.

"Come clean?"

"Don't! Yes! God, yes!"

"Who paid you?"

"Dazzy Nagle—"

"How much?"

"A thousand bucks! Jeeze, Skipper—"

MacBride let him drop to the floor. "What a piker you were!" He stood up, his clothes wrinkled, his face gray and granite-hard. "There's nobody going to beat this rap, Louie—nobody!"

Chapter VI

THE news was a bomb-shell in Headquarters. Many cops are clannish. Many will even try to hide the duplicity of one of the Force's members. Some of these growled. A few here and there sighed and wagged their heads.

But MacBride, the old war-horse, did not give two hoots what anyone, cop or otherwise, thought of his own irregular tactics on Swartzman. In his heart he had believed Swartzman guilty of treason. He had used an unvarnished method to bring the truth out. He told the doctor who came that he didn't think any of Swartzman's bones were broken.

"I used only my paws," he said. "I didn't use a hunk of hose, a billy, a gun-butt or any of the furniture. I might have—but that double-crossing —— has no guts."

Said Inspector Starin: "At least, Steve, you might have called me in and maybe we could have handled it gently."

"Hot air!" boomed MacBride. "It would have given him time to sober up. Besides, Charlie, I was sore. You know what we do to a guy kills a cop. We hit him with everything but the radiators, and I once saw a hunky cop try to use that. Well, this is the same. This punk cheated on us. He's in with the gang and some day he'd walk off the beat when maybe you or I or another cop was on the spot."

Starin shrugged. "I guess there are only a few of us old-timers left, Steve. What are you going to do now?"

"Well, I just broke up a pool game by telephone Moriarity and Cohen were having at Max's. The reserves are dousing their mugs with ice water to wake up, and Keyser's gone after the squad car."

"But what are you going to do?"

"Do? Hell, I'm going to get Nagle and his boy friends!"

He yanked open the desk drawer and pulled out a .38 Police Special, a duplicate of the one he carried in an armpit holster. He loaded the extra gun and dropped it in his overcoat pocket.

Starin looked worried. "Smoke, Steve?"

"Ten to one somebody in Swartzman's Pomano party is on speaking terms with Nagle."

The door opened and Moriarity and Cohen trooped in.

"Now what are you up to?" Cohen complained. "Damn it, every time I go and make a late date you go into a huddle and find something to do."

"I hope," MacBride said, "you didn't hock your gun."

"Oh, is that the kind of a party?"

Keyser poked his head in. "The damn' squad car blew a gasket, Cap. We'll have to take the flyer."

"Take it."

"I did. It's downstairs."

Six cops were hanging around in front of the desk when MacBride reached the central room. He called off names:

"Bauer, Kostika, O'Hagan, Finnegan, Oberdorfer and Fidelago. Okey, gang. Let's."

He barged out through the door with Moriarity and Cohen on either side of him and the cops tramping behind.

The flyer was a special seven-passenger job, painted black, with a one hundred and forty inch wheelbase and an eight cylinder motor capable of doing ninety miles an hour. The windshield, of nonshatterable glass, was slanted way back at a rakish angle. The body was constructed of quarter-inch metal and the tires contained puncture-proof tubes. In the compartment back of the front seat were two Thompson submachine-guns and ten drums of .45 caliber bullets, each drum containing fifty cartridges, and two sawed-off shotguns.

Keyser was gassing the motor. Moriarity and MacBride jammed in beside him and Cohen went in the back with the uniformed cops.

MacBride got his pipe started and said: "Go to the *Red Lantern*, Keyser, in Jockey Street."

The gears meshed silently. The car gathered speed in second, slipped into high, and wheeled around the next corner.

MacBride half-turned in the seat and said: "Remember, boys, this may mean a fight. I'm not going to hand you a line about tradition, honor and valor. Nagle is a big shot, and he bribed a copper to act dumb while his wagons sailed up Hummel Street. If we can, we're going to get this baby and most of his gang quietly. But if news got to him tonight—he'll know we've got the goods on him—and the bird'll get snotty. And if it's fight, use everything you've got—guns, rocks, clubs, feet and your brains. Okey. Swing right here, Keyser, and beat that crosstown traffic light."

"I'll give 'em the siren and we'll go right through."

"Nix on the noise, Keyser."

The long black car swung right and went purring down a dark street. It got a crosstown green light at the next left turn.

"To think," brooded Cohen, "that I've been trying to date that jane up for a month."

"How'd you make it finally?" Moriarity slurred.

"Well, I told her I had a friend in the silk business, and I'd get her stockings and things."

"Hey, you," MacBride said, "cut out shaking down the silk houses."

"That's only what I *told* her," Cohen said absently.

They bantered and chided each other on their way across the town. When they drew up a block away from the *Red Lantern* and got out, Officer Fidelago crossed himself and O'Hagan, grimly humorous, wondered if his insurance policy were paid up to date.

"Never mind," Finnegan jibed back, "I'll pay it up in the morning."

MacBride got them in a huddle. "Keyser, you stay at the wheel. Mory and Ike, you come with me. You other guys spread out across the street. All except you, Oberdorfer. You beat it around the back and see they don't try to bust out into the next street. If they do, give us the whistle. Keyser, two quick blasts will mean you drive up to the front. Three quick ones mean you shoot around with the car to the back street. All straight now?"

The men nodded and said, "Yeah," all around.

"Ike, Mory," MacBride said, and started off.

THE three of them walked in through a narrow door level with the street. A row of ten tables ran back on either side. Three waiters were idle. A short fat man in a black suit looked up from behind the cash desk.

"Where's Dazzy?" MacBride asked.

The fat man started. His face assumed a blank expression.

"He lives here," MacBride said. "A guy just told me. He owns this building and he owns you."

"Dazzy—who?" the man gulped. He was sitting on a high stool and his body seemed to twist downward a bit.

MacBride cursed and dived behind the counter. He kicked away the fat man's rigid left leg. He saw a button on the floor.

"Ike, Mory," he barked, "keep this guy and the waiters nice."

He went down the length of the restaurant like a blast of wind. He found a stairway leading upward from a rear room and went up quickly, both guns drawn. Reaching the top he saw a lighted transom. A second later the transom was dark. But there was a light in the hall.

MacBride heard a window grate open. He crept towards the door and listened. He heard the ring of shoes on metal. Men going out by way of the rear fire-escape!

He stepped back and rushed the door. Wood strained. He tried again, slamming into the door with his right shoulder. Wood crackled, snarled—and the door burst open. He saw one man crouched on the fire-escape platform outside the window—one man with a gun raised, waiting to slow down the chase.

MacBride let the impetus of his lunge carry him to the floor. Three jets of flame burst from the fire-escape. MacBride fired both guns with his elbows on the floor. He saw the man heaving on the metal grating, and then the man vanished and MacBride heard his body tumbling down.

The skipper crossed to the window and looked down into a dark yard. He saw no one. He raised his whistle to his lips and blew three short blasts. Then he climbed out and went clattering down the metal rungs. He jumped over the dead man in the yard and looked around for an opening. He saw only a high board fence. He rushed towards it and was about to scale it when he noticed a small door. The door gave and he went through into the adjoining yard.

He heard a motor roaring. The roar seemed confined within walls. He went grimly towards the back of the next building, down into an areaway. There was a door there, heavy and barred from the inside. He went back to the yard and crashed his way through a window. He landed in a dark room. He clawed around for another door while the thunder of a motor echoed throughout the building. He found the door and knocked it down in time to see a car swing out into the street ahead. He raised his guns and fired.

He ran towards the entrance and saw spurts of flame coming from behind a pole across the street. That would be Oberdorfer. He saw flame spurting from the gangster car. As he reached the doorway he heard the scream of the siren on the flyer. The black car roared down the street. He saw visored caps jutting from the tonneau. He leaped to the running-board. He saw Oberdorfer leap to the other side

"Step on it, Keyser!" MacBride clipped.

He hung on while the car whipped sharp right into the next street. Keyser opened his cut-out and the exhaust hammered behind them in the darkness. The siren kept screaming. Cars jolted to a standstill ahead of them, and they went through red lights at fifty miles an hour.

The gangster car hit River Road and opened everything wide. The flyer was doing sixty-five and the cops were loading the Tommy guns. Quick bursts of flame spat from the car ahead and lead tore through the flyer's mudguards.

"For God's sake, get in here, Cap!" shouted Keyser.

"Hey," MacBride yelled, "hand me one of those Tommy guns."

"For God's sake, Cap—"

"Ah, pipe down, Keyser." MacBride grabbed the Tommy gun and lay down between the left mudguard and the vibrating hood. He laid the barrel of the Tommy gun across the horizontal headlight supporter. The flyer was doing seventy when the skipper opened fire. The rattle of the gun was almost lost in the hoot of the wind and the roar of the motor beside him. He heard lead bang into the thick grating in front of the radiator. He heard the crash of the left headlight and felt shattered glass whip across his face. He cursed a blue streak, yelled for more speed, and started the Tommy gun again. And heard the beat of the other gun handled by Finnegan from the other side.

They gained on the car ahead. They were doing eighty miles an hour, and MacBride could hardly keep his eyes open in the wind. He lost his hat and the wind hauled at his hair. He hammered the back of the gangster car with another burst, and the smoke whipped back into his eyes, stung his nostrils.

Then he saw the car ahead swerve from side to side. He heard the squeal of brakes on the flyer. He saw the gangster car skid, wheel around three times and slam broadside into a telephone pole. While the flyer was skidding to a stop he saw two men hurled from the gangster car and heard the yells of others.

He leaped from the running-board with his .38s and found his men spreading beside him. He saw one of the men lying on the street raise a gun. MacBride made a flying tackle and landed heavily on the man, bearing him back to the pavement. In the glare of the flyer's headlight he saw the agonized face of Dazzy Nagle.

A shot barked from the gangster car. Oberdorfer said, "Hell," and turned away sidewise. The police battery opened fire as one man and their lead pounded into the tonneau of the car.

Oberdorfer was walking around in a circle saying, "Hell, now, hell, now!" in an annoyed voice. Then he sat down abruptly and looked vacantly about him.

MacBride, having knocked Nagle out with a gun-barrel, came towards Oberdorfer, saying, "Are you hurt, Oby?"

"Well," said Oberdorfer, "suppose you had a bullet in your leg?"

MacBride looked up. "Hey, Keyser, take Oby to the hospital."

"Sure. How about them punks?"

MacBride was lifting Oberdorfer. "Hell," he said, "third class is good enough for them. We'll get an ambulance."

He looked around at his men and the bristling guns they held. He looked at two gangsters lying on the street, at another draped over the side of the car, at the visible arm of another whose body was inside the car.

"Well, Oby," he said, "you boys o' mine didn't do so lousy."

Chapter VII

KENNEDY took the first drink out of the new bottle of Dewar's. "Have you connections in London—or Montreal, Cap?"

"Why?"

Kennedy winked at the bottle. "So Swartzman played two-time, eh, old tomato?"

MacBride scowled at the desk. "Now don't rub it in, bozo."

"You know. Cap, I'm great on fairy stories. Tell you what. Give me a bottle of this stuff, seal unbroken, and maybe I'll go out and find another fairy story. Only"—he raised the glass—"you don't believe in fairy stories."

MacBride pulled open a drawer, drew out a cigar box.

"Thanks," said Kennedy.

MacBride held his hand on the box. "Kennedy, I'll tell you a fairy story. There's a family I know. The mother is being a great help to the State. The kid is in the hospital with the grippe. The father is out of work. I'm getting the guy a job next week on a county road gang. But it costs money for medicine and doctors, and meantime the guy and his wife have got to live."

He opened the cigar box. It was filled with bills and change.

"I'm collecting," he went on. "I've been around to five station-houses and canvassed Headquarters. Turn out your pockets, Kennedy."

Kennedy touched his lips with a handkerchief. "Glad to. I'll have my check in the mails tomorrow morning."

"I have no use for rubber checks. Dig down, bozo."

Kennedy shrugged, drew a ten dollar bill from his pocket. "It makes no difference to me, Skipper. I'll only borrow it back from you before the week's over."

"When I borrowed five from the wife today? Horse on you, sweetheart!"

Death for a Dago

Capt. Steve MacBride gets all steamed up—and the murdered man was only a poor dago.

Chapter I

RICHMOND CITY'S Little Italy is a neighborhood of color and smells. Not a particularly tough layout. The dagos work there from sunup until after sundown. Fruit markets, big and little, flank the crooked streets; spaghetti joints; grocery stores and meat markets.

By day the streets teem with women and children. Gossip travels up and down. The dago laborers come home about five, laughing-eyed, boisterous. Over the back fences you can see the railroad yards. Many of the inhabitants speak little or no English and all of them are ambitious in their modest way: work hard, make a pile, and some day go back to Italy.

Not a night-owl neighborhood. The vice, the dives, are over in Rock Hollow; the light o' loves, the sleek-faced wops, the window-tappers, the alky-cooking joints and the guinea ink at one-fifty a bottle. At ten p.m. Little Italy is pretty quiet, while Rock Hollow, the modernistic woptown, is just starting.

At half-past ten that night Pietro Matteo was closing up his vegetable store in Garibaldi Street, Little Italy. He was the last to close. He was lugging his crates of fruits and vegetables into the store and humming a song of the gondoliers. He was happy. His wife had recovered from an illness, his two sons had been promoted, and he had recently acquired a second-hand towing car for five hundred dollars cash. True, there'd been a little trouble with the car, but—

Pietro lifted the last crate of tomatoes in his arms and started for the doorway of his store. He heard footsteps coming resolutely down the other side of the street. The footsteps were sharp in the otherwise empty street, and Pietro looked over his shoulder as he paused in the doorway. There was the possibility of yet another sale. He was shrewder than most Italians, and worked harder than many.

Yes, the two men were cutting diagonally across the street.

"Hey, Pete—"

Pietro turned all the way around, squinting.

Suddenly the two men stopped. Their hands became flame. Four interlocked explosions burst in Garibaldi Street and Pietro Matteo, aged thirty-three, crashed down with his case of tomatoes.

The two men turned and sped swiftly away, diving into an alley thirty yards up the street.

Crushed tomatoes and a crushed body. Red tomato juice and the red blood of a dago fruiterer.

A window grated open.

"Pietro!"

A woman's head thrust out, far out.

"Pietro!... *Mother of God!*"

That was Chiara, the late Pietro's widow.

In a minute she was down on the sidewalk. She slipped on the mashed tomatoes. She skidded and fell upon Pietro, screaming and hauling him and then sitting down and holding his bloody body in her arms, against her ample bosom.

Gradually other windows opened. A man appeared in the street and came towards the pair hesitantly, asking "Whassa mat'?"

Cries began to come from the windows.

Then two cops came running. The people could see their shields and buttons flashing. The people took heart and began to flow into the street from every hall door.

The cops slowed down to a walk and reached the woman holding the man in her arms. She didn't see them. Tears streamed from her eyes. Her two children were clawing at her and crying.

"Hey, Joe," said one of the cops, "keep the crowd back."

"Okey, Benny."

The first cop bent over and tried to unfasten the woman's arms. She fought with him.

"Come on, missus. I ain't gonna hurt him."

"He's-a d'ad! My Pietro he's-a d'ad!"

"Ah, nix, he ain't dead."

"He's-a d'ad—"

"Well, lemme look. Come on, missus. Ah-r-r— Hey, Joe, come over. This frau's got a stranglehold on this guy—"

"Yeah? Jeeze, that guy's dead, Benny!"

"Well, gimme a hand."

Between them they pried loose Chiara, and Joe had to hold her back while Benny spread Pietro out. The two children kept holding the mother's skirts. The crowd surged close, babbling, exclaiming.

"Yeah," Benny said, "he's dead." He stood up and took out a book. "What's the name, missus?"

She didn't hear him. She was blind with horror, with remorse. A tall, gaunt Italian stepped up.

"His-a name Pietro Matteo. Dis-a his wife Chiara, and dis-a his kid."

"Which one?"

"Dis-a two his kid."

"Okey."

At that moment the wife fainted and Joe had a dead weight in his arms. But he held on grimly, setting his jaw.

"What's your name, buddy?" Benny said.

"Orazio Cafarelli."

Benny looked blank, then said: "Well, I'll just put down O. and spell the last name."

He got mixed up with the Fs, Rs and Ls.

"He lived upstairs, eh?"

"Shoo. Run-a dis store; shoo."

"All right. Now, did you see the shooting?"

"No."

Benny raised his voice. "Did anybody see whatsizname get shot?"

A great hullabaloo started, hands waved.

"Hold on!" barked Benny, raising his hand.

It simmered down that almost everybody had heard the shots but no one had seen the shooting. Joe looked grim and red-faced holding up the woman.

"Ah, plant her somewhere," Benny said.

"I'll take her upstairs. You report, Benny. Hey, big shot, give me a hand with this woman."

Cafarelli stepped forward and they went upstairs with the widow, followed by the wailing children. Benny put his hands on his hips, stepped over the corpse, and entered the store. He found a telephone on a desk in the rear and called a number.

"Patrolman Benjamin I. Nussbaum reporting…. That's the old name, Sergeant. Get this…."

Chapter II

MacBRIDE stood with his hands clasped behind his back, chin on chest, eyes looking moodily down his nose at the woman rocking in the chair. Her black hair was all over her head, stringing down her cheeks. Her face was red as a beet. Her eyes seemed unable to focus; they were vacant of all but a wildness; wide-staring, fierce with a blind intensity.

Women had come and taken the children into another room. Their voices could be heard faintly through the door.

MacBride sighed. He lifted a chair and planted it in front of Chiara. He sat down heavily, for a heaviness was in his heart. He was tired of death, tired of waiting out scenes like this, of seeing a woman suddenly alone in the world.

"Now, Mrs. Matteo—there, there now—"

" 'S my Pietro—d'ad!" she moaned.

"He was a swell guy," MacBride said. "He was murdered. All right now, Mrs. Matteo—we have to get the murderer."

"Whassa good—when-a my Pietro he's all d'ad?"

"I know, I know. But—well, you've got to pull yourself together. You've got to think of your kids, Mrs. Matteo. And yourself. They say you've been very ill. Well, if you don't try to pull yourself together you'll have a relapse—you'll be sick again."

She tried to straighten up, gripping her hands together in her lap. She kept convulsing.

"Whatcha want, sir, mister?"

"Well, have you any idea who might have killed your husband?"

"Pietro he's-a got no enemy. Everywan he's-a like Pietro. He's-a brave man too, and gotta good head. Oh-o-o, whatcha talk—whatcha talk!"

She buried her face in her hands and broke out crying again.

MacBride rose and took a slow turn up and down the room. For half an hour he had been trying to get something out of her. He had been patient, understanding; had suppressed the natural impatience attendant to the business of trying to talk rationally with a woman who had just lost her husband and spoke very broken English.

But she knew nothing. That was the truth. She had no idea at all as to who might have killed her husband. Pietro was law-abiding, honest, hard-working. MacBride knew that. Little Italy was one of his hobbies. Nor had Pietro been in any kind of racket; he hadn't even sold wine. He had been prosperous enough through his fruits and vegetables. Had bought a car. Was going to take a week off and go touring with his family, leaving Orazio Cafarelli to run the business. Orazio was downstairs cleaning up the sidewalk. The morgue wagon had taken Pietro's body and an undertaker would pick it up the next day.

Kennedy, of the *Free Press*, poked his head in. "What's the dope, Cap?"

"Nix, sweetheart."

One of the women came in to look after Chiara. MacBride went downstairs with Kennedy to take the air. He stuffed a pipe and lit it, looking up and down the street. The people had gone back into their doorways. Orazio was inside the store, straightening things.

"So some gun landed right smack in your hobby, eh, Cap?"

"Listen, sweetheart." MacBride tossed away a match and puffed up on his pipe. "Just that. Some wiseacre landed in my hobby. It took me two years to weed out Little Italy. I did, didn't I?"

"Yeah. And then what? Rock Hollow, woptown wide-open and shaking its belly in mirth."

"Huh! What's the matter with that? It's a swell idea if you ask me. It's a smaller community, and we know what it is. But I cleaned up Little Italy and ever since then the merchants and honest wops here have been mentioning me in their prayers."

"Conceited slob."

"Listen, Kennedy." He thumbed the reporter's ribs. "I'm going to get the jazzbo that horned in. The whole town knows that Little Italy's been taboo."

"First, master mind, would you mind telling me why Pietro was bumped off?"

MacBride snorted, walked six paces, looked into the store and came back again. "You just leave that to me, Kennedy. I'm a great little finder-out."

"Your hat should be getting tight these days, Skipper."

"It's just this, Kennedy: There's just a gang of hoodlums on the muscle. Pietro had no enemies in Little Italy. There's a new racket in the bud, or maybe it's been going on for some time. Maybe he bought the wrong kind of vegetables. Or fruit. Hell, it's not just liquor any more. It's everything. But I didn't think they'd have the nerve to bust in here."

Orazio came out and locked the store door.

"Hey," MacBride called, "you were a good friend of Pete's, eh?"

"Shoo. Me an' Pietro come over on de same boat."

"And you're sure you don't know who might have gunned him out?"

"Please, no, Cap. Pietro's quiet, see. Happy like a fool, but no go around an' shoot off de mouth. Everywan around say he wan swell guy, dat's shoo."

"All right," MacBride muttered.

Orazio went upstairs.

MacBride and Kennedy started across the street. MacBride stooped to pick up an empty cartridge case he had scuffled.

"Thirty-eight," he said.

"Here's another," Kennedy said. "Only it's a .45."

"H'm. That means two guys." MacBride looked around the street. "There's an alley over there. These shells were ejected in the middle of the street. The guys would have turned, say, and rather than chance a cop at the corner they would have, say, ducked down that alley."

"That doesn't call for a lot of brainpower."

"Who said it did?"

MacBride reached the opposite sidewalk, followed the curb to the alley and started down the alley. It was cobbled, about five feet wide, and there were garbage cans at intervals. The other end of it emptied into Venice Street. MacBride traversed the alley, swinging a small pocket-flash in front of him, from side to side; playing it on the garbage cans. Some of the refuse lay on the cobbles and between many of the cobbles were patches of damp mud. MacBride went slowly.

"What do you expect to find?" Kennedy asked.

"I never expect to find anything, Watson."

As he said this he stopped, then bent down on one knee.

"Here, Kennedy. Hold this light."

"Where?"

"Hold it just the way I've got it. See that banana peel over there? Well, somebody slipped on it."

"Should I hold it on the banana peel?"

"Don't be a goof. Hold it here—right down here on this mud." MacBride extracted a pocket-knife, opened a large blade. He cut out a square of the damp solid earth, slid the knife beneath and pried it up carefully. When he had it loose, he took a sheet of paper from his pocket, worked it beneath the square of mud he had loosened, and then lifted the square intact on the sheet of paper. He stood up, holding it carefully on his palm.

"Come on, Kennedy. Maybe this is all wrong but there's no harm in trying."

"Heel print?"

"No. Some guy slipped on the banana peel, took a header and slapped his mitt down on this chunk of mud. He left prints of three fingers. Now razz me and I'll sock you."

"Once in a while you get a notion, don't you?"

Chapter III

THE skipper came to work next morning through the rain. He trooped into Headquarters with his gray slicker crackling and dripping, with water streaming from a battered felt hat he used on rainy days.

"Morning, Otto," he said.

"How's every little thing, Steve?" said Bettdecken from the central room desk.

"This rain's good for the flowers. My garden needed rain like nobody's business."

MacBride plowed on down a corridor, up a flight of stairs, down another corridor and into his office. He heaved out of his slicker, swung his hat back and forth, knocking the rain off, and hung up both. He sat down, drew off his rubbers, which his wife had made him wear, and swung the swivel chair to face his desk and the morning's business. He massaged his palms vigorously.

He made a telephone call. "Hello, Charley. Steve.... D'you do anything with that hunk of mud?... I see. Well, let me know soon as you get finished.... Well, it's good for the gardens."

He hung up and dived into the mail. He whistled a popular air, separated the important letters and notices from the unimportant.

The door opened and Ike Cohen, one of his right-hand men, came in humming. Cohen, wearing a snappy mackintosh, came to the desk and, still humming, opened a crumpled package and laid four spent bullets on the desk.

"Oh, you were down to the morgue, Ike."

"Yeah. Here they are. Two .38s, two .45s. One of the .45s was lodged in the right shoulder, the other busted open his stomach and lodged in his spine. One of the .38s smacked him in the chest and the other stuck in his right thigh, high up."

"Instantaneous, huh?"

"Yup. The .38's were dipped in garlic."

"No!"

"On the up and up. Dipped in garlic."

"The guy must have been strictly torpedo. Take your coat off, Ike, you're getting my desk all wet."

Cohen slipped out of the mackintosh and revealed himself as a natty dresser of medium height and build. He started life as a cabaret dancer and was accomplished on the banjo.

MacBride fingered the slugs. Garlic. If a bullet dipped in garlic didn't kill a man right off it drove him crazy and quite often pre-cipitated a hemorrhage.

"Real bad guys, Ike," MacBride mused.

"Yeah. The kind of a punk I'd like to plug in the back. Find out anything about the hunk of mud?"

"Burch is working on it. Where's Moriarity?"

"Trying to muscle out some info in Little Italy."

MacBride sighed. "It's a damned shame, Ike. The dago had every-thing to live for. Nice wife, nice kids—and he was making dough. Liked all over the neighborhood. I knew him—sort of. Used to stop by and chat with him and he used to brag about his fruit and vege-tables. He gave me an idea how to grow lettuce. I was always having bum luck with lettuce. And then for some reason—I wish the hell I knew what it was—he's drilled."

"Ah," Cohen snarled, "there's a lot of small-time droppers in this burg can be hired to fog a guy for fifty bucks."

"Anyway," MacBride growled, making a slow fist, "I'll bet the punk did it fries on the hot-seat—or I gun him out personally."

"Two guys, Cap."

"Well, what the hell! Two guys, then!"

"Well, don't take *my* head off."

MacBride settled. "Okey, Ike. Hang around till we get word from Moriarity."

"Jake." Cohen took his mackintosh and went out, humming.

Five minutes later Burch, the fingerprint man, came in with a green eyeshade slewed over one eye. He carried some photographic prints.

"I can't locate anything in the files, Steve," he said. "It was tough. I had to go careful with the mud. I sprinkled my trick aluminum powder on the impression, transferred it to the black tape I use, and then photographed that, having to reverse the print, of course. See, I've got a pretty good job, good enough to locate anything if it were in the files. But it isn't."

MacBride studied the prints and gloomed for a minute. Then he shrugged. "All right, Charley. Just hang on to them, will you?"

"Sure."

Burch went out and MacBride started his first pipe of the day, puffing up slowly. It had been a stab in the dark that had come to nothing. The person that had fallen in that alley was likely an honest one. The bare chance had fizzled. But it didn't squelch the skipper's appreciable opinion of himself. He still believed that he had done right by lifting that chunk of mud and taking it to Burch. You never could tell. His ego was a healthy one: he believed himself the equal of any gunman and a shade better than most. This may not make a master mind, but it's the stock in trade of a good cop. And the skipper was not a bad one. Long service had ground him to a tool that while it had not the fine cutting edge of steel, still had the wallop of iron.

The door opened and MacBride sensed trouble before he looked up. He was not wrong.

Kennedy came in, coughing. He wore an old spring topcoat, bedraggled, and a crumpled wet hat.

"You're going to slam out one of these days," MacBride said.

"Not if you give me a little nourishment."

"Got none."

"In that right-hand drawer. I saw it yesterday."

MacBride gave up and dragged out the bottle. Kennedy took a drink large enough to floor an ox. His cough vanished instantly. His young-old face brightened, then became droll.

"I just dropped around," he drawled, "to see what became of your precious bit of terra firma?"

"Huh?"

"The mud."

MacBride looked guilty. "Nothing." He took a drink himself. "So far," he added, and the guilt vanished. "If that's all you want, get the hell out!"

Kennedy lit up. "Get the slugs?"

"Yeah. Two of them'd been dipped in garlic. You know what that does."

"Imagine!"

"If they were in your guts you wouldn't have to imagine."

Kennedy held the cigarette before him and stared dreamily at the window. He sat down and took half a dozen slow meditative puffs, sopping his wet shoes on the floor. Gradually a light came into his weary eyes.

"Cap."

"M-m-m."

Kennedy got up slowly and dragged his wet shoes up and down the floor. His wet coat left raindrops on the floor and on the chairs he passed.

"Cap." He stopped and turned. "Five months ago... over on the South Side. In one of those creep-joints. You remember that gunfight over a stud game?"

"I was on leave. Besides, I don't often get over that way."

"Well, I was there. Johno the Spic was running the creep-joint—moving it every night or so to a new flat. It happened finally in Sara Street, in a Greek rooming-house, top floor. Johno, Bubby Kline, Rocky Moorehead—and two dinges, Sam White and Wash Johnson, a couple of lippy-chasers. I think Nasson and Hoppe, out of the Sixth Precinct, were on the job. Well, it wasn't much. I mean, Johno the Spic was down to case-dough and Rocky Moorehead accused him of pulling an acecrey-outcrey."

"What's that?"

"Putting an ace on the bottom of the deck so he—Johno was the dealer—so he could extract it to fill a suit. In a minute there's heat. Johno goes for his rod and so does Rocky, and Johno gets it in the arm. There were no arrests. But Johno was laid up for a long time. You see, old tomato, Rocky's bullet had been dipped in garlic."

MacBride picked up the bottle and thumped it down again. "Have another drink, Kennedy."

"Johno swore to hell he'd get Rocky, but I don't think be ever did."

"What was Rocky doing for a living at the time?"

"They say he was on the muscle in the cleaners' and wet-wash

racket. He used to be an airdale on the river, too. Never very impor-tant. Hell, I don't think he was ever booked. I haven't seen him around. But Bubby Kline said he sure looked like a torpedo the night he fogged Johno—and the two jiggabos there damned near turned white."

"And Nasson and Hoppe were on it?"

"Well, they just went around. It was kind of a private scrap, and nobody'd press a charge. Nasson and Hoppe and I chased them out and sat around finishing the liquor. It was good, too—real McCoy, old horse."

MacBride corked the bottle. "You're really a good guy to have around, Kennedy. You remember things. That's the only other time I heard of a gun in this burg using garlic-dipped bullets. If it's Rocky Moorehead—and I'm not saying it is—what the hell was he doing in Little Italy? There's no graft there—for the cleaners and wet-wash."

"A hot torpedo doesn't stay in one racket long, Cap. He might have changed bosses."

MacBride leaned back, thinning his eyelids. "I think it wouldn't do any harm to see if Rocky is in town." He reached for the phone, said into it, "Tell Cohen to come up here... I don't care if he is playing rummy!" He hung up, growled: "Sometimes I think Headquarters is a kind of country club, no fooling!"

Chapter IV

RICHMOND CITY had never been a cop's paradise. It was a tough town from the roots up, and growing fast. It had woolen mills, shoe factories, some garment trade, and a big novelty jewelry business. It was only a few miles from the Atlantic, on a navigable river; and its railroad yards covered a lot of territory. If its gangs were itinerant, they at least raised havoc any time an opportunity presented itself. Under-policed, the city was naturally the way-station of many a gangster notorious in a dozen states.

MacBride could remember the days when its trolley cars burned wood-stoves in winter, and when a cop's job was considered a snap. He had hardened as the town hardened. A lot of guys called him bullet-proof, shock-proof, and graft-proof. The last was a brass-bound fact; else today the skipper would have been driving a Cadillac instead of a Ford nor would he be worrying about the heavy premium on insurance policies.

"You remember that case, don't you, Nasson?" he said to that detective in the Sixth Precinct house.

"Sure. Now I remember it. Is that slob Rocky a red-hot?"

"I don't know. But I'll consider it a favor, Nasson, if you'll nose around and see if he's working this neighborhood. Tell Hoppe, too. I'm probably up a wrong tree, but I'll take a chance."

"Do all I can, Cap, and sure glad to."

"Thanks, Nasson. I won't forget it."

Meanwhile Ike Cohen was prowling the city with his nose to the ground. He had his stoolies on the walkabout. Moriarity was on the job, too. He hadn't found anything in Little Italy. So far as he could determine, Little Italy was temporarily clean. The fruit and vegetable trade had not yet been smacked by the extortionists, and the killing of Pietro Matteo was indeed a mystery.

Leaving Nasson, MacBride made an aimless tour of the South Side. Once it had been his precinct, long years ago, when a stabbing was something to talk about and a murder rated headlines for a week. Now, the killing of Matteo was not even on the second page—and it was only three days old. And Mrs. Matteo was in the hospital: relapse. The neighbors were taking care of the kids.

Rounding a corner cigar store, MacBride ran into a familiar figure. "Well, hello, Johno."

Johno the Spic looked like money. "Well—if it ain't Captain MacBride himself!"

"You're looking good, Johno."

"Yeah, I'm swell."

"In the real dough, eh?"

Johno laughed good-naturedly. He was a small, white-faced, chubby man, with black, shiny eyes and red, soft lips. His clothes were the extreme of the prevailing mode and he wore ridiculous sideburns, a small-brimmed derby.

"Cards?" said MacBride.

"Nix. It ain't a gentleman's game no more."

"Booze, eh?"

"If I'm greasin' it with the right guys, what's wrong with that, Cap?" He laughed, saluted. "Happy days!"

MacBride drowsed on the curb, watching Johno strut away. When a guy talked fast like that he was getting up in the world. Alky? No doubt. And it would be all right so long as a guy didn't go for the heat. Those who had risen from the gutter and flopped back, or taken hot lead at the peak of their glory—their names were legend over the past ten years.

"I wonder," MacBride thought, "if he still holds that grudge against Rocky Moorehead."

He moved on, and his peregrinations began to assume a purpose. He made half a dozen stops: in restaurants, barbershops, two speakeasies. In each he drew a man aside and said:

"I'm looking for Rocky Moorehead. If you get wised where he's hanging around, tip me off."

Invariably the answer was: "Sure—sure, boss."

They were all copper-hearted—stoolies—not by inclination but by force of circumstances. Once, or maybe a couple of times, they had slipped: petty robbery, a lush job; and they enjoyed the freedom of the city by informing the man whose retarded hand had kept them from jail. This had the effect of keeping them to the straight and narrow, too.

Another two days passed. Pietro Matteo was buried on a hill that overlooked the city. His wife was in the hospital. Friends gathered around the grave and Father Viviani read the service. MacBride sent flowers and went up the hill to stand in the background. Little Italy had been his hobby. He had cleaned up—or thought he had. They were simple, good-natured folks, these poor dagos. It was the wiseacre wops that caused all the trouble.

"It is but the beginning, Captain," Father Viviani said, his round red face beatific.

MacBride, who had it figured out he was a Presbyterian, but was never certain, nodded and said: "Yes, Father," and walked down the hill, thinking. Then the city was around him, roaring; work flooded him; and death went gently into limbo.

ON the sixth day, at noon, the skipper was munching a liverwurst sandwich and taking swigs at a bottle of five percent beer, when he heard a commotion outside his door. He took a last drag at the bottle and hid it; finished the sandwich and began rustling papers industriously.

The door whipped open and a man took a header in. MacBride watched him regain his balance, and looked at Moriarity and Cohen as the two dicks stalked in and Cohen slammed the door shut so hard that a picture of a former police commissioner dropped from the wall and smashed.

MacBride said: "Now look, Ike—now look!"

Cohen was mad. "Well, this punk tried to give us an argument."

"Who is he?"

Moriarity was cooler, but no less angry. "Rocky Moorehead."

Rocky weaved around and then flopped into the nearest chair, his eyes bitter and his mouth working. "Where do you rate that stuff, you two flatfoots!"

"Sock him, Ike," clipped Moriarity.

"I'll sock him! I'll bust a radiator over his head!"

"Hey!" barked MacBride.

The two plainclothes men stood glowering.

"I don't care!" snapped Cohen. "The punk's been spieling dirty names ever since we picked him up. He's a wise guy; that's what he is! A tough baby! A real big shot! Yes, he is—he is—my eye!"

"All right, all right," MacBride said. "Hamburger down, boys—"

"You dirty flatfoots!" Rocky snarled.

"You too!" roared MacBride. "Cut your chops—mind your own business!"

"Well, for cryin' out loud—"

"Well—well—well!" MacBride crackled. He slammed down his fist. "Shut up! Who's running this joint? I'll take a swing at the whole damned lot o' you!"

Gradually the electricity in the room subsided. Rocky breathed heavily in the chair and the two plainclothes men bit their lips to silence, though their eyes were still mutinous. MacBride sat back creaking his chair slowly and watching Rocky fidget with his hat. Rocky was a lean, tight-jawed tough with straw-colored hair clipped close, and glassy blue eyes.

"Now," MacBride said, "I hope everybody is calm."

"Ah-r-r," growled Rocky.

"Where were you on the night of May fourth, Rocky, between ten and eleven o'clock?"

"I was in a movie."

"Anybody with you?"

"A frill."

"I suppose she'll come here and swear you were with her."

"Say, nix on that, Skipper. I only seen her once. She said she was leavin' town next day."

"Where'd she go?"

"I didn't ask her."

MacBride shook his head. "That doesn't go, Rocky."

"The hell it doesn't! And thanks for the feelers! I'm strictly kosher, see—I'm clean and on the up and up. You hams ain't got nothin' on me—"

"Hold on, Rocky." MacBride leaned elbows on the desk. "What's your racket these days?"

"Ixnay on that, too. I'm clean, see. I don't have to answer any questions. What the hell am I here for anyhow?"

MacBride looked at his men. "D'you get his rod?"

"Yeah," Cohen said, and handed over a .38 automatic. "The slugs are clean, Cap, but that don't mean a thing."

MacBride looked at the gun. "When did you give up using garlic, Rocky?"

"What you mean now?"

"You used to use it, Rocky. You used it on Johno the Spic six months ago."

"What—is that punk been bumped off?"

"No."

Impatient, Rocky got up. "What the hell am I here for?"

MacBride shoved back his chair and rose. "Come on," he said.

He took Rocky down to the Bureau of Criminal Identification, in the basement. Burch got up from a stool.

"Take this guy, Charlie," MacBride said.

Rocky recoiled. "You guys can't do this! I'm clean. You ain't got no right—"

MacBride shoved him and Burch caught hold of his right hand. Rocky cursed a blue streak, but the two men rough-housed him to the desk. Burch splayed Rocky's fingers and placed them on a square of black. Then he raised the hand and placed each finger, one at a time, in five small squares on a sheet of white paper. Then he released the hand.

MacBride said: "Check that against the one you took from the hunk of mud, Charlie. Call me.... Upstairs, Rocky."

Back in MacBride's office, Rocky became sullen.

When Burch called up, MacBride listened, sighed, said: "Thanks, Charlie," and hung up.

Moriarity and Cohen were watching him closely. He shrugged and shook his head. Cohen cursed.

Rocky sprang up. "Okey. You guys have been up a blind alley. Gimme my hat. I'm goin' outta here. Wise guys, eh? Ah-r-r, horse-feathers—for all o'you guys! You, Cohen; and you, Moriarity and you, too, Skipper! Rats for all of you!"

"Ike, Mory," MacBride said, "take this loud-mouthed jazzbo downstairs and lock him up for a while."

"Hey!" yelled Rocky.

Moriarity went towards him. Rocky made a pass at Moriarity and Cohen jumped over and clipped Rocky on the jaw. Then both dicks gripped him and ran him out of the office.

When they had gone, MacBride paced up and down slowly, gnawing his lips. Suddenly he stopped by the desk, opened a drawer and drew out two of the spent slugs that had helped kill Matteo. His hand closed over them.

He made a telephone call. "Joe, I've got a gun up here and some slugs. I'd like you to see if they match. Are you busy?... All right, I'll bring 'em down."

At two o'clock the gun expert said that the spent slugs had not been fired from the gun that was taken from Rocky Moorehead.

At two-thirty Rocky sailed out of Headquarters snarling: "Horse on you, Skipper."

"Some day I'll nail you, Rocky."

MacBRIDE was stumped. He hadn't a thing on Rocky and he knew it. The findings of the Department's experts, both in the matter of the fingerprints and the gun, had automatically cleared Rocky. What MacBride believed was a different matter. He knew Rocky was a gunman, one of those rare gunmen still to reach a police blotter. But he couldn't hang anything on the man.

Cohen said: "Anyhow, I believe that guy's in the know. I've got my stoolies watching him."

MacBride said: "If Matteo had been a big shot, this case would cause a lot of attention. As it is, only a dago was killed—a dago nobody'd ever heard of. But we're hot on it, Ike. There's a racket of some kind on the make that we don't know about. Matteo was killed because of it. I don't believe it was a personal feud. Matteo knew something and very likely he threatened them if they didn't let him alone. He must have thought that would stop it. He wasn't the kind of guy to run to the police."

"But you never know in Little Italy," Cohen argued. "They're close-mouthed, those babies. What we should have done was hold that guy Rocky."

"He would have been out by now anyhow. A writ's so easy to get nowadays that if you haven't got a red-hot cold it's a la-de-da for him and a kick in the pants for us. Don't tell me my business, Ike. I know when to hold a guy. And I know when not to hold him. I'm getting the razzberry in certain quarters as it is. I'm not going to be a complete goof by holding a guy just for spite. If he knows I'll get him, Ike—I'll get him."

"Wire me when you do, Cap."

"Listen, you! If you don't respect me at least respect the fact that I'm your boss!"

"I think I'll go around and shoot some pool."

Chapter V

MacBRIDE continued to get the gentle razzberry. He might have dropped the case, let it die a natural death. It would have joined many others. Who was Matteo? Why should a captain attached to Headquarters bother himself with small fry?

But the rub lay in the fact that MacBride was beginning to get his dander up. He could stand a certain amount of razzing, but his powers of resistance in that respect were not manifold. He had pride, a temper, and in some ways he was stubborn.

He would not dump the Matteo kill into oblivion. He got his own stoolies working. He kept Moriarity and Cohen in the jump. He sent out two under-cover men. In two days he found out the mob Rocky Moorhead was running with. Cohen had said this couldn't be done. It was irony for him when one of his own stoolies turned in the information.

"Now," said MacBride, "maybe you know who's running this end of the Department."

"Oh, well," said Cohen, good-naturedly.

MacBride took a cab across town to Jockey Street. It was three in the afternoon when he entered the *Hunt Club*, a flashy dive run by Maxie Bloomberg. The cabaret was dark and the bar off the side was empty but for a couple of waiters and the barman.

"Maxie in?" MacBride said.

"No, Skipper."

"Well, that's all right. I want to see Baxter anyhow. Just a friendly call."

The barman made a telephone call and five minutes later Case Baxter came downstairs and asked MacBride into a back room. Baxter was an easygoing racketeer.

"What have I done, Cap?"

"You're strictly alky, aren't you?"

"You know me."

MacBride started a pipe. "You've got a torpedo in your mob, Baxter, that may run into a lot of grease one day."

"Who?"

"Rocky Moorehead."

"A couple of your guys picked him up the other day. Hell, Cap, Rocky don't go around Little Italy."

"How do you know that I wanted him for anything around Little Italy, Baxter?"

Baxter's eyes became blank for half a minute. Then he chuckled and shot smoke through his long nose. "That was a fast one, wasn't it? Well, I'll tell you. There was a dago over there shot with garlic-dipped bullets. There used to be a rumor around that Rocky did that sort of thing."

"You're pretty fast yourself, Baxter."

"Hell, Rocky came back here all steamed up. He didn't even know why he'd been picked up. Until I told him." He wagged his head. "No, Cap, you're on a bum steer here. When Rocky came with me I broke him of that habit of using garlic. And he's no torpedo, Cap, if that's what's worrying you. He drives one of my trucks. That's open and shut."

MacBride scowled. "You're sure it's nothing but alky you're in, Baxter. You're sure about that, eh?"

"Positive. Just an everyday bootlegger, Cap, trying to make ends meet. It's been rough sledding lately. We lost a truck of real McCoy last week on the North Road. Was this dago Matteo a big shot after all?"

"No. If he was a big shot it would be easy. He was just a plain honest dago that got a dirty deal."

"That's too bad."

"All right, Baxter. But get this: I don't care what you say, Rocky's a torpedo. He's a snotty guy, too, and that don't go with me. Tell him that."

There was a furious knocking on the door.

"Come in," said Baxter.

The barman knocked open the door and shouted: "Telephone!"

"I'll go along," MacBride said.

Baxter went out ahead of him into the bar and picked up the telephone.

"Hello…. Yes…. What!… Where, Louie?… Okey." He hung up and his lips tightened, the color drained from his face.

MacBride stopped. "Trouble, Baxter?"

"No." Baxter headed for the back room.

"Hey," MacBride said.

Baxter turned, his eyes blazing. "Well, if you want to know—Rocky just got the works."

"Where?"

"Warren Street and Commercial—Rock Hollow. And ten to one it was one of your lousy cops!"

THE skipper arrived at the corner of Commercial Alley in a taxi-cab. An ambulance was standing by and a couple of policemen were trying to keep the crowd back. MacBride elbowed his way through.

"Where is he?" MacBride asked.

"Right by the wall, Cap," one of the cops said. "There's another guy up the alley a bit."

MacBride took one look at Rocky Moorehead and then headed up the alley. There was another crowd, and when he plowed through it he found the ambulance doctor kneeling beside the body of a man. The doctor stood up.

"Well, that's that," he said.

"What?" barked MacBride.

"Who are you?"

MacBride flashed his badge.

The doctor said: "Well, he's dead, too—that's all."

"This his gun?"

"I guess so."

MacBride pocketed a revolver and bent down to look at the dead man. It was a face he had never seen before. He stood up and swore under his breath; strode back to the corner and found Patrolman Hahn hefting a big .45.

"This was this guy's," Hahn said.

"Yeah," said MacBride. "Anybody see the shooting?"

"No. There's a jane inside, though. This guy must have come out and met the hot stuff right here."

"Where's the jane?"

"Room at the back of the hall, left."

MacBride entered the red brick house and found Kennedy sitting on a bed looking at a girl.

"You certainly get around, Kennedy."

"Yeah, I get around."

The girl was a red-head, and she held a blue dressing-gown tightly around her waist.

"Who are you?" she snapped.

Kennedy said: "Oh, he's only Captain Stephen J. MacBride, a boy scout from Headquarters."

"What's your name, sister?" MacBride clipped.

"Marge Wilshire. And what's the boy scout want?"

"Now, don't get hard-boiled, girlie. I'm not going to pick on you. Was Rocky in here?"

"Sure. Sure, he was in here. He went out of here, though. He wasn't shot in here. He wasn't shot in here at all."

"Did you see the shooting?"

"No. I was in here. How could I?"

Baxter appeared and leaned indolently in the doorway. "I came right over," he said. "I bury my men."

"Well. I guess you found out it wasn't a cop did it," MacBride shot back.

"Who's the broad?"

"Friend of Rocky's."

Baxter eyed her dully. "I never heard of you, sister."

"And I never heard of you, brother."

"I was Rocky's boss."

MacBride cut in: "Blow wise and beat it, Baxter."

"I'm waiting for an undertaker."

"Send him around to the morgue tomorrow."

Baxter shrugged, took another sinister look at the girl, and then went out slowly.

"Look here," the girl began. "I've got nothing to do with this. Is it my fault if a guy walks out and gets shot outside my door? How can I help it?"

"If you'd only calm down," MacBride said. "How long have you known Rocky?"

"A year—on and off."

"Did Rocky tell you anything, girlie?"

"Oh, well—just a lot of noise. He always was a lot of noise—but funny sometimes. And he had the dough. Today he was kind of drunk. Not much. Just kind of. He was shooting off about a rough raw deal the cops handed him. And he said something about—I don't know—something about he was getting the lowdown on some guy. I guess he thought some guys tried to frame him with the cops. He said: 'I'll show that skipper. I'll find the guy pulled that job in Little Italy and I'll wise up a dick who's a particular friend o' mine,' he said. He said: 'I'll give the pinch to this dick and leave that wise skipper holdin' his hand on his neck.' He was all steamed up and plastered. Don't think I'm in on this!"

"What time did he leave here?"

"Ten past three. I heard him walk down the hall. I heard the front door open. It didn't close, because right then I heard two shots, and then one more—close—like as if Rocky fired back, And then there were some more. I don't know—maybe three or four. I was so scared."

MacBride thought for a moment. Then he said: "Well, stay in here. I'll see you're not bothered, if I can help it. Just take it easy, girlie."

She laughed jerkily. "Gosh. Captain, you ain't as bad as a lot of guys say you are. You're a pretty swell guy, ain't you?"

He grinned. "Come on, Kennedy."

MacBride reached the street as the morgue bus was drawing up. Baxter was standing against the house-wall with two of his men. He was smoking a cigarette with quick puffs. His eyes glittered.

MacBride went over and tapped him on the chest. "Remember, Baxter, I'm on this job."

Baxter said nothing. He kept on puffing rapidly, shifting his eyes over the crowd.

"Remember," MacBride said. "I've got a hot hunch, see. And I don't want you or any of your wipers busting around town with a lot of loose artillery."

"You think you're the berries, don't you, Skipper?"

"Just remember, Baxter."

Chapter VI

AT seven that night MacBride sat at his desk. Before him were two guns. One was a .45 automatic, with three bullets discharged. Rocky had used this gun against his assailants. MacBride assumed that Rocky had been attacked, had fought back, spending three shells before he collapsed.

The other gun was a .38 Colt's special, with every chamber empty. This was the gun MacBride had taken from the dead man in the alley. The man was still unidentified. No likeness of him was in Headquarters; no fingerprint. Why had he waited for Rocky outside that shady red brick house? Had the woman lured Rocky there? He spoke the question aloud.

Kennedy, sprawled in a chair, spoke from beneath his hat brim: "I don't think she did, Cap. This guy must have tailed Rocky there and waited for him to come out. He was waiting for him. No doubt about that. And he was a real torpedo. No guy but a hot torpedo would empty a gun that way."

"And we don't know him. Case Baxter took a look at him and said he didn't know him. It has all the earmarks of a mob job, and yet the guy is unknown."

"A visitor no doubt, old tomato. Rocky knew him. Anyhow, I think the broad was telling the truth. Rocky had a line on the guy that killed Matteo. The guy found out—and silenced Rocky. Now—well, why not say that's the guy that killed Matteo and pigeon-hole the whole shebang?"

MacBride frowned, puzzled. "But that seems too simple, Kennedy."

"It would satisfy me."

The telephone rang and MacBride unhooked it. "Yeah, this is MacBride.... I get you.... Six, eh? What's that?... And two were... Yeah, I get you."

The skipper hung up, leaned back slowly, and bent squinted eyes on Kennedy. "What do you think, Kennedy?"

"Shoot."

"Rocky had six bullets in him. Six .38's. Only one, kiddo—just one—was dipped in garlic."

Kennedy whistled and came up from beneath his hat brim. "Why only one, Cap?"

"Just this, Kennedy." MacBride extended a fist across the table. "There were two guys waiting for Rocky. Not one. *Two*. One of them was the guy we find in the alley. The other got away."

He reached into his coat pocket and drew out a slip of paper. He had taken it from the dead man's pocket. Written in pencil were the names and addresses of six persons. Beside each name was written an amount of money, the items ranging from two hundred to four hundred dollars. MacBride studied them for a moment, then stood up. He grabbed his hat.

"I'll be seeing you, Kennedy."

He buzzed Keyser from the reserve room and told him to get out the flivver. He waited out front, and when Keyser drew up to the curb MacBride gave him an address. The first address MacBride chose was in a Polack neighborhood—not far from Police Headquarters. Kowalski was the name.

Kowalski ran a candy shop and spoke very little English. He had been in the country five years. His wife spoke no English at all. But there was a clerk in the store who acted as an interpreter.

"It's this way," MacBride said. "We found a list of names on a guy was bumped off this afternoon. Your boss's is one of them, and it looks to me like a shake-down. What I want to know is, was a guy in here trying to extort money out of Mr. Kowalski?"

The clerk spoke with Kowalski at length, and the Pole, looking mystified all the time, finally shook his head. MacBride went on harassing him for fifteen minutes, then gave it up. He told the clerk to notify him immediately if anybody tried to shake down the boss. He walked out and gave Keyser another address.

By nine o'clock he had made his fifth call, with no material success. What impressed him, however, was that all the men were foreigners. They spoke very little English, and they were located all over the town. The law frightened them. They knew very little about the law, and it took a lot of fast talking on MacBride's part to put them at ease.

This was not an ordinary extortionist racket. All of the men were in different lines of business, in different neighborhoods. None of them ran a speakeasy. All of them seemed like honest, hardworking men, with families. The list of names, MacBride reasoned, was of those men who had not yet been approached by the dead man or his accomplice.

"Well, Keyser," he said, "there's one more."

Adolph Koenig ran a bakeshop on the South Side. He was closing up when MacBride walked in. He was a short fat man, with red cherubic cheeks.

"Mr. Koenig, I'm Captain MacBride, from Police Headquarters."

"Ja?"

MacBride leaned on the counter. "I want to know if anybody's been here bothering you. I mean, if any man or men have come in here and tried to make you give them money."

Koenig blinked and shook his head. "Nein."

"Your name's on this paper here along with some others. We believe somebody's been working the neighborhood. We found this on the body of a man who was killed by another gangster this afternoon."

"Himmel! Killed!"

"Yes."

Koenig shook his head. "Dere vass nobuddy come here, Captain." He picked up a late edition, pointed to two faces on the front page. "Dis?"

The newsmen had taken pictures of the dead men and touched up the faces.

"Yes," MacBride nodded, and pointed to a vague likeness of the unidentified man. "This was the man I thought might have bothered you."

Koenig took off his spectacles, polished them, and put them back on his nose again. "You vait just vun minute, Captain." He went to the rear and telephoned. He spoke in German for a couple of minutes, getting excited toward the end. Then he hung up and came back to the counter.

"You vait just anodder minute, Captain."

Presently a hatless man came in. He resembled Adolph Koenig, but looked younger.

"Dis is mein brudder," Adolph said. He picked up the late edition again, spread it, looked at Adolph and pointed to the picture of the unidentified man. "Hans, dis is it, no?"

Hans, nervous, not yet sure of himself in the presence of the law, nodded and said: "Ja!"

"Den tell de Captain, Hans! Himmel, tell him!"

Hans was still reluctant. He was afraid. But his older brother kept urging him, and finally he began.

Hans ran a small meat shop in the next block. He was married and had two children and was fairly prosperous. He had been in America six years and his brother had loaned him money in the beginning to start his business. Everything went along fine.

A month ago he had bought a car. It was second-hand and cost him four hundred and fifty dollars. He was proud of it, even though friends had warned him against buying a second-hand car. About three weeks ago, two men had come into his store. One of them showed a badge and had a lot of important-looking papers in his hand. The men wanted to see his car. They were from the Motor Vehicle Bureau.

Hans showed them the car. They lifted the hood and looked at the engine number and serial number. They looked at the papers. Then one of them said that it was a stolen car and would have to be given up. Hans argued. He had paid good money for it. The two men shook their heads and said that it was a penal offense, that he would be jailed for receiving stolen property. Hans got all hot and bothered and pleaded with them. Finally they offered to say nothing about it on receipt of two hundred dollars. Hans paid, with the understanding that he would not mention a word of the deal to anyone. Then they left.

"Und dat," said Hans, pointing to the picture of the unidentified man, "vass vun of dem."

MacBride began to expand. "Hans, you've been gypped. Those men were not from the Motor Vehicle Bureau. Their badges and papers were faked. It's too bad, Hans."

"Just vhat I told you!" reprimanded Adolph.

MacBride left and revisited the other five men upon whom he had made calls. Each of them had bought a second-hand car within the past six weeks.

He drove off with Keyser, saying: "Now I begin to see it, Keyser. The second-hand car racket. Pietro Matteo bought a car too. They approached him. He bluffed them, and they thought he might spring their racket to a cop. So they bumped him off."

"But there were two guys, Cap. Who was the other guy?"

"Hans gave me a sort of hazy description. It fits several guys I've seen around town lately. I'll take a Brody. I bet I get the real guy. How much you want to bet, Keyser?"

"I'm broke."

"And Kennedy is always broke, so I'm out of luck."

Chapter VII

ALONE on foot, the skipper was prowling the South Side at eleven that night. He knew the district of old; he'd policed it in days gone by. He heard a muffled jazz band in a dark quiet street. He slowed down and entered a doorway beyond which was a wide wooden staircase that led him to regions above.

A cabaret was upstairs, a cheap joint. The lights were dim and fifty-odd persons, women and men, sat at tables and drank second-rate liquor. The four-piece band was taking a breathing spell, and a buzz of conversation came through the skeins of cigarette smoke.

MacBride went through to an office in the rear and found Mike O'Hara, the owner, drinking with two men. O'Hara looked up and shifted his cigar.

"Hello, stranger!"

"Hello, Mike. Like to have a talk with you."

O'Hara said: "Beat it, boys," to the two men. They went out.

MacBride sat down. "I've been walking my feet off, Mike."

"On a tail?"

"Yeah. And maybe you can help me. I gave you many a break in my day, Mike."

O'Hara tightened up and stopped puffing on the cigar. "Well—sure, Cap."

"Johno the Spic."

"He ain't in my scatter, Cap. I don't do business with that guy. Not me, Cap."

MacBride was patient. "I know, Mike—I know. But he hangs around the South Side and this is one of the joints he stops in."

"Well, what can I do?"

MacBride shifted his pipe. "I just want to know where I can find him. I'd like to have a quiet little talk with him."

"You're liable to find him in any joint around here."

"I don't mean that, Mike. Where does he flop."

O'Hara fingered his collar. He got up and lunged around the room.

He stopped short and spread his palms.

"Jeeze, Skipper!"

"Lay off, Mike. He's not in your crowd. He doesn't mean a thing to you. For all I know—so far—he might not mean a thing to me. But I want to talk to him. And you know where he is. Don't try to pull an act on me."

O'Hara flopped back to the chair. "Well—well, I sent a case o' Scotch around to Twenty-two Low Street a couple o' weeks ago."

"How come a guy that's in the alky business buys it from you?"

"Who said he's in the alky business?"

MacBride got up, put on his hat. "Well, many thanks, Mike."

The jazz band burst forth as MacBride tramped among the tables. He descended the stairway to the street and walked downhill. The night was mellow, and the jazz band didn't sound so bad at a distance. There was a pool-parlor at the next corner, dingy, with stained windows. The sound of balls smacking re-echoed sharply in the quiet night.

MacBride rounding the corner into Low Street, glanced negligently through the open door and then stopped. Johno was standing behind one of three tables leaning on a cue. There were eight other men in the place. MacBride took a pull at his hat and drifted in. Most of them did not know him and gave him only a passing glance. Johno was bending over the table and MacBride stopped to watch him make a shot.

"Not so bad, Johno," he said.

Johno the Spic looked up. He remained bent over the table, rings shining on his fingers, his black lustrous eyes looking up absently at the skipper.

"Well—well, Cap! Ain't you out late?" He straightened and stepped back to allow the other man room, and while watching his play, said: "How's your game these days, Cap?"

"Lousy."

"H-m-m."

"Because I'm too busy playing other games, Johno."

"H-m-m. That so?... Watch the English on this."

MacBride watched. "That's really swell, Johno."

Johno shrugged in a self-deprecatory manner. "Punk, that shot."

"When you're finished, Johno, let's you and me take a walk around the block."

"Huh?" Johno looked up quizzically.

MacBride sighed. "Yeah, Johno. Just around the block. Maybe you can help me in a certain little thing. I'm stumped, Johno. I need help. Be a good guy."

Johno wrinkled his forehead and looked perplexed. Then he turned and set by his cue. "Sure, Cap. The game can wait."

They went out and MacBride turned down Low Street. "It's about an old enemy of yours, Johno."

"Who?"

"Rocky Moorehead. You know he was bumped off. He was bumped off in Rock Hollow. And," MacBride lied, "somebody said you were in the neighborhood. Wasn't that coincidence?"

"You hard up for a pinch?"

MacBride chuckled. "Me? No. Didn't the guy that plugged Rocky get his, too?"

"Yeah. But where do I fit in?"

"You were in the neighborhood, weren't you, Johno?"

Johno's eyes glittered in the darkness and his shoulders rolled. His footsteps were soft alongside MacBride's. Dark store fronts moved by.

"Weren't you, Johno?"

"No. No, I wasn't." He stopped short, his white face hunched between his shoulders. "Cut the comedy, Skipper. What's the idea of pickin' on me?"

"Have you ever seen the inside of Police Headquarters, Johno?"

"No! And I ain't gonna!" snarled Johno, his teeth showing in the gloom. "Don't take me for a gofor, Skipper. Speak your piece and then blow."

MacBride was oddly placid. "Don't get tough, Johno."

"I ain't gettin' tough. I'm just tellin' you, Shamus—just tellin' you. Thanks for the walk. Good-night."

He swung on his heel. MacBride started after him and fell in step beside him.

"You're taking the wrong attitude, Johno," be said. "You're getting all steamed up."

Johno stopped again. "Listen, flatfoot. Beat it. I don't know anything, see. I'm clean."

MacBride made a grab for his arm. "Then you've got to prove it, Johno."

Johno twisted violently, a short snarl in his voice. He broke loose, struck an ash can and toppled with it. MacBride drew his gun and was swinging towards Johno when he saw a shadow detach itself from a doorway twenty yards up the street. Flame burst from the shadow. A bullet clanged in the ash can. MacBride, twisting, fired across his stomach twice and heard a scream.

Johno was up and bolting across the street, looking over his shoulder, his gun raised.

"Johno!" yelled MacBride.

Johno's gun belched red and the bullet clicked close past MacBride's head. The skipper cut loose. His gun boomed twice. Johno buckled, hit his knees and slammed into the curbstone head on. But he writhed away frantically, moaning, clawing the pavement. He looked back with blazing eyes and raised his gun. His hand shook. The muzzle spewed flame into the darkness. The shot went wild.

MacBride fired again at the crawling man, barking: "You're asking for it, Johno."

Bang! went Johno's gun again. His whole arm shook. He could not have hit a pole at twenty feet in that condition.

He screamed: "I'll get you, Skipper!"

"Not in these pants, Johno."

Bang! went MacBride's gun.

Johno heaved over the curb and sprawled on his back. He let go his gun and rocked from side to side, arching his back, beating the pavement with his fists.

MacBride bent down and picked up Johno's gun. He thrust it into one of his pockets and looked up the street. He saw two men running towards him. He caught the dim flash of buttons.

"Oh!" Johno groaned.

"Well," said MacBride, "you went and asked for it."

Chapter VIII

AT three in the morning Kennedy, Moriarity and Cohen (and a news photographer named Wilson) were sprawled around Mac-Bride's office. The desk was littered with paper napkins and the men were drinking black coffee and munching hot hamburgers which had been brought in. Kennedy was lounging on the desk among the paper napkins. Nobody was talking. All were eating. Until Kennedy finished his sandwich and looked at the clock on the wall.

The door swung open and the skipper barged in. His hat was dented in and slewed over one eyebrow and he looked drawn.

Finally Kennedy sighed and said: "Well, Cap, too bad it was a false alarm."

MacBride looked up—glared. "Who said it was a false alarm?"

"Open up, Skipper."

MacBride drained a mug of coffee and banged it down. He leaned back expansively, hooking thumbs in vest.

"All right, you guys that gave me the razzberry—get this: Johno the Spic is in the hospital. He'll recover, and when he does he'll go on trial for the murder of Pietro Matteo. Also for killing Rocky Moorehead, which is a minor offense in my mind—but it helps. He'll fry on the hot-seat, bimboes.

"I got his fingerprints while he was unconscious in the hospital. The guy tried to slam me was a punk named Billy Griff from Toledo. I fogged that baby clean. The guy took the dose from Rocky was a red-hot from Kansas City named Speed Davis, Jack Davidson, and Dave Jackson—all in one. The three of them were running their racket in this burg: Johno, Davis and Griff.

"The gun we found on the guy in the alley in Rock Hollow was Johno's. Johno dropped his and picked up his pal's and beat it on through the alley. The gun he dropped was the one from which the garlic-dipped bullets were fired. Johno was a lousy shot.

"Well, I got his prints, guys. And what do you think? Well, his prints tally with the ones we got from that chunk of mud I lifted the night Matteo was killed. They're Johno's fingerprints. He babbled a lot before he went unconscious. He thought he was going to die. He got the garlic idea from the time Rocky used one on him in that card fight on the South Side."

"How many guys did they gyp in their racket?" Kennedy asked.

"Hell knows. A lot. They had it all figured out. They used to make out they were in a cut-rate equipment outfit. They'd get the names from the second-hand car dealers and then weed them out. They always picked on a guy in one of the foreign settlements. I've got the forged badges and papers from Johno's flat. Pietro Matteo was the first guy that called their bluff. Billy Griff was the real torpedo of the mob and he talked them into killing the dago. Rocky got wise somehow.

It was the garlic-dipped bullets, I guess. Because Johno once said he'd get square with Rocky for that fight over the cards—and give him a dose of his own medicine. Rocky talked too much though, and somebody tipped Johno that Rocky was looking for him. So they got Rocky."

Kennedy smiled. "You're sure some old tomato."

"Thanks for the flowers, Kennedy. But I haven't forgot the razzberries."

Some Die Young

Capt. MacBride follows a murder trail to the bitter end.

Chapter I

SHE was dead.

She was young and she was dead and she lay on the ochre-tiled floor of the roof-garden. On her back. Her body was twisted at the waist and her white arms were outflung and her head—with its spun-gold hair—lay on one side. Her green frock had dark spots on it and—twisted as she was—the inside of her left knee rested on the inside of her right.

The chair on which she had sat lay beside her, overturned. Warm summer stars twinkled and a warm breeze clicked in the fronds of potted palms.

A blue screen, decorated with birds of paradise, mercifully hid her from the rest of the roof-garden.

Ohms, the hotel manager, short, bald, spade-bearded, took nervous steps up and down in the roofed anteroom and kept patting his pink cheeks with a silk handkerchief.

Duffy, the house officer, stood with his hands thrust into hip pockets and glared truculently at the hundred-odd persons who sat at tables beneath the stars and waited.

Fessenden, the roof-garden steward, fidgeted with his white cuffs and watched with anxious, troubled eyes the pacings of the hotel manager. Beside him Dr. Mavery, the house physician, drew reflectively on a cork-tipped cigarette.

A waiter motioned from the wide entrance and Ohms stuffed his handkerchief into his breast pocket, Fessenden gave a last flick to his immaculate cuffs, Dr. Mavery turned quietly, and Duffy pivoted and got a firm grip on his ragged cigar.

Moriarty and Cohen wandered into the anteroom from the corridor, and Moriarty was saying: "I don't care if it was the biggest

tournament in the world. And I don't care who played in it. A man can't castle if he's put in check—all right, he can't—but if he ain't in check at the moment, and if he was in check before that and got out, he can castle."

"Says you," shot back Cohen. "Listen, I played chess before you could count right— Hello, Duffy. Hey, Duffy, do you know anything about chess?"

Duffy gritted, dramatically: "It's murder, boys." Dramatically he swiveled, leveled a stubby arm towards the blue screen.

MacBride came swinging in wiping the sweatband of his hard straw hat. "Hello, Duffy. Who was the doctor?"

"Jeeze, Cap," Duffy gritted. "It's murder."

Dr. Mavery put in, quietly: "I was called up, Captain MacBride. Death was instantaneous. One bullet slightly below and to the rear of the left ear. One in the right side, below and back of the armpit. Both bullets are lodged in the body. It is over behind that screen."

"Thanks, doctor—that's all for the moment. Who's the head-waiter?"

"Listen," put in Duffy, "it was this way, Cap—"

"I am the headwaiter," said Fessenden, tall, dignified, headwaiterish.

MacBride turned from Duffy, said to Fessenden: "Okey. What's her name?"

"No one knows."

"Anybody with her?"

"No. You see, the table—you will observe that the table is a corner one, in the southeast corner—it was reserved this afternoon. By a Mr. Philip Lake. Reserved for two—at ten-thirty tonight. The lady came at ten-thirty, said that Mr. Lake might be late. I seated her."

MacBride looked at his watch. "It's eleven-ten now. The guy didn't show up, eh?"

"No."

"What time was she bumped off?"

"Ten-fifty."

"Everybody's been kept here?"

Duffy said: "I kept 'em all here, Cap. I wasn't gonna let anybody get away. Not me!"

Ohms said, gesturing: "Please, Captain, be as politic as possible, for the sake of the establishment, for the sake of—"

"Who are you?"

Duffy said: "Mr. Ohms, the manager."

A sergeant in uniform and a squad of cops trooped in and MacBride said: "Just hang here a minute, boys." He looked around. "Where's Moriarity and Cohen?"

They had gone over to the blue screen. MacBride put his hands in his coat pockets and walked out, firm-heeled, beneath the stars. Duffy followed.

Moriarity and Cohen were kneeling, the girl's body between them. Cohen pointed.

"She was shot here and"—he pointed again—"here."

"Do you know her?"

"We don't know her," Moriarity said.

MacBride put his hands on his hips, drew his under lip in between his teeth, wagged his head. He sighed, barely audible.

Duffy said: "She was sittin' there, Cap, right in that chair. The chair was there. Nobody heard any shots. Hell, nobody even saw her fall. One of the waiters was bringin' some ginger ale and he found her layin' right there."

"Who was sitting near her?"

"Nobody. There was a dance goin' on, and the tables between here and the dance-floor were empty."

MacBride looked around at the tables. His eyes, keen and yet oddly weary, moved back to the body, across the table at which the girl had sat, up to the intersection of the south and east rails, where a white globe of light shone at the top of a short wrought-iron post.

"What's funny, Cap," Duffy was saying, "is this guy Lake when he calls up makes it plain he wants this corner table. And then"—Duffy leaned closer, dropped his voice—"he don't show up."

"Yeah," MacBride said absently, nodding. "Yeah." He reached over and took a small beaded purse from the table. He searched it, found nothing of consequence. He dropped it into his pocket, looked blankly at the body, then went around the screen and returned to the anteroom.

"Harry," he said to the sergeant, "take your boys and percolate. Names and addresses. Frisk the men."

He went out to the center of the dance-floor and said in a loud, blunt voice: "As you know, murder's been committed. Answer all questions plainly, don't argue and don't crack wise. The men will have to be searched and there'll be a couple of policewomen over any minute to search the women."

A man stood up, indignant; said: "Nonsense! Searching the ladies!"

MacBride looked at him, looked slowly around the tables, eyeing every face. Then he said: "That'll be all," and went over to the blue screen.

"What I say, Cap," Moriarity said, "is that if she was sittin' the way Duffy says she was—with her left side to the dance-floor, then she must have been shot from the dance-floor."

"How bright you get," Cohen said.

Moriarity spread his hands. "Well, mustn't she have?"

"Listen," said MacBride. "You two master minds go downstairs and circle the hotel grounds. See if some guy pitched a gun over."

Moriarity and Cohen left and MacBride said to Duffy: "Young, Duffy. Nineteen or so... eh? And pretty. ——! she must have been pretty. I've got a daughter, Duffy—that age."

"Yeah?"

MacBride muttered: "Yeah," vacantly, and half-grimaced.

Kennedy of the *Free Press* drifted up beside MacBride, dribbled cigarette smoke from his nostrils. "I would have been here sooner, old tomato, only I have athlete's foot and—"

"You weren't missed."

"My pal." Kennedy smiled. "My old pal.... Crime of passion—or was she tired of it all?"

"Murder," gritted Duffy.

Kennedy leaned over, pursed his lips for a whistle, didn't whistle. "Blossom Marghary should look stunning in black."

MacBride looked sharply at him.

Kennedy was still leaning over, his eyes narrowed, the spectre of a sardonic smile on his pale, tired face.

"Cripes!" burst out Duffy.

Kennedy looked at him, raising his eyebrow.

Duffy pointed. "Say, is *she* Blossom Marghary's daughter?"

OHMS, the manager, perspired and perspired. He complained. He soaked one handkerchief with perspiration and produced another. He watched the cops proceed inevitably. He watched a policewoman lead two women at a time into the dressing-room, where another police-woman searched. He forgot all about the dead girl. He worried about profits, headlines, notoriety. He almost collapsed.

But everything progressed smoothly with a minimum of altercation. Moriarity and Cohen came up still arguing, but they found nothing. No gun was found on any of the guests. No one had heard any shots.

MacBride went out to the center of the dance-floor, a little nettled, his hands thrust hard in his pockets and a narrowed-down glitter in his eyes. The crowd was not as silent, as tense, as it had been. Bits of talk bubbled here and there; here and there, a light laugh. They had been searched, questioned; they were relieved, some of them slightly contemptuous of the police, forgetting the girl who lay dead behind the screen.

One hundred and six persons… and no one had heard any shots. No gun had been found below.

"There might," said Moriarity alongside MacBride's shoulder, "have been a guy planted down on the lawn to get the gun was pitched over—if there was a gun. Still, cripes, a silencer would ha' been used—would ha' had to be used."

"The way she was sitting," MacBride said, "she would have had to been plugged from a table along the south rail, and nobody was sitting at any of those tables. No, Mory," MacBride went on, "I hate to get fantastic ideas, but take a look at that apartment house across the street. Two stories higher than this—but, at the angle she was shot, the bullets would have come from the roof or the top story."

"Hell," said Moriarity, "somebody would have seen the muzzle fire."

MacBride said: "A revolver or an automatic couldn't have done it, at least from that distance. Looks like small calibre but high velocity. It would have to be a rifle. That poor young kid was on the spot the minute she sat down at the table."

"Philip Lake, eh?"

"It figures that way. Call the morgue and have them take the body over there. Ring Headquarters and give 'em the dope. They'll have to telephone her mother." He shook his head, "I'm damned if I will."

He raised his voice, addressing the crowd. "That's all. You're at liberty to leave."

Ohms rushed over, beaming. "Ah, I am so glad, Captain! This strained tension… I am so relieved, so glad—"

MacBride cut him with a dour look. "So glad, eh, that we didn't find the murderer?"

Ohms swallowed, reddened, made silly gestures.

MacBride chuckled, without humor. "In other words, Mr. Ohms, on with the dance. To hell with the dead. Yeah. Oh, yeah. No, don't apologize. Say," he said in a voice suddenly rusty with sarcasm, "you'll get lots of business. The cockeyed world'll want to see the table where Bess Marghary croaked!"

Disgusted, he turned away—almost bowled over Kennedy.

Kennedy smiled drolly. "You have your moments, Cap."

Chapter II

AT exactly midnight MacBride strode out of the hotel, walked a
few yards west on Baxter Boulevard to where Spruce Street
formed the western boundary of the hotel. On the other side of Spruce
reared the Lancaster Apartments. White, slim, the building impaled
the darkness.

MacBride crossed, entered the Baxter Boulevard door and found
a clerk drowsing behind a small desk.

"From Police Headquarters," he said. "I'd like to see a list of the
people living on your top floor."

The clerk blinked, opened his mouth to say something, but got a
book out of a safe instead. He began reading off names in a nervous,
halting voice.

"Hold on," MacBride cut in. "Lake. Philip Lake."

"Yes," nodded the clerk. "Philip Lake."

"Yes," nodded MacBride. "Is he in?"

"I don't know. I can ring."

"No, don't ring. Get a pass key and come up with me."

The clerk went back to the safe, said over his shoulder: "He was
in, though. There was a wire came for him. The elevator boy took it
up."

"What time?"

The clerk left the safe, dangling a keyring. "Eleven—about eleven."

MacBride stared at the clerk for a long moment. The clerk became
uneasy and said: "Yes—honest."

"Okey. Come on up."

They went up two steps and entered an elevator where a black boy
yawned.

"Was this the boy?" MacBride asked.

The clerk nodded and MacBride said to the boy, as the elevator
started upward: "Was that at eleven?"

"Yassuh. Ah heard the radio, but Ah guess Mustuh Lake was turnin'
in, 'cause he said I should shove it under the door."

The elevator whispered to a stop at the fourteenth floor. The clerk led the way out and MacBride followed him down a wide, green-carpeted corridor.

"Know him well?" MacBride asked.

"No." The clerk was squinting, choosing a key. "I'm new here. This is the door."

MacBride put a restraining hand on him. The clerk stepped back and MacBride knocked. The top floor was silent. No one responded to the knock, and after several more sharp raps, MacBride turned, took the key from the clerk and told him to get away from the door.

The skipper drew his revolver. Cautiously he inserted the key in the lock, moved the key until he felt it pass the greatest pressure and heard the lock click faintly. He put his left hand on the knob, turned it, edged it inward slightly then flung it open and ducked in sidewise.

He bumped against a heavy chair recoiled and felt a bridge lamp teeter. He steadied it with his left hand, crouched behind the chair and listened intently. Heard no sound. He reached up with his left hand, found the bridge lamp's dangling cord, jerked it and ducked again as the lamp glowed.

His hard head free of his straw hat, rose from behind the chair and his keened eyes darted swiftly about the large living-room. He saw no one, felt no intimation of another presence. He rose to his full lank-boned height, crossed the room, paused for a moment near an open door, then reached in and snapped on a light.

It was a bedroom. The bed had not been slept in. MacBride entered, a frown between his eyes, his eyes sharp with a bright, blue, predatory look. He swiveled silently on soft rugs, went back into the living-room, crossed to the corridor door and motioned to the clerk.

The clerk swallowed, offered a sickly smile and entered. MacBride put away his gun, went to one of two windows that faced the west side of the Boulevard Hotel and overlooked the now deserted roof-garden. But a few lights still glowed there.

MacBride's eyes settled on the southeast corner, where Bess Marghary had met her death. The angle was sufficient for a man to shoot over the heads of the dancers and, if he were a good shot, shoot anybody sitting at the corner table.

The window was open.

MacBride turned, went to a closet, searched it. He entered the bedroom and searched the closet there. He came back into the living-room scowling.

"D' you see Lake go out about eleven?" he growled.

"No."

"Get that elevator boy."

The clerk got the negro, and in response to MacBride's questions, the boy shook his head and—white-eyed—said: "N-no, suh."

"Did anybody leave this floor between ten-fifty and twelve?"

"N-no, suh."

"You weren't tipped to say that, were you?"

"N-no, suh."

The clerk ventured, tremulously: "But—but what's happened?"

MacBride, ignoring him, looked in the bathroom, looked under a divan, under a bed, turned up the mattress. He tramped into the living-room, found his hat.

"What office would a telegram come from?" he asked.

The clerk said: "That one in Charles Street."

"Okey. Now get this! Keep this door locked. Don't let anybody in here—maid or anybody. If anybody stops by and asks for Lake, have 'em wait and then get in touch with me right away. Understand—I don't—I don't want anybody—you or the manager—or anybody—in this room. Until I say so."

"Yes, sir."

"Get out."

He waited until the clerk and the negro had gone into the hall, then turned out the bedroom light, went to the bridge lamp and turned it out, and left the room, locked the door.

The clerk said: "W-what shall I tell the manager?"

"Tell him that your orders were from Captain MacBride."

"But—"

"That'll do."

OUTSIDE, the skipper hopped a taxi and, dropping back in the leather cushions, lit up his dead pipe and puffed hard for the space of a minute. It took him five minutes to reach the Charles Street telegraphic office and he barged in on a young man who was eating a sandwich.

He showed his badge, said: "There was a message delivered to the Lancaster Apartments tonight about eleven or so. For Mr. Lake. Got a copy of it?"

"J's a minute."

The man picked up a sheaf of papers, began thumbing them rapidly, drew one out and slapped it down on the counter.

The message was brief:

> *I think something is up anyhow watch it stop will remain at the Forester but meet you at Carlos.*
>
> *Max*

MacBride squinted, took a drag at his pipe, said: "Got a pencil?"

He copied the message—it was dated at Wendell—and left.

Chapter III

KENNEDY lounged in the chair on the small of his back, his fingers interlaced on his stomach, his weathered fedora tilted down over half of his face. A half-smoked cigarette, dead, hung from the center of his lips.

Moriarity, striding up and down, was saying: "Have it your way, then. Go ahead, have it your way. But that don't cut any ice with me. *I* know. See?"

"Why," broke in Cohen, "only the other night me and Nussbaum were playing, and Nussbaum—"

"And as for Nussbaum—"

"As," said Kennedy, "a matter of fact, I don't think either one of you morons know what the hell you're talking about. In the first place—"

The office door opened and MacBride came in.

But Kennedy went on: "In the first place, ten to one neither one of you has ever seen a rule. Very well. The king was in his original position. The rook—"

"My ——!" said MacBride. "Are you getting weak-minded too?" He glowered, first at Moriarity, then at Cohen. "No more of this damn' chess business. You hear! By cripes, it's all I've heard since eight o'clock was rook and king and castle this and castle that."

He banged his hard straw hat on the desk. "Another crack out of either one of you birds—and you too, Kennedy—and I'll take a swing at you! What's a lousy chess game in comparison with—with that poor kid that was bumped off? And"—he made a fist—"those pink-faced bums from the tabloid wanting to take a picture of her—the way she was—all bloody there—for the first editions! Bah!"

From beneath Kennedy's battered hat brim—"Your nerves, Skipper—your nerves!"

MacBride sat down. "First, this guy Lake. He was in his room—and get this: he lives in the Lancaster, across from the hotel. Well, the boy friend was in at the time the girl was fogged. But he left. There'd been a wire for him. He's got a pal down in Wendell."

"That's on the river," Cohen said.

"At the Forester." MacBride passed around his copy of the wire, reloaded his pipe, screwed down one keen eye.

Kennedy blew a meditative mushroom of smoke towards the ceiling, watched it. "Eighteen she was, Cap. Bess Marghary. They just had her old woman over the morgue. Or should I say 'old woman?' Still, she's seen better days. Some live on and on—and some die young—"

There was a sharp rap on the door and Sergeant Otto Bettdecken looked in. "Jeeze, Cap, who's downstairs but the Marghary girl's mother!"

"What's she want?"

Bettdecken shrugged. "I should know. She just wanders in like a dame in a trance and keeps demandin' I know who bumped off the kid. You should see her!"

MacBride said: "Bring her up, Otto."

SHE was tall, Blossom Marghary. And gone to weight a bit, but not much. She had a white evening dress on, a wrap flung over it. No hat. Her hair bordered on henna and she had a white columnar neck. Transfixed, she stood in the doorway.

MacBride was standing. "Come in. Sit down," he said.

"Who did it, MacBride?" she said slowly.

MacBride raised a palm-upward hand. "Sit down."

"Who did it, MacBride?"

Kennedy, from under his hat brim, said: "Sit down, Blossom."

Her glazed eyes jerked to him. She seemed not to see him, yet she said: "Another *gentleman* of the press," bitterly. Then she flared, turning to MacBride: "Who did it? My ——! who did it?"

The press—and those on the inside track—knew her as Blossom Marghary. But she had married a second time and was now Mrs.

Jackman, wife of the racketeer, Big Dan Jackman. Nightclub hostess in her own right, blues singer, wisecracker extraordinary. She didn't wisecrack now. Her face was white as marble, except for a feverish patch of crimson on either cheek.

"You know, MacBride—you know who did it!"

She came to the desk. Stiff-legged, each fall of her high heels sharp and distinct.

MacBride drew on his pipe, said quietly: "Sit down, Mrs. Jackman—right there—in that chair."

She dropped into the chair suddenly.

MacBride leaned forward, put his elbows on the desk's flat surface, clasped his long, strong hands together, stared levelly into Blossom Marghary's eyes.

"I know," he said. "I'd offer you sympathy—but I know that doesn't do any good. I've got a daughter. I know how my wife would feel. I've got an idea how you feel—and I know how I would feel. I'm going to get the rat that did her in. Depend on that. It won't do you any good—but it's my job, and I intend doing it. You can talk my language and I can talk yours. You can help me get the rat. Just"—he made a soothing gesture with two palms—"try to hold together, try to hold together."

Quivering, she said: "She was good, MacBride. Good as gold. Not like me. You know what I am. The great old war-horse, redheaded, giving the boys a thrill in the *Club Mex*, glad-handing the crowd— But she was good and clean, and I kept her away from all that. And she was lovely, MacBride.

"I changed her name and faked all kinds of references to get her in a good school. I hoped to polish her off, to send her to Europe, to get her married to some decent guy there. Elizabeth Wentworth... swell name, eh? And you, Kennedy," she grated, "I heard that you popped off right away, with a wise-crack, that she was Bess Marghary. Now the hell you find things out, I don't know."

Unperturbed, Kennedy said: "It had to come out."

"Now wait a minute," MacBride said. "Who is Philip Lake, Mrs. Jackman?"

"Philip—" She squinted.

"Yeah," said MacBride. "Lake."

"I don't know," she said hoarsely.

"What time did your daughter leave you last night?"

She shook her head. "Don't you see—didn't I tell you? She wasn't staying with me. She used to come in twice a week. But she shouldn't have been in town last night. She was staying with a French family at Wendell for a couple of months—between terms—learning French and how to act decent."

Kennedy sat up, said: "Wendell!" while looking at MacBride. He pushed back his hat. "Jake. I'll catch a bus down to Wendell and interview this French family. What's the name, Blossom?"

MacBride rapped out: "You'll stay right here, Kennedy! If anybody goes to Wendell, I will. And I mean that, sweetheart. I do right by you—and by cripes, you'll do right by me. Or get your jaw busted."

Kennedy felt his jaw, sighed, relaxed. "After all, it's the only jaw I have."

MacBride turned to the woman. "Do you know what time she left there?"

"Nine. At nine. They said she got a telegram that afternoon. They didn't ask her about it. They're not nosy—like a lot of newspaper guys I know. She told them she was going down to the movies they have there. She did that a lot. She must have come in town instead. That telegram—"

"Yeah," nodded MacBride. "That telegram."

She stared at the flat surface of the desk with eyes that became more glazed, her lips moved in inaudible whispers. She kept shaking her head slowly, absent-mindedly.

MacBride started to say something, but didn't. He started again and managed to get it out. "Better get along home now, Mrs. Jackman. I'll have one of the boys drive you home."

She didn't move.

He got up and went around the desk, laid his big hand on her shoulder, patted it.

"It's just one of those awful things, Mrs. Jackman. Come."

She looked at him, said, with a half-hysterical little laugh: "And they used to tell me you were hard as hell, MacBride."

MacBride shrugged and said nothing and helped her up. He took her downstairs, got out Dooley and had him use a squad car. He went to the car with her. He stood on the curb, his hands on his hips, and watched the tail-light disappear around the next corner. It was after one in the morning and tattered scud raced across the stars.

HE barged back into his office. "Ike—Mory, get the lead out of your pants. We're taking a ride down to Wendell."

Kennedy got up and yawned, stretched his arms, wiped his tired eyes. "Sometimes I think Blossom isn't such a bad-looking wench. Take her man, now: Big Dan. There's a gorilla for you. Sometimes Blossom has a hard time painting over the marks on her jaw. Big Dan hauls off more frequently than occasionally and knocks her for a row of filling stations—or something. Someday"—he stifled a yawn— "someday Blossom is going to give that baby the works. I often wonder why the hell she sticks with him.

"Maybe she's that way. Take Mike Marghary. Before he died they said he used to burn her with cigarettes. Sadist. I mind the time he put on a show at his South Side Club. A guy who didn't pack a gun there was considered a wildflower.

"Mike got his kid—Bess—down there in tights and a smile—she was only twelve. That was the night Blossom broke a chair over his head. Now—she's got another egg on her hands. Just one of those broads, Blossom." He smiled reflectively, ironically. "Just the kind of gal that guys slam down."

MacBride was lighting his pipe. "She may be a hot number. Hell knows, she's been notorious. But she always married her men, Kennedy. And—that kid—she sure tried her best for that kid.... Okey. Let's go. There's a guy in Wendell we may have to kick out of bed and spoil his night's sleep."

Chapter IV

THE police phaeton rolled through dark streets, crossed Main Avenue past the late restaurants, the flashy chop suey joints; swung down Jockey Street past pool-parlors, hit the river road where thin clouds of fog rolled in. Headed west, big balloon tires hissing on the fog-wet cobbles.

MacBride sat beside Dongan, the driver. Moriarity and Cohen were in the back, with Kennedy between them. Three red ends of cigarettes in the back and a glowing pipe bowl in front.

Out of the freight yard and packing district, through a settlement of hunky shacks. Along the river wall, where the cobbles gave 'way to shiny-wet cement. West on River Drive, with the thin fog blowing into the car, showering sparks from cigarettes.

Dongan began stepping on it. The faintly lighted dashboard showed fifty-five an hour. Filling stations flashed by. The canvas top drummed and clapped and the motometer needle went to a hundred and sixty. The speedometer went up to sixty.

MacBride said: "Now don't be Barney Oldfield, Sam."

Wendell lies on the outskirts of Richmond City. Wendell is a suburb with a small casino built over the river, a sandy beach, a couple of modest hotels and some good homes on the low hills beyond.

The phaeton rolled into a town gone to bed. The fog was more like a weak mist here and moonlight lapped on the quiet river. Dongan turned a couple of corners and then headed towards a small lighted

sign that said, *Forester House,* in black letters on white glass.

Dongan applied perfect brakes. The car came to a noiseless stop.

MacBride said: "You boys stay here."

He climbed down, knocked out his pipe against the hard heel of his left hand and climbed six wooden steps, crossed a veranda and entered a small, unpretentious lobby.

A man in shirt-sleeves leaned over a narrow wooden desk. He wore a green eyeshade and was figuring in a big ledger. He looked up and MacBride made himself known briefly.

"You've got a man staying here," MacBride said. "His first name is Max and I thought maybe if we looked over the books, we might be able to get some dope."

"We're not full up," the clerk said. "I remember getting a wire or two for a Max Engleberg. Don't think—in fact, I'm sure—we've no other Max staying here."

"How long has he been here?"

"A few weeks, offhand, I'd say. He's in twenty-four, second floor—halfway down the hall."

MacBride nodded aloft. "Up there now?"

"I couldn't say."

"Ring him."

The clerk turned to a small switchboard, plugged in. After a minute he pulled the plug out, shook his head.

"No answer."

MacBride said: "Suppose I look in his room."

The clerk handed him a key.

MacBride went upstairs, walked to number twenty-four, inserted the key and opened the door. He found a light switch just inside. The room was small, plain.

MacBride closed the door. He saw only one bag—a black Gladstone. It was empty. One suit hung in a closet. He searched the pockets. By the size of the suit he reasoned the man to be small, thin. But nothing was in the suit.

He crossed to a small bureau. Opened the top drawer. A few shirts there, two ties. In the second drawer: socks, a pair of pajamas, two suits of underwear. No papers. No letters. He turned the name over in his head—Max Engleberg. No, he had never heard it before.

He turned and accidentally kicked over a tin waste basket. A crumpled ball of paper rolled out. It was yellow. MacBride picked it up, flattened it out. It was a telegram. From Richmond City. Sent at ten p.m. the night of the murder; received ten-twenty.

> *Will be down about midnight meet me at Carlos*
> *Phil*

MacBride whistled softly, folded the message and tucked it in a vest pocket. He turned out the light, went out, locked the door and descended to the desk.

"Is there a place around here named Carlo's?" he said.

"Down by the river. A speakeasy."

"How do I get there?"

The clerk told him and MacBride went out and climbed into the phaeton.

"Are plaudits in order?" asked Kennedy.

"Sam," said MacBride, "take the next left. I'll direct."

Forty-five Lewis Street was a two-storied brick house, the first floor flush with the pavement. The street was dark and the river was nearby. MacBride spoke to Moriarity and Cohen and they got out and went with him to the door. The door opened and they went down a corridor, pushed open another door and entered a bar.

The bar was empty and the sleepy-eyed barman behind was counting change.

"I'm closin' up," he said.

"We're from the city Police Headquarters," MacBride said.

"What you drinkin'?"

Cohen said: "I'll have a—"

"We're not drinking," cut in MacBride. "Do you know a guy named Max Engleberg?"

The barman yawned. "I know a guy named Max—just over the bar, kinda."

"Was he in here lately?"

"Left about one. How I know his name is Max: he said, 'If a guy comes in here lookin' for me, tell him to ring me at the Forester.' So he left. Won't you guys have a drink?"

"I—" Moriarity began.

MacBride said: "Well, give these two tanks something. Well—on second thought, make mine Scotch."

The telephone rang and the bartender said: "Just a sec," and picked up the instrument; said: "Hello," into the mouthpiece and then: "Yeah, Carlo's.... Huh?" He frowned. "Wait a sec." He put his hand over the mouthpiece, craned his neck, said: "Guy askin' for Max Engleberg."

MacBride bounded behind the bar, took the telephone, held it tensely. "Hello," he said.

"Max!" exclaimed a man's voice.

"Yeah."

"For —— sake, Max!... two-o-six Clemons... quick ... or I'm done for!"

There was a click and MacBride said: "Hello—hello," quickly, but the line was dead. He hung up, came around front saying: "Come on, boys."

Moriarity and Cohen grabbed two drinks from the bartender,

gulped them down. MacBride, hesitating, grabbed one also.

"Now let's go," he clipped and led the way out to the car.

"Plaudits?" asked Kennedy.

MacBride said: "Sam, back to the city—and this time play Barney Oldfield. Pass the Forester. You, Ike, stay at the Forester. This guy Max Engleberg is wandering around. If he comes back there, nab him. His buddy's in dutch at two-o-six Clemons." He landed in the front seat. "D' you get that address, Sam?"

"Oke."

They dropped Cohen off at the Forester, and then Dongan opened up, sliding through the town, hitting the main pike and rolling the phaeton through the night like a bat out of hell.

The wind hit the canvas top hard, whistled past the windshield. The speedometer quivered at sixty. Twin headlights charged beams close to the road. Twin spotlights on the windshield frame hurled beams far ahead, picked out turns in the cement road, trunks of trees.

"Clemons... two-o-six," Moriarity was saying between claps of wind. "Ain't that down near Harrow?"

MacBride barked back: "This guy must be in a tough spot. He was coming down to meet this Max Engleberg at that speak. At midnight. He never got there. Max must have gone out on the look-see."

"Maybe it was a case," Dongan said, taking a curve at fifty-eight, "of this heel gettin' cold feet after he bumped off the jane and he's countin' on Max to get him out."

The phaeton boomed past a filling-station. Mists whipped into the car. They swung nearer the river, hitting River Drive.

"The jane was mixed up in it," Moriarity yelled. "I'll bet the jane was mixed up in it. She was put on the spot and she was mixed up in it. I'll bet you'll find it was some mob of hoods fogged her to get even with her step-papa Big Dan Jackman. She got a telegram, didn't she? Sure. This mug Phil Lake sent it. I'll bet he said: 'Meet me at the Hotel Boulevard roof-garden.' Then he fogged her."

The phaeton streaked through the hunky settlement, past the freight yards.

"Intimates you," said Kennedy.

"Well," Moriarity said. "Well! Well, wisenheimer, what do *you* think?"

"Thinking," said Kennedy, "has ruined many a good cop. And it makes poor novelists out of good reporters, too."

Dongan slewed into Harrow Street, grazing a milk truck, screeching his tires on the pavement. He slowed down and rolled up Harrow at forty. He slowed down to thirty.

"Park along here, Cap?"

"Yeah—anywhere, Sam. Right here."

The phaeton stopped. Moriarity stepped to the footboard, struck a match against a fire-hydrant, lit a cigarette. MacBride stepped down beside him, knocked out his pipe against the hydrant and then Dongan came around the front of the car.

Kennedy, from the rear of the phaeton, said: "I'll keep house while you boys go out and play."

MacBride was glaring at Moriarity. "Fathead, douse that butt!"

Moriarity tossed it away.

They crossed the street, kept walking until they reached Clemons and then turned left. It was a dark and dismal neighborhood at this hour, shadow-ridden and silent: blank-faced stores rubbed shoulders with two- and three-story red brick flats and these in turn rubbed shoulders with ancient frame houses set back from the sidewalk—all weather-beaten and ramshackled, making passive resistance against wholesale houses and warehouses. A narrow street of narrow, cracked sidewalks, motley smells, indifferent virtue.

"There it is," MacBride muttered, stopping Moriarity and Dongan and nodding diagonally across the street. "Next that warehouse."

It was a two-story frame house, with a patch of grubby ground in front, and a small stoop. Between it and the warehouse ran a cobbled alley wide enough for vehicles. The windows of the house were dark.

MacBride made a motion with his chin, led the way across the street to the warehouse, went along in the shadow of it, stopped when he came to the corner nearest the house. After a moment he ducked into the alley and Moriarity and Dongan followed. They could see that the alley ran straight through to a street in the rear.

In the yard back of the house they found a big Cadillac sedan. They got behind it and looked up at the back of the house. The windows were dark, but MacBride saw a faint sliver of light on the second floor, where a dark shade had worn.

He took a penknife, opened the door of the car silently, reached under the dashboard and severed the ignition wires. He cut them in two places, threw away odd ends, so that the wires could not be respliced. He backed out and rejoined Moriarity and Dongan.

Chapter V

"I'M going in this dump," he said.

"Let's," said Moriarity.

"Nix. You guys stay out here. You in front, Mory—and you back here, Dongan."

He walked up the alley to the front, climbed to the stoop and rapped hard knuckles on the glass panel of the door. He did not draw his gun. His hands rested in his coat pockets. He waited a minute, sensed that someone was looking at him from behind the curtained glass.

The door clicked, opened, and darkness yawned beyond.

MacBride said to the darkness: "Captain MacBride, Police Head-quarters."

For a long minute the darkness did not answer him. He stood on wide-planted feet, motionless, cool as an iceberg.

Then a voice said: "What do you want?"

"I want to come in or I wouldn't have knocked. I'm here to play ball—and you'd better play with me. Put some light on the subject."

There was a pause, a whisper—then a yellow light went on and revealed a drab hallway.

Three men stood there. They were young, well-dressed, but they looked like rats.

MacBride stepped in, kicked the door shut with his heel. He kept looking sharply from one to the other.

One of them made a sad attempt at a grin. "Sure… how you, Cap?"

"I'm fine, Gatz. How are you?"

"Just great. Just great."

"Happy and conscience-clear, I suppose, and going to prayer meet-ings, regularly."

Gatz had a glassy grin. "Sure. All that."

MacBride eyed the others. "I don't know your friends from the choir."

Gatz laughed it off. "Oh, they're good boys."

"Do they always carry their right hands in their pockets?"

The two men shrugged, removed their hands and then didn't seem to know what to do with them.

Gatz grinned again. "Well, come in, Skipper."

They went down the hall, into a room off the side where a lamp burned on a table littered with newspapers and magazines.

Behind the lamp sat a girl, straight in a chair, holding a magazine before her with both hands but looking over the top of it fixedly with dark, expressionless eyes.

MacBride gave her a brief, keen stare. Gatz, a dapper tall man, red-lipped and white-skinned, lit a cigarette with an air of nonchalance that didn't get over.

The woman stared at the print on the magazine.

No one sat down.

Gatz, rocking on his heels, held up his cigarette and regarded the end of it. "The houses, Skipper, are up in the next block. Funny... I didn't think they'd shoved you on the vice squad."

"I didn't think Big Dan Jackman let you stay out so late—in this end of town."

"You know, Skipper, I just can't sleep at night."

The girl looked up—looked down again.

MacBride chuckled sardonically. "You know damned well what I'm here for, Gatz. Where's the guy?"

"Guy?"

The girl looked up—looked down again.

"Yeah," MacBride said. "I'm here to play ball, Gatz. You guys want him. I want him. But you guys 've got no right to have him and I have. I know you're Jackman's bodyguard. Bess Marghary was bumped off and you guys know who did it. You've got the guy. I want him. Now don't try to stand there and spiel me a song and dance. I was tipped he was here—and in good faith I came in this dump on my lonesome."

Gatz sobered, thinned down his eyes. "You just got a bum steer, Cap." He shook his head. "There's no guy here. There's only me and the two boys and the girl friend."

MacBride began to look unpleasant. "I said, Gatz—don't hand me any half-baked song and dance. I want that guy. Hand him over and I'll forget all about this monkey business. It's murder, and I've got to get that guy. You've got to play ball, Gatz."

The woman slammed the magazine on the table, got up, said: "Hell!" disgustedly and started out of the room.

"Come back here, you," MacBride said.

She stopped, turned, snapped gum with her teeth and tongue, warped her mouth and said: "Ah, ——!"

MacBride said: "Sit the hell down in that chair and keep your trap shut."

Gatz said: "Now there's no use gettin' tough, Skipper. I don't know how the hell you got here, or why, but we're strictly kosher in this little scatter tonight. You got a steer, but it was a bum one. I'm tellin' you, see."

"And I'm telling you, Gatz." MacBride scowled. "I'll look this scatter over."

The girl snapped: "Like hell you will, you will! You get a search warrant and you can look it over. But not unless. I should have a lousy shamus busting around my house. Go on, get the hell out of here."

Gatz smiled crookedly, saying: "No hard feelin's, Skipper—but just as a kinda matter of principle"—he shrugged—"you'll have to get a search warrant. See? No hard feelin's. Just, you know, a matter o' form. Sure."

"Yeah?" growled MacBride, darkening.

"Yeah—yeah—yeah!" snapped the woman, and punctuated it with a crack of her chewing-gum.

Gatz—the other two—moved slightly. Hawk-eyed, they watched MacBride. Their hands had returned to the vicinity of their right-hand pockets. There was something sinister in Gatz' fixed, self-satisfied leer.

MacBride knew. An old cop, he knew the danger line.

He said: "You heels are only making it hard for yourselves. There's a lot of dumb bunnies in this man's town that've tried to read me the law. Yeah, and they're warming their pants in the pen right now. Do I search this joint now—or do I walk out?"

"You—walk—out," said the girl.

"That okey by you, Gatz?" MacBride said.

"Okey, Skipper."

MacBride said, "Okey, Gatz."

He left the room, and Gatz and the two men followed him to the hall door. Standing in the open door, MacBride tapped Gatz's chest with a rigid forefinger.

"O—key, Gatz."

"Toodle-oo, Skipper."

MacBRIDE walked long-legged away from the house. Moriarity loomed up out of an areaway and joined him.

"Three in there, Mory," MacBride said in a clipped whisper. "Gatz, two imported wipers, and a jane I'd hate to meet in a dark room.... Quick. We go around and up back that alley. Those lame-brains started talking search warrant." He chuckled brittlely. "I'll search-warrant them! Yes, I will. Beat it to the car and get the Thompson gun and then hike up the alley. I'll be there with Dongan. Quick, Mory, because those guys 'll lam out o' that dump pronto."

Moriarity went off at a run.

MacBride turned into Harrow, walked a short block, turned left and reached the alley; turned left into it and hung to the shadows of a board fence as he neared the rear yard of the Clemons Street house.

Dongan ducked in the shadows. MacBride whispered his name hoarsely. Dongan joined him behind the Cadillac.

"Out front, Dongan. Quick! If any guy pokes his knob out challenge him. We're going to clean this scatter out. Hop to it."

Dongan crept up the alley.

Moriarity came quietly out of the shadows, his pockets sagging with fifty-cartridge magazines, one magazine in the Tommy gun.

"Kennedy ain't there," he whispered.

"Now where the hell do you suppose that gonof went?"

"Probably for a drink."

Bang!

The shot was muffled.

Moriarity clipped, "That's inside!"

Bang! Bang!

MacBride gripped Moriarity's shoulder. "Again, eh? That's funny, Mory! The shots are upstairs!... Here, let fly with that Tommy. Come on, the back door. Blow it open, kid."

They ran up eight steps to a landing outside the rear door. Moriarity held the Tommy gun low. He let the gun rip. Lead blazed through the lock—ten terrific shots.

MacBride kicked the door open and Moriarity passed him a pocket-light. MacBride flashed it on. They landed in a kitchen.

A door beyond was closed, but they saw a streak of light at the bottom of it. They looked at each other, nodded. MacBride went to the door while Moriarity stood squared off in front of it. MacBride reached out diagonally, caught the knob, turned it and whipped the door back inward.

One of the men spun around with a Luger automatic to which was attached a special sixty-cartridge magazine, sticking down from the butt—an improvised but deadly weapon. But he never used it.

Flame ripped from the Tommy gun.

The man fell backward over the table and, taking the electric lamp with him, broke the wire and plunged the room in darkness. His body went clear over to the floor. Magazines—bottles—the table—went down in a resounding crash with which the throbbing echoes of the sub-machinegun mingled.

Footsteps pounded upstairs.

MacBride knocked over chairs on their way to the hall, where lights still burned. Moriarity covered the staircase while MacBride opened the hall door and called to Dongan.

Dongan came on the jump, hefting his gun.

A door opened at the head of the staircase, slammed shut again—violently—as a short spurt snapped from Moriarity's Thompson. He went bounding up the stairs two at a time. MacBride, barking: "Watch yourself, Mory!" bounded after him. Moriarity reached the top, crouched. The gun hammered his shoulder as a stream of lead junked the knob, shattered the lock, knocked the door open and demolished window panes beyond.

In the dark room—suddenly—another Tommy gun flamed and a string of bullets shattered six uprights in the banister.

Moriarity cut loose, sweeping his gun from side to side as he fired into the darkened room. There was a scream, a dull thump and the sound of a heavy gun falling.

Dongan leaped for another closed door, kicked it open. The woman stood behind a bed, holding an automatic. The gun exploded as Dongan dived in. The bullet whanged past and buried itself in the banister. Dongan hit the bed headlong, carried it with him. It struck the woman and toppled her and Dongan landed on the bed, bounced from it upon the woman, tore the gun from her hand. He jumped up, yanked her with him, manacled her to the bed post.

MacBride poked in his head. "Swell work, Sam."

"You dirty lousy—"

"Pipe down, sister," MacBride said.

"You dirty double-crossing—"

Dongan slapped her face and said: "And the next time I'll put my fist down your throat!"

Bang!

MacBride started, looked up at the ceiling. "That's up in the attic, Sam!"

"Yeah."

They swung out into the hall again, saw Moriarity standing in the room at the back, which was now lighted. On the floor lay a man. Moriarity was looking upward. MacBride and Dongan went in and saw a ladder leading to a trapdoor aloft.

"Was that last shot fired at you, Mory?" MacBride said.

"No. It's up there."

They looked quizzically at one another.

Suddenly two shots banged—then three from another quarter of the attic. The house shook. A heavy object fell down with a dull thud, then rumbled a distance over the attic floor. A hoarse, congested voice began cursing. One-two lagging footfalls. The bang of a gun—the bang of another, echoes interlocking. An arm shot down through the open trapdoor; a body came plummeting, corkscrewing downward. MacBride and Dongan broke the headlong fall. The feet whipped over and the heels struck the floor hard. MacBride and Dongan let the head and shoulders down and Moriarity kept the Thompson trained on the trap opening.

Gatz lay on the floor, quite dead.

From aloft a voice—"Road clear down there, old tomato?"

"Kennedy! By ——!" MacBride poked Moriarity. "It's Kennedy!"

Came Kennedy's weary voice: "You must come up, Cap."

MacBride went up with the flashlight. Its beam bored through the darkness. It fell on a man who lay prone on his face. It leaped up, picked out Kennedy leaning against a barrel, sweat showing like silver streaks on his face.

"How the hell did you get in here, Kennedy?"

"Through that attic window. The house next door is empty. I found a busted window in the cellar and got in and went up and I found some boards in the attic and leaned one across to this window. Don't fall over the stiff."

"Who's it?"

"I bumped into him. Hell, it gave me a jolt and I hopped back.

They heard me downstairs. I didn't know for sure whether the guy was dead, so I cut him down—"

"Cut him down?"

"He was hanging from a rafter. By the neck, I mean. Hell! Whew! Who was the guy I nailed?"

"Gatz."

"Ah, one of Big Dan Jackman's protégés."

"This guy," said MacBride, "should be Philip Lake. Dongan, go downstairs and watch out the jane doesn't try to do the dutch or something. Here, Mory, give that Thompson to Kennedy and help me with this stiff."

"They hanged the poor slob, Cap," Kennedy said.

Moriarity, looking at the dead man's face, said: "Yeah, they sure must ha' hung him. And look—cigarette burns on his arms and chest."

A chill quivered up and down MacBride's spine. "The two kinds of pups, those eggs! Yeah? Jackman thinks he can send his hoods out to pull this kind of stuff? Yeah? Like hell, like hell! The— Here, Mory, come on—give me a hand. If this is Lake... but it's got to be Lake—"

"Then there's still his pal," Kennedy said. "Max Engleberg."

Chapter VI

FOUR in the morning....

She said her name was Arline Kleinsic. Thirty or so. Her long, mannish jaw jutted and red spots burned on her high, knobby cheekbones. Close-set eyes burned beside a long, wide-nostriled nose.

She sat in the big armchair in MacBride's office, her hair disheveled—Dongan had had to take another crack at her—and her lips were tight and hueless. A powerful light with a bright reflector streamed mercilessly on her face, picking out its irregularities, its latent viciousness.

MacBride sat at his desk, facing her—his face in shadow. Moriarity and Dongan were eating hamburgers and drinking home-brew they had pilfered from Sergeant Otto Bettdecken's desk. Kennedy had gone to his newspaper.

"Nix," she clipped with her tight lips. "I'm like the dagos, big boy: no spikka Eng-leesh."

"You'll talk, baby," MacBride said. "Did Jackman order that job?"

"You heard me, shamus, you heard me. Rats for you and the rest of these mutts around here."

"Gatz and those other two rods were on Jackman's payroll. I want to know if Jackman ordered this. You'll fry, sister, unless I make it easy for you—and I'll make it easy for you only if you'll play ball with me."

She laughed. "Big-hearted, you are! Great big-hearted Captain Stevie J.—for Jackass—MacBride. Sell your boloney somewhere else, you ——. I won't fry. And I won't do a stretch, either."

"You were an accessory, sister. You were there when that guy was strung up, when he was tortured. How did he make that telephone call?"

"Gatz wanted his pal, too. He told this gofor that if he'd get his pal to my shack he'd be sprung clean himself. The guy said he would. He telephoned, and then instead of saying what Gatz told him to, he started yelling something else."

"I know what he said. Well, the guy had guts anyhow. He tried to warn his pal and save himself—at the same time. But I got the call instead. Go on."

She took a swing at the desk lamp and knocked it over. "To hell with you!"

MacBride set the lamp up again.

The woman shoved back the chair, started to get up. Moriarity planted a hand on the back of her neck and shoved her down.

"Remember, honeybunch, where you are."

She struck the desk. "Damn it, let me telephone my lawyer! I ain't gonna hang around here. Go ahead. Call up Jackman." She thrust out for the phone. "I'll get—"

"Oh-oh," said Dongan, grabbing her hand.

The door opened and Ike Cohen came in manacled to a small, thin, wiry man who had keen eyes and a concentrated air.

"Engleberg," Cohen said, and unlocked the manacles.

MacBride swiveled his chair a bit. "You're Engleberg, eh?"

"He said so. Yeah, I'm Engleberg." He put a cigarette between his lips, eyed the woman narrowly, lit up and then eyed each man in the room.

"Would it interest you to know," MacBride said, "that your partner Lake is at the morgue?"

"Yes, it would."

"He is."

Engleberg's black eyebrows went together. He stared at MacBride a long time. His hand, lifting to the cigarette in his mouth, trembled. His face remained unchanged, however, and his voice remained clipped, flat.

"On the up and up?"

"Yeah," MacBride nodded.

Engleberg took his cigarette, gestured towards the woman. "She did it?"

"She helped."

Engleberg regarded her keenly. "She looks like the kind of wren that would."

"Never mind her for the time being," MacBride said. "Let's talk about you—and your pal. We had him picked for a red-hot. Why? Have you heard yet about the Bess Marghary kill?"

Engleberg blinked, took a quick, quiet puff at his cigarette. "No. What about it?"

MacBride said: "She was put on the spot—on the Hotel Boulevard roof-garden. She was bumped off by a rifle—I just got the two bullets up from the morgue. Twenty-five-twenty—high speed. It couldn't have been done from the roof. It was done—we figure—from the window of your pal's apartment. Then he lammed. This brat and her mob picked him up and gave him the works. What about Bess Marghary and Lake?"

Engleberg had the poise of a potentate. "He fell in love with her. She fell in love with him."

"Where'd they meet?"

"Wendell."

"Lake sent you a wire that he'd meet you at Wendell at midnight. That would have been an hour or so after the girl was bumped off. He never showed up. Where did you go when you left that speakeasy?"

"I called up the Forester and asked if he'd called there. He didn't."

"Then what did you do?"

Engleberg blinked. "What would you do?"

"Look for him."

"Well."

MacBride squinted. "What did you mean when you sent Lake that telegram?"

"What it said. I warned him. I got a tip from a friend in the know that they had a line on him."

"They—who?"

"Big Dan Jackman—and friends. He was out in the open more than I was. More chance of a lousy break. I kept under cover a lot. That was my end. I warned him to go easy on the jane, but he went crazy over her—and got careless. He mixed up hearts and flowers with a tough, rough and nasty racket. But I couldn't have stopped him. I had to play my end. He had to play his. He was a nice kid. College kid. Liked the excitement. Game, too. Too game. And crazy over the girl. Well, she was something to be crazy over. Swell girl."

"How well did you know her?"

"As between acquaintances. I met her on the sly in Wendell. That's why I stayed there. She used to go to the movies. She'd pick out a certain seat. We had that arranged. I'd be next to her. We'd talk. She loved Lake. She'd do anything for us.

"Then one night some guy—I was walking down by the river—some guy took a pot shot at me. I jumped overboard—there was no other way out—and stayed under the pier. The heel must have thought he finished me. I stayed there half an hour—"

He reached and grabbed the back of a chair. He swayed. He looked tense, and moisture rushed to his face. Then he went suddenly limp and crumpled on the floor.

MacBride dropped beside him.

"I'm okey," Engleberg said. "Just a weak spell again." He tapped his side. "That wound. I'm all bandaged up. Just a drink of water and I'll be jake."

Cohen got him a drink, said to MacBride: "Hell, I didn't know he was wounded. He wouldn't tell me a thing."

MacBride stared at Engleberg, frankly puzzled. "You're a queer one, guy. You've got a way of getting a guy interested, but you don't tell an awful lot. What mob are you running with?"

Engleberg laughed weakly. "I hoped I wouldn't have to tell this. It's just a business formality: don't tell the cops any more than you have to, unless you have to. Lake and I came from New York two months ago. I'm a private dick. Lake was. But only for the excitement, Lake; he had plenty of jack."

"Who were you working for?"

"Your Richmond City's Crime Commission."

"Getting evidence against—"

"Jackman." Engleberg closed his eyes, breathed slowly, with an effort. "I put Lake on the girl—Bess. He fell for her. And she helped us with—information. She had reasons of her own. Jackman hated her. She hated him. He used to torture her mother. He was fresh with her. The girl, I mean. The girl wanted to beat it to Europe with her mother.... I may pull a faint any minute now, but I'll come out of it. Just... give me air... you know...."

He went off to sleep quietly, with a faint whisper of a sigh. MacBride carried him to the window, spoke to Moriarity and Moriarity put three chairs in a row. MacBride laid him there, put a thick telephone book under his head.

He looked up at Cohen, Moriarity, Dongan. "You got a load of that, didn't you?"

Cohen said: "Cripes, you get it! You—" He stopped, shook his head violently, said: "Hell's bells!"

MacBride, glitter-eyed, spun on the woman, grabbed her shoulder. "What the hell time did they bring Lake to your shack in Clemons?"

"I didn't look at the clock. Say, take your paws—"

He lifted her up with his left hand, his mouth bitter, his right hand raised in a knotted fist. "Shut up! What time did they bring Lake there? Answer me, you dirty little brat! Or I'll hand you the punch in the mouth you deserve!"

She swallowed, snarled—then rasped, suddenly: "Little before eleven, damn you!"

MacBride let her go. She landed in the chair like a wet sock and lounged there, white with fright, her eyes aquiver, her upper lip jerking spasmodically.

MacBride pivoted on one heel, inhaled deeply, brought his right fist down hard into his left palm. Then he strode hard-heeled to a costumer, slapped on his hard straw hat, strode to the door, yanked it open, leveled an arm at the woman.

"Lock that up, Mory," he said, bluntly. "Ike, take care of Engleberg. If Kennedy comes in, don't tell him where I am. Keep him here. If you have to break open my new bottle of Scotch. And, Mory, call up that greasy spoon down the street and tell 'em to send up an order of ham and eggs in an hour. I'll be hungry."

Chapter VII

THE phaeton purred through the summer dawn, sliding across town through empty streets. Down Broad Avenue, where a street car swayed and rattled over switches, the sound accentuating other absence of sound.

MacBride pulled up in front of an apartment house and shut off the ignition. He looked up at rows of windows, saw only a couple lighted. He left the phaeton and swung in beneath the rococo façade. He roused a dosing clerk behind an Italian marble counter.

"Jackman's apartment number," he said, identifying himself.

"Mr. J. Daniel Jackman?"

"Have you any other Jackman?"

"No."

"Then that ought to be the Jackman I want, oughtn't it?"

The clerk blinked. "Yes—of course." He looked in a book. "Eight-twelve. Eighth floor. Shall I tell him you're coming up?"

MacBride looked pained. "No—no. Just—just resume the doze."

He sloped across the lobby, gave a sleeping elevator boy a gentle push against the head. He got off at the eighth floor, waited until the elevator doors had closed and then looked at nearby door numbers. He went down towards the front of the building, turned left into an intersecting corridor.

There was a brass knocker shaped like a bell cut in two, and Mac-Bride raised it twice. He heard some movement inside, but he waited for longer than a minute before the door opened.

Blossom Jackman (once Marghary) looked out, swollen-eyed. She was dressed in a navy blue tailored suit.

"Kind of funny hour, Mrs. Jackman, but…." MacBride shrugged.

She opened the door and said nothing and MacBride walked into a large, luxurious, living-room where twin wall-lights glowed behind shields of frosted amber glass.

Blossom closed the door, cleared her throat. "You—you've got news, MacBride?" She came over as he turned to face her and gripped his arm. "You—got the bird—did it?"

"Not yet—I don't think."

He looked over her red hair. "I want to speak to Big Dan."

"He ain't here—yet."

"Where's he?"

"Oh—I guess at the *Club Mex.* They don't close till the sun comes up. I came home. But I couldn't sleep —— ! MacBride!"

He walked past her towards an open bedroom door through which he had caught a glimpse of a traveling bag. He saw a suitcase and a handbag on the floor. He turned around and eyed Blossom.

"Going somewhere?"

She made a feeble gesture. "I was thinking—yes. I want to duck reporters. I can't stand them. I'm going out on the river somewhere. I'm burying Bess out that way."

He kept regarding her—quizzically. "Couldn't Big Dan come home with you—at a time like this?"

She shrugged, grimaced. "I don't know. Business— Well, you can't stop a place of business— Oh, hell." She sobbed once or twice, then said, casually: "What do you want Dan for?"

"This bird named Lake: some of Dan's boys rubbed him out."

She started, put a hand to her throat. "Dan's boys!" She looked around the room in a daze, then snapped out of it. "Listen, MacBride, you wouldn't yank Dan down for that, would you? If this guy Lake— well, don't you see, if Dan did it— Look, if you had a kid...."

"I've got a daughter."

"Well—don't you see?"

He eyed her steadily. "I'm going to see Dan. Have a little talk with him, anyhow."

He went to the door.

Blossom gripped his arm. "Please, MacBride, give us a break."

"I give any guy a break, Mrs. Jackman, if he deserves it."

He opened the door, went to the elevator, went down to the lobby, out.

THE electric sign above the *Club Mex* had been turned off, but imitation lanterns glowed on either side of the street door. The phaeton stopped. MacBride sat looking at the door while he stuffed and lit his pipe. He heard no music, no sounds of gaiety.

The skipper climbed out of the phaeton. His pipe was drawing well. He pushed open the door and entered a low-ceiled lobby where thick rugs muffled his footsteps. At the end of the lobby was a grilled iron rail, and two steps below, the restaurant and dance-floor. On either side was a grilled balcony with little dining booths.

The place was empty of guests. The cloak-room was dark. A couple of waiters were gathering up table-cloths and both stopped and looked as MacBride went down the two steps from the lobby. His heels echoed on the polished dance-floor.

"Where's Jackman?"

One of the waiters said: "Who wants him?"

"I'll go with you. Get along."

"Who wants—"

MacBride shoved him. "Don't you know a cop when you see one? Shake it up."

The waiter walked towards the rear with MacBride at his heels, entered a narrow corridor off the left corner and knocked at a door. It opened and a small, dark youth with side-burns and a close-clipped mustache looked out.

MacBride, looking beyond him, saw Jackman sitting at a table. He pushed aside the waiter, but the dark youth said: "Hey, wait a minute, you."

MacBride thrust him aside and went in saying: "Hello, Dan."

Jackman sat in shirt-sleeves and white double-breasted waistcoat, his tie off and his winged-collar open. Bombino, the club manager, was fat and soft and white in evening clothes. The dark youth closed the door, scowling.

Big Dan leaned back expansively, cocking one whimsical eye. "Am I honored, Cap?"

"It's the way you look at it. Hello, Bombino.... Who's"—he jerked a thumb towards the dark youth—"the fresh guy?"

Jackman said: "Oh, forget it, Cap. He didn't know you. He's a sax player. Drinking?—or does it spoil your breakfast?"

"Nothing spoils my breakfast, but I'm not drinking. You know why I'm here, don't you?"

"Suppose *you* tell me."

"Gatz. Gatz and his boy friends. Your heels, Dan." He eyed Jackman steadily. "And a guy named Lake. Your heels rubbed him out. You know why I'm here."

Jackman took a drink without removing his eyes from MacBride's.

"That's damned unfortunate, Cap. I'm sorry about Gatz and those guys. I just kept telling them to watch Bess. I told 'em not to take the law in their hands. But—it was their idea of loyalty. You guys sure raised a hell of a racket down in Clemons Street."

"We've still got that jane, Jackman."

"Yeah. Well, I'll have to get her out of it. It was a dumb play Gatz and the boys made. I warned them. But—I'll have to stand by the jane. Get her out."

"You won't get her out, Dan. Not that jane. She was an accomplice and she took a shot at Dongan and she's going to fry. That is, if she don't come clean. She'll come clean, though. I know my janes. She's yellow at heart and she'll spring the truth."

"What truth?"

"About who told Gatz and his boys to get Lake—"

"You're crazy!"

MacBride looked at the dark youth, at Bombino, whose fat jowls shook—back to Jackman, whose pale hard eyes were narrowed. Jackman took a drink and looked at the dark youth. Bombino began breaking up matches. Jackman shoved back his chair, cursing.

"You're beginning to give me a pain, MacBride. Some guy bumps off my step-daughter—"

"You tried to get fresh with her once."

Jackman glared, his mouth hardening. He lit a cigarette and flung the match across the room.

"You better go home, Joe," he said to the dark youth.

The youth crossed the room, picked up his hat and saxophone case.

MacBride said: "You stay right here, fresh guy."

"I'm goin' home."

MacBride shoved him back and Bombino got up and wiped his hands nervously with a silk handkerchief. Jackman got up, spurted smoke through his nostrils.

"What the hell's wrong with you, MacBride?" he growled.

"There's a hell of a lot wrong with a lot of things. Mainly this murder. It looked at first as though some gang was trying to muscle in on your rackets. You might have given them a raw deal. They came back at you by bumping off the kid. But that doesn't figure at all—now. Not at all, Jackman. Because there was no gang. You know what I'm going to hang on you, Dan?"

"What?"

"A murder rap."

"Hell you are."

"Hell I am. You put Bess Marghary on the spot, Dan. You put her on the spot because she was giving information to a couple of private dicks. And she was doing that because she hated you and because you're a louse that Blossom, God help her, has stood by."

The dark youth said: "I'm damned if I'm gonna hang around here and listen to this guy yap all night. I'm goin' home."

"You are like hell. You're going with me. And so are you, Dan. To Headquarters—for breakfast—and other things. There was no gang. There was only one dick—in love with Bess—and his partner. Working for the Crime Commission. Getting the lowdown on your profits—on your vice rackets.

"Lake was picked up by Gatz and his boys before eleven because they slammed in the Clemons Street house before eleven. Some guy got his key and went to his apartment. That guy was in Lake's apartment at eleven, because the elevator boy shoved a telegram under the door to a guy that told him to—at eleven. There was a light in the room. A rifle was used on the girl. It had a silencer and it was fired from a lighted room because the guy knew that if the room was dark somebody might see the muzzle fire. The radio was playing too, to kill any pop the gun would make. One of you guys had sent a wire to Bess telling her to meet Lake at the Boulevard Roof. Signed his name. Reserved a special table—"

"I—I must check up the cash," said Bombino.

"Get back, get back," said MacBride. "Gatz took Lake to the Clemons Street dump to sweat out of him how much information he'd got so far. They tried to get his partner down there. They hung Lake in the attic and we busted in before they could get rid of the body. Get your duds on, Dan. And you, fresh guy—you look like a punk to me—you bring along your saxophone."

Jackman had a vein throbbing on his forehead. He snarled out a short oath, took his coat off the back of the chair and got into it. Put on his tie. His eyes burned whitely beneath his brows. He swung on Bombino in a sudden burst of fury, rough-housed him to the wall. He came out of the tangle, spinning, with a gun he had yanked from Bombino's armpit.

"Yeah, MacBride?" he snarled. "Yeah?"

MacBride let his hand slide down from his pocket. "That was fast, Dan. And swell headwork."

The dark youth had a gun out too.

Bombino sat dumfounded on the floor.

"Well?" rasped Joe. "Well, Dan, what's the verdict?"

"Go out the back way, Joe. Get the big Packard out of the garage, back it in the alley. Fast, Joe. Here—frisk this guy first. Bombino, shell out all the dough you got on you."

MacBride said: "I never thought you'd make a dumb move like this, Dan. I thought you'd at least try to get a lawyer to get out. This is dumb, Dan. Dumb as hell."

"Yeah, but I'm goin' to make room for a new skipper on the Force," Jackman said.

Joe came around and took away MacBride's gun.

Chapter VIII

THE door whipped open and Blossom stood there holding a big automatic. Her face was white, bitter.

The muzzle of her gun spewed flame and the gun convulsed in her hand.

Joe cried out and fell against MacBride.

MacBride fell against Jackman and his left hand shot up quickly and caught Jackman's. They crashed into the table and Jackman's gun went off, a bullet whanged through the ceiling.

Bombino fell in a corner and huddled there.

Joe lay writhing on the floor.

Blossom came in, closed the door, locked it. Her eyes glittered. The big gun shook in her hand. She watched the two men tip the table and crash to the floor with it. She looked at Bombino. Bombino covered his face with his hands.

Blossom crossed the room. "Cut it out, Dan. Cut it out or I'll let you have it."

Jackman rolled his eyes upward. He lay on his back. He saw Blossom standing near his head, pointing the gun downward. He relaxed. He let his gun go and MacBride took it and stood up. Jackman lay there, on his back, his breath beating hoarsely from his open mouth.

Blossom said: "I heard it all, Dan. I was outside the door, I came down here—after MacBride—to help you out of a jam—to shoot MacBride if—" Her voice shook. Her legs shook. "But I heard it all. And right out there I began to see how dumb I was. You hated her. She loved me and she knew I hadn't the guts to break away from you. So she tried to do it her own way. Get me—away from you. I—I wondered why you brought Joe here from Dayton two weeks ago. But I didn't— Hell, I was just dumb. I—I—but—now, Dan—"

MacBride made a quick movement and wrenched the gun from her hand.

She screamed: "Give me it! I've a right to—to—"

"The State'll finish him, Mrs. Jackman. You got an old cop out of a bad spot—and I'm telling you I appreciate it. But—nix on the other thing.... Roll over, Dan."

He leaned down and clicked manacles on Jackman's wrists.

He stepped over Joe—dead Joe, now—and opened the saxophone case. There was a rifle in it. A silencer. The rifle was a 25.20 Savage. It used a bottle-neck cartridge—high power.

ENGLEBERG, sitting in the chair in MacBride's office, said: "We had quite a bit on him. Bess got to his books and copied a lot. I have the notes in a safe-deposit box. I sent Lake that warning wire because I was wandering up on the hill around the house where Bess was staying. I saw a guy hanging around there. I picked him for a rat but I didn't say anything. I just began to hang around too. After a while he went away. I tailed him, and did it so that he knew it. He took a bus back to the city.

"It looked as if something dirty was on the make. So I wired Lake. He was always taking chances. He picked up this jane—Arline Kleinsic—in the *Club Mex*. I told him that was dangerous. It was. She probably sprang the trick that cooked his goose.

"Lake even wanted to kill Jackman. He loved the girl. The things Jackman had done. Once Jackman tried to fix a date with her for a city magistrate—no use mentioning names. Like a fool—the kid never told her mother."

MacBride cut into his eggs. "He was a louse from the word go. And Blossom is a great girl. Joe got the key to Lake's apartment. The jane—Kleinsic—had been up there once and she got the idea of the kill. Joe went up there carrying his sax case. Instead of getting off at the top floor, he got off the elevator four floors below and walked up. He walked all the way down and went out the side entrance. He was the guy phoned for the reservation."

Sergeant Otto Bettdecken looked in and said, fretfully: "Damn it, Cap, there ain't nothin' we can do with that Kleinsic jane. She wants a lawyer. She's been yammerin' and cursin' so dirty that even the guys over in the other cell block can hear and they're beginnin' to get sore. She spit in the matron's face and, gosh, I dunno, a man can't just shut her up."

MacBride held a piece of crisp ham poised on a fork before his mouth. "Has anybody bopped her in the jaw yet?"

"Jeeze, Cap, we ain't laid a hand on her. We ain't touched her. She just goes swearin' and spittin' and—"

"Okey," MacBride said. "Bop her."

"Bop her?"

"Bop her and then gag her. But bop her."

The Quick or the Dead

Capt. Steve MacBride calls it murder wherever he finds it.

Chapter I

BRODERICK came in with the ungainly haste of a fat man, made a dramatic pause, then put his hand behind his back and closed the door, half-leaning against it. With the other hand he drew a handkerchief from his pocket, dabbed at his florid face, dragged the handkerchief from one ear down around his throat to the other. His breath was hoarse between agitated thick lips.

Colfax stood by a window looking down into the courtyard. He neither turned nor said anything.

Broderick looked at Colfax's fragile back, made an exasperated grimace, strode clumsily to the massive desk, tried brandy. He licked his lips and stood glaring at the fragile back of Colfax. A thin, tranquil column of smoke rising from Colfax's cigarette irritated Broderick.

He muttered: "No word of Chadbourne yet?"

"None," murmured Colfax, not turning.

Broderick stared in a sort of repressed fury at the empty glass. His thick voice rushed out bitterly: "This is a hell of a jam! Where is he?"

Colfax said enigmatically: "God knows. God knows everything."

"Don't talk like a fool!"

"Don't act like one."

Broderick erupted. "Don't act like one! By—"

"Shut up." Colfax pivoted and was like cold drawn steel. "Don't come in here and flop around like a lump of jellyfish. You may be manager of this establishment, but I am managing director."

His voice was clipped and brittle. He was small and thin. His white hands looked transparent.

Broderick raised a fist, shook it. "But this is murder! This is something we can't fool with! Don't you realize that this is murder?"

"Don't you realize what financial power Chadbourne wields in Tudor Towers?" Colfax threw Broderick a look of contempt, went to the phone.

"Hello— Anything yet?... You tried all the places?" He hung up, put the phone down slowly.

"Huh?" Broderick asked.

"Of course not."

Broderick's voice got guttural. He thumped his fist down on the desk. "We can't wait any longer. It's murder and we can't wait any longer. We've waited half an hour now and there'll be hell to pay. We can't wait any longer."

Colfax sighed, picked up the telephone again.

Broderick began pacing the floor, mopping his red neck with his handkerchief.

Colfax said: "Police Headquarters."

TUDOR TOWERS was the most luxurious apartment house in

Richmond City. Maintaining full hotel service, it did not cater to transients, accepted no lease for less than a year. It stood on a rise of Marshall Drive, in the swank West End. Its entrance was in a private flagstone courtyard. Twin brownstone gate-posts showed on Marshall Drive. But no name—no name anywhere. From any number of its many quaint turrets the lights of mid-town could be seen.

Two police cars swung in between the brownstone gates, rolled across the flagstone court and drew up beneath the glass marquee. MacBride got out of the first, thrust hands into the pockets of his conservative gray overcoat, waited with a show of weary patience for Moriarity and Cohen to follow. Meanwhile a squad of cops got out of the second car, and two bellboys standing in the yawning doorway put their heads together.

Moriarity appeared and with an exaggerated expression of tenderness helped Cohen to the flags. Cohen looked a little pale.

MacBride snorted. "If it's not one, it's the other. Headquarters is beginning to be like a college dormitory or something."

Cohen shrugged. "I had to be sociable, didn't I?"

"Oh, so drinking a bottle of brandy and six bottles of beer is being sociable, eh?"

Cohen coughed. "Was only five bottles, Cap."

Moriarity said: "It wasn't the liquor, Cap, it was something he ate. Ha!"

"So now," said MacBride, "you're going to act that way…. Hey, Sergeant, leave two men here. If any reporters come, boys, don't let 'em in. The rest of you guys with me…. Come on, Ike, make believe you're sober."

A man in the doorway was rubbing his hands together nervously. "Is this the police?"

"Believe it or not," Moriarity said.

The lobby was vast, with a floor of stone. It was deftly lighted.

The nervous man said: "I am the second assistant manager. This way, please. The north tower."

They went through a passageway to an elevator. The elevator carried them silently to the fifth floor. At the end of the corridor Simms Colfax stood in his elegant morning clothes.

"Good morning," he said. He opened the door, went in with it and stood at one side.

MacBride walked past him, kept walking across the large living-room till he came to the body of a woman lying on the floor. He stood for a moment looking down at it. Then he turned.

"Who is she?"

Colfax said: "No one *seems* to know."

"No one seems to know."

"You see," Colfax said, "she is a stranger to me—I am the managing director—and to Mr. Broderick, the manager, and to the three assistant managers. Also to the chambermaid—who found the body—and to the housekeeper, the head porter and the bell-captain."

"What time was the body found?"

"At eight o'clock."

"It was reported at eight-thirty-five. Did it take you that long to make up your mind whether this was a police job?"

Colfax raised his palms. "We were upset."

"Who lives here?"

Colfax raised his chin a trifle, clasped his hands behind his back. "Magistrate Chadbourne."

"Chad—"

Cohen said: "Oh-oh."

MacBride turned to look at the body again; turned back to Colfax, regarded him with blunt eyes. "Where's Chadbourne?"

"He is—he doesn't seem to be here."

"She's been choked," Moriarity said, kneeling. "Some guy choked hell out of her. Lookit—will you lookit!"

MacBride stared until Colfax turned halfway and flicked a finger at an imaginary spot on his trousers. MacBride swiveled, entered the bathroom, the bedroom, the library, the kitchenette. He returned slowly to the living-room.

"Did the maid find the body after she made up the beds?"

"The beds," Colfax said, "were not slept in last night—the maid says."

"Was the door locked when the maid came in?"

"Yes."

"There's only one door?"

"Yes."

Moriarity was saying: "Choked…. Hey, was there a doctor in here? Did you—"

"Dr. Pyne, the house physician," Colfax said. "He was on his way out when the maid ran into him. He came in directly. He left word that he thought the woman had been dead from eight to ten hours."

Cohen said: "There's her coat and hat. Did anybody see a purse around here?"

"No," Colfax said. "I asked the maid."

Cohen nudged MacBride. "There ain't a label in her hat or coat. But it's good stuff. I used to be in the business. This coat here set her—or some guy—back four or five hundred."

Colfax drew MacBride into an alcove. "Frightful mess. Captain. You well acquainted with Jim Chadbourne?"

MacBride eyed him. "Sure. I always thought he was a pretty swell egg. You?"

"I know Jim quite well."

"All right." MacBride indicated the body. "What do you think about this?"

Colfax arched one thin eyebrow. "What can I say?" He paused. "Except"—he paused again—"it's rather hard."

"I'd say it's hard on the girl. Cripes, I've got a kid of my own. This one's only a kid."

"Ye-es. But take Jim. Young—forty, isn't he?—young and one of the outstanding magistrates, headed for a big place. Wealthy. No one's ever dared try to bribe him. And now—"

"Listen. You might be a swell guy, Mr. Colfax. I don't know you. But say you are." He shook his head slowly and nodded towards the dead girl. "That's something a guy can't straighten out—not with me, ever. I don't care what she was—good, bad, or on the edge. If she was good, the guy's a louse. If she was bad, the guy's a louse too. He was screwy to do a thing like this and it's bad news all around. Down on the South Side we get a hunky who up and beans his frau with an ax for playing around. We send him up for life or fry him on the hot-seat. And that"—he touched his chest—"gets me hard, but we have to do it. And I can understand a poor bohunk doing a thing like that. But this—nix. It's over my head. It's murder."

Colfax stared at him with cool tranquillity.

MacBride turned away and went to the telephone, called Police Headquarters.

"MacBride. Otto.... Yeah. Tudor Towers out on Marshall Drive.... An unidentified woman dead in Magistrate Chadbourne's apartment.

Was found at eight this morning by one of the maids. Strangulation. Chadbourne's not here. His bed was not slept in last night. It looks punk to me.... Yeah. Buzz the Medical Examiner's office and if Charley's awake have him shoot over here to look things over. Better tell the morgue too.... No, don't give it to the papers until we straighten out a bit. I haven't got a single clue yet.... Well, you fat-head, if you'd seen her face you wouldn't ask me if she's beautiful. You've been hanging around with tabloid newshawks too long."

He slammed the receiver on to the hook, then put the phone down quietly.

Cohen said: "I'm going out and get me another pick-me-up."

"You stay here and suffer," MacBride said.

He crossed to the body, knelt down on one knee, leaned with his elbow on the other. His lean, chiseled face looked grim, yet there was something of weariness, too, in the lines about the mouth. The morning sun had crept across the tamarack-brown carpet and now shone on one side of the woman's dead face. Standing, she would have been tall, high-breasted, long-legged. Not a frail woman. There was something Scandinavian about her features. Her hair was straw-colored. Her hands were large, but only in proportion to her build. The fingernails were squarish.

The skipper stood up and looked at Colfax. "I want your staff up here. Everybody—bellhops, maids, porters, clerks, all your managers. Everybody."

"But if everybody is here, there will be no one to—"

"Send 'em in relays—but I want everyone. And I mean right now—not half an hour from now.... Ike! *Ike!*"

"Honest, Cap, I won't be a minute. Just rye and Worcestershire—half and half."

"Okey, then—okey. But snap on it. So help me, I never saw the likes of— Excuse me, Mr. Colfax. Please start shooting your staff up here. The maid first—the maid found the body."

Colfax made a slight motion with his lips, tightening them. Very stiff, poised as an icicle, the managing director left the apartment.

MacBride relaxed, looked at Moriarity. His voice dropped to a rumbling mutter: "Cripes, Mory, this is going to be tough on Jim. I went to school with that guy. Grew up with him. Of course, his family had dough. But he always stuck with his old friends. He was always a white guy. I'd give ten years of my life not to be on the case. Ten years! You think I wouldn't, eh?"

"What the hell," Moriarity said vacantly.

MacBride stared hard into space. "I don't know… the higher a guy rises nowadays the more strings get hung on him. Politics—yeah!" He chopped off a short, hard laugh. "And this: women. Wine, women and politics. Song never hurt any guy."

The sunlight was now a white bar across the dead woman's face. Fingers had left marks on her columnar throat.

Chapter II

POLICE COMMISSIONER HARRY STERNS sat back in his leather-upholstered chair and tapped his lower lip with rimmed pince-nez.

MacBride said: "I put the whole shebang over the jumps. But it was a waste of breath. I even had the chef up. I figured while I was at it I might as well do things up brown. Colfax, the guy runs the place, gave me a little trouble—but I guess I just don't speak his language. He's a dry kind of guy and I kept thinking he was trying to make a pass at me all the time. Nobody heard a thing all night. Nobody saw Chadbourne. Nobody saw the dead woman."

Sterns nodded. "And the bed wasn't slept in."

"No. I telephoned all over town trying to locate Chadbourne, but nothing doing. He's pulled a fade-out."

"Tough." Sterns shook his head.

"Tough. I like Jim. Good ——, this will start something," he said with sudden vehemence; relaxed, exhaling heavily.

"The flash goes out, huh?"

"What do you think?"

MacBride dropped his voice. "You know what I think, Harry. You know what I think of Jim." His voice dropped lower still, he laid a hand on his knee. "There's only one thing to do."

Sterns grimaced, nodded. "Okey, Steve."

"MacBride left the office, went down two flights, into the Missing Persons Bureau. Sergeant Oberkopf looked up from a crossword puzzle.

MacBride said: "Magistrate Chadbourne, Joe: get him."

"What'd he do?"

"Don't you work here?"

Oberkopf laughed.

"That job at Tudor Towers," MacBride said. "If a jane was found dead in a guy's room, and the guy wasn't around, what would you do?"

"Okey. I'll shoot the boys out."

Back in his own office, MacBride called the dispatcher. "Bill, flash all the precincts. We're out after Magistrate Chadbourne, missing since last night. He was last seen at dinner in the dining-room of Tudor Towers, at six."

As he hung up, Moriarity came in. "Ike show up?"

"Listen, Mory." MacBride jabbed a finger at him. "A nice friend of yours is going back to harness faster than that. Show up? Hell, I knew when I let him go that the dirty son-of-a-gun would never show up. For three mornings this month he's shown up here looking like something a cow kicked around. And that's not counting the two mornings he didn't show up at all and the night the jackass got plastered and joined a circus bound for Boston."

"He's a good guy, though."

"Sure, you'd say that. The only reason you ain't drunk all the time is because your wife would beat you up. I'd like—"

The phone bell jangled. MacBride reached for the instrument. His face darkened.

"Oh, it is, is it?... Well, pipe this, you rat—.... I don't want any alibis. I told you to come right back, and I'll bet the minute you got out of my sight you said 'Hell for you, Skipper!' and—... What?" MacBride's voice dropped. "*What?*... Yeah, Grove and Parkway— shoot.... You did, eh? That's the boy, Ike. Great stuff!... What then?... *What!* You mean to stand there and tell me that— Good cripes!... No—no, go on, go on.... Yeah, I got it.... I'll be a son!... Blue sedan, Buick, Pennsy pads, F-66400-X...." His pencil flew over a sheet of paper; notes grew. "Okey, kid, take it easy.... S'long."

He hung up with a bang, slammed both palms down on the desk. "Now what do you think of that?"

"What?"

"Ike came out of a speakeasy in Grove Street and saw a hold-up at Grove and Parkway, two blocks away. And what do you think was held up?"

"Huh?"

"The morgue bus! And what do you think was stolen? *The dead girl!*"

Moriarity smiled. "After all, Cap, there's no telling what Ike was drinking—"

"Listen, drunk or sober, Ike doesn't see things. I trained that guy. Besides, we'll get it from the precinct in a minute. The two guys on the morgue bus were winged. Ike says he came out of the speak just as the shooting started. He busted into a run and he thinks he wounded one of the guys in the Buick. He picked one of the morgue guys up out of the gutter and the guy said the body was lifted. Can you tie that!"

He grabbed up the phone and gave the news to the Commissioner. He had barely hung up when he received the same news from the dispatcher's office, relayed from the Seventh Precinct house. The Seventh's squad car and flyer were out. MacBride sent orders to the Fourth and Eighth Precincts to send out their cars, and a Headquarters flyer boomed across town towards the North Side, whither it was rumored the blue Buick had gone.

Ike Cohen landed in the office with a torn hat, a torn tie and a worn and haggard look.

"Did I have fun? You know, I thought I was crazy. I thought I was completely gone. But no—there it was: the morgue bus being stuck up. So indignation began to burn in my breast—"

"Indig-what?" slurred Moriarity,

"Well, maybe I'd better not go into that. But don't this stand you on your toes? Will you please tell me what these guys want with that dead jane?... Imagine, coming out of the speakeasy and seeing— Well, just imagine!" He lit a cigarette. "Any news about Chadbourne?"

The door opened and Kennedy, of the *Free Press*, drifted in, saying: "Is everybody unhappy?"

"I've decided to ignore you," MacBride said.

"Good old tomato!" Kennedy chuckled lazily. "You can't ignore the facts of life, Cap, and I'm one of the facts…. By the way, I hear there's been murder done—most foul. What were you doing running away from that scrap at Grove and Parkway, Ike?"

"Oh, were you the guy I saw hiding behind that lady?"

"Cap—" Kennedy dropped wearily to a chair, his whimsical young-old face falling into gray lines. "Cap, why do you suppose that body was stolen?"

"Why do you?"

Kennedy blew a smoke circle. "It might have been stolen by a gang of enthusiastic young students."

"Horseflies!" Moriarity grunted.

"Swell sense of humor," Kennedy smiled. "Marvelous reflex…. Look, Cap. Did she have any rings on, any bracelets, necklace—what-not?"

"No. If she did I would have taken them off."

"Not robbery then." His gray face dropped. "I thought you might have left something on—something that might have incriminated somebody. If it's not that—then identification of the body might have meant that somebody would have been caught. Man, this is rich! Swell copy! The berries!… But what's the meaning of it all?"

"All I know," Cohen threw in, "is that these guys were heels—hot rods. And the swellest pick-me-up I ever had."

Kennedy mused. "Funny guy… Colfax."

MacBride's ears pricked up. "What makes you think so?"

"He's so anxious about Jim Chadbourne. I understand that half an hour elapsed between the discovery of the body and the report to the police."

"That's happened before," MacBride said, still watchful.

Kennedy wore a droll smile. "You're telling me history? But would it mean anything if during that elapsed half-hour Colfax tried hard to locate Jim Chadbourne? By phone, you understand, popping out SOSs thither and yon."

MacBride drummed hard fingernails on the desk, put a callous eye on Kennedy. "What's this, a buck and wing, or are you on the up and up?"

Kennedy raised a hand and looked at it. "Way up and up. I wouldn't fool you, Skipper. Not me—not you."

"What did I tell you?" MacBride flung at Moriarity. "I had a hunch right off the bat that Colfax was too sure of himself. He'd rehearsed too much. He gave me a smooth song and dance…. Where'd you muscle in on that dope. Kennedy?"

"Pul—lease!"

"Okey, pardon my foot." MacBride scowled. "But this is God's honest, Kennedy?"

"By the beard of the prophet."

The phone rang. MacBride answered it; boomed: "What!" In a minute he hung up and massaged his palms. "They found the jane. Out on Farmingdale Road. In a culvert. Stripped."

Chapter III

COLFAX, who had changed to a lounge suit, sat behind his massive desk smoking an after-luncheon panatela. He was a small, pale man amid huge, dark furnishings. In repose he was steel undrawn. When MacBride entered like a gust of rowdy wind, Colfax moved a transparent hand, indicating a large chair.

"A hectic day for you, Captain."

"I'm naturally a hectic guy, Mr. Colfax."

Smoke rose tranquilly from Colfax's excellent cigar.

MacBride said: "I want to know why you killed half an hour this morning trying to get in touch with Jim Chadbourne."

"I see," Colfax said quietly.

"That was a boner, but it was a worse boner when you didn't think it important enough to tell me. I'm a lousy guy when you pull a fast one like that, Mr. Colfax."

"I did not intend it to be a fast one, Captain MacBride. Nor did I think, subsequently, that it was essential I tell you."

"I'm to be the judge of that."

Colfax smiled bleakly. "Yes, of course. The police are always to be the judge—"

"Now don't make any cracks. I know what you think of me. You think I'm just a cop, kind of rough and ready and not up on the nice things in conduct. And you're right. Your business is being—well, diplomatic. You do it swell. Mine isn't. I want to know why you tried so hard to locate Jim Chadbourne."

"My reaction to the finding of the body, I think, was a quite natural one. I know Jim—well. When I saw the body in his apartment, my first reaction was one of disgust. That passed. I am not a policeman. My second reaction was in the interest of Jim. I tried to locate him, to get things straight. I have a strong personal interest in him."

"Do you know that when the morgue bus left here this morning it was held up and the body was stolen?"

Colfax made a quick motion with his lips. "No."

"The body was just found again—stripped. What do you think of that?"

"I really don't know what to think."

MacBride eyed him levelly. "You're a tough nut to crack, Mr. Colfax. I don't know whether you're telling the truth or not. Murder's been done. Two men on the morgue bus were wounded. I think that if you really wanted to help us out you could drop a hint."

"I am in complete ignorance."

"Only because you don't want to make any cracks until you see Jim Chadbourne."

There was a knock on the door.

Colfax said: "Come in."

Magistrate Chadbourne came in. He wore tweed knickers, a tweed coat.

"I just got back," he said.

He was a tall, burly man, with a heavy jaw, sandy hair. He closed the door softly.

"I met Broderick," he said.

He made a gesture with a curved pipe, took a puff at it.

Colfax seemed to grow remote.

MacBride got up and stood looking quizzically at Chadbourne.

Chadbourne shrugged, frowned. "Broderick told me," he said. "Yes, Broderick told me. Who was the woman?"

"Hello, Jim," MacBride said.

"Hello, Steve. What's eating you, old master mind?"

"Maybe you think you're not in a jam."

Chadbourne looked thoughtful. "That's what I was thinking on the way up in the elevator, after what Broderick told me."

"It was murder, you know," MacBride muttered.

"What Broderick said. Any leads?"

"Only you."

Chadbourne had a husky chuckle. "You're not taking that very seriously, are you, Steve?"

"What the hell else am I supposed to do? A jane is bumped off in your apartment some time around midnight. Your bed's not slept in. You're nowhere to be found. Cripes, Jim!"

"I catch on." Chadbourne puffed his pipe. "I was up country. Left at seven last night."

"Where?"

"Riding Lakes. You can drive it in an hour. I went up to see about a camp for a couple of weeks. Telephoned the caretaker a few days ago and he said he was going away for a week but he told me where he'd hide the key. I drove up there, that's all."

"And just got back, eh?"

"Yes. I stayed in the camp overnight. I got away late this morning."

MacBride said: "Anybody see you up there?"

"You're not quizzing me, are you?"

"I don't know what else you'd call it."

Chadbourne scoffed. "Don't be an ass, Steve! I'm telling you the truth, damn it!"

"I want to believe you like hell, Jim, but this is something you can't be offhand about. No kidding. This goes deep. This is murder. For crying out loud, wake up! I'm only in charge of the Detective Bureau."

Chadbourne's lips tightened. He flicked a look at Colfax. Colfax's head might have moved a fraction of an inch—negatively. His white fragile face remained expressionless. In that massive room he looked like a piece of rare bric-a-brac.

MacBride said thickly: "You'd better come down and see the Commissioner with me, Jim."

Chadbourne's big jaw hardened. "You're cop, aren't you, Steve? For all the years you've known me, you stand there and say I'm guilty of murder."

"I haven't said that. You know the rough details. If a guy came up against you wrapped up in evidence like this, what would you do? What the hell can I do?" His voice went down deep, throbbed a bit when he said: "Maybe you think I'm happy to be on this. If you do, you're crazy. Come on, Jim."

THE afternoon papers flung the news to the public. The tabs didn't pull their punches and the name of Magistrate James Chadbourne was taken for a ride. A man whose private life thus far had been impeccable, whose career on the bench was meteoric but, on past performance, justifiable. The tabs played up the fact that he was a bachelor—"young, handsome, charming personality."

Dozens of people had tried to identify the dead woman. None had succeeded. Who she was, whither she had come, remained a mystery. The bolder news sheets suggested the skeleton in Chadbourne's closet. Pitching mud at a supposedly clean record makes racier reading. The tabs did it to a turn.

The long arm of the law reached out, groped for the gunmen who had wounded two morgue attachés, stolen a dead woman, left her stripped on a lonely county road.

It hit MacBride hard. There was nothing he could do about it. The facts lay before him. He had seen good men go wrong before and he knew that good men do sometimes go wrong. There was not the vestige of an alibi upon which Chadbourne could lean. He cursed MacBride.

"You blockhead," he said. "If I'd planned to kill her, don't you think I would have tied up all loose ends? I never saw the woman before. I tell you I left the city at seven last night and spent the night at Loon Camp. Nobody saw me. Of course not."

MacBride said: "Don't get steamed up, Jim. I'm not trying to hang anything on you. I want to get you out of this, if you're innocent. If you're not, it's just too bad."

"To you a pinch is a pinch, Steve. I know you. You'd pinch your own brother if you had one."

"And if he committed a crime," nodded MacBride. "You're doing a hell of a lot of squawking, Jim. A lot of yapping. That's not like you. Put me straight. Give me a chance to prove where you were last night."

"To hell with you. I'm sore."

"Which is dumb for an enterprising magistrate."

"To hell with you."

MacBride, unabashed, said: "Could a woman prove you were at that camp last night?"

"No. Can you prove I was at my apartment?"

MacBride wagged his head. "Can the wisecracks, Jim. It's not going to get you anywhere and if you keep it up I'm going to get sore."

An hour later municipal bigwigs convened in a large room on the top floor of Police Headquarters. Party chiefs, lesser gods from the outlying aldermanic precincts, the vital cogs in the mechanism of the municipal government. Comptroller Hourig, with his thick-lensed glasses; Wellsboro, President of the Board of Aldermen; State's Attorney Michaelsen; Justice Lowenbrau, with his one baleful eye; His Honor the Mayor, Henry Chilton, with his purring voice at odds with his massive build.

The Mayor said: "It looks as if Jim is in bad and something must be done about it. Our party can't stand a blow below the belt like this, gentlemen. Did you see the papers? It is a most disgraceful situation. It seems to me that when the body was found we should have been notified."

Commissioner Sterns said: "What was done was the proper thing. Steve MacBride went to the scene, reported. We all like Jim. But we were duty-bound to start a search for him when he could not be located through the usual channels."

"Crap!" snapped State's Attorney Michaelsen. "There was no attempt whatever made to keep the soft pedal on this. MacBride's goofy over this thing called loyalty to the badge—"

"Is that so?" growled MacBride. "You tell me, huh? You'd do well, mister, to sweep out some of the corners in your office."

"You heard what I said."

"I heard you. I've been in the Department over twenty years. I've seen administrations come and go, and I'm still here. And not because I pandered to guys like you. I've been suspended, demoted, kicked out to the sticks, but, by cripes, I always come back. I know Jim better than any of you birds know him. I like him but if he's ratted on his job I'll break my neck to give him the limit."

The Mayor smiled indulgently. "We value men like you, Captain MacBride. But they are making a party issue of this. You acted too quickly. You should have considered us."

"Murder is murder, Your Honor. There's no consulting anybody about it. You're trying to tell me my job. Nobody can tell me my job. When I find murder I know what to do about it."

The Mayor had a feline smile. "I know, I know. But you're taking a fundamental attitude. We are bound by party loyalty to help Jim Chadbourne."

"Whether he killed the woman or not," MacBride said.

"Exactly."

MacBride laughed harshly. "I'm not a politician. I'm a policeman. We don't talk the same language. And besides, do you think you can shove this bunk down the newspapers' throats?"

"We've got to," the Mayor said.

The State's Attorney said: "Jim says he was out at some camp at Riding Lakes. We can find some guy out there to back that up. It's open and shut. It's the simplest thing in the world."

"You think it is!" MacBride growled. "How are you going to account for the stolen body, the two men from the morgue that were wounded? There's the rub. There's more than just Jim Chadbourne mixed up in this."

"There must be a new mob," the State's Attorney said, "that makes a practice of stealing dead bodies. Get a couple of newspapermen to write it up dramatically. We can do it. We've got to do it."

MacBride said: "I've got men out after those gunmen. Suppose we nail them—what then?"

"The thing is," His Honor said, "we've got to get Jim in the clear. I don't want him detained any longer, and when I say that, I mean it. And you will do well, Captain MacBride, to walk gently. This is a strong administration."

"I won't be told my job, Your Honor."

"You have a family, haven't you, to support?"

MacBride closed his fists. "I get you," he muttered.

Commissioner Sterns stood up. "I owe my appointment to you, Mr. Mayor, but I will say that this is the dirtiest, rottenest bit of mental coercion—"

"Oh, don't be noble," the State's Attorney scoffed.

MacBride rumbled: "Would it interest you gentlemen to know what I really think about this case? I've got a hunch, based on no reason I can grab hold of. Only because I know Jim. I thought I knew him all the way. Maybe I do. And he's acting queer. And it's possible— get this straight—that he didn't kill that girl. It's possible that the same line of bunk that you birds call party loyalty has got hold of him!"

"Well, well!" sing-songed the State's Attorney. "Now isn't that interesting!"

"Whatever your hunch is," said the Mayor, "I'm not interested. Jim may have got tangled up with a woman. Many good men do. The thing is, we think more of Jim than we do of her. That, in a nutshell,

is it. The party—first, last, always. United we stand, divided we fall—
and that sort of thing."

"Hurray!" said the State's Attorney.

Chapter IV

A T six that night MacBride sat in his office. He was a bit dazed.
His desk was bare and his big hands rested on it, side by side,
and he stared at his hands vacantly. Chadbourne had been released
on a writ. The State's Attorney's office had made a statement relative
to the fact that it had proof Chadbourne spent the night at Loon
Camp, Riding Lakes.

An unclaimed, unidentified body lay in the morgue. Murder had
been committed and the powers that be did not want the murderer
brought to justice. This was hard against the grain of MacBride. It
made a lump in his chest and sometimes the lump rose and almost
gagged him. He was, as he had said, no politician. He was not attuned
to the political mind. The magnitude of the political machine over-
shadowed him; the rumble of its machinery was a dull, persistent roar
in his ears. He was floored—knocked flat. They had not even wanted
a fall-guy.

Kennedy came in—gray-faced, whimsical-eyed. "You don't look
like the hard-hitting, energetic Captain MacBride I've been hearing
about."

"Hello, Kennedy."

"Down-hearted?"

"Liver."

Kennedy tangled up his legs. "I've been thinking, believe it or not.
I've been thinking about those eggs swiping that body, stripping it
and then ditching it. It's interesting as hell."

"Yeah? So what?"

"You said there were no rings—no jewelry. A woman—any
woman—is bound to wear some bit of jewelry. This one didn't. Ah—
clue! But no kidding... huh?"

"So what?"

"It was removed at death. Through jewelry dead persons are often
identified. We'll say the jewelry was removed. All right. What else
can persons be identified by?"

"Clothes— By cripes!"

"Easy, old tomato!"

MacBride relaxed. "I forgot—there were no labels."

"All right. Suppose there weren't. Clothes can be identified without labels. Ready-made clothes carry labels. I've seen tailor-made clothes that didn't. But in a city of this size a good tailor can trace a garment—through the stitching, the model, that certain something that a certain tailor will put into a garment."

MacBride leaned forward. "You mean those clothes were stolen because some egg figured?... I get you, Kennedy." He leaned back.

"I see they released Chadbourne." Kennedy's smile was sly.

"Yeah. They found a guy can prove Jim was at a camp in the Riding Lakes section all night."

"Did they?" The sly smile remained.

"What the hell are you talking about?"

Kennedy shrugged. "Let it slide.... But, pipe this. Those clothes were stolen for one reason. I'd say the girl was a model, not because all models go to guys' apartments, but because some do. That's just a hint. It may be lousy."

"Thanks, Kennedy."

"Got to be going.... And another thing: Chadbourne's through. Guilty or not, this has licked him. He'll never sit on the bench again." He moved to the door. "Toodle-oo, Skipper."

MacBride sat alone, his shoulders hunched up alongside his ears.

Suddenly he swore—out loud—a violent, guttural oath. He got up, kicked back his chair, grabbed hat and coat and put them on and went hard-heeled down the echoing corridor.

"Where you headed, Steve?" Otto Bettdecken said, in the Central Room below.

"For a fall, probably."

"What a guy!"

"What a *sap!*" MacBride flung back.

THERE was a shop in Cravath Street with one word on the oblong window: *Paul.* It was the fifth shop in front of which MacBride had stopped. Four he had visited. He entered Paul's, and futuristic decorations enveloped him. A woman came towards him—a platinum blonde with slanted eyebrows and a big mouth.

"Yes, sir?"

"I'd like to see the owner."

"He's not in. Can I do something for you?"

"I was thinking about my wife."

"Surely. A gown… lingerie?"

"Complete."

She led him to a room in the rear, showed him gowns, explained about them. Her voice was husky. She showed him lingerie, draped it this way and that, flashed him smiles with her big lips and her slanted eyes.

He said: "It's hard to tell unless you see them on a woman. Last place I was to had some swell pictures."

"They do give one an idea. We have some."

She went into another room, humming to herself. MacBride stood with his hands in his pockets, his eyes keened and darting about the luxurious room. The girl came back, carrying a portfolio and laid it on a slim-legged table. She began turning the pages, explaining about each gown.

MacBride said: "All these originals with you?"

"We make no copies."

"You have beautiful women."

"Yes, we do."

The pages were turned, one by one. MacBride watched each gown, each face. Suddenly he put his finger down.

"That one. I like that dress. Blue, isn't it?"

"Why, this one…" She paused.

He said: "But then I want something that's never been out before. Come to think of it, I've seen one like that."

"Like this?" She seemed confused.

"Like that. The only thing is, I never saw that girl in it. The girl I saw in it was a kind of blonde. She must have bought it here. It was just like that—exactly. Since you said you make no copies. Maybe you can remember."

"You mean—you mean this dress—this one right here?"

"Yes. That one. That one right there."

She said: "You saw this dress on a lady—"

"Yes. She was kind of tall. Well, that one's tall there. But this one I mean had more heft and she looked like a Swede. She wasn't a bad-looking girl. Ten to one you sold the dress to her, because you said— Tell you what. You come with me and I'll show you the girl."

The platinum blonde said: "Really, I can't leave the shop. Perhaps something else would interest—"

"No. This dress right here interests me more than any dress I've ever seen—anywhere. Take back here—back six pages.... You see that girl? Well, she used to interest me, in a purely professional way. I pinched her once for pulling the badger game on a hick from Kokomo. Nellie Cassidy, yes, ma'am! And this girl back here: she's redheaded and her name's Louise Kempfer. And you—now, you—"

The platinum blonde let the pages slip from her fingers. Her shiny slanted eyes crept up along MacBride's chest, paused on a point just below his chin. She stood with her body slightly twisted. Color ebbed from her face.

"Well, I don't know you," MacBride said. "But if you'll close shop I'll take you around and show you this girl I've been telling you about."

She said: "I can't leave the shop."

"What are you shaking about?"

"Nothing."

MacBride dropped his voice: "I've got a memory for mugs in this city. I've never seen yours. Do you want to get a break?"

"I don't know what you mean."

MacBride heard the front door open. His hand dropped into his overcoat pocket. He heard footsteps. A tall man in a tight-fitting blue overcoat strolled into the room and stopped short. The platinum blonde was trembling violently now and staring at the newcomer. The tall man had a thin black mustache, neatly pointed.

"Pardon," he said curtly.

He walked towards the office door, his back to MacBride and the platinum blonde.

"You!" clipped MacBride.

The man stopped, pivoted on one heel, his nose in the air. He said nothing.

MacBride said: "Take your hands out of your pockets."

"I beg your pardon—"

"To hell with that crap! I know a heel when I see one! Get 'em out, baby—and up!"

The man blinked flat gray eyes, withdrew long, thin hands and held them up.

"Over here," MacBride ordered.

The man advanced towards MacBride, blinked his flat gray eyes at the woman. Suddenly the woman cursed and flung herself against MacBride. His left elbow jerked upward, jammed against her throat. She gagged and squirmed to one side. MacBride stepped on the thin man's foot and brought his left arm around to block the thin man's draw from the overcoat pocket. His left hand closed on the thin man's right wrist and he used his service pistol to chop a short blow to the thin man's jaw.

The thin man squealed and tried to fling back, but MacBride's heel held the other's foot to the floor and he had the man's left arm doubled up between their chests, elbow locked to elbow. The thin man used his knee but MacBride twisted and slid the blow off his left thigh; brought his right side around in a sharp pivot and sent the thin man hurtling away from him. The thin man struck the glass panel of the connecting office door. Glass exploded as the door whipped inward and the thin man sprawled into the office. MacBride was over him; wrenched a gun from the man's coat pocket.

MacBride turned and saw the woman tugging at a drawer in the table. He leaped as he heard the drawer grate open. He stuck out his right foot, sent table and woman to the floor. He saw a small automatic bounce on the floor, saw the woman reach for it. MacBride kicked gun and hand. The gun spun away. The woman yelped.

The thin man had streaks of blood on his white face and he was rising unsteadily, rolling his eyes so that the whites were mostly visible. His jaw hung slack and he looked like a half-wit.

MacBride tugged the woman to her feet and ran her into the office. He manacled her to the man. The platinum blonde's hair was disheveled, her slanted eyes were wild.

"I don't know who started this," MacBride said, "but by —— I'll finish it. So I suppose you're Paul."

The man rolled his eyes and made a sickly face.

MacBride squinted. "Yeah… and maybe I've got you figured out too. I don't often go wrong on types." He looked around the office. "I'm going to get ideas in this scatter…."

There was a green steel filing cabinet, with one drawer open. MacBride went to it. There were portfolios in the open drawer, all numbered. One picture was not in a portfolio. It had been stuck away in the rear.

MacBride heard a sound. He looked around. The girl and the man were stealing towards the door.

"Oh, yeah?" said MacBride.

They stopped. The man looked very sick and seemed about to cry. The woman's face was like a painted mask, wild and unreal.

MacBride looked at the picture. His face got long and hard and somber.

He said: "I've had enough of this song and dance." He strode to the pair, blue wind in his eyes. "Who's this girl? What's her name?"

"It's so warm in here," the thin man said weakly.

MacBride struck the photograph with his knuckles. "What's her name, damn you?"

"Karen Lanstrom," the thin man choked.

"Worked here until yesterday and was murdered last night!"

"Oh, it's so warm—"

"Murdered, by cripes! And then stolen—her dead body stolen from the morgue bus and the clothes taken so that no connection would be made with your scatter here. And what a scatter I've fallen into!"

The thin man whimpered: "Elsie, why did you let this man get in the back room?"

"Did I know he was a cop?"

MacBride said: "Where did this girl go last night?"

"I read in the papers," the man said, "that she went to Tudor Towers."

"Fat-head, you knew all about that before you read it in the papers, because the body was stolen before even the papers got wind of the murder."

"Oh!" whimpered the thin man.

"Don't say anything," the woman said.

"You'll change that tune, sister," MacBride said. "We'll hold court right here."

MacBride walked to the desk, picked up the telephone. He called Police Headquarters.

"Hello, Otto. Moriarity and Cohen there...?" He sat on the desk, dangling one foot. "You, Ike?... MacBride. Hey, you and Mory come down here to 241 Cravath right away.... Yeah. And listen, keep it under your hat. And Ike—in the top right-hand drawer of my desk is a nice new piece of hose.... Don't ask questions. Grab Mory and pop down."

He hung up.

"So you're Captain MacBride," the woman said.

"Yeah," the skipper nodded. "Good old kind-hearted Steve Mac-Bride. Is that bad news?"

Chapter V

IT was raining. Where Marshall Drive became a low hill the wide pavement was dark and shiny under the moving glare of auto lights. Tudor Towers looked fabulous, with its great gate-posts, its lanterns, its quaint turrets and towers dotted here and there with lighted windows.

MacBride arrived unostentatiously, in a taxi. The taxi clattered across the courtyard. A doorman in a capote waited with a big umbrella. MacBride lunged from the cab, passed beneath the marquee, entered the vast, deftly lighted lobby with something undeviating and grim in his walk and the set of his jaw.

An elevator lifted him upward. His neat gray coat and neat gray hat had spots of rain on them. Rain had spotted the bright polish on his shoes. He smoked a cigar and he smoked it furiously, filling the elevator with pungent fumes.

He got out and walked doggedly. He stopped and knocked at a door. It was opened by Chadbourne. Smoke and voices were in the living-room. Chadbourne had been drinking.

"Hello, copper."

"Hello, Jim."

MacBride pushed past him.

State's Attorney Michaelsen was there; Mayor Henry Chilton and some others MacBride had seen at the Party gathering. All the men were in shirt-sleeves. Some looked haggard. They had been talking, arguing, smoking and drinking.

"You again?" Michaelsen said.

MacBride said: "Your Honor… gentlemen." He tossed his hat on to a console, unbuttoned his overcoat, laid aside his cigar.

Simms Colfax came in from another room. Cool as an icicle. Elegant. Clothes did not entirely make Colfax, but they helped.

"This is a surprise, Captain." His Honor said, purring, running his thumbs up and down lavender suspenders.

One of the other men tried to be jocular. "Herr Captain looks very lowering," he said thickly.

MacBride said nothing. He stood on wide-planted feet, moving his weary, bitter gaze from face to face, slowly.

Colfax stood remote in a corner.

"Well," the State's Attorney snapped, "be dramatic now—now be dramatic. Ready: one—two—*three!*... What—no?"

Chadbourne shuffled across the tamarack-brown carpet in black slippers, dropped to a chair near the Mayor, smoked listlessly.

Somebody said: "Try some of this Scotch, MacBride."

"Mr. Mayor," MacBride said, ignoring the invitation, "I had a run of luck tonight. This'll interest all of you. I found out who the dead woman was."

The men sat back, looked at one another. But Chadbourne kept looking at MacBride.

The State's Attorney said: "Now what are we supposed to do? Cheer? Weep?"

"I found out something else," MacBride said. "I found a new racket in town. The mannequin racket. This ought to interest you. A so-called swell shop hires girls as mannequins. It's done like this. Guys with jack go down there, watch a revue of the models. Later—at night as a rule—a girl goes out to a guy's apartment to show him a dress—or lingerie. Sometimes she knows what it's all about. Sometimes she don't. The shop where she works gets a split.

"This girl Karen Lanstrom was a hick from Iowa. She'd run away from home and she landed here and she landed in Paul's shop. She was a new type and she was dumb. Last night she went out wearing a blue dress to show. She came to this apartment at nine. She was murdered here because she didn't know what it was all about and was set to give the guy away.

"The guy cleared out through a stairway down the back of the tower, the same way he'd come in. And that same guy had a finger in this racket. A mob was sent to swipe the body from the morgue bus and get the clothes the girl wore, so they couldn't be traced. The guy that murdered that jane is in this room right now."

"Will you listen to him!" exclaimed the State's Attorney.

"You'll listen to me!" barked MacBride. "If it costs me my job, you'll listen! And the guy that murdered that girl is going to take it on the nose!"

"Look here now, look here now!" cried His Honor.

"And you know who I mean!" MacBride flung at him. "You can't slide out of this, Mr. Mayor! You killed that girl and—"

The State's Attorney was on his feet. "Shut up!"

"You make me! I've got the evidence. I beat hell out of Paul to get it, but the blonde in the store came through quietly, to get a break. So you can say the guy's story is no good because I beat him, but the woman came through of her own accord. Tie that and see how you like it!"

All the men were on their feet. The Mayor was pale, dry-lipped. His eyes glittered.

"You idiot, what did I tell you today? Didn't I tell you to drop this? You cheap upstart of a lousy police captain, do you think you can run this municipal government?"

"No. And I'm not. I'm running my own job."

The State's Attorney snapped. "This punk can't get away with this. We can buy the woman back."

The Mayor flung at MacBride: "I told you to lay off. Jim here was willing to play ball with us. There wouldn't even be a trial—"

"And then Jim would be through," MacBride said. "Through!"

"We'd take care of him—"

"Says you! The dirt of this thing'd hang over him—always. It'd kill him. You guys think that I was trying to hang something on him. By ——! I wasn't! I ain't now! I'm going to—"

The Mayor walked across to him. "You're not going to do a damned thing, MacBride. This is too big. Too many things are involved. Party loyalty—"

"To hell with your party loyalty! You're throwing Jim to the wolves to save your hide and he's jackass enough to stand for it—because you helped put him where he is—or was, until last night."

Chadbourne said, irritably: "Stay out of this, Steve. I know what I'm doing."

"Yes," said MacBride. "You knew what you were doing when you lent the key to your apartment to His Honor. Yes, you did!"

"Never mind that," cut in the Mayor. "You're not going to do anything."

"I'm not? I'm going to pinch somebody for that murder. I'm going to force a trial if I have to go to the governor. You can't stop me.

Because I've got the goods on you, Mr. Mayor."

The State's Attorney said: "Jim can deny everything that girl and Paul said. Jim's willing to take the rap because we can clear him inside of twelve hours."

Sweat dripped from MacBride's face. He gritted: "You heard me. You heard what I said. There's nobody taking any rap. The pinch I'm making is right here. You, Mr. Mayor."

He put his hand on the Mayor's arm.

The State's Attorney cursed and yanked a gun from his pocket.

Another gun smacked. The State's Attorney said: "Oh!" softly, staggered two steps, fell to the carpet.

Colfax said nothing. His face was white and cool and the Mauser .25 was steady in his fragile hand.

"Good ——!" whispered a tall, thin man.

MacBride had his gun out, covering the men. The State's Attorney sat up, breathing hard.

"Who shot me?" he snarled.

"I," said Colfax tranquilly. "You attempted assault upon a police officer in my establishment."

"I thought," gasped another man, "he was on our side!"

"I was," said Colfax. "But Chadbourne has a lot of money in Tudor Towers. He is one of the biggest backers. We cannot afford to lose him, to run the chance of his *not* getting clear, of perhaps going to jail. I am managing director of this establishment. Its interest is close to my heart. A change in mayors will not affect us in the least. Incidentally, this apartment is soundproof."

MacBride said: "Put your coat on, Mr. Mayor."

"Yes… my coat."

MacBride looked over at Chadbourne. Chadbourne was sitting with his head in his hands.

"What a dope you were, Jim," MacBride said.

Chadbourne didn't say anything.

The Mayor groped. "My… coat."

Backwash

Capt. Steve MacBride rides the trail of a big kidnaping.

Chapter I

KENNEDY, leaning on the bar with his left elbow and with his chin propped on his left hand, laid his right palm on the top of the siphon, pressed down with the heel of his hand and fizzed seltzer hard into a glass of rye. Rye and seltzer geysered, splashed down on a newspaper George the barman was reading.

George looked up. "Well!" he growled.

"My error," Kennedy said, absently. He raised a hand to his lips to camouflage the disorders of indigestion, then stirred his drink with a glass swizzle stick.

"You're drunk," George said indignantly, patting the despoiled newspaper with a towel.

Kennedy raised his drink. "I say with Dryden, 'Bacchus ever fair and young.' This bootleg is the fairest color and the youngest in age I've ever guzzled."

"What are you talking about? That there liquor is a month old."

Kennedy's eyes drooped; he opened them with an effort. "What the hell is that radio mumbling about?"

"Dunno." George turned and gave one of the dials a twist. "Police alarms," he said.

"Is there no escape from monotony?"

"Shut up a minute," George growled.

A blunt voice was broadcasting:

"Richmond City Police Headquarters. Attention all cars. All cars attention. Governor-elect Cortland Wayne left his home on Westover Boulevard at seven o'clock this evening. He was driving a black Cadillac coupé; license number six—B as in Bottom—four—six; license number six—B as in bottom—forty-six. A black Cadillac coupé. He was to speak at the Foursquare Club at thirty minutes past seven

o'clock. He did not arrive there. He is not home. It is now eleven-fifteen o'clock. Foul play is indicated. Stop and investigate any black Cadillac coupé. Report. Again: Attention all cars. All cars attention. Governor-elect Cortland Wayne...."

Kennedy stood back on his heels, blinking.

George said: "Cripes, did you hear that?"

Kennedy weaved. "Where's my coat?"

"Over on that hook."

Kennedy wheeled, lost his balance, regained it and lunged towards a wall rack. He unhooked his topcoat, got his right arm into the left sleeve, dropped his hat. George bounded around the bar and

straightened him out. Kennedy stepped on his hat. George picked it up and slapped it, battered as it was, on Kennedy's head. Kennedy smashed into the door, got it open and barged out.

Before the door had stopped swinging, it whipped open violently. Kennedy ran headlong into the bar, drained his drink, turned and sloped out again. He hove on to the sidewalk, overran the curb, regained the sidewalk and broke into something between a skip and a hobble. A block farther on he reached a main drag, stood swaying breathless

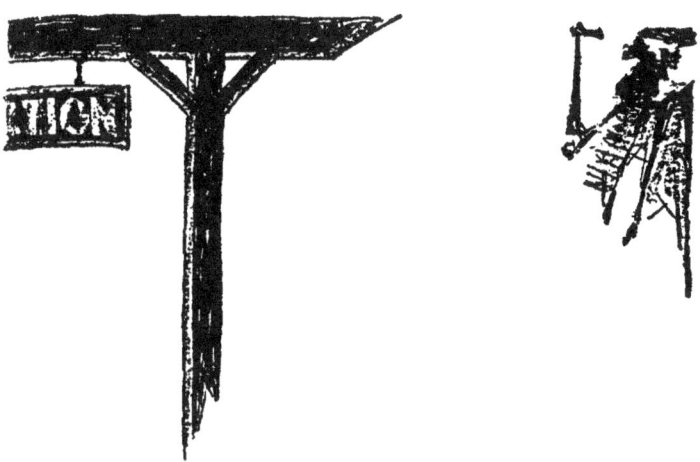

on the corner. He put fingers in his mouth and whistled. A taxi's brakes screeched.

Chapter II

CORINNE WAYNE was a tall woman of thirty. Her hair was russet and full of unexpected gleams and shimmers. Her eyes were large, luminous, her mouth full and exquisite. She had pale satiny skin touched with a faint glow of damask on the cheeks. Her throat was columnar. At college she had been adjudged the most beautiful girl in her graduating class.

MacBride, appearing in the drawing-room doorway, ducked his spare-boned head.

Corinne, rising from a tapestry wing-chair, said: "I'm so glad you came, Captain."

She extended a hand whose wrist was encircled by a bracelet of hammered silver links. MacBride, carrying his derby in his left hand, crossed the room and took her hand with his right.

"I came right over," he said.

Her eyes were red-rimmed and she held a crumpled damp handkerchief in her left hand. She put the handkerchief to her lips, gestured wearily to a divan, sat down in the wing-chair, MacBride unbuttoned his dark blue Chesterfield, dropped to the divan and held his derby on one knee. His blue suit was neatly pressed, his black shoes shone, his shaven face was ruddy from the cold.

He said: "Cort left here at seven, huhn?"

"Yes."

"Sharp?"

She nodded. "He left at seven. It was Mason's night off, so Cort drove the coupé himself."

"He wasn't nervous, was he?"

"No. He was in the best of spirits."

"When did they call from the Foursquare Club?"

"At eight I told them he'd left. I began to worry. I called them again at nine and he hadn't arrived. I spoke with Carl Davenport. He told me not to worry. Then they started telephoning a lot of places—where they thought he might have gone. I did also. We didn't want to notify the police and start a hullaballoo until we were sure. At eleven I couldn't stand it any longer. I called Carl Davenport. He hadn't been successful. I told him I was going to report. What do you suppose has happened?"

MacBride said: "We've got all the patrol cars on the lookout. I've ordered out special squads and all the flyers from every precinct. We've notified the authorities in surrounding towns."

"Do—do you suppose it's—abduction?"

MacBride looked at the inside of his hat. "It has the earmarks, Mrs. Wayne."

"Oh!"

He gestured with his hat. "In which case we can rest assured that he's come to no bodily harm."

"But—but it might be political opposition. It might be some gang. You know that as soon he gets in office he's going to push through the Rittenmoore Bill. And if a gang—"

The skipper frowned. "I wouldn't think of that, Mrs. Wayne."

She muffled a sob in her handkerchief.

MacBride said: "If it's a kidnap job, you'll get word by tomorrow. A phone call. Or maybe they'll make Cort write a letter. Whatever it is, let me know right off the bat."

"But if they demand money—and if you interfere…."

"Cort's an old friend of mine," MacBride said. "You can bank on it that I'll do whatever I think's best for him. For the time being, try to be calm. You're not going to gain anything by worrying. That's an easy thing for me to say, but try it, anyhow. And do as I say. As soon as you hear, let me know."

She said, haltingly: "And if you're not in the office?"

"When a job like this breaks, I sleep at Headquarters."

There were footsteps on a hardwood floor: they became muffled on a rug; drummed louder again on wood. Corinne looked towards the reception hall. A man came long-legged in through the doorway.

"Corinne—"

Seeing MacBride, his voice stopped and his footsteps slowed down. He was a tall man, darkly handsome; young and with a lean smooth poise. He bowed.

"I didn't mean to interrupt."

Corinne had risen. A hand started towards her breast, fell away back to her side.

"Captain MacBride," she said. "Mr. Figueroa."

MacBride got slowly to his feet.

Figueroa bowed again but remained where he had stopped. "How do you do." And to Corinne: "I just heard over the radio—"

"Yes, yes," she sighed, looking away.

"I came to see if there is anything I might do."

She sighed. "Nothing. Nothing yet. Thank you so much, Manuel."

Figueroa had taken a handkerchief from his breast pocket. He rubbed his palms on it, then patted his temples and shrugged his shoulders at MacBride. "It's quite terrible," he said.

MacBride, thinking of the woman, said: "I wouldn't say that. It's nothing to give a rousing cheer about, but on the other hand there's no sense getting all steamed up."

Corinne sat down, rested her elbow on an arm of the chair and sobbed quietly in her handkerchief.

Figueroa said: "Is there no clue?"

"We only got the report half an hour ago and everything's being done." MacBride buttoned his Chesterfield. "Remember what I told you, Mrs. Wayne. Good-night. Good-night, Mr. Figueroa."

Figueroa's voice was off-key— "I'm glad to have met you, Captain."

"Thanks."

MacBride strode to the door, went across the reception hall towards the front entrance. A maid appeared and opened the latch. MacBride, glancing in an elongated mirror beside the open door, saw Figueroa standing in the drawing-room doorway, watching him. MacBride's step faltered. But he picked it up. He did not look around. He went out. He went down four veranda steps, passed beneath a white porte-cochère and took a pale cement walk that crossed a lawn between blue spruces. He could see the right front cowl-light of the police phaeton. He heard low querulous voices.

Achermann, the driver, was holding a spare figure by the arm and saying: "Nix, I said; nix."

"Hey," MacBride said.

"It's this pest," Achermann complained.

Kennedy said: "It's getting so nowadays that a private citizen takes his life in his hands every time he goes out."

"Yeah?" MacBride muttered. "Who's been picking on you?"

"Achy, here—"

"Oh, yeah?" MacBride muttered. "Well, I told Achy to kick any stray newshawks where it would do good if they clowned around."

"Ah, my pal," Kennedy sighed.

Achermann said: "The reason I'm holding him up, Cap, is that the souse can't stand. He fell out of a taxi, fell over the curb and started crawling up the path there on hands and knees."

Kennedy's tired smile wavered. "I've got to get a statement from Mrs. Wayne."

"Put him in the back, Achy," MacBride said. "Get in, Kennedy! Get in!" Impatient, he took Kennedy away from Achermann, lifted him bodily and piled him into the tonneau. Climbing in, he said: "Shoot, Achy."

The phaeton moved, purred two blocks to an automatic traffic light, made a U-turn on the green and headed back towards mid-town. The wind was raw and rowdy. Stars twinkled back of a mackerel sky. The canvas top rat-a-tatted petulantly and the wind whistled in varied keys past lights and braces.

Kennedy was slumped in one corner, his hat still as battered as when he had left George's. Knuckles of his right hand were skinned. There was a ragged tear in his trousers.

"You make me sick," MacBride complained. "What the living hell induced you to take a header off the water wagon again?"

"Well, it was about seven o'clock, and I was off duty, and at the time it bore the hallmark of a swell idea."

"If you were off duty, you gonoph, then what's the idea of this do-or-die monkey business over an interview?"

Kennedy hiccoughed. "I never—uh—thought of that."

MacBride leaned forward and said alongside Achermann's ear: "Twenty-five Olympia Street."

Kennedy went to sleep. Number 25 Olympia Street had an electric sign swung out over the sidewalk. It said: *Turkish Baths.*

MacBride said: "Give me a hand, Achy."

Chapter III

SERGEANT OTTO BETTDECKEN was holding down the central room desk. He lowered a half-eaten hamburger from his red jowls when MacBride came in and clamped a half-drunk bottle of Canadian ale between his commodious knees.

"Anything?" MacBride clipped, preoccupied.

"A lady's Pomeranian pup ran away at 10:35 and answers to the name of Goo-goo and—"

"I mean about Wayne."

"Oh, Wayne. Oh, yes. Oh, that Caddy coupé: Sorensen found it parked on Luke Street between Jockey and Havemeyer. It was empty. Jaekel went right down to look for fingerprints."

"Any blood?"

"Sorensen says nope."

"When'd he find it?"

"Just after you left. At twenty minutes past eleven."

MacBride said: "Give Sorensen special mention. That was snappy work. And for crying out loud wipe the beer suds off your chin."

He went down the wide corridor and climbed a flight of stairs. He walked with his hands thrust into his overcoat pockets and his eyes were still preoccupied. He entered his warm neat office, took off his coat, draped it on a hanger and clipped the hanger on a costumer. He absent-mindedly flipped specks of dust from his hat and then put the hat on top of the costumer.

He went to his desk, picked up a charred briar and stuffed it from a glass jar of tobacco. He lit up. He watched the match burn till the flame almost touched his fingers. He popped the match into a glass tray.

Dropping into the swivel chair with the worn leather cushion, he leaned back and propped his heels on the desk. Thought went round and round in his eyes.

He pressed a button and turned towards a rectangular brown box. A voice said: "Yes, Captain?"

"Did you notify all cars that Cortland Wayne's coupé was found?"

"All them."

"Okey. Broadcast to cars 36 and 38 in the Fourth Precinct to investigate every house in Jockey, Havemeyer and Luke Streets. Vacant houses also. Question residents and report. Broadcast to all cars: Search blind alleys, stop all speeding cars and investigate. Investigate any suspicious character."

He returned to his pipe.

A knock sounded on the door.

"Come in," MacBride said.

Carl Davenport loomed in the doorway. "Glad I found you, Captain."

"Hello, Mr. Davenport. Sit down."

They shook and Davenport took a straight-backed chair, laid one hand on the other atop a silver-knobbed walking stick. He was in evening clothes. A great rock of a man nearing seventy, the rock was crystallizing at the edges. A mane of hair, white and flowing like white silk, swept back from a broad impressive forehead. White thatching for eyebrows. A jaw that still defied loose jowls. Blue eyes like a glacial lake, deep-set and penetrating.

"No word, I understand."

"No," MacBride said. "They found the car."

"Where?"

"Luke Street. Abandoned."

The blue eyes had a touch of frost. "What do you make of it, Captain?"

MacBride puffed. Puffed again. Said: "Offhand, I'd say it's a kidnap. We'll get the shake-down in the morning."

"We?"

"Mrs. Wayne, of course."

Davenport cleared his throat. Latent power was evident in his voice when he said: "I came here to ask you, Captain, in no shape, manner or form to attempt to interfere."

"I don't get you."

"I mean insofar as the safe return of Cortland is concerned. Mrs. Wayne has money. We, his aides, have plenty and we intend putting forth any amount to insure his safe return. This gubernatorial campaign was a stiff one. Cortland won by a fair margin. His inauguration will mark an epic in the history of the state. We who have stood beside him do not want this to have been all in vain. As a boy, I held Cortland on my knee. I saw him grow to be the youngest governor-elect this state has ever known. I coached him. I might say I have been his mentor. Anything I could have done, anything I can do, was and is not too much."

MacBride said, pointing his pipe-stem: "I know. I get you. Well, I've known him too—ten years. I knew him when he was Assistant State's Attorney. I tell you I think he'll be the swellest governor this state's ever had or ever will. Take it from me, I'm just as anxious as you are to get him back safely. When that's done—if it is a kidnap—"

"You don't think it might not be?"

"There's no telling. The Rittenmoore Bill will make carrying a gun without a license a penal offense carrying a minimum sentence of fifteen years. He's sworn to put that bill through. If it is a kidnap, and when he's back safe, I'll go after the guys. My word of honor that there'll be no police interference beforehand."

Davenport stood up. "Captain...." His hand was extended.

MacBride rose and gripped it.

Davenport said: "I am infinitely happy that we both realize in Cortland Wayne the man of the hour. I am glad that through the years I have been his guiding light, willing to sacrifice anything in order to put him one notch upward, always. I am not bragging. Forgive me my elation."

"Any idea who's behind this kidnap—if it is a kidnap?"

"None," Davenport said. "You?"

"No-o."

"You say that peculiarly."

MacBride straightened. "I was just thinking. It's nothing. Be seeing you, sir."

Davenport's keen eyes flicked MacBride's spare-boned face. He started to say something. Cleared his throat instead. He went out with a slow sedate step.

MacBride reached for a phone. "Moriarity or Cohen around?...

Send him up."

It was Cohen. Dapper, well-dressed, one-time a fast lad in the prize ring. "And me holding four kings."

MacBride said, looking at his pipe-bowl, "Name of Manuel Figueroa. Friend of Mrs. Wayne. Find out what he does, where he goes, who he knows. And keep it to yourself until you tell me. Start now."

"Where should I start?"

"That's your job, Ike."

INDEFATIGABLE in his haphazard way, Kennedy drifted in at a quarter to one, found MacBride in shirt-sleeves over a bowl of chili and a mug of coffee. Kennedy looked refreshed, though weariness was still in his eyes, around his mouth; a droll weariness that seemed more of the soul than of the body.

"Thanks for the bath, Skipper."

"Don't mention it. Boy-oh-boy, were you crocked!"

Kennedy expired into a chair, his weathered hat lopped over one ear. "Please omit the post mortems. It was from *Othello:* 'O God, that men should put an enemy into their mouths to steal away their brains.' Remember?"

"How the hell would I remember something I've never read?"

"Ah… that leads around to something else again. Something Spanish this time."

"Huh?"

"You read it once. You should remember."

MacBride finished the chili. "Go on, go on."

"Manuel Figueroa."

MacBride choked on a mouthful of coffee, spattered the desk.

Kennedy went on drowsily: "A year ago. A play called *Spanish Bayonet* put on by the Amateur Art Theatre. The feminine lead was played by Corinne Wayne; the male by—you guessed it the first time—Manuel Figueroa. Quite a lot of pawing on the part of the male in the third act. Recollect?"

"No."

"You should."

"All right, then. Now what's the connection?"

"Well, I was pretty whoofled tonight, but not so whoofled that I didn't recognize Manuel hot-foot into the Wayne casa. You were there. Must have seen him."

"I did."

"Two and two make—what?" He laughed. "Or rather, one and one—make what?"

MacBride scowled. "All right. What?"

"Love's a funny thing," Kennedy sighed.

"Are you still drunk?"

Kennedy pushed his hat down over his eyes, bent his head so that only his mouth was visible. His mouth began wearing a droll smile.

MacBride swiveled his chair. His voice dropped to a hard, blunt tone. "Whatever you think, Kennedy, you keep it to your sweet self."

"A crack like that indicates that you think similarly."

"You heard me!"

"Could I help hearing you?"

MacBride glared at the mouth that was wicked and wise—and gentle—and a little weak.

A steam radiator began clanking and went on clanking while neither MacBride nor Kennedy said anything.

Chapter IV

THE morning papers cut loose. It was something to shout about, the disappearance of a governor-elect. Newsmen arrived from other cities by train, bus, car and plane. They hit Headquarters like a deluge and circulated throughout its chambers. They practically took over two rooms in the building, robbed other offices of chairs and tables.

High pressure special correspondents arrived in baggy coats and carrying portable typewriters. A bootlegger succeeded in delivering a case of gin through a back entrance. Two Boston newshawks drove up with two cases of ginger ale and a gunnysack of ice. An enterprising New York correspondent tried to get the local electric company to wire the room and then tried to get a special wire directly from the room to his home office. MacBride sat on that idea like a ton of brick.

He was pointed, saying to the gang: "Now pipe this, you eggs. I'm on this job—me personally. What I say around this scatter pretty much goes and I'm telling you now, one and all of you, that I'll not stand for any lousy shenanigans. It's only through a kind-hearted commissioner that you're being allowed to stay in these rooms. I don't want any prowling around halls. I don't want to hear raps on doors. I don't want any spitting on the floor or see any bright cartoons on the walls. When there's any news—you'll get it. In the meantime, no monkey shines or you'll get slid on to the pavement."

A wiseacre, winking at a confrère, said, "Any pungent supplement to add to that, Captain?"

"Maybe a punch in the kisser for smart Alecks like you," MacBride said, and went out.

When he strode into his office Ike Cohen was sitting on the desk.

"So you got back," MacBride said. "Well?"

"Figueroa's a young sculptor. Like Mrs. Wayne, he's still a member of the Amateur Art Theatre. He's got a studio on West Walnut Street. He owes two months rent there. He owes his tailor three hundred and ten dollars. Owes his bootlegger a hundred and twenty-five. Has a balance in his bank of eight hundred and six dollars and forty-three cents."

"Where'd you find all this?"

"I went around to art museums first thing this morning. I saw one of his figures. I got his address there. I went over and he wasn't in. I got the door open and fanned his studio. I busted open a trunk—fixed it again—and found six photographs of Mrs. Wayne. He's also modeled a bust of her—from the waist up. It was locked in a closet. I saw letters from an insurance company reminding him he was two hundred bucks in arrears. There was also a letter from an auto finance company reminding him he was four hundred in arrears. I didn't find a bill marked 'paid' in the whole place. I found a lot of photographs, all locked up, of other women with tender sentiments on the backs. I also found—this."

He drew a folded sheet of paper from his pocket, passed it to MacBride. It read:

Dear Manuel,
Please accept this, darling. I hope it will tide you over till better times. I won't be able to get over until Thursday afternoon at three. Please arrange to have no one there. Love, love.

Corinne.

MacBride looked up. "Oh, yeah?"

"Uhuhn."

"Where'd you find this?"

"On the floor back of his desk. It must have fallen down."

MacBride folded the note carefully, tucked it into his wallet, looked keenly at Cohen. "Keep this to yourself, Ike."

"Sure. What do you think?"

"What do you?"

Cohen shrugged. "Maybe I'm naturally bad-minded."

"Well, I'm not. And I think with you."

"That makes Corinne Wayne a nice girl then."

"Yeah, swell."

"And Figueroa a gigolo."

MacBride said: "I've got an old-fashioned word for that guy."

"What's that?"

"Since I joined the Boy Scouts I promised not to swear."

Cohen yawned. "On the eve, so to speak, of the governor-elect's inauguration. And umpteen reporters with their teepees pitched downstairs."

"There's one thing we've got to do, Ike." MacBride squared off in front of Cohen and chewed on his lip. "We've got to keep Cort Wayne's name as clean as we can."

"You're my boss, so what now?"

"Okey, Ike. Pound your ear a while and come up smiling."

NUMBER 48 West Walnut Street was a three-storied stucco building with a broad skylight on the north slanting roof. The broad glass hall door was open. MacBride climbed the stairs and knocked on the door of the top apartment. Figueroa opened the door. Cigarette smoke made blue-gray skeins across his face.

"Oh, yes—Captain MacBride."

"Hello," MacBride said.

Figueroa let him in, closed the door. A small cubicle served as a reception hall. Off to the left was a living-room. Beyond, a broad airy studio. Figueroa regarded the back of MacBride's bony head as the skipper strode into the living-room.

"Nice place," MacBride offered.

"Won't you sit down?"

"Thanks."

"I have some rather fair Scotch—"

"No thanks. Never touch it till I've had lunch." He crossed his legs, regarded the inside of his derby. "I see you're an artist...." He gestured towards the studio.

"Sculptor."

"Busy?"

"Moderately so."

MacBride turned his hat around and looked at the crown. "You act too, don't you?"

"Just as an amateur. I'm a member of the Amateur Art Theatre."

"That's right. You've played with Mrs. Wayne there, haven't you?"

"Quite a bit."

"I take it you're a friend of the family."

"Yes. Yes, indeed."

MacBride nodded. "Yes, I noticed you ran right over to see if you could help Mrs. Wayne. Cort's an old friend of mine. Great guy. I've got a hunch he's very much in love with his wife. She's a very good-looking woman. Should make a swell hostess at the capital. I believe in that. I'm old-fashioned that way. I believe a wife should help her husband in every way she can; stick by him; do nothing that might embarrass him—or even ruin him. It's her duty. Don't you?"

"Why, yes. Why, yes of course."

MacBride had been stuffing his pipe. He lit up. "Have you any other source of income besides what you get out of your profession?"

"No, none."

MacBride puffed. "We've been checking up on all of Cort's friends and so-called friends. We happen to know exactly how much you have in the bank. I hope you don't mind. It's just a sort of precautionary measure. We've done the same on lots of others. You don't, do you?"

"Well—I'd never thought about it. But if—if that comes in line of police routine—why, of course, I can't help minding."

MacBride stood up and looked at the inside of his hat. "You kind of catch on then how tough it would be on you if, say, in a day or a week or a month or so your bank balance jumped a number of thousand dollars."

Figueroa stepped back. "I don't quite see—"

MacBride put on his hat. "Think it over." He walked to the door, opened it. "Good morning, Mr. Figueroa."

He went out.

Chapter V

CORINNE'S hand shook and that made the plain white sheet of paper shake and rustle. She dropped on to the divan and read the message over again. She looked at the clock on the mantel. It was three o'clock in the afternoon. She sat staring at the message and, after a while, not seeing it. Her eyes filled and a few tears rolled down her cheeks.

She rose with a little outcry followed by a sob which she muffled in her handkerchief. She stood for a moment staring at a sunlit window and sobbing softly. Her tall body shook. She went by fits and starts across the room, into the reception hall. She sat down at a telephone table. She read the message again. She unpronged the receiver and put it to her ear. The hand that held it trembled.

"Please… Police Headquarters."

While she waited she blew her nose softly and used the knuckles of her hand to wipe her eyes.

"Captain MacBride, please…. Hello—hello. Captain MacBride?… This is Mrs. Wayne. Will you come right over?"

The receiver going back into the prong made not a sound.

It took MacBride twenty minutes flat to get over. He came in like a clean blast of wind bringing some of the cold outdoors with him.

"Yes, Mrs. Wayne."

She gave him the letter. He read it:

Dear Mrs. Wayne:

Your husband is safe and sound. To keep him this way and to have him returned safely, you will have to give us $15,000 in $100 bills. On the Old West Road, two miles beyond Sandy Crossing, is the Bullock house that was burned down three months ago. In front, on the road, is an old R.F.D. mailbox. Place the money in this box. Do not come yourself. Send a man who isn't connected with politics or the police. If these orders aren't carried out your husband will be killed. And no tricks, either. The road will be watched a mile on either side of the house. Send it at ten tonight.

There was no name signed.

"How'd it come?" MacBride said.

"Special Delivery."

She showed him the envelope. He folded the letter and inserted it in the envelope, on which name and address had been printed.

"At least," the skipper said, "he's safe. Who'll you send?"

She thought. "All of our friends are one way or another connected with politics. Except Manuel Figueroa."

MacBride blinked.

She looked at him. "Cort thinks so much of him. He'll do anything for me, Manuel will. I'll—call him."

"Wait. Can you get the money?"

"I've a small checking account. But Carl Davenport told me not to worry. He said as soon as I heard I should call him and he'd turn over the proper amount."

MacBride went to the phone and made a call. "Mr. Davenport, this is MacBride.... Can you come right over to Wayne's place?... Can you bring fifteen thousand in centuries?... Good. Yeah, right away."

He hung up and turned to find Corinne regarding him. "Now if you'll call Mr. Figueroa...."

She put the call through.

They went back into the drawing-room and she sank exhausted into the divan. "I hope everything will work out."

He could see her profile. His lips drew tightly across his teeth and relaxed when she turned towards him.

He said: "Everything'll be okey."

"Oh, I hope so—I hope so."

Davenport arrived first, breathing heavily. The maid tried to take his overcoat but he detoured around her and went straight into the drawing-room, doffing his hat.

"Mrs. Wayne. Captain."

"The letter came through," MacBride clipped and passed it to Davenport.

Davenport put on pince-nez and read, his lips moving silently. "Well," he said, "it is bitter medicine, but nothing compared with the assurance of Cort's safe return. I trust, Captain, that there will be no interference."

"I gave you my word."

"Who is going?"

There was the sound of footsteps and Figueroa strode quickly into the room, stopped short, made a curt bow.

Corinne was saying: "Manuel, you've got to do something for us, if you will."

"Of course...."

His dark eyes shot from MacBride to Davenport.

"Manuel," she went on, "we have a letter from Cort's abductors demanding fifteen thousand. We—Mr. Davenport has the money. Will—will you take it?"

Figueroa squinted. "What?"

"Will you take the money to the place they specify in the letter?"

A flush seemed to creep over his dark cheeks, his eyes appeared to become dazed.

"Manuel, will you?"

"But—but—"

MacBride cut in. "Mrs. Wayne thought you'd be only too glad to do this for her."

Figueroa started to draw his handkerchief from his breast pocket. He didn't. He fussed with the cuffs of his coat, twisted his neck in his collar.

Davenport was leaning back on his heels, looking for all the world like a fat critical prelate. But his eyes were narrow-lidded, his lips a little tight.

Figueroa coughed. "Yes—yes of course. Only too glad to—to do whatever I can."

Davenport beamed and his voice came heavy-timbered: "This is very fine indeed." He drew a long brown envelope from his inside pocket.

MacBride was saying: "You'll take your car, Mr. Figueroa. Hit the Old West Road out of town. Two miles beyond Sandy Crossing, where the railroad's built an underpass—two miles beyond there you'll see the ruins of a farmhouse on the right. Check by your speedometer. In front of the house is one of those old R.F.D. boxes. Slip this package in there and drive on. Don't wait. Drive like hell once you've planted the money."

Figueroa's dark eyes were glazed. "I see. Had I better go armed?"

"No. Absolutely no."

"I see. Will you—will the police cover me?"

MacBride shook his head. "No. We want to get Cortland Wayne back whole. If police followed you there might be a jam and he might get hurt."

Figueroa's voice had become a whisper. "At what time?"

"Reach there at about ten. Leave here at nine-thirty."

Figueroa straightened, moistened his lips. "Of course," his whisper said.

Chapter VI

MANUEL FIGUEROA entered his studio apartment, kicked the door shut with his heel, scaled his hat clear across the room, heaved out of his swanky polo coat. Stopping short, he stood erect, very tall; placed a hand at either temple and then drew the hands backward over his ebon hair. His lips were set in a tight ironic line, his dark eyes were alive with crossfires of thought.

"So, Manuel, old fellow!" he said aloud.

He used a key to unlock a closet door. From the closet he drew a bust of Corinne Wayne. He used a hammer to chip away any likeness. He opened a trunk, took out six photographs of Corinne Wayne. In a fireplace where embers still glowed he burned the pictures, knelt and watched the paper become waferlike ashes.

Rising, he stood spread-legged and massaged his palms slowly together. From his inner pocket he drew the long brown envelope. He crossed to his desk, sat down and carefully counted the bills. Exactly fifteen thousand.

He went out and down to a corner drug-store, entered a telephone booth and called the ticket office at Union Station.

"Reserve for—ah—Courtney Blaine a drawing-room on the nine-fifty p.m. train for New York. That reaches New York at eleven-fifty, doesn't it?... Yes, I want a reservation on the fast express."

He hung up and thumbed the telephone book. He made a call to a local agent for a transatlantic steamship company. "Can I get a stateroom on the *Magnetic* leaving New York at twelve-thirty tonight?... Well, please arrange and see. I shall drop by at four o'clock... Mr. Figueroa."

He caught a taxi outside and went to a luggage store. He carried two suitcases to the Hotel Ardmore and checked in as Louis Massara. He went out again and took a cab to his bank, where he withdrew seven hundred dollars, leaving a hundred and six dollars and forty-three cents.

It took him an hour to buy two new suits, a sports outfit with knickers, shirts, socks, underwear and shoes. He specified that these articles be delivered at his hotel not later than five o'clock. Then he picked up his reservation at Union Station; went to the steamship ticket agency and found he was able to secure a stateroom to Le Havre, France. When he arrived back at his apartment he had eighty dollars in cash—sufficient to get him to New York and aboard the *Magnetic*.

Into a gladstone he threw odds and ends; shaving articles, slippers, a silk robe, his passport. And in one of the compartments he stuffed the packet containing fifteen thousand dollars.

He mused aloud! "And when that is gone there will be women abroad eager to support a handsome young man. Ah, yes, Manuel!" He chuckled liquidly to himself.

He left the paraphernalia of his profession. He left his trunk, a large valise, some objects of art. He left three suits in the closet, and an overcoat. He left four pairs of shoes. Going out with the gladstone, he left the door unlocked. His car was in a garage up the street, but he did not take it. A taxi carried him to the Hotel Ardmore.

Chapter VII

KENNEDY said: "On the up and up, Skipper, hasn't there been any word from Wayne—or about him?"

"Kennedy," MacBride said, "I told you that when there is any news it'll be broadcast. Another thing I'd like to know is, who the hell invited you in my office?"

"Pardon me if I seem not to have been made aware of the fact that you were issuing invitations. Are they engraved 'n' everything?"

"Waltz me around a little more and it'll be engraved on your nice sweet jaw, my son."

Kennedy seemed very comfortable in the armchair. "Captain, I like the atmosphere of your office. The warmth, the genial and abounding good-will exuded by the Department's chiefest exponent of right makes right and wrong, wrong. I carry home with me to my drab hall bedroom a vision of your kindly, smiling face, the tranquil benediction of your smile—"

"Oh, yeah?"

"The feeling of good fellowship, the remembered homilies, the beatific aspect of your profile and, by the way, how is Mrs. Wayne?"

MacBride took his eyes from the clock, which indicated a quarter to nine. "You heard me, sweetheart. Scram."

"And by the way, what do you think of Manuel Figueroa?"

MacBride stood up, darkening. "Kennedy, I'm no mood to be monkeyed with."

"I was just getting around to telling you, O Captain, that I've found out things about Figueroa. Three years ago he lived in Boston, was supported by Mrs. K.T.P. Weems-Colbrooke, the wife of the president of the Western Ocean Mercantile. Supported for a year. He has no standing as a sculptor anywhere. He's never had a piece exhibited, has never sold—well—not even a miniature of the Washington Monument. The lady's daughter fell for him. He got in Dutch with the girl and lammed. No complaint could be made because he held the whip-hand over mama. This never got in the papers. I remember the name, though—Figueroa. Will Smythe gave me the yarn two years ago. He used to be publicity agent for the Western Ocean Mercantile. I've a good memory.

"It recalls another anecdote from the amours of our hero. At a newspaper club in New York three years ago I met Jim Mapes, late of the Indianapolis *Star-Express*. Love in the midlands. Mrs. Jennifer Carnes, wife of a potent midland banker, had Figueroa under her wing. One day her husband noticed a twenty-thousand dollar rope of pearls missing from her collection. She said she'd lost them. You figure it out. A month later our hero spreads himself in a Boston studio. Cute?"

MacBride drummed on the desk with his fingers and bored Kennedy with a hard stare. "Kennedy, you spring that in your lousy rag and you're through in this city. You spring that and blow up Cort Wayne's balloon and I'm on you like hell-fire."

"I'm just telling you, old tomato. I'm just trying to suggest, possibly, the X quantity behind this abduction. I'm just trying to give you a faint idea of what kind of a crum this greaseball is."

MacBride sat down. "Thanks, Kennedy. Thanks. I've got ideas about that baby myself. But you give me more. You make me begin to—" He cut himself short and snapped a look at Kennedy. One eye narrowed. He unlocked a drawer and hauled out a bottle of Golden Wedding. He uncorked it, set two glasses side by side.

"This calls for a drink, Kennedy."

"Ah… 'drink down all unkindness,' Skipper—with the Bard of Avon."

"I still think you're going ga-ga, but what the hell."

They had two more drinks. MacBride rose then, saying, "I'll be back in a minute." He left the bottle on the desk. He went out, locked the door, went down the hall and entered another office. He picked up a phone.

"MacBride…. Switch all calls for me to extension twenty-one. Pay no attention to any calls coming from eighteen…. That's right. Now try locating Moriarity."

He sat down at the desk, knocked out his dead pipe, restuffed it and lit up. He looked at his watch. Five minutes to nine. Put the watch away in his vest pocket and puffed furiously on his pipe. He got up and paced the room, back and forth, back and forth.

Moriarity came in saying, "Moved?"

"Listen, Mory. I locked Kennedy up in my office with a bottle of rye. It's a dirty trick but I don't want him pulling a tail on me. I'm going places. I may even do things—if I see scenery. Here's the key to my office. You stay in here and take any calls for me. And don't let Kennedy out till you hear from me."

"Oke, Cap."

"If any of these reporters crowd you tell 'em I'm in the building. I'll want to borrow your hat and overcoat."

"Down in my locker. It's open."

"Thanks."

MacBride went downstairs and got into Moriarity's coat. It fit well enough, but the fedora was a little small. It set quaintly on MacBride's bony head, but he pulled the brim down all around and that helped. He took the tunnel to the garage and found the mechanic there.

"The Ford touring with the curtains, Jerry."

"You drivin'?"

"Yeah. But don't tell anybody. I'm supposed to be in the building."

"I gotcha."

The flivver was black, had no police markings. MacBride drove it out of the garage and lit out for the West End. At nine-fifteen he passed Wayne's house, saw Figueroa's roadster parked in front. He drove on and parked at the next block. Traffic plowed past continuously. He twisted around in the seat and kept his eyes on the little cowl-lights that marked Figueroa's roadster.

At exactly nine-thirty the lights moved, were replaced by headlights that swung into westbound traffic. MacBride started the flivver, saw the roadster go by and stop at a red traffic signal beyond. MacBride crawled into the traffic and was the third behind Figueroa when the roadster started again.

Westover Boulevard climbed upward beyond Laurel Street and the traffic ascended like an escalator. It reached a peak, then sloped away westward, going down gradually to the corporation limit, leaving the big houses behind. The flivver ducked around slow movin' vehicles, maintained a comparatively equal distance behind the roadster, never approached it too closely.

Traffic thinned out but three cars were still between the roadster and the flivver. Ahead, MacBride saw the white blur of the railroad underpass. He saw the roadster pass beneath it. MacBride passed beneath, and now Westover Boulevard became the Old West Road. Three hundred yards beyond, Riding Pike crossed it north and south.

The roadster made a left turn into Riding Pike. MacBride slapped his foot down on the accelerator, let a southbound sedan head him off and then swung in behind it. He took his gun from its holster and laid it on the seat beside him. A few oaths sizzled on his lips and then his lips clamped tightly shut and he tipped Moriarity's hat lower on his forehead.

The roadster was picking up speed. MacBride had to pass the sedan, and when he did he saw the roadster taking a turn in the Pike fast. The straightaway ended. The Pike became serpentine and MacBride kept his foot jammed down on the throttle. On a moonlit rise ahead he saw the silhouette of the roadster; then it dropped from sight, and when MacBride topped the rise he saw the roadster sweeping ahead and far below. The flivver roared and shook and the wind hammered the loose curtains.

He saw the roadster make a left turn into Black Horse Road. He followed it and had to go a mile before he picked up the red tail-light again. Houses appeared, then a settlement, then a suburb of the city. The roadster shot beneath a raised grade-crossing, turned sharp left, climbed a short hill.

MacBride was going too fast to make the turn. He jammed on the brake and sat tight while the flivver skidded fifty feet. Then he backed up, shifted and swung left hard. He gave the motor the gun to make the short grade and saw Figueroa hauling a bag from the rumble. He went over the hump, jammed on the brake and raised dust skidding past the roadster. On his left was a suburban station of the main line.

He knocked open the door and scooped his gun off the seat as he bounded out. Figueroa saw him and dropped everything but the gladstone. He leaped and ducked beneath the station platform. MacBride went under after him, stumbled over a track and rebounded to his feet.

Figueroa jumped from behind a supporting pillar, scaled the tracks and went under the platform opposite. MacBride followed and crowded him against a stone wall. He walloped his gun against Figueroa's stomach and flattened him upright against the wall.

"Give me that dough, you punk!"

"I—I—"

"You heard me! I've got to get out on the Old West Road and deliver it. Wayne's a friend of mine and if I had the time to pinch you I'd do it. But I'll get you later. Wayne's the only guy matters now. Shake it out, you two-timing so-and-so!"

Far up the line a locomotive whistle hooted.

"I can kill you," MacBride gritted. "I can let you have it in your dirty guts and by —— I will if you don't fork over that money!"

Figueroa's breath was stifled. He shoved his hand into his inside pocket, dragged out the brown envelope. MacBride snatched it and stepped back.

"Remember, greaseball," he said, "I'll be after you inside of an hour. But there's no time now."

He turned and raced across the tracks, beneath the platform. He reached the flivver and as he whipped it down through the underpass he heard the train puff into the station. He hit the Black Horse at sixty miles an hour, wheeled the car into Riding Pike and held the accelerator flat to the boards on the way north. For once he wasn't a cop. He was a friend of governor-elect Wayne. He had to deliver shake-down money to insure the release and safe return of Cortland

Wayne. It was against his code, against his principles. It griped him, but a life that mattered was at stake.

He took the turn into Old West Road much too fast. He felt the car heave. He toiled with the wheel, heard the rasp of the rubber, felt the rear end slew, then snap back again. He was off the road. He saw the windows of a filling station rear up in front of him, heard a man's hoarse cry. He hit. Glass exploded and flew. Metal snarled and cracked and the hard stone of the filling station did not budge.

He went through the curtains, did a somersault and landed asprawl on cinders. He lay slightly dazed and blinking while figures ran around him and bent over him. Time seemed to fly, but somehow an ambulance got there and he was still blinking while a white-coated figure ran fingers over his body. Suddenly he made a sweeping motion with his hands and sat up. "Hey, take it easy," a voice growled. MacBride saw things clearly. He saw the ambulance, the doctor, a motorcycle cop, and the flivver. The crushed and hardly recognizable flivver.

"Now, now," the doctor was saying.

"I'm MacBride," the skipper declared.

The doctor said: "I don't give a damn—"

"Oh," the motorcycle cop cut in. "That's right! Captain MacBride! This is Enders, Captain; Ninth Precinct."

"Hello, Enders."

MacBride was on his feet. Moriarity's hat was ruined and the seat was completely removed from Moriarity's overcoat. But MacBride slapped the hat on and looked comically pugnacious. He brushed the doctor out of the way and jumped to the wreck of the flivver. From its ruins he drew the brown envelope. But somehow it had been gashed in two. He held the pieces up and looked at them. The envelope had been stuffed with newspaper.

He whipped around. "Enders! Enders, where the hell are you?"

"Here, sir!"

"Lend me your motorcycle."

He forked the machine, gunned it hard, walked it off the cinders and went booming away towards the city.

Enders scratched his head. "The Skipper always was wild as a coot."

Chapter VIII

THE maid let MacBride in. He went past her without seeing her. He even forgot to remove his hat. Moriarity's hat was cocked over one eyebrow and the seat of the skipper's pants showed through the ragged hole in Moriarity's coat. His jaw looked teak-hard and a bitter glint was in his eye.

He ran into Davenport. "Mr. Davenport, more dough—and as quick as you can get it. That greaseball pulled the old two-time and Cort—"

"Sh! Sh!"

"Now don't shush me. I figured that guy was a heel and I tailed him. He didn't take the Old West Road. He lit out down Riding Pike and went over Black Horse to the Wentwood mainline station. I took the envelope away from him. I wanted to pinch the sweet double-crosser but I had no time. I wanted to get that dough to the spot. I piled up the car into a filling station—and lucky I did. The envelope contained newspaper. He'd taken out the dough and was on the lam. Come on now—rake up some dough—"

"Not so loud. Not so loud. Cort just came back."

"What!"

"He's in bed. Upstairs. Mrs. Wayne is with him."

"You mean to say—"

"Please, Captain, please!"

MacBride straightened and his jaw set. He clipped: "Okey." He pivoted and walked hard-heeled to the telephone. Davenport heaved after him and grabbed his arm.

"What are you going to do?"

"Get Figueroa. I know what train he's on."

Davenport got between MacBride and the telephone. He shook his white-maned old head. "No, Captain. No."

"What the hell do you mean—no?"

Davenport's blue eyes keened to fine glacial points. "You promised you'd do everything within your power to keep Cort's name clean."

"What's this got to do with Cort? Get away from that phone."

"No. Listen. Figueroa is on his way. Everything has worked out as

I hoped. I know where he's going. New York. He's booked on the steamship *Magnetic* for France. I had a secret agent following him. I know just what he did."

MacBride narrowed his eyes. "I don't get you."

Davenport took a deep breath. "You know how I feel about Cort. You know I said that I would do anything to prevent a blemish on his name or his household. I know I can tell you this in strictest confidence. I know or suspect that you already have some knowledge of how things stood.

"In Cort's kidnaping I saw an opportunity to get rid of Figueroa. It was a long chance but I took it. Had not Mrs. Wayne suggested that he go with the money, I should have done so. I wanted him to go. I knew from what I'd heard of this leech that once he got fifteen thousand in his hands he would abscond with it. I wanted just that to happen."

"But—"

"Let me finish. I knew that Figueroa and Mrs. Wayne were more than friends. I was resolved one way or another to get rid of Figueroa without breaking an inch of scandal and without making Cort aware of the fact that this liaison was existent.

"So Figueroa was to take the money to the designated point. A trusted agent of mine followed him. This man also carried an envelope containing fifteen thousand. If Figueroa had gone to the designated point, my agent should have gone on about his business. But we had Figueroa reasoned out. He absconded. My agent, who was only a block behind you when you reached the underpass, carried the money to the rendezvous and shortly afterward Cort walked in that door, haggard and worn but all right otherwise. He had been kept blindfolded all the time. He was helped from a car at a North Side street corner, still blindfolded, and the car had driven away before he got the blindfold off.

"Figueroa is gone. You might say I could have offered him a sum outright, but with bribery there is always backwash, later on. Now he has committed robbery, grand larceny. But no one knows but you and my trusted agent. He will not come back. Leave it that way, Captain."

MacBride rocked on his heels. "What am I going to tell that flock of newshawks? Here I've been clowning all around town, busting up cars and a filling station."

"You could say that you saw a car trailing my agent. You were afraid it contained a newspaperman or perhaps even gangsters who may have found out the identity of the man carrying the ransom. You hailed the car and it started off. You chased it. You noticed it had no rear license plate...."

"I get you, Mr. Davenport. In other words, I take the merry razz from the boys and likely a hot calling-down from the chief."

"You like Cort, don't you?"

"Sure."

"And your shoulders are broad, Captain."

MacBride cracked a hard tight grin. His voice was low, saying: "Okey. I'll be the goat then. But just let somebody try riding me! Just let them!"

Doors in the Dark

Everyone said it was suicide, but Capt. MacBride smelled murder, and went on the trail alone.

THE sounds of motor traffic on Marshall Drive rose in a muted, not unpleasant medley to the topmost floor of Tudor Towers. Eastward, the glow of mid-town hung like a will-o'-the-wisp in the crisp winter sky. A breeze plucked fitfully at the northeast turret apartment.

MacBride, admitted by the oldish maid, brought with him into the warm apartment a breath of the cold outdoors and a vital sense of his own personality. He shook his head when the maid reached for his hat. His windy blue glance flicked her frightened gargoyle's face, darted away and leaped nimbly about the foyer as he trailed her short, rapid footsteps towards the living-room entry.

He saw Halo Rand standing at the far side of the room. The room was dimly, discreetly lighted. A parchment-shaded floor lamp stood back of the woman and built an amber halo about her amber hair.

"I'm so glad you came, Captain."

The Aubusson muffled the blunt fall of his heels as he went towards her extended hand. His spare-boned head dipped; in his eyes was a candid, straightforward look.

"Got here as quick as I could, Mrs. Rand."

The maid vanished with a breathless look flung over her shoulder.

Though Halo Rand's tall, slender body was relaxed, one knee slightly bent, there was an air of repressed excitement in her face. MacBride, holding her hand for a brief instant, felt tension transmitted to his own. He was aware of a vague, well-bred perfume.

"What's the matter, Mrs. Rand?"

She said: "Come." She led the way across the dropped living-room, up three steps to a mezzanine; opened a door and motioned the skipper into a large room furnished with leathers and hardwoods—a man's room.

"Dan's room," she said. "His den. Sit down, Captain."

He was strangely moved, puzzled; but he sat down. Halo Rand chose to stand, resting the fingertips of one hand on a mahogany desk. The other hand toyed with a string of pearls suspended from her neck.

"I may be foolish," she said, "but I'm afraid. I can't help it. I'm afraid for Dan. It's ten o'clock and he hasn't come home yet."

MacBride said: "Why are you afraid?"

Her violet eyes were luminous in the dim light. "He came home at noon today. I—I hardly recognized him. He looked—well, crushed. Dreamlike. And that isn't like Dan. You know that. Well, he walked in quietly, kissed me, though I think he barely saw me, and then went to this room. I was disturbed. I came and knocked on the door and asked what was wrong, and he said nothing was wrong and asked to be left alone. So I didn't bother him."

"What do you think was wrong?"

She breathed deeply, said in a hushed voice: "I don't know. But he was worried. That much I do know. For the past two months, every now and then, he would sit and stare absently—and suddenly ask me what I had said. When I appeared curious, he'd rouse up and be his own self." She shook her head. "He never was the one to bring his business into the home."

"Think it's business?"

She shook her head wearily. "I don't know. I feel so helpless. That's why I asked you to come over. I knew you two were old friends. He's been hit hard in the market, you know. And I guess you know he's had trouble with the Colosseum. He is in debt heavily—but he hoped to pull out of it."

"Did he say where he was going?"

"No, he didn't. He came out of his room after an hour. I don't think he'd even taken his overcoat off. He came out and stood for a moment at the window. Then he said he was going out. He kissed me good-bye and held my hand for a minute, and then he went out. He said he'd be back at six. Well, he hasn't come."

MacBride slapped his knee. "Well, Mrs. Rand, I wouldn't get all worked up, if I were you. Maybe—"

"Wait," she said, and opened a desk drawer. "An hour ago I came in here. I don't know why. I don't think I expected to find anything. It was just chance. I—I opened this drawer. You remember the gun you gave him two years ago?"

"Yes."

"It's gone," she said. "It's not in his drawer."

MacBride stood up, muttered: "H'm."

"Emma, our maid, straightened this room yesterday. She said she saw the gun in this drawer yesterday. Now it's gone." Her eyes stared fixedly across the room. "That's why I'm afraid," she said. "That's why I asked you to come over."

She slumped a bit where she stood, brushed a hand across her forehead. MacBride's eyes were thought-fixed on the amber casque of her hair. He remembered the day she had ceased to be the première danseuse of Dubinoff's Ballet and had become Dan Rand's wife.

He said: "Just be calm, Mrs. Rand. You're imagining things. No use taking this thing so hard. I'll find him. He'll be okey. I'll phone you when I find him." There was a rough note of reassurance in his tone. A smile cracked his lean, spare-boned face. "Just take it easy."

They went into the living-room and she laughed brokenly. "I suppose I am a little fool. But I kept thinking about his finances. So many men nowadays, when they can't see their way ahead...." She made a limp, hopeless gesture.

"Not Dan," MacBride said. "He can take it. He always could take it and come up smiling."

She nodded. "I know. But lately—he hasn't been smiling."

They passed into the foyer and the oldish maid with the gargoyle's face appeared mysteriously and stood by the door.

The phone rang. The maid left the door and answered it and then said: "It's for you, Captain."

He went towards it, saying: "I left word at the office I'd be here." He picked up the instrument. "Hello.... Yeah, Otto." He listened, and presently his brows bent, a shine appeared in his eyes. His low voice said: "Okey, Otto." He hung up, put the instrument down, staring hard at it.

Then he raised his bony head and looked at Halo Rand. A corner of his wide mouth twitched.

KENNEDY, the eyes and ears of the Richmond City *Free Press*, slammed into the dusty little office at the base of the pier, ricocheted from door to wall to chair to desk, where he finally, sprawled with a relieved sigh and calmly placed the telephone receiver to his ear, using the same hand to prop his head.

"Central 1000."

An astonished watchman stood spellbound against the wall. "Hey," he said. "Hey!"

"Now, now," Kennedy said with wrinkle-browed remonstrance. "Shush, shush. Don't you see I'm on the telephone?" He rolled over languidly on his back, propped his heels on the edge of the desk, his knees in the air, and held the telephone transmitter above his mouth.

The watchman dried his hands on a soiled towel. "This here is a private office and I'd like to know who the hell give you permission to use that phone!"

Kennedy said into the mouthpiece: "City desk, flower." He looked sidewise at the watchman. "Pardon me. I'm Kennedy of the *Free Press*. May I use your phone?"

"Sure—go ahead."

"Thanks.... Hello, Abe," he said into the transmitter. "Kennedy. Dust out your ears and get a load of this. Daniel Cosgrove Rand, sportsman, fight promoter, owner of the Colosseum; dead, by his own hand, at 9:50 tonight, on River Road, near the foot of Pokomoke Street, in an abandoned warehouse. Shot heard, body found, by Patrolman Henry Pflueger. No witnesses. Got that?... Okey. More later."

He hung up, turned over on his stomach, put the phone down and pushed himself back off the desk to his feet. He was calm again, a little sallow-faced beneath his battered fedora. His roving, world-weary eyes alighted on a pint flask standing on a shelf above the desk.

"Is that," he said to the watchman, "something to drink?"

"Nah. Nah. That's rubbing alcohol." Kennedy reached up, took down the bottle, uncorked it and smelled it. He took two long swallows, corked the bottle, sighed and replaced the bottle on the shelf.

"Somebody's been kidding you, my good friend. That's gin." He buttoned his flimsy topcoat, said cheerfully: "Thanks for the use of your phone," and went out.

Winter wind, freighted with river damp, smote him and he shivered beneath his inadequate topcoat. He strode, a scarecrow figure, along the edge of the river wall; saw red and green lights of tugboats moving, heard deep-toned whistles. Up ahead, in front of the abandoned warehouse, the red-tinted lights of an ambulance glowed like swollen eyes. Figures moved in the glare of a spotlight, paced by their elongated shadows. Breath spumed whitely and hard heels struck and scraped on cold cobblestones.

Kennedy said: "I thought I recognized your Harvard accent, Skipper."

"Oh, you, huh?" MacBride said. He had just stepped from a police squad car. He blew his nose loudly into white, crisp linen. His cheeks were reddened by the cold; his eyes flashed like dark coals in the beam of the spotlight. "You always go where I go, huh?"

"Only this time I was here first. You're slipping, Cap."

A rotund man appeared in the entrance of the old warehouse. He blinked in the glare of the spotlight, then came forward with a bobbing, cheerful walk, a small black bag swinging in his hand.

"Hello, Doc," MacBride said.

"Dead, Steve—very dead," the ambulance doctor said. "In fact, he must have died instantly. Shot in the heart.... Well, I must get going."

MacBride nodded. He set his jaw and suddenly started off in a hard-heeled stride. The sound of his footfalls echoed in the large, bare warehouse. Far beyond, near the head of the wharf, he saw a lantern and several hand torches glowing; they made a wan, lonesome aureole of light around the shapes of several men. He walked through chill, damp air that seeped to his marrow; heard, beneath the floor, the lapping of water among pilings.

He saw, as he drew nearer, the narrow chalky face of Eggleson, the Deputy Medical Examiner. Eggleson was standing spread-legged, torchlight spraying upward over his gaunt body to his narrow face; and he was writing absent-mindedly in a book. Patrolman Pflueger was in silhouette, arms akimbo, his back to MacBride. Moriarity and Cohen were kneeling, getting two lights from a match.

No one said anything as MacBride came up. He stopped, stood with hands thrust in overcoat pockets, slouching a bit, the torch- and lantern-light picking out sharply the bony irregularity of his face, the slitted eyes.

Then Kennedy's quiet voice from behind: "You knew him well, huh, Skipper?"

"Yeah."

Patrolman Pflueger pointed: "There's the gun, Captain—layin' there."

"Yeah." MacBride's voice had a dull flat sound. "Yeah. I can recognize it from here. I gave it to him. You can see on the barrel: 'From Steve MacBride to Dan Rand.'"

Eggleson, the D.M.E., looked up from his notebook. "Suicide, Steve. Tough." He shook his head profoundly. "Tough, tough. He got pie-eyed drunk and then did the Dutch."

"Drunk, huh?"

"Pie-eyed. Can't you smell it?"

"Yeah."

Kennedy touched his arm. "Snap out of it, Steve."

"I liked him, Kennedy. I grew up with him. It's kind of swell to see a guy you grew up with make a name for himself. It ain't exactly the nuts when you find him dead." He wagged his bony head. "I never figured Dan would do the Dutch. He wasn't that kind. Not him. But…." He sighed, moved his broad shoulders. Then he flexed his hands, his voice picked up: "Moriarity, get the lead out of your pants. Get the morgue bus down…. Hey, Pflueger, did you touch that gun?"

"Just by the barrel."

"I trained you, didn't I?"

"Yes, sir."

MacBride looked at Kennedy. "Hear that?" He bent down, caught hold of the gun by the barrel and lifted it. He wrapped the gun in a fresh handkerchief and slipped it carefully into his pocket.

"Who trained you, Skipper?" Kennedy said.

"Experience.... Hey, Moriarity, I thought I told you—"

"Okey, okey!" Moriarity started off at a fast walk.

Eggleson scoffed: "Suicide! It's as plain as the nose—"

"On my face," MacBride nodded. "I know. But I also knew"—he leveled an arm at the dead man—"Dan Rand. I guess if I want to take prints off this gun I have a right to!"

"What a man!" Eggleson sighed; then said: "Okey, Steve. Well, I'll be seeing you."

Police photographers came and took flashlight pictures of the body on the floor.

MacBride roamed through the warehouse, picking his way with the help of a torch borrowed from Pflueger. He pushed through a small door and stood on the pierhead, in the wind, watching the lights of river traffic. Kennedy came out and huddled in his topcoat, using MacBride's bulk to break the wind.

"Don't be a sap, Cap," he argued. "It was suicide plain and simple. You know Dan was in a bad way financially. Ever since he refused to let the Ricks-Gowanus boxfight take place in his Colosseum Cardiac boycotted him. It's cost Dan a lot of dough. He couldn't afford to lose it. Well, he lost it. And what happened?" He shrugged. "A Dutch out. He got drunk as hell and getting drunk either weakened or strengthened him to rub himself out. Depends on how you look at it."

MacBride remained silent, staring at the river lights.

Kennedy raised a cigarette to his mouth. The wind whipped sparks from its red end. His tone was lazy, ruminative: "He had an expensive wife... his apartment at Tudor Towers set him back $500 a month.... a front to keep up." He shrugged. "A guy like Rand would have hated to take one backward step in the scale of living."

"Yeah," said MacBride. "He hated defeat. And he could take it. I've seen him take it before."

"Sure. But a man can take it just so long, Skipper, and then the lights go out. A short circuit in the nervous system."

MacBride turned. "I know, I know, Kennedy. You're using your head, you're reasoning things out. Swell! But I can't reason the same way because I knew Dan, I know he had guts. It's not like him to pull a stunt like this. It's all goofy! It's a cap that don't fit his head!"

Kennedy leaned back on his heels. "Listen, am I talking to a hard-headed cop or am I talking to a fat-head?"

MacBride growled, swung on his heel, yanked open the door and heaved into the warehouse. The lantern was swinging now in someone's hand. The morgue bus had come and they were carrying out the body of Dan Rand.

Kennedy caught up with MacBride and said: "So don't make a horse's neck out of yourself just because you happened to play at cowboys and Indians with this guy when you were kids!"

"I'm in the dark right now," MacBride ground out. "In the dark, get me?" His eyes shimmered between narrowed lids. "In a dark house. But I've got a feeling that there's a lot of doors around me in the darkness—and if I look hard enough, and take your wisecracks as just so much bushwha, I might find a streak of light—you know, at the bottom of a door."

"Listen to the man!"

"Razz me, sweetheart. I could take the razzberry when you were just a hope in your father's chest."

COHEN was sitting on the desk, swinging a leg, flipping a coin in the air, when MacBride strode into the office next morning. The skipper removed his conservative blue overcoat, his conservative gray fedora, and hung them on a costumer in the corner. Crossing to the desk, rubbing his chilled hands smartly together, he stared down at the morning edition of the *Free Press. Dan Rand Commits Suicide*, the headlines said. MacBride looked at Cohen. Cohen continued flipping the coin.

"What's that, Ike, a new kind of endurance contest?... Come on, come on—with six chairs in this office, do you have to park yourself on my desk?"

Cohen stood up. "So I dusted the town last night, Cap. Rand hit *The Panama* at 2:30 yesterday afternoon, stayed an hour drinking alone. At 3:40 he walked into Joe Paloma's place, in Senate Street. Joe says he knocked off three highballs and left there about four o'clock. Plenty looking-glass drinking. At 4:30 he landed in Nick Raitt's place, on Division Hill. Rye highballs again; three. Nick said he didn't talk, didn't say a thing. Just looked at himself in the mirror and took on the liquor. Nick says he bailed out at about 5:30.

"At about a quarter of six he walked into the *Old English Grill* and got himself a meal, and Al says he drank rye there. He was pretty crocked when he came in, but the food kind of straightened him out. He left the *Old English* at a little past seven and went down to Elmo Street, to Mike Cahill's place. He threw dice with Mike, but Mike says he kept his trap shut except to open it to pour in rye. He left Mike's place at 8:30.

"Tony Gatto, down in Jockey Street, says Rand sloped into his joint between eight and nine. He was pretty drunk. He took two highballs fast and left at about 9:15. Tony says Rand said: 'Well, Tony, I think I'll go home to my wife. Listen, Tony; never give up ship. Stick to it.' Tony didn't know what he meant. 'Some of us slide out, Tony,' Rand said. 'Some of us stick, hang on. I guess I'm that kind, damn my guts.' And he went out." Cohen shrugged. "So I guess Tony Gatto was the last guy to see him alive."

MacBride said: "Good work, Ike. Did you mark those places and times down?"

Cohen scaled a slip of paper on to the desk.

MacBride studied the memoranda, mused aloud: "What did Dan mean by that speech, Ike?"

"Hell, do drunks mean anything by the speeches they make? I read a book once—"

"Okey, okey. Suppose we don't go into that. Here"—he pointed to the telephone—"call McGovern and ask him if he got the prints off that gun yet."

Cohen telephoned the Bureau in the basement. Hanging up, he said: "In about half an hour."

MacBride took a turn up and down the room; stopped, eyed Cohen darkly. "You've got an idea I'm nuts, haven't you?"

"Well"—Cohen leaned on the desk—"it looks like suicide to me, Cap. Of course, if you want to make a case out of it, okey. I know about seventeen guys I could pick up, frame, box and deliver—"

"Do drunks mean anything by the speeches they make?… You asked me that, Ike. And I'll tell you. They do! Dan would, anyhow. He was going home to his wife. He might have thought about doing the Dutch. But in the end, tight as he was, he changed his mind." He leveled an arm. "When Danny Rand walked out of Tony Gatto's he was going home to his wife. He might have been flat broke, up to his ears in debt—but he was going to stick, kid—he was going to stick."

He struck the desk with his fist. "Danny Rand didn't commit suicide!"

Cohen was unimpressed. He shrugged. "Okey, Skipper, okey. He didn't commit suicide. Okey. Now tell me who bumped him off and I'll go out and pinch the guy—"

"Cut it, Ike!" MacBride chopped in savagely. In a quieter voice he said: "Scram. I'll call you if I want you."

He crammed a pipe, lighted up. He had fought the Medical Examiner's office tooth and nail for an autopsy. Halo Rand had sobbed. "An autopsy's cruel in his poor dead body," she had said. The Medical Examiner had chided, wheedled, opened a bottle of Napoleon brandy. But MacBride had stood his ground—grim-faced, obstinate, on a single track of thought and purpose.

He smoked out his pipe, knocked the ash into a tray. He sailed out of his office, went down to the central room, on down to the Bureau of Criminal Identification. McGovern, the fingerprint man, chewed a cigar beneath a brilliant light. The smoke foamed and rolled beneath the green eyeshade he wore, and he spoke laconically:

"No prints but Rand's on this gat, Steve. Nice gun. I always did like a .32."

MacBride muttered: "You're sure of that, Mac?"

"That's my business—being sure. But wait." He picked up the gun. "Smell it."

MacBride leaned down, sniffed. "What?" he said.

McGovern shrugged. "Smells—that's all. Can't you smell it?"

"I think I can. What's that mean?"

"Oh"—McGovern shrugged—"nothing, I suppose." He slapped palms softly together. "Suicide, Steve. You can't get away from it."

MacBride pointed: "Turn the gat over to Lewis. We ought to have that slug from the morgue this morning." He turned on his heel, strode away; stopped, returned to the desk and picked up the gun again. He sniffed along the barrel, along the butt; sighed, shrugged and walked away again, a puzzled frown shadowing his forehead.

In the central room, Otto Bettdecken lowered a half-eaten liverwurst sandwich behind the desk and called: "Cap, a guy just called up from 313 Diamond Street. His name's Rossman. He said if you could come down there maybe he can tell you something."

"About what?"

"Well, he said he'd read the paper this morning—"

"Okey. Thanks, Otto."

The skipper hiked up the steps two at a time, barged into his office and saw Kennedy was sitting at the desk. Kennedy was holding a glass in one hand, a bottle in the other; and he was grimacing painfully.

He said: "Honest, Cap, this last batch of liquor of yours is crummy—absolutely crummy." He was indignant.

MacBride grinned tightly, nodded. "I know, sweetheart. You got it out of that lower left drawer, didn't you? Swell! The good stuff is in the lower right—under lock and key. And I"—he thumbed his chest—"have the key!"

"Ah, my pal, my pal! Is it true that Rand was shot down by four Chinamen disguised as Princeton professors? I understand that there is a certain captain in Headquarters who insists that they were not four Chinamen; he says they were four dwarfs disguised as two dark, swart men wearing false hair eyebrows. This captain is principally known as an oboe player."

MacBride slapped on his hat, shrugged into his overcoat, said scornfully: "I hope you choke, Kennedy. And I hope if you ever get married your kids 'll turn out to be saxophone players. In three words"—he reached the door, yanked it open—"nerts to you!"

In the central room he ran into Eggleson, the Deputy Medical Examiner. Eggleson's chalky face wore a dry, broad grin. "I hear, Steve, that only Rand's prints were on the gun. Tsk, tsk!"

MacBride said grimly: "You're just breaking down with regret, ain't you." And he went on, red-faced, warm with chagrin.

Cohegan was waiting at the wheel of the shabby squad car.

MacBride said: "Down to 313 Diamond Street, Bert."

"Okey."

MacBride climbed in, slammed the door. "The razzberry market is cheap these days," he rasped out.

"Me," said Cohegan soberly, "I like blueberries. My wife now, she likes strawberries; but take a good bowl of blueberries—"

"You take 'em," MacBride sighed. He nipped savagely at the end of a cigar, cupped hands in the wind and lighted up.

The car purred across town, hit Broadway Avenue and weaved through traffic. It pushed westward past mid-town hotels, shops, theatres. Its canvas top clapped and pattered in the wind, and the wind kept MacBride's cigar at a bright glow, tore smoke from his nostrils and whipped it away, reddened the right side of his face. Winter sunlight glittered on plate-glass windows, automobile radiators, the shields and buttons of white-gloved traffic officers. Pedestrians hurried. Discarded newspapers skipped and planed and looped above the sidewalks.

Cohegan made a left turn into Diamond Street, a narrow thoroughfare that sloped downhill, walled on either side with food shops, noisy radio stores, cut-rate drug-stores, pawnshops, novelty stores, cheap haberdashers. Number 313 was a pawnshop.

"Park here, Bert," MacBride said.

He climbed out, made a half-turn against the driving wind and strode into the pawnshop. Inside it was dim. Lights glowed dimly. Counters and showcases were cluttered with cheap odds and ends; and behind a brass wicket a small, pink-cheeked man was studying the inside of a watch.

"Your name Rossman?"

The little man was cheerful, bright-eyed. "Yes—yes, I'm Rossman."

"I'm Captain MacBride—"

"Oh, yes!" The little man laid down the watch, turned and shouted: "Charley! Charley, come here and take care a minute." And to MacBride: "Right in the back, Captain, if you don't mind."

MacBride strode to the rear of the store. Rossman met him at the end of the counter and bowed him into a small office where a coal stove glowed warmly. He closed the door quietly, changed spectacles and picked up a copy of the *Free Press*. A smile twinkled in his eyes, tugged at his lips.

"This," he said, pointing to the Rand story. "I read about it this morning, and I thought it over. I saw your name connected with it. I remembered that once you were kind to my son-in-law, Benny Lisk, and I thought maybe this would interest you." He paused, darted a shrewd, smiling look at MacBride. "I read here about the gun—the gun it says you gave him. I looked a long time at Mr. Rand's picture here. Sit down, Captain."

MacBride sat down.

"This man," went on Rossman, striking the picture of Dan Rand, "came into my store at about two o'clock yesterday afternoon. I'm sure. I remember the face. And, Captain"—he dropped his voice significantly—"he wanted to buy a gun."

MacBride's face remained expressionless, but his eyes steadied on

Rossman's cherubic face.

Rossman nodded. "So I sold him one. A .32 Colt automatic. And a box of 73 grain, metal case, cartridges." He paused. "You see, Captain, I want no trouble with the police. Usually I don't sell guns to anybody, but this man had a permit to carry one. He loaded the gun here, and then, after he left, I found he didn't take the rest of the cartridges."

MacBride's eyes glowed. "Thanks, Mr. Rossman. I appreciate this a hell of a lot." He stood up, shook Rossman's hand vigorously. "This will help. This will help, Mr. Rossman. Any time you feel you're in a jam, let me know. I don't forget."

Leaving the room, he strode briskly through the shop, a hard windy glitter in his eyes and a firm jut to his jaw. Outside, he found the shabby squad car empty. He sent a sharp glance about the street, took a few steps, swore irritably; and then he saw Cohegan stroll casually out of a fruiterer's, eating a banana.

"Bert!"

Cohegan reached the car with his mouth full of banana.

MacBride jerked his chin, growled: "In, bozo!" And as they drove off: "Always on the muscle! Always on the make! If it's not fruit you're mooching, it's cigars, or socks, or candy for some jane you know, or liquor!"

Cohegan said soberly: "Where was we headed for now?"

There was a note of vengeance in MacBride's short laugh. "Back to H.Q., you racketeer!"

MORIARITY and Cohen were rolling dice on MacBride's desk when the skipper breezed into his office. His two aides did not look up. The dice clicked, tumbled; coins rang on the desk.

"Hot-cha!" Cohen exclaimed. "After it's over, Mory, you can borrow from me—at seven percent."

"What I found," MacBride said, rocking on his heels, "was that Dan Rand bought a gun. Bought a .32 Colt auto from a guy named Rossman in Diamond Street. Yesterday afternoon. And loaded it and walked out!"

The dice clicked and Cohen said: "You should never roll the bones, Mory; you were born unlucky."

"Now why did he buy that gun?" MacBride said impressively. "Why did he buy a gun when he had a perfectly good gun of his own? And how come the gun we found on him was the gun I gave him and not—not, you understand—the gun he bought? What happened to the gun he bought? Boy, oh boy, if I— Listen, you apes!" he suddenly exploded. He caught up the dice and flung them against the wall.

Cohen whistled, picked up the money and dropped it into his pocket. Moriarity lighted a cigarette and said reasonably:

"It must have disappeared."

"It means this," MacBride hammered out, shaking a fist. "It means that I'm no fat-head! It means that maybe all the razzberry you and a lot of other guys shoveled at me is going to be dumped right back at you! It means," he said, thinning his voice, "that when Dan Rand walked out of his house at noon yesterday he didn't carry a gun. He went and bought one—"

"And with it," nodded Cohen, "committed suicide."

MacBride barked: "No!" He walked around the room and came back and barked again: "No!" He folded his arms. "This is murder. I know what to do about murder, wherever I find it. We'll see what kind of bullet they've taken out of Dan Rand and—"

The phone rang and MacBride scooped it up. "Okey," he said. He hung up. "Come on down. That was Lewis."

They went down to the basement. Lewis, the ballistics expert, was wiping off a gun.

He said: "There's the slug they took out of Rand. I matched it with this gun you gave him. It matches. There it is—a lead slug. Came out of a 98 grain Smith & Wesson cartridge." He laid the revolver down. "Suicide, I guess."

MacBride picked up the slug, studied it closely, then rolled it round and round between thumb and forefinger. His eyes flashed, his lips warped. He tossed the slug back to the desk.

"Murder," he clipped.

"Suicide suits me," Lewis said.

But MacBride was striding away. Moriarity and Cohen went along, exchanging hopeless glances. MacBride stopped short, swung about, returned to Lewis' desk and picked up the gun, thrust it into his pocket. He bore down on Moriarity and Cohen with a hard, preoccupied stare.

"Look at it this way, Cap," Moriarity said. "Maybe this guy Rossman made a mistake. Maybe it wasn't Rand after all."

"I'll bet that's just what happened!" Cohen said decisively.

MacBride went past them with his hard, fixed stare. He picked up Cohegan in the central room and they went outside and climbed into the car. MacBride sat motionless, staring ahead, while Cohegan started the motor and waited. After a while MacBride relaxed, looked about them as though surprised, then said:

"Okey, Bert. Drive to the Metals Building in Simpson Street." He leaned back, sighed as the car started. "I'm a sap," he muttered. "I get all steamed up over nothing."

The Metals Building was a seven-story brick affair, not new. The elevator was large, old, tarnished, and wheezed on the way up to the fifth floor. MacBride got out, slapped his heels down a linoleum covered corridor floor and stopped before a ground-glass door bearing the inscription: *Acme Sporting Enterprises, Inc.*

"Yes, sir?" chirped a blonde over a noisy typewriter.

"Mr. Cardiac." He champed the tip off a cigar. "MacBride's the name."

The girl flounced into one of two inner offices; reappeared in a moment and said: "Okey."

MacBride swung into the inner office, scaled his hat on the desk and flopped down into a leather upholstered armchair; scowled down at his cigar and then licked a piece of the wrapper back into place.

"What do you think about Rand's suicide, Cardiac?"

Cardiac said: "Shocked. I was shocked. Sorry as hell to hear of it."

"Yes, you were!" MacBride chuckled sardonically.

Cardiac was a tall, handsome man, blond and rounded about the head. He had broad, neatly tailored shoulders, a jaw shaped like a spade, big white hands.

"Okey, then. I'm not sorry." He chuckled.

"That sounds better. With Dan Rand out of the way I suppose things will be easier for you, huh?"

"In what way?"

"Oh… I suppose it'll be easy for you to get control of the Colosseum. Listen, Cardiac." MacBride leaned forward. "Dan Rand hated you and you hated him. I'll tell you why he hated you. He didn't like your business methods. He kept you and your stable of fighters out of the Colosseum because he didn't believe in robbing the fight public. He had no use for set-ups. He believed the Ricks-Gowanus thing was a set-up.

"Before that, he crossed you on a number of other deals. He lost money doing it but he was willing to lose money to keep the fight game clean. You tried to stage fights in the old Hessler Arena. He stopped that by proving the place was a fire-trap. The only place big enough to make money in was the Colosseum, and he shut you out of there. You got back at him by talking other sport promoters into taking their jobs elsewhere—the smaller jobs, hockey, bicycle racing, wrestling. The Colosseum became an empty barn. He lost money and kept on losing it but no matter what you did you couldn't make him change his mind. Dan could always take it."

"Sure," Cardiac nodded. "Until finally he was flat broke and did the Dutch."

MacBride's eyes narrowed dangerously. "It always surprised me, Cardiac, the way all these small fry suddenly slid away from the Colosseum and pulled their stuff elsewhere. All of them!" He held aloft a rigid forefinger for a taut split-minute, then swung it levelly towards Cardiac. "I hope you've kept your nose clean, boy."

Cardiac delivered a bland smile. "You're steamed up about something." An eyebrow went up. "Will a drink help?"

"No.... I'm dumb," he confessed. "When I look back, I see how dumb I am. The more I think of it, the funnier it seems… I mean the way all these enterprises—wrestlings, bike races, hockey, smokers—the way they all slipped away from the Colosseum to outlying dumps. You're the only man big enough in this town to've worked a racket like that, Cardiac!"

Cardiac looked bored. "Rave on, Skipper," he said offhand, waving a cigarette languidly.

There was a thump—and the gun lay on the table. And there was MacBride's blunt voice: "Ever see that?"

Cardiac folded his hand on his flat stomach, shook his head, said quietly: "No."

"It's the gat that killed Dan Rand."

"So-so! H'm… nice-looking gun. Suicide's queer—"

"Damn' queer. So queer, Cardiac, that this time it's not suicide."

"Well, that *is* news!"

"Would you mind," said MacBride, "letting me see that nice silk pocket handkerchief?"

Cardiac tensed, his eyes flickered. He flexed his lips, then shrugged, chuckled jerkily. "Sure! Here." He tossed the handkerchief across the desk.

MacBride smelled it, making noises. Then he threw it back to

Cardiac, rubbed his bony hand around the nape of his neck and sent a couple disgruntled smoke-puffs from one corner of his mouth. The skipper and Cardiac regarded each other for a long minute.

"Plan to get the Colosseum, don't you?" MacBride asked.

"I plan to organize a holding company and try to do business with the executors of Rand's estate."

"You wouldn't," MacBride said, "by any chance have already formed this holding company?"

"I was just thinking about it."

MacBride picked up a clipped sheaf of papers from a wire desk basket. "I've got good eyesight, Cardiac. It says here, 'Prospectus of the Colosseum Holding Company.'"

Cardiac nodded. "Yes, I know. I was just playing around with the idea this morning. Got down to the office early and ran off my ideas on the typewriter before my secretary arrived."

MacBride nodded, turned and went to the connecting door and opening it said to the blonde in the outer office: "Typewrite on a piece of paper, miss, one line—anything—and bring it in."

Cardiac was annoyed. "Why all the horseplay, Captain?"

MacBride, reading the prospectus, made no reply. In a moment the blonde entered with a sheet of paper. MacBride took it, slowly read the single line.

"Miss," he said, "how many letters have you typed since you arrived this morning?"

"Oh, about three."

"Thanks. You can go."

She went out, puzzled, a little frightened.

MacBride tossed the prospectus and the newly written sheet of paper on the desk.

"Take a look at them, Cardiac. You said you wrote that prospectus on the typewriter this morning. The girl said she's written only three letters this morning. Yet—look close, Cardiac—the typewriting on your prospectus is in fresh, heavy black type made by a brand new ribbon. The line the girl just wrote is very faded—the ribbon hasn't been changed in weeks."

"Oh, nonsense!" Cardiac scoffed.

"Nonsense your grandmother! That prospectus wasn't written this morning, Cardiac. It was written weeks ago—maybe months ago. It

was written because you had a good idea that pretty soon the Colosseum would be in the bag!"

Cardiac rose slowly, his mouth twisting, his pale eyes hard as chips
of ice. "I'm getting tired of listening to a lot of hot air, MacBride!"

"You'll listen, baby—and like it. You're the only man big enough
in this town to've wanted Rand's scalp."

Cardiac came around the desk, swaggering, a hard set to his spade
jaw. "Watch those cracks, copper! I'm not taking dirty cracks from
any cheap shamus." He held his hands out, palms up. "These hands
are clean, Skipper. Suppose you tuck your tail between your legs and
scram."

The phone rang and Cardiac lifted it, growled "Hello" into the
mouthpiece. Then, his eyes blinked, he shook his head, clipped: "Call
back. No, I'll call you back when—… No—no, not now!" His face
colored, he seemed uneasy; he shouted: "I said I'll call you back!" He
hung up violently. There were a few beads of sweat on his forehead.

MacBride said: "I'll be seeing you oftener." And went out.

MacBRIDE dropped into Tony Gatto's *Jockey Street Club* and found
Kennedy drinking gin and Perrier at the bar.

It was not quite noon, and Kennedy was the only customer. Tony
Getto stood behind the bar grinning, polishing a glass.

"No see you in a long time, Cap. How's t'ings?" Tony said.

"Hello, Tony. Bottle of ale…. You ever drink water, Kennedy?"

"Sure. But I always put liquor in it to kill the germs. It turns out
they weren't two dwarfs, Steve; just the Four Marx Brothers up to
their old tricks—"

"Enough o' that, honeybunch." MacBride took a drink of ale;
about-faced and hooked his elbows on the bar, his heel on the brass
rail. "So all you mugs still think it's suicide." He clucked. "I'm con-
tinually grateful for the swell support I get from my friends. It just
breaks my heart with gratitude. Some fine day I'm going to start out
and systematically change the shapes of a lot of schnozzles in this
man's town."

Kennedy also turned about, hooking elbows on the bar, a heel on
the rail, and stood shoulder to shoulder with MacBride. Both stared
at the blank wall opposite.

Kennedy said: "Ah," and took another drink. "How about the
woman?" he asked.

"What woman?"

"Halo Rand."

MacBride said nothing. He took a long swallow of ale and cleared his throat; but still he said nothing.

"This gun business," Kennedy said. "If it's true that Rand bought a gun, that means his own gun wasn't in his desk at home."

"My, but you're a thinker, Kennedy!"

"And yet the gun found on him was the gun that wasn't in his desk and the gun he was supposed to have bought was—where?"

"So you still think it's suicide?"

"Come over to one of the booths."

They went to the rear of the bar, entered a small booth and drew the curtains. Kennedy flopped on to a chair, planked down his glass.

"There's no reason," he said, "why a man would buy two guns to commit suicide. So we must believe that his own gun wasn't in his desk."

"It wasn't there when I went over."

"Right. We must believe that it wasn't there when Rand came home. If we believe that, then it stands to reason that somebody removed it."

"It was in the drawer on the day before."

"That narrows down the time element. It was removed between then and the time Rand came home."

"Why wouldn't Rand have mentioned it to his wife?"

"Maybe he thought she'd removed it for fear he might use it. Guys about to commit suicide are very clever. So he said nothing about it. He just went out and bought another." He dropped his voice. "What do you know about his wife?"

"Not much. I never saw Dan much in the home. I guess I met his wife only about three times. They seemed happy."

"A lot of people seem happy."

MacBride frowned. "Hell, I don't think she'd—"

"Okey, okey. It was just a thought I had. Only the way you talked, it seems to me she tried hard to stick it into your mind that he was hard up financially."

"He was!"

Kennedy smiled drolly. "I've been poking around this morning. I went down to Rand's office. I talked with his stenog. I got the names of the men who called on Rand yesterday morning. One of them was a man named Osgood—the only name I didn't recognize. So I looked up the business directory and found out a man named Charles Osgood was connected with the Packillac Motor Car Company. I sloped around and looked him up. Yes, he'd called on Rand. They'd had a long talk. When Osgood left it was practically settled that Rand was to sell his Colosseum to the Packillac people for $300,000."

MacBride barked: "Sell the Colosseum— What for?"

"The Packillac people intended to convert it into an assembling and distributing plant."

MacBride smacked the table. "Then it wasn't money! It wasn't money worried him! It wasn't, then, suicide!"

"Hold on. We've got to believe that he intended to commit suicide. The sale could have been consummated through his estate. When he bought that gun, we must believe it was with the intention of committing suicide. Then, maybe, he changed his mind."

"So why, in the first place, if he had a chance to sell the Colosseum for $300,000—why did he even think about suicide?"

Kennedy was dry: "There might have been another reason. Men do do the Dutch, you know, because of women. Not often. But now and then."

MacBride's voice was low, hoarse: "Then you've changed your mind about the suicide theory?"

"Blushingly," bowed Kennedy.

"Kennedy," MacBride said. "I always liked you. I never said I didn't like you, did I?"

Kennedy chuckled. "Old tomato!… How's the chances of buying me a drink?"

MacBride stood up. "Nah. Not this bellywash Tony sells. Here's the key to my private stock. Go back to my office. Lower right drawer."

"Where's your white whiskers, Santa Claus?"

THE shabby phaeton roiled into the flagstone courtyard of Tudor Towers. A liveried chauffeur opened the door and MacBride stepped out, passed into the large, deftly lighted lobby. No hurry here; no noise: Tudor Towers was strictly residential, quietly austere. The elevator that carried the skipper to the top floor was a vehicle of black and chromium, noiseless in its ascent.

MacBride's hard heels were ably muffled by the thick cushioned runner in the corridor. The oldish maid with the gargoyle's face let him in. When he entered the living-room he saw Halo Rand sitting in a vis-à-vis couch beside a man wearing a correct morning suit, with a winged collar, dark-rimmed pince-nez. He was about fifty, black-haired, black-eyebrowed. He rose.

Halo Rand, wearing a black crêpe negligée, did not rise; but she said: "Captain MacBride, this is Dr. Landau." She had been crying. Her eyes were red-rimmed, her face sapped of color; and she was listless, tired.

Landau gripped MacBride's hand, eyed him with a dark, keen, direct look. "I am delighted to know you, Captain. I have heard a lot about you. I was just trying to console Mrs. Rand." He threw a profound look at her. "It is not easy, Captain."

"Family doctor?"

"Well, I've attended Dan Rand for quite a few years." He stopped, inhaled deeply, said in a low, level voice: "I am glad you came, Captain, when you did." He stared fixedly, remorsefully, into space. "You know, Dan Rand came to my office yesterday morning. We had a long talk together. He wasn't well, you know. It was marvelous, the way he kept it from everyone. But he was that way… proud; he hated pity. He'd been coming to me regularly and I'd been treating him, but finally, yesterday, he wanted to know the truth. I tried to evade telling the truth. But when a man like Rand becomes angry— And, well, he wanted to know. So I told him. Lungs." He nodded reflectively, bitterly. "I told him the truth. I told him to give up business. I said it was necessary for him to go west—New Mexico—if he hoped to prolong his life. He thanked me. He walked out of my office. So you see, Captain"—he shrugged—"what happens when a man demands the truth of a doctor."

Mrs. Rand said: "Do you want something, Emma?"

The maid was still hovering in the doorway. "N-no, madam."

"Then please go." For a brief instant Halo Rand seemed angry. Then it passed, and she relaxed, was limp again.

"That's news, doctor," MacBride said.

"I daresay it is. Regrettable news. I hope you will understand my position. I hope you will understand that I tried to keep the truth from Rand a long time."

"Would this change of climate have helped him?"

"It would only have prolonged his life a little while. I daresay the poor chap took the bravest way out. I only regret that in a way I was responsible—"

MacBride scoffed. "Wasn't your fault."

They were silent for a moment and then Landau said: "Well, I shall have to get on."

When he had gone, MacBride sat down on a straight-backed chair and regarded Mrs. Rand.

He said: "Well, that seems to straighten out the motive for Dan's suicide."

"P-poor Dan," she said in a tiny voice, half-sobbing.

"Only I came here," MacBride went on, "pretty firmly convinced that it wasn't suicide."

She looked up, startled. "Wasn't suicide!"

"Yeah."

"But-but if it wasn't—"

He said: "Mrs. Rand, your husband, when he left here at noon yesterday, went and bought a gun of a pawnbroker in Diamond Street. I have a complete description of the gun. It wasn't the gun we found in Dan's hand; that was the gun I gave him; it wasn't the gun that killed him."

"Oh!" She felt her throat. "You can't mean—"

He dragged out sardonically, half to himself: "It kind of bears the dirty earmarks of murder."

She sat bolt upright. "Murder!"

"Mrs. Rand, it appears that the gun I gave him was not in his desk drawer when he came home yesterday at noon. It appears that though he left this house and bought a gun with the intention of committing suicide, he changed his mind later in the day."

"But his gun must have been there!"

He thought this over. "No," he said, "it mustn't have been. He went out and bought another."

She was taut, white-faced, shaking. "This—this is all incredible, Captain!"

He was point-blank: "Is there another man in your life?"

She jumped to her feet, her eyes flashing. "How dare you say a thing like that?" she cried.

"My job," he said, rising, eyeing her levelly, "is not always the pleasantest under the sun. I asked you a question."

"It is so absurd that I don't feel called upon to answer it!"

He said: "Of course, you don't have to answer me—not now, anyhow. Later, you might."

Her eyes shimmered. For a long moment she stood tall, quivering, shiny-eyed. Then she burst into tears and covered her face and her handkerchief fell to the floor.

"How cruel you are! How utterly cruel!"

He bent, picked up the handkerchief, passed it in front of his face, sniffed, caught the faint odor of perfume. She took her hands from her face and stared at him with tears streaming from her eyes. He gave her back the handkerchief. She broke out into an incoherent hodgepodge of words, wringing her hands, shaking her head.

He raised palms towards her and said: "Please, Mrs. Rand."

She fell suddenly to the divan and fainted. The oldish maid came swiftly, silently, into the room; flicked a cold, contemptuous look at MacBride.

He offered: "I'll help you—"

"You needn't!" the maid snapped.

He colored, stepped back. "Very well. Tell Mrs. Rand I'll see her again—soon."

She snapped: "I will tell Mrs. Rand nothing of the sort!"

"Suit yourself," he said.

He pivoted and walked across the living-room, into the foyer; opened the door and went down the corridor to the elevator, his hands in overcoat pockets, his shoulders hunched and a dogged, obstinate look in his windy blue eyes.

Cohegan was asleep at the wheel.

MacBride punched him. "Well, sleeping beauty!…"

The shabby phaeton left a cloud of acrid exhaust smoke in the flagstone courtyard, hummed eastward on Marshall Drive.

"AFTER all, Steve," the Police Commissioner said, "if there was another man in her life, and Dan committed suicide because of this, you can't—you really can't convict anyone of murder."

Pacing the floor grimly, MacBride threw up his hands in a violent gesture. "But it's murder! I say it's murder!"

Commissioner Sterns smiled drily. "I know. I know you've been going around saying that, but you haven't shown one shred of evidence that would hold in court. Very likely this pawnbroker made a mistake. Very likely it wasn't Dan Rand who bought that gun of him. I'm not trying to pigeon-hole anything, Steve, I—well, I just don't like to see you make a fool of yourself."

"Oh!" MacBride stopped, glared. "I just should be a strong, silent guy, huh? Well, listen to me, Harry. I've noticed that a strong, silent guy is usually that way because he don't know anything. I'm willing to beef around, talk my head off, *make* a fool of myself—if it'll get me anywhere."

"Trouble with you, Steve," Sterns said good-naturedly, "is that when a case concerns someone you knew and liked, why, you get all steamed up; you cause yourself a lot of heartache and headache.... Just because the gun happens to have an odd smell, you think that—"

"That's only one of the things, Harry."

He hammered his heels back to his office, crammed his pipe, lighted it and sat in his swivel chair and filled the office with smoke. Somehow he couldn't bring himself to believe that Halo Rand had had a hand in it; and when Moriarity and Cohen drifted in, he said:

"Now if Dan Rand wanted to kill himself because his wife was in love with someone else, why would he have sold, or planned to sell, the Colosseum? He left everything to his wife. I asked his lawyers an hour ago. It seems to me that if he felt he was losing his wife to another man, he'd have left his estate to someone else. But he didn't. He meant, you apes—he meant to leave his wife well-fixed!"

Moriarity and Cohen exchanged subtle winks.

"You, Mory," MacBride clipped. "You go to the telephone company and find out about a telephone call Jim Cardiac received at 11:30 this morning. Find where it came from."

Moriarity went out and Cohen said: "Ah, so we're going to make Jim Cardiac the fall-guy."

"Razz on, Ike; razz on. Even the Commissioner's doing it. I'm getting used to it."

Moriarity returned in half an hour and said: "The call came from Southern 509—the Apex Laboratories, in the Marks Building, 199 South Endicott Street."

MacBride grabbed his hat, put on his overcoat and left his office. He ran into Kennedy in the central room, barged past him, went down to the basement and on into the garage. Cohegan was working on the phaeton's bright work.

"Knock off, Bert."

The skipper climbed in back, sat down, and was joined in a moment by Kennedy.

"I don't remember asking you to join me, Kennedy."

"Oh, I'm sure you did."

"Where to, Cap?" Cohegan said.

"South Endicott Street—199."

The phaeton rolled out of the garage.

"How about the woman?" Kennedy said from beneath his hat brim.

"I think she's okey."

"She say she was?"

MacBride snorted, made no reply.

Kennedy said: "Where are we going now?"

"Call on Mr. Apex Laboratories…. Hey, Cohegan, you color blind? That was a red light you passed through!"

"Oh, was it?"

The phaeton crawled through a mid-town traffic jam, turned south past the Empress Theatre, entered South Endicott Street and pulled up before a narrow stone building.

"I'll be right down," MacBride said.

Reaching the elevator, he found Kennedy beside him.

"Me and my shadow!" he muttered.

"Think of all the guys who haven't got shadows. Up!"

They got out at the fourth floor and turned left. The legend Apex Laboratories was in black on the ground-glass panel of a door at the end of the corridor. The door was locked. There was a white card tacked to the wood:

Gone for the day. Phone Midland 214 or call at 26 Cypress if urgent.

"Let's go, Skipper."

MacBride complained: "Listen, Kennedy. Haven't you got a room of your own, or just some nice quiet place where you can go and sit for a while?"

"Sitting is a vice, Skipper. Continuance of the practice leads to a multitude of evils."

They went down to the lobby, strode out to the phaeton. Cohegan was not in sight, but in a moment he was seen coming across the street with a package in his hands.

"Peanuts?" he offered soberly.

"Idea!" said Kennedy. "It stimulates the liquid appetite."

They climbed in and MacBride said: "I bet some fine day I manacle Cohegan to that wheel!... Drive to 26 Cypress."

Kennedy munched hot peanuts. "Translated into English, Steve, what would Mr. Apex Laboratories' name be?"

"I'll let him translate it."

NUMBER 26 CYPRESS was a large fieldstone house in the West End; there was a broad lawn in front planted with shade trees. A driveway ran past the right side of the house, and on this side was a white porte-cochère. The phaeton was parked in the street. MacBride and Kennedy walked up the driveway and MacBride hammered a knocker on a broad, heavy door.

A vellum-skinned butler opened the door.

MacBride said: "I want to see the head of the Apex Laboratories. My name is MacBride."

"Have you an appointment?"

"No."

"Is the call professional?"

"Absolutely."

"Please step in."

They entered a high, dim foyer paneled in dark wood.

"Please take a seat," the butler said. "It won't be long."

He padded off down the hall, vanished.

MacBride and Kennedy did not sit down. They heard the low sound of voices somewhere near, behind a closed door. Kennedy roamed around, came back and pointed.

"In there, Skipper. That's the talk-talk room. Mr. Apex Laboratories is probably busy."

"So am I."

MacBride went down the large foyer towards the door Kennedy had indicated. It was broad, heavy, and he stood eyeing it speculatively. Then he knocked. The low sound of voices ceased. After a moment the latch clicked, the door opened noiselessly.

MacBride stared; then his eyes narrowed, his low blunt voice said: "Hello, Dr. Landau."

"Why—Captain Mac—"

Kennedy chuckled: "You old translator, you!"

"Come on, Kennedy.... This is Kennedy, doctor—of the *Free Press*—"

"Just a moment, Captain. Please! I am very busy and—"

"I won't take long."

Hard-eyed, MacBride elbowed Landau aside and entered a large, sumptuous room. Kennedy trailed amiably behind him. Landau closed the door quietly.

Cardiac was standing on the other side of a tremendous library table. In a large, straight-backed chair sat a youth dressed in tweeds.

"Cardiac," muttered MacBride.

"Hello, Skipper."

Landau removed his pince-nez, dabbed at his face with a hand-kerchief, came briskly from the door.

"Really, Captain, this is a most pleasant surprise—"

"Pleasant?" MacBride said dully.

"Naturally I didn't expect—"

"Just a minute." MacBride raised a palm. "I'll talk first." He flexed his lips, shot a dark glance at Cardiac, at the youth in tweeds, at Dr. Landau.

"You phoned Cardiac at 11:30 this morning, doctor, didn't you?"

"Really, I can't remember—"

"You don't have to. You phoned him. That's settled. I was in his office then. Your phone call upset him. It upset him because I happened to be in the office and he couldn't talk to you then. Why couldn't he?"

The youth's eyes traveled slyly from one to another.

Cardiac cut in: "You're certainly making a nuisance of yourself, Skipper. Why don't you get wise to yourself?"

"Why couldn't you talk to him, Cardiac? I know. Because I was there. Because the things you had to talk about were not for my ears.... Who's the pink-cheeked boy?"

"Mr. Avarill," Landau said.

MacBride said: "So you were Dan Rand's doctor, Landau? You were the man who told him he'd have to leave Richmond City? Was that the first time you told him?"

"Of course!"

"Hell! I don't believe it! His wife told me he'd been acting queer for the past few months. You told him before yesterday. And what happened? He wouldn't leave. He wouldn't leave his business interests. Do you use perfume, doctor?"

"No."

MacBride looked around. "Someone in this room does. How about you, Mr. Avarill?"

The pink-cheeked boy grinned. "Why, Captain!"

MacBride crossed to him, bent down. "No, it's not you."

"My ——! this is rich!" Cardiac exploded.

Kennedy was sitting on the edge of the large library table. He fished in his pockets for a cigarette, found none. He knocked open a large box on the table. It was empty. He knocked open another and found cigarettes; put one between his lips, started to strike a match, paused. He frowned, picked up the empty box, opened it and sniffed.

Landau complained: "You certainly make yourself at home, Mr. Kennedy."

"Don't I, though!... Nice sandalwood box, doctor."

MacBride was standing at his shoulder. "That's what I smell," he said. He snatched the box from Kennedy's hand, inhaled. He tossed the box back on the desk and said: "That's the smell. That's the perfume I've been looking for."

Landau said warmly: "This is becoming ridiculous, Captain!"

"Is it?" MacBride snarled, turning on him. "It's the smell of sandalwood in the gun that killed Dan Rand. The gun was kept in that box for a while. The odor of sandalwood—if that's what Kennedy called it—was absorbed by the oil in the gun. It stayed with the gun, not as strong as the smell in the box—but it was there; it was faint but it was there!"

The pink-cheeked youth smiled brightly but said nothing. Cardiac lifted his chin, pursed his lips hard. Dr. Landau looked about the room in nervous fits and starts, shrugging, saying: "Of course... this is peculiar.... I hardly know what to say... to think... but of course—"

"You had access to Rand's home," MacBride cut in. "When were you there last—before his death? And don't lie, because it'll be easy to check up."

Landau cleared his throat, touched his necktie. "I think—yes, I dropped in there for a few moments the evening before his—ah—death."

"How long do you consider a few moments?"

"Well"—he cleared his throat—"I daresay I was there for about—well—half an hour."

"In Dan's den?"

"I—ah—yes, of course: Dan's den. To be sure!"

MacBride said: "The gun was in his drawer during the day. The maid saw it when she was cleaning up. It will be easy for me to check up and find out if anyone was in that room between the time she cleaned up and the time you were there."

Cardiac picked up his coat, flung it over his arm. "I wouldn't take cracks like that from any cop, doc. Remember, you don't have to answer him.... Well, I've got to run along."

MacBride turned. "Get back, Cardiac!"

"Now look here, you flatfoot—"

"Get back, Cardiac. I've stepped into something that's just burning my toes. Dan Rand was double-crossed by somebody—"

"I'd watch," drawled Kennedy, "the young Joe College over there. I don't like his smile."

Landau wrung his hands. "This is positively the most absurd situation I have ever—"

"Of course," said MacBride sarcastically, "sandalwood boxes are as common as egg crates in this burg!... You get the hell back there, Cardiac. I told you you're not leaving this room!"

"I'll be damned if I won't!" whipped back Cardiac. "If you want to hold me, shamus, go out and get a summons! I'm a busy man! I've got no time to play tag with a second-rate police captain!" He jerked his thumb. "Come on, Ralph. We're leaving."

The pink-cheeked youth rose cheerfully. "Right with you, Jim, old boy!"

MacBride pivoted, caught hold of the youth's vest and flung him back into the chair. The youth's teeth clicked. He jumped right up again. MacBride flung him into the chair a second time, and this time the chair went over, the youth sprawled on the floor. He lay there, propped on his elbows; he smiled wistfully, sadly, reflectively, a lock of golden hair curving down over one golden eyebrow.

MacBride roared: "When I tell you to sit down, mister, I don't mean stand up!"

"Captain, Captain!" Landau panted. "Don't—don't aggravate him that way. Don't—"

"And will you," ripped out MacBride, swiveling, "stop sticking your nose in my business!... Cardiac, come back here!"

Kennedy yelled: "Look out!"

MacBride swung around, his gun half-drawn.

Landau cried out and dived for the youth. The youth was chuckling liquidly, resting on one elbow. The gun exploded in his other hand and stopped Landau in mid-career. MacBride fired and his slug nailed the youth to the floor. Landau started stumbling forward, choking. He gathered unbalanced speed, went careening across the room, knocked over a floor lamp, crashed head-on against the wall and slumped to the floor. The youth writhed on his back chuckling wildly, beating his palms upon the floor.

A door banged.

"Cardiac," said Kennedy.

"You stay here!" MacBride said.

He broke into a run, yanked open the door, collided with the butler and fell down as the front door slammed shut. The butler cried out. MacBride untangled himself, rose, lunged for the front door and yelled:

"Cohegan!"

But Cohegan was not in the phaeton. Through the trees, MacBride saw Cardiac at the wheel; heard the blast of the motor and saw the car lurch forward, gather speed. He galloped down the graveled driveway, reached the sidewalk, turned left and stretched his legs in a hard-heeled run. Raising his gun, he did not fire. There were other automobiles moving in the street. But he fired in the air. Beyond was a main highway and he thought a cop might be in the neighborhood. Running, he fired again.

And then he heard, ahead, three blasts from another gun. He saw the phaeton whip from side to side; heard the scream of its brakes and the scream of other brakes as other cars sought to avoid it. Heeling over, the phaeton slammed across the curbstone; its radiator and hood doubled up like a folded accordion, and the sound of the crash was drowned instantly in the roar of the explosion that followed. Flame daggered its way through smoke; bricks flew from the building into which the car crashed.

KENNEDY picked up the telephone, sat on the library table and swung his legs. "Central 1000," he said into the mouthpiece. His world-weary eyes traveled from the dead youth to the dead doctor, and he sighed. "City desk, flower." He lay down on the table, held the mouthpiece above him.

"Abe," he said, "this is that famous journalist and bon vivant,

Kennedy.... So now dust your ears. Old Stephen J. MacBride did it again.... I'm telling you! Listen. A young punk named Ralph Avarill accidentally shot and killed Dr. Amos Landau in the latter's home, 26 Cypress Street.... Yeah, the punk meant to kill the skipper, but things got balled up. Then MacBride knocked off the punk. At that moment Jim Cardiac took it into his head to lam, and MacBride high-tailed after him in the well-known MacBride manner. They're not back yet.

"Meantime, get a load of this nice little bed-time story. Landau told it to me and then died. The punk—Ralph Avarill—killed Dan Rand. He was a hop-head.... No. sweetness, not Rand; the punk. The punk was a friend of Cardiac's, and Landau was a silent backer of Cardiac's interests. Ostensibly a fine medico, he was also a dealer in dope and an addict himself. He met Dan Rand seven years ago at a box-fight where he attended a boxer who later died from the effect of a blow to the heart. He became Rand's personal physician.

"When this trouble between Rand and Cardiac began, grew hotter, Cardiac went to his silent partner Landau and wanted him to put Rand out of the way. Landau thought of a better method. He began working on Rand mentally, telling him he was a lunger and advising him to sell out all his business interests here and go West and live the simple life. Well, it didn't quite work out. It wore Rand down, but he was a sticker. Finally Landau told him he would die if he didn't leave. But before he told him that—in fact, the evening before—he dropped in at Rand's apartment and while Rand was out of the room Landau swiped his gun, went home and put it in a sandalwood box until the punk called for it. Next day he told Rand his chances of living were mighty small. He thought Rand would go home and tell his wife and that his telling her would make an open and shut suicide case when the cops found the body....

"What?... Sure, the punk was to tail Rand. And he did. Tailed him all afternoon and finally, at between 9:30 and ten o'clock, walked him to that abandoned warehouse and let him have it with the gun Landau had stolen from Rand's desk. And when Rand fell, his hand came out of his pocket and he dropped the gun he'd bought. The punk picked it up, left the other— Just a minute."

MacBride had come darkly into the room. "Tell him Cardiac's dead, Kennedy. Cohegan objected to the squad car being stolen."

"Where was Cohegan?"

"Down in a fancy grocery store on the corner, mooching apples."

Publication History

in-interest to Popular Publications, Inc.

BLACK MASK	The Richmond City Free Press	BLACK MASK

All the Stories from 1928 to 1936

THE COMPLETE CASES OF MacBRIDE & KENNEDY

IN FOUR VOLUMES

BY FREDERICK NEBEL

Crimes of Richmond City

CAPTAIN STEVE MacBRIDE was a tall square-shouldered man of forty more or less hard-bitten

Dog Eat Dog

WHEN CAPTAIN MacBRIDE was suddenly transferred from the Second Precinct to the Fifth, an undercurrent of whispered speculations trickled through the Department, buzzed in newspaper circles, and traveled along the underworld grapevine.

It was a significant move, for MacBride, besides being the youngest captain in the Department—he was barely forty—was known throughout Richmond City as a holy terror against the criminal element. He was a lank, rangy man, with a square jaw and windy blue eyes. He was brusque, talked straight from the shoulder, and was hard-

INTRODUCTION BY DAVID LEWIS

Coming This Fall From Altus Press

The Law Laughs Last

TOUGH precinct was the Second of Richmond City, lying in the backyard of the theatrical district and on the frontier of the railroad yards.

A hard-boiled precinct, touching the fringe of crookdom's elite on the north—the con men, the night-club barons; and on the south, the dim-lit, crooked alleys traversed by the bum, the lush-worker and poolroom gangster. On the north were the playhouses, the white way, high-toned apartments, opulent hotels, high hats, evening gowns. On the south, tenements, warehouses, cobblestones, squalor, and the railroad yards. The toughest precinct in all Richmond City.

Law Without Law

KENNEDY chuckled. "So you're back in the Second, Mac."
"See me here, don't you?"
"Ay, verily!"
The old station-house, blown up during the last election, had been rebuilt, and the office in which Captain Stephen MacBride sat and Kennedy, the insatiable news-hound, stood, smelled of new paint and plaster. Something of the old atmosphere was lost—that atmosphere which it had taken long years to create: dust, age-colored walls decorated with news clippings, "wanted" bulletins, likenesses of known criminals.
Two days ago MacBride had been

New Guns For Old

POLICE Captain Steve MacBride was on leave. He had it coming to him. As one of the main factors in the scouring of Richmond City's corrupt municipal government, he was due some little respite from the shield and the gun. With the passing of a self-seeking Mayor

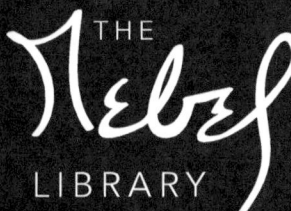

THE *Nebel*
LIBRARY

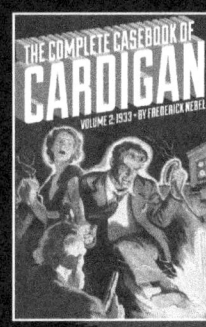
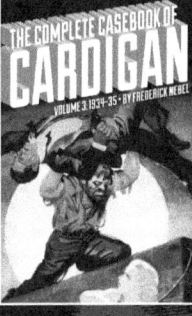
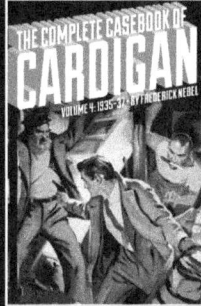

www.ingramcontent.com/pod-product-compliance
Lightning Source LLC
Chambersburg PA
CBHW051127030726
47504CB00004B/740